THE SIGNET CLASSIC POETRY SERIES is under the general editorship of poet, lecturer, and teacher JOHN HOLLANDER.

Mr. Hollander's first volume of poetry, *A Crackling of Thorns,* won the Yale Series of Younger Poets Awards for 1958. He was a recipient of a National Institute of Arts and Letters grant (1963) and has been a member of the Wesleyan University Press Poetry Board and the Bollingen Poetry Translation Prize Board. Mr. Hollander is Professor of English at Hunter College.

John Keats

SELECTED POETRY

Edited by Paul de Man

The Signet Classic Poetry Series
GENERAL EDITOR: JOHN HOLLANDER

A SIGNET CLASSIC
NEW AMERICAN LIBRARY
TIMES MIRROR
NEW YORK AND SCARBOROUGH, ONTARIO
THE NEW ENGLISH LIBRARY LIMITED, LONDON

COPYRIGHT © 1966 BY PAUL DE MAN
ALL RIGHTS RESERVED

Library of Congress Catalog Card Number: 66-23616.

𝄮

SIGNET CLASSIC TRADEMARK REG. U.S. PAT. OFF. AND FOREIGN COUNTRIES
REGISTERED TRADEMARK—MARCA REGISTRADA
HECHO EN CHICAGO, U.S.A.

SIGNET, SIGNET CLASSICS, MENTOR, PLUME AND MERIDIAN BOOKS
are published *in the United States* by
The New American Library, Inc.,
1301 Avenue of the Americas, New York, New York 10019,
in Canada by the New American Library of Canada Limited,
81 Mack Avenue, Scarborough, 704, Ontario,
in the United Kingdom by The New English Library Limited,
Barnard's Inn, Holborn, London, E.C. 1, England.

FIRST PRINTING, JULY, 1966

5 6 7 8 9 10 11 12 13

PRINTED IN THE UNITED STATES OF AMERICA

Table of Contents

Introduction   *ix*
A General Note on the Text   *xxxvii*
A Note on This Edition   *xxxviii*
Chronology   *xxxix*
Selected Bibliography   *xlv*

I. The Early Keats   49

Epistles:
   To George Felton Mathew   51
   To My Brother George   54
   To Charles Cowden Clarke   58

I Stood Tiptoe   63

Sleep and Poetry   70

Sonnets:
   O Solitude   82
   How Many Bards   82
   Written on the Day that Mr. Leigh Hunt Left
     Prison   83
   To One Long in City Pent   83
   On First Looking into Chapman's Homer   84
   Keen, Fitful Gusts   85
   On Leaving Some Friends at an Early Hour   85
   To My Brothers   86
   Addressed to Haydon   86
   Addressed to the Same   87
   Written in Disgust of Vulgar Superstition   88
   On the Grasshopper and Cricket   88

TABLE OF CONTENTS

 After Dark Vapors   89
 On Seeing the Elgin Marbles   89
 To B. R. Haydon, with the Foregoing Sonnet
  on the Elgin Marbles   90
 On the Sea   90

Endymion   91

II. The Middle Period   203

Hyperion   205

The Eve of St. Agnes   230

The Eve of St. Mark   242

Ode to May   246

Ode to Psyche   247

Ode to a Nightingale   249

Ode on a Grecian Urn   252

Ode on Melancholy   254

Ode on Indolence   255

Sonnets:
 On Sitting Down to Read King Lear Once
  Again   257
 When I Have Fears   258
 To a Lady Seen for a Few Moments at
  Vauxhall   258
 On Visiting the Tomb of Burns   259
 Written in the Cottage Where Burns Was
  Born   260
 Read Me a Lesson, Muse   260
 To Homer   261
 Why Did I Laugh?   261
 To Sleep   262
 On Fame, I   262
 On Fame, II   263
 On a Dream   263
 On the Sonnet   264
 O Thou Whose Face   265

TABLE OF CONTENTS

To J. H. Reynolds, Esq.   265

Lines on Seeing a Lock of Milton's Hair   269

Where's the Poet?   270

Welcome Joy . . .   271

Stanzas: In a Drear-nighted December   272

Fancy   273

La Belle Dame sans Merci   276

III. The Late Keats   279

   Lamia   281

   The Fall of Hyperion   301

   To Autumn   315

   Ode to Fanny   316

   Sonnets:
     The Day is Gone   318
     To Fanny   318
     Bright Star   319
     To——   320
     This Living Hand   321

IV. Selected Letters   323

Introduction

In the course of time, the reputations of the main English romantic poets have undergone considerable and revealing fluctuations. It would nowadays be considered eccentric to rate Byron above Wordsworth or Blake, yet during his lifetime Byron's fame far surpassed that of his contemporaries. Not till the end of the nineteenth century did Blake begin to receive full recognition, and we are now no longer surprised to find critics give him a central position that none of his contemporaries would have remotely suspected. We may have some difficulty in sharing the excitement with which the young Yeats discovered the audacities of Shelley's more speculative poems, but, on the other hand, Arnold's judgment in rating Wordsworth above Spenser, Dryden, Pope and Coleridge might again find some support, albeit for reasons that have little in common with Arnold's.

These fluctuations reflect changes in critical temper that are themselves the result of a continued reinterpretation of romanticism. Time and again, literary and critical movements set out with the avowed aim of moving beyond romantic attitudes and ideas; in America alone, Pound's imagism, Irving Babbitt's neo-humanism and the New Criticism of T. S. Eliot are relatively recent instances of such a trend; the same anti-romantic (or anti-idealist) bias underlies neo-realist and neo-Marxist tendencies here and abroad. But time and again, it turns out that the new conceptions that thus assert themselves were in fact already present in the full context of European romanticism; instead of moving beyond these problems, we are merely becoming aware of certain aspects of romanticism that had remained hidden from our perception. We certainly have left behind the Victorian image of Wordsworth, but Wordsworth himself is far from having been fixed and determined by a poetic or critical itinerary that went beyond him. What sets out as a claim to overcome romanticism often turns out to be merely an expansion of our understanding of the movement, leading inevitably to changes in our images of individual poets.

The poetry of Keats is no exception. As the amount of biographical and critical studies augments in quantity and in quality, our knowledge of Keats has increased considerably, yet many questions remain unresolved, as if the work had not yielded all the possibilities of significance that it may contain. The curve of his reputation shows perhaps less dramatic ups and downs than in the case of Blake or even Shelley: it has constantly risen since his death at the age of twenty-five in 1821. He had already earned the enthusiastic appreciation of several close and loyal friends during his lifetime, but his career was too short to give him the real critical recognition that would have been so useful: Wordsworth paid little attention to him; for all his apparent sympathy, Shelley was deeply uncongenial and remained aloof; Coleridge was already on the decline and Keats hardly knew him; Hazlitt was the object of his admiration rather than a full admirer, and even Hunt's ultimate loyalty went to Shelley rather than to the earlier disciple. Later in the century, the Victorians were never able to forgive Keats his plebeian birth and the unbridled erotic despair of the love letters to Fanny Brawne; Arnold has to strain a great deal to find in the life and letters traces of the moral high-seriousness that he cannot fail to detect in the greater poems. Some of this Victorian snobbishness still echoes in Yeats's reference to Keats as a "coarse-bred son of a livery-stable keeper" who made "luxuriant song" out of his frustrations. But the poetry had always found considerable appreciation, not only for its decorative aspects that so delighted the Pre-

INTRODUCTION xi

Raphaelites, but for its thematic depth as well. In our own century, when the relationship between life and work is understood in a somewhat less literal manner, a considerable exegetic effort has been directed especially toward the elucidation of the shorter poems. Continued interest in the biography and in the letters—a new edition of the letters edited by Hyder E. Rollins appeared in 1958 and W. J. Bate's biography appeared in 1963—indicates that the problem that preoccupied the Victorians, the contrast between the banality of Keats's life and the splendor of his work, has not been fully resolved. Arnold's remarks about an element of vulgarity in Keats have cut so deep that recent biographers are still writing polemically in an effort to dispel their effect. This almost always results, even among Keats's warmest admirers, in a trace of condescension or defensiveness, as if one were forced to look for attenuating circumstances. The facts are distorted either by making the life appear darker and more tragic than it was, or by exalting Keats's very genuine courage and self-sacrifice to the point where it obscures his poetry. Except for the last few months, the life is in fact more banal than tragic; it is one of Keats's most engaging traits that he resists all temptation to see himself as the hero of a tragic adventure. The unfavorable circumstances of his birth—he was the eldest of four orphaned children cheated out of their modest inheritance by an unscrupulous guardian—were such that he lived almost always oriented toward the future, keeping his capacity for personal happiness in reserve, so to speak, for the better days he saw ahead. The pathos, of course, is that he never reached these days, but he was no longer able to write by the time he realized this. In reading Keats, we are therefore reading the work of a man whose experience is mainly literary. The growing insight that underlies the remarkably swift development of his talent was gained primarily from the act of writing. In this case, we are on very safe ground when we derive our understanding primarily from the work itself.

The pattern of Keats's work is prospective rather than

retrospective; it consists of hopeful preparations, anticipations of future power rather than meditative reflections on past moments of insight or harmony. His poems frequently climax in questions—"Was there a poet born?", "Did I wake or sleep?"—or in statements such as: "and beyond these/I must not think now . . .", "but now no more,/My wand'ring spirit must not further soar"—that suggest he has reached a threshold, penetrated to the borderline of a new region which he is not yet ready to explore but toward which all his future efforts will be directed. *I Stood Tiptoe* announces *Endymion*, *Endymion* announces *Hyperion*, *Hyperion* prefigures *The Fall of Hyperion*, etc.; Keats is steadily moving forward, trying to pull himself up to the level and the demands of his own prospective vision. None of the larger works—and we know that the larger works mattered most to him—can in any sense be called finished. The circle never seems to close, as if he were haunted by a dream that always remains in the future.

The dream is dramatically articulated from the very start, in a naïve but clear mythological outline that even the awkward diction of the early poems cannot altogether hide from sight. It reveals Keats's original conception of the poet's role and constitutes the thematic center around which the history of his development is organized.

In one of Keats's longer early poems, the title line as well as the last word suggest a soaring, Icarus-like urge to "burst our mortal bars" and leave the human world behind. But nothing could be less like Shelley's skylark, a "scorner of the ground," than Keats's young poet. Icarus's rise as well as his fall are acts of overbearing that destroy balance and "burst" beyond natural limits. Even in the earliest poems, Keats never conceives of poetry in this manner: to the contrary, poetry is always the means by which an excess is tempered, a flight checked, a separation healed. In terms of the material sensations toward which Keats's imagery naturally tends, this tendency is expressed in the impression of a temperate breeze that cools excessive heat, but never chills—a sensation so all-pervading throughout the early poems that it cannot be considered merely conventional or derivative:

INTRODUCTION

> ... pebbly beds;
> Where swarms of minnows show their little heads, ...
> To taste the luxury of sunny beams
> Tempered with coolness.
> *(I Stood Tiptoe*, ll. 71 ff.)

> Where had he been, from whose warm head outflew
> That sweetest of all songs, that ever new,
> That aye refreshing, pure deliciousness ...
> *(Idem.*, ll. 181 ff.)

> The breezes were ethereal, and pure,
> And crept through half-closed lattices to cure
> The languid sick; it cooled their fevered sleep ...
> *(Idem.*, ll. 221 ff.)

The early Keats discovers the narrative equivalence of this restoring, balancing power of poetry in the Greek myths, which he interprets at the time as tales in which the distance between mortals and immortals is overcome by an act of erotic union. As a story of love between a goddess and a mortal shepherd, Endymion attracts him even more than Psyche or Narcissus, and he announces it as his main theme before embarking on the narrative poem *Endymion* itself. But the symbolic function of the poet as a narrator of myths immediately widens in significance: since he can "give meek Cynthia her Endymion," he not only restores the natural balance of things, but his exemplary act extends to the whole of mankind. The union between the goddess and the shepherd prefigures directly the communal celebration of mankind liberated from its suffering. By telling "one wonder of [Cynthia's] bridal night," the poet causes the "languid sick" to awake and

> Young men, and maidens at each other gazed
> With hands held back, and motionless, amazed
> To see the brightness in each other's eyes;
> And so they stood, filled with a sweet surprise,
> Until their tongues were loosed in poesy.
> Therefore no lover did of anguish die:
> But the soft numbers, in that moment spoken,
> Made silken ties, that never may be broken.
> *(Idem.*, ll. 231 ff.)

Here we have Keats's original dream in all its naïve clarity: it is a dream about poetry as a redeeming force, oriented toward others in a concern that is moral but altogether spontaneous, rooted in the fresh sensibility of love and sympathy and not in abstract imperatives. The touching tale of a lovelorn goddess replaces the Ten Commandments, a humanized version of Hellenic myth replaces biblical sternness, in an optimistic belief that the universe naturally tends toward the mood of temperate balance and that poetry can always recapture the freshness of ever-rising springs.

The optimism of this myth is tempered, however, by the negative implications it contains: if poetry is to redeem, it must be that there is a need for redemption, that humanity is indeed "languid sick" and "with temples bursting." The redemption is the happier future of a painful present. One of the lines of development that Keats's poetry will follow reaches a deeper understanding of this pain which, in the earlier texts, is merely a feverish restlessness, a discordance of the sensations that creates a tension between warring extremes of hot and cold. Some of his dissatisfaction with the present is transposed in Keats's image of his own situation as a beginning poet on the contemporary literary scene: the greatness of the major predecessors—Spenser, Shakespeare and Milton—measures his own inadequacy and dwarfs the present:

> Is there so small a range
> In the present strength of manhood, that the high
> Imagination cannot freely fly
> As she was wont of old?
>
> (*Sleep and Poetry*, ll. 162 ff.)

Totally oriented toward the future, Keats cannot draw strength from this past grandeur; his use of earlier models will always be more a sympathetic imitation than a dialogue between past and present, as between Milton and Wordsworth in *The Prelude*. Hence that Keats's use of earlier poets is more technical than thematic: however Spenserian or Miltonic the diction of *The Eve of St. Agnes* and *Hyperion* may be, Spenser and Milton are not present as such in the poems; Keats has to derive all his power from energy he finds in himself or in his immediate vicinity. But he experiences his own times as literarily deficient: a curious passage from *Sleep and Poetry,* where the entire movement of the poem, as well as the allegiance to Leigh Hunt, would demand the unmixed praise of contemporary poetry, turns into a criticism of Byron and Wordsworth for failing to deliver the message of hope that Keats would like to hear. As a criticism of *The Excursion* the observation would be valid enough, but it is presented instead as a source of personal discouragement. A certain form of despondency and stagnation seems to threaten Keats from the start and forces him to take shelter in falsely idyllic settings like the one at the end of *Sleep and Poetry,* where the problem that concerns him can be temporarily forgotten but not resolved.

Retreats of this kind recur throughout the work, but they gain in poetic significance as the predicament from which he retreats grows in universality. This progression can be traced in the changed use of Ovidian myth from *Endymion* on, as compared to the earliest poems. Originally, the myths serve to gain access to the idyllic aspects of nature: they are "delightful stories" about "the fair paradise of Nature's light." The sad tales alternate with joyful ones merely for the sake of variety. This, of course, is by no means the dominant mood in Ovid himself, who often reports acts of refined cruelty with harsh detachment. From *Endymion* on, the movement of mythical metamorphosis, practically absent from the early poems, achieves a striking prominence that will maintain itself to the end; the very narrative pattern of *Endymion,* of *Lamia* and, in a more hidden way, of *Hyperion* and the Odes, is based on a series of transformations from one order of being into another. The various metamorphic combinations between the inanimate, the animal, human and divine world keep appearing, and the moment of transformation always constitutes the dramatic climax toward which the story is oriented. Far from being merely picturesque, the metamorphoses acquire an obsessive intensity in which one recognizes a more mature version of the original, happy dream of redemption.

The erotic contact between the gods and man in Ovid is anything but the idyllic encounter between Cynthia and Endymion in *I Stood Tiptoe*; it results instead in the brutal degradation of the human being to a lower order of life, his imprisonment in the rigid forms of the inanimate world: Niobe's "very tongue frozen to her mouth's roof" (*Met.* VI, 1. 306), Daphne's "swift feet grown fast in sluggish roots" (I, 1. 551), Myrrha, the mother of Adonis, watching her skin change to hard bark (X, 1. 494). This state of frozen immobility, of paralysis under the life-destroying impact of eternal powers, becomes the obsessive image of a human predicament that poetry is to redeem. A long gallery of human beings thus caught in poses of frozen desire appear throughout the work: the lovers in Book III of *Endymion* imprisoned in a sea cave "vast, and desolate, and icy-cold" (III, 1. 632), the figures on the Grecian Urn, the knight-at-arms of "La Belle Dame sans Merci" caught "On the cold hillside," the knights and ladies at the beginning of *The Eve of St. Agnes* "sculptured dead, on each side, [who] seem to freeze,/Emprisoned in black, purgatorial rails," Saturn at the beginning of *Hyperion* "quiet as a stone,/Still as the silence round about his lair." There hardly exists a single of Keats's important poems in which a version of this recurrent theme fails to appear, though the outward form may vary. It is most frequently associated with the sensation of cold, as if the cooling breeze of *I Stood Tiptoe* heralding the benevolent arrival of the gods had suddenly turned icy and destructive. The myth is a paradoxical version of the mutability theme: the passage of time, the loss of power, death, are the means by which the gods announce their presence; time is the only eternal force and it strips man of his ability to move freely in the direction of his own desire; generations are wasted by old age, "youth grows pale, and specter-thin, and dies" and "Everything is spoiled by use" ("Fancy," 1. 68). Under the impact of this threat, mankind is made powerless in the stagnation that Keats felt at times in himself and saw around him. Mutability causes paralysis.

His dream then becomes a kind of reversal of the Ovidian metamorphosis, in which man was frozen into a natural form: the poet is the one who can reverse the metamorphosis and reanimate the dead forms into life. Again, Book III of *Endymion* gives a clear mythological outline of this process: by a mere touch of his wand, warmth is restored to the frozen lovers and the reanimated figures rejoice in an exact repetition of the redemption scene from *I Stood Tiptoe* (*Endymion*, III, ll. 780 ff.). This dream, by which dead nature is restored to life and refinds, as it were, the human form that was originally its own, is Keats's fondest reverie. A large measure of his poetical power stems from this. It allows him to give nature such an immediate and convincing presence that we watch it take on effortlessly human form: the ode "To Autumn" is the supreme achievement of this Ovidian metamorphosis in reverse. His ability to make his conceits and metaphors spring out of a genuine identity of nature with man, rather than out of an intellectual awareness of an analogy between both, is also rooted in this dream. It is so strong that it forces itself upon the narrative of his longer poems, even when the original story does not allow for it. In *Hyperion*, one can never conceive of Apollo as the warring opponent of the Titans. Instead, the story inevitably turns toward a repetition of the Glaucus episode in *Endymion*: Apollo tends to become the young man whose task it is to free and rejuvenate Saturn, the victim of old age. We are dealing with still another version of Keats's humanitarian dream. He will reach maturity at the end of a rather complicated itinerary, when the last trace of naïveté is removed from this vision.

The power by means of which the poet can redeem the suffering of mankind is called love, but love, in Keats, is a many-sided force. On the simplest level, love is merely the warmth of sensation: Endymion's ardor is such that it seems to melt the curse of time away at sheer contact. Till the later "Ode to Psyche" when love has been internalized to such an extent that it bears only the remotest relationship to anything physical, the epithet "warm," associated with Eros, preserves the link with sensation in a world that is otherwise entirely mental.

> A bright torch, and a casement ope at night,
>   To let the warm Love in!
>   ("Ode to Psyche," ll. 66–67)

The importance of sensuality to Keats has been abundantly stressed; when some biographers, with the laudable intention of rescuing Keats from the Victorian reproach of coarseness, have tried to minimize the importance of erotic elements in his poetry, they present an oddly distorted picture. Yet, even his most straightforward eroticism easily turns into something more than sensation. First of all, sensuous love for him is more readily imagined than experienced; therefore it naturally becomes one of the leading symbols for the workings of the imagination. One of his most elaborate conceits on the activity of the mind, the final stanza of the "Ode to Psyche," spontaneously associates Eros with fancy; the same is true of the poem "Fancy," in which Eros is present as an activity of the mind. Moreover, since Keats is the least narcissistic of romantic poets, love is easily transferred by him to others and becomes a communal bond: one remembers how the union of Cynthia and Endymion spontaneously turns into a public feast, the kind of Rousseauistic brotherhood that recurs in romantic poetry as a symbol of reconciliation. In *Endymion* also, one passes without tension from love to a communal spirit of friendship with social and political overtones; something of the spirit of the French Revolution still echoes in these passages. In the optimistic world of *Endymion*, love and history act together as positive forces and historical redemption goes hand in hand with sensuous fulfillment.

Another aspect of the love experience, however, leads

to more complex involvements. Aside from sensation, love also implies sympathy, a forgetting of the self for the sake of others, especially when the other is in a state of suffering. In the earlier poems, when the poet's sympathy goes out to Narcissus, to Psyche or to Pan, or even when Endymion is moved to tears over the sad fate of the woodnymph Arethusa, these movements of the heart could still be considered a conventional form of sensibility. But in the recurrent image of frozen immobility, the suffering is not just an arbitrary trick of fate or a caprice of the gods: it becomes the generalized statement of the human predicament, man stifled by the awareness of his mortality. Sympathetic understanding of these threatened figures, the attempt "To think how they may ache in icy hoods and mails" (*St. Agnes,* l. 18), tears us away from the safety of everyday experience and forces us to enter a realm that is in fact the realm of death. The ordinary life of consciousness is then suspended and its continuity disrupted. Hence that the experience can only be expressed in metaphors such as "trance" or "sleep," suspended states of consciousness in which the self is momentarily absent. The "romantic" setting of certain dream episodes in *Endymion* or in "La Belle Dame sans Merci" should not mislead us into misunderstanding the connection between love and death that prevails here: love is not a temptation to take us out of the finite world of human experiences, still less an impulse toward a platonic heaven. Keats's love impulse is a very human sense of sympathy and pity, chivalrous perhaps, but devoid of transcendental as well as escapist dimensions. Endymion cannot resist the "sorrow" of the Indian maiden, Glaucus is taken in by the feigned tears of Circe, the knight of "La Belle Dame . . ." is definitely lulled to sleep only after his lady has "wept, and sighed full sore," and Lamia, also, woos her lover Lucius by appealing to his pity as well as to his senses. Keats's imagination is fired by a mixture of sensation and sympathy in which the dual nature of love is reunited. The sympathy, however, is even more important than the sensation: love can exist without the latter but not without the former, and some of Keats's heroes are motivated by sympathy alone. This adds an important dimension to our understanding of the relationship between love, poetry and death in his work: because poetry is essentially an act of sympathy, of human redemption, it must move through the death-like trances that abound in Keats. One misunderstands these moments altogether if one interprets them as a flight from human suffering; to the contrary, they are the unmistakable sign of a sympathetic identification with the human predicament. There are moments of straightforward escape in Keats: we mentioned the end of *Sleep and Poetry* as one instance; several of the more trivial poems fulfill the same function. But the "tranced summer night" of *Hyperion*, the Cave of Quietude in Book IV of *Endymion*, the "drowsy numbness" of the Nightingale Ode, the "cloudy swoon" of *The Fall of Hyperion*, do not stand in opposition to human sympathy; as the subsequent dramatic action of these poems indicates, they represent a necessary first step toward the full unfolding of humanitarian love as it grows into a deeper understanding of the burden of mortality.

This expansion of the theme of love, which takes place without entering into conflict with the other, sensuous aspect of love, leads to a parallel deepening of the theme of history. In the easy simplicity of *Endymion*, Keats can herald, at the opening of Book II, the "sovereign power of love" over history: love suffices to bring about universal reconciliation and to make the slow labor of history superfluous. By the time of *Hyperion*, a considerable change has already taken place: the myth of the defeat of the Titans by a new generation of gods is interpreted as the very movement of history. Oceanus's speech (*Hyperion*, III, ll. 114 ff.) as well as Mnemosyne's initiation of Apollo to

>   Names, deeds, gray legends, dire events, rebellions,
>   Majesties, sovran voices, agonies,
>   Creations and destroyings . . .
>   (*Hyperion*, III, ll. 114 ff.)

make very clear the increased importance of the theme. But it is not till the late *Fall of Hyperion* that Keats's historical consciousness is fully developed. In *Hyperion,* it remains obscure why the knowledge of the historical past which "pours into the wide hollows of [Apollo's] brain" suffices to "make a god of [him]." The corresponding scene in *The Fall of Hyperion* may be confused in some respects, but not as far as the poet's attitude toward history is concerned: history, in its most general aspects, is for him a privileged subject, because the gift of sympathy which he possesses to a larger degree than any other man allows him to understand the sacrificial nature of all historical movement, as epitomized in the downfall of Saturn. Far from reasserting the consoling law stated by Oceanus "That first in beauty should be first in might" (*Hyperion,* II, l. 229), the historical awareness in *The Fall* returns to the deeper theme of man's temporal contingency. The poet is the chosen witness of the damage caused by time; by growing in consciousness he gains no new attributes of beauty or might, merely the negative privilege of witnessing the death of those who surpassed him in greatness. The suggestion of a conquering, youthful Apollo has entirely disappeared. The dynamic thrust of history itself is frozen into immobility by the deadly power of time and the poet now has to expand his capacity for sympathy until it encompasses the full range of this tragedy:

> Without stay or prop
> But my own weak mortality, I bore
> The load of this eternal quietude,
> The unchanging gloom ...
> (*The Fall of Hyperion,* I, ll. 388 ff.)

History can only move by becoming aware of its own contingency. From his earliest poems on, Keats had conceived of his own work as a movement of becoming, a gradual widening of his consciousness by successive stages. The pattern is present in the prefigured outline of his own career in *Sleep and Poetry,* in the structure of *Endymion* which, for all its apparent disorder, is nevertheless organized as a consistent "growth of a poet's mind," in the famous letter to Reynolds of May 3, 1818, on the poet's progress from the thoughtless Chamber to the "Chamber of Maiden-Thought." This prospective scheme now no longer appears as a reassuring projection, since every step in the progression takes on the form of a tragedy beyond redemption, though not beyond the power of understanding. Nowhere does Keats come closer to a historical consciousness that recognizes and names the full power of negativity. Traveling entirely by his own pathways, he comes upon some of the insights that will shape the destiny of the nineteenth and twentieth centuries.

Yet it seems that Keats never achieves an authority that is commensurate with the quality of this perception. The conception of the poet's role, in *The Fall of Hyperion,* appears at once so lofty in its impersonality and disinterestedness, yet so humane in its concern for the grief of others, that we would expect a more serene tone in Keats's later work. Instead, he frequently sounds the strident note of someone who sees through the fallacy of his own certainties. There seems to be little room for self-deception in the stern wisdom of *The Fall of Hyperion*; where are we to find the point where Keats lies open to his own reproof?

Nothing could be more genuine than the positive aspect of Keats's concern for others: neither in the poetry nor in the letters can one discover a jarring tone that would reveal the presence of affectation or pose in his humanitarian attitude. Keats's generosity is total and all the more admirable since it is never based on an idealization of himself or of others, or on an attempt to emulate a chosen model. Perfect good faith, however, does not shelter us from the intricacies of moral inauthenticity. Keats's gift for sympathy has a negative aspect, and the significance of his complete evolution can only be understood if one takes this into account.

Already in *Endymion,* when Keats is speaking of love

and friendship as central formative experiences, he refers to these experiences as "self-destroying":

> But there are
> Richer entanglements, enthrallments far
> More self-destroying, leading, by degrees,
> To the chief intensity: the crown of these
> Is made of love and friendship ...
> (*Endymion*, I, ll. 797 ff.)

"Self-destroying" is obviously used in a positive sense here, to designate the moral quality of disinterestedness—yet "destroying" is a curiously strong term. The phrase is revealing, for a recurrent pattern in the poetry indicates a strong aversion to a direct confrontation with his own self; few poets have described the act of self-reflection in harsher terms. For Endymion, the most miserable condition of man is that in which he is left to consider his own self in solitude, even when this avowedly takes him close to teaching the "goal of consciousness" (II, l. 283):

> There, when new wonders ceased to float before,
> And thoughts of self came on, how crude and sore
> The journey homeward to habitual self!
> A mad pursuing of the fog-born elf,
> Whose flitting lantern, through rude nettle-brier,
> Cheats us into a swamp, into a fire,
> Into the bosom of a hated thing.
> (*Idem.* II, ll. 274 ff.)

The inward quest for self-knowledge is described here in the very terms used by Milton to represent the triumph of Satanic temptation (*Paradise Lost,* IX, ll. 633 ff.). The "hated thing" to which Keats refers is the situation, rather than the content of his own consciousness: the condition of the "sole self" is one of intolerable barrenness, the opposite of all that imagination, poetry and love can achieve. The experience of being "tolled back to one's sole self" is always profoundly negative. He almost succeeds in eliminating himself from his poetry altogether. There is, of course, much that is superficially autobiographical in *Endymion* and even in *Hyperion,* but one never gains an intimate sense of Keats's own selfhood remotely comparable to that conveyed by other romantic poets. The "I" of the Nightingale Ode, for instance, is always seen in the movement that takes it away from its own center. The emotions that accompany the discovery of the authentic self, feelings of guilt and dread as well as sudden moments of transparent clarity, are lacking in Keats. Poetic "sleep" or "trance" is a darkening, growing opacity of the consciousness. Suffering plays a very prominent role in his work, but it is always the suffering of others, sympathetically but objectively perceived and so easily generalized into historical and universal pain that it rarely appears in its subjective immediacy: a passage such as the opening scene of *Hyperion* gains its poetic effectiveness from the controlled detachment of an observer who is not directly threatened. The only threat that Keats seems to experience subjectively is that of self-confrontation.

Keats's sympathetic love thus appears less simple than it may seem at first sight: his intense and altogether genuine concern for others serves, in a sense, to shelter him from the self-knowledge he dreads. He is a man distracted from the awareness of his own mortality by the constant spectacle of the death of others. He can go very far in participating in their agony: he is indeed one "to whom the miseries of the world/Are misery and will not let [him] rest" (*Fall of Hyperion,* I, ll. 148–49). But the miseries are always "of the world" and not his own, a distinction that should disappear when the suffering referred to is so general that it designates a universal human predicament. Although it would be entirely false to say of Keats that he escaped out of human suffering into the idealized, trance-like condition of poetry, one can say, with proper caution, that he moves away from the burden of self-knowledge into a world created by the combined powers of the sympathetic imagination, poetry and history, a world that is ethically impeccable, but from which the self is excluded.

The tension resulting from this ambivalence does not remain entirely hidden. It comes to the surface, for instance, in the difficult choice he has to make in his literary allegiances, when he has to reconcile his admiration for Shakespeare and Milton with his consideration for Wordsworth, whom he considered his greatest contemporary. His own term for the "self-destroying" power of the poetic imagination is "negative capability," the ability of the mind to detach itself from its own identity, and he associates this characteristic of the poetic temperament primarily with Shakespeare. It is typical, in this respect, that he would consider Shakespeare's life as exemplary: "Shakespeare led a life of Allegory . . ." (letter to George Keats, February 19, 1819) in the full figural and Christian sense of the term, when it is precisely a life so buried under the wealth of its own inventions that it has ceased to exist as a particular experience. This stands, of course, in total contrast to what we find in Wordsworth, for whom the determining moment occurs when the mind exists in and for itself, in the transparency of an inwardness entirely focused upon the self. Even in the absence of the posthumously published *Prelude,* Keats knew the direction of Wordsworth's thought and felt the challenge it offered to his own orientation. W. J. Bate, in his biography of Keats, has well seen the decisive importance of this confrontation when, in the letter of May 3, 1818, to Reynolds, Keats rates Wordsworth above Milton ("who did not think into the human heart") because he is the poet of the conscious self. But Keats did not choose, at that time, to follow Wordsworth into the "dark passages" which he had begun to explore. The poem that stems from these meditations, the first *Hyperion,* is certainly not Wordsworthian and not altogether Miltonic either: the emphasis on characterization, the deliberate variety of tones, the pageant-like conception of history, are all frankly Shakespearian, and in many ways *Hyperion* resembles an optimistic, humanized version of *Troilus and Cressida* more than *Paradise Lost.* It definitely is a poem founded on negative capability. The sense of human sympathy has grown considerably since *Endymion,* but we are even further removed from real self-awareness than in the early poem. Only at the very end of his career will these unresolved tensions come fully into the open and disrupt the continuity of his development—but this happened, not as a result of literary influence but under the pressure of outward circumstances.

Interpreters of Keats have difficulty agreeing on the significance of his latest work: after the almost miraculous outburst of creative activity in May, 1819, when he wrote practically all the great odes in quick succession, there still followed a period of nearly six months until the final onset of his illness. *The Fall of Hyperion, Lamia* and several other shorter poems were written at that time. There is some logic in considering the entire period from June till the end of the year as one single unit—the "late" Keats—that includes the poems to Fanny Brawne, dating from the fall of 1819, and frequently considered as poetically unimportant and slightly embarrassing documents written when he was no longer in full control of his faculties. In truth, it is from *The Fall of Hyperion* on that a sharp change begins to take place; it is also from that moment on that the differences among the commentators begin to increase. For all the divergences in the interpretation of the main odes, there exists a clear consensus about the general meaning and merit of these poems; the differences refer to matters of detail and are certainly to be expected in the case of rich and complex poems studied in such great detail. But *The Fall of Hyperion* is considered by some as "the culmination of Keats's work" and the dialogue between Moneta and the poet as a "dialectical victory" over Moneta's attack on poetry; for others, however, the same passage is read as symbolizing "exhaustion and despair" at "seeing the world of poetry doomed to destruction."[1] *Lamia* has also given rise to incompatible readings and to general puzzlement. The hesitations of the critics are the unmistakable sign of a change that is so

---

[1] Edward E. Bostetter in *The Romantic Ventriloquists* (Seattle: University of Washington Press, 1963), p. 171; the preceding quotation is from Harold Bloom, *The Visionary Company* (New York and Toronto: Doubleday & Company, Inc., 1961), p. 418.

far-reaching that it requires a radical readjustment on the part of the readers. The particular difficulty and obscurity of *The Fall of Hyperion* and *Lamia* stems from the fact that they are works of transition toward a new phase that is fully revealed only in the last poems Keats wrote.

The striking fact about Keats's last poems is that they contain an attack on much that had been held sacred in the earlier work; one is reminded, at moments, of Yeats's savagely derisive treatment of his own myths in some of the *Last Poems*. There is something indecorous in the spectacle of a poet thus turning against himself and one can understand the desire of commentators to play down this episode in Keats's history, all the more since illness, poverty and increased bitterness invaded his life at the time, offering a convenient explanation for this radical change in tone. It would be a reflection, however, on the strength of Keats's earlier convictions if they had not been able to stand up under the pressure of these events, however damaging they may have been. Even among his near contemporaries—one thinks of Hölderlin, Maurice de Guérin and Gérard de Nerval—some of the most assertive poems are written in a comparable state of physical and mental distress. We must understand that, far from detracting from his stature, the negativity of Keats's last poems shows that he was about to add another dimension to a poetic development that, up till then, had not been altogether genuine.

We can take as an example the poem dated October, 1819, and entitled "To ——," sometimes referred to as "Ode" or "Second Ode to Fanny Brawne." The term "Ode" in the title is fitting, for the dramatic organization of the poem is very similar to that of the famous great odes; it is, in fact, the exact negative counterpart of the "Ode to a Nightingale." The paradox that was partly concealed by the richness of the language in the earlier odes is now fully revealed: the poems in fact set out to destroy the entities they claim to praise; or, to put it less bluntly, the ambiguity of feeling toward these entities is such that the poems fall apart. In the October poem, the absurdity of the dramatic situation is apparent from the first lines, in which Keats begs Fanny to assist him, by her presence, in curing a suffering of which this very presence is the sole cause:

> What can I do to drive away
> Remembrance from my eyes? for they have seen,
> Aye, an hour ago, my brilliant queen!
> Touch has a memory. O say, love, say,
> What can I do to kill it and be free
> In my old liberty?
>
> ("To ——," ll. 1 ff.)

The prospective character of Keats's poetry, which we stressed from the start, stands out here in its full meaning. The superiority of the future over the past expresses, in fact, a rejection of the experience of actuality. Memory, being founded on actual sensations, is for Keats the enemy of poetic language, which thrives instead on dreams of pure potentiality. In the last stanzas, the poem turns from past to future, with all the ardor of the sensuous desire that tormented Keats at the time, and with an immediacy that produces the kind of language that already proved so cumbersome in the erotic passages of *Endymion:*

> O, let me once more rest
> My soul upon that dazzling breast!
> Let once again these aching arms be placed,
> The tender gaolers of thy waist! . . .
> Give me those lips again!
>
> (*Idem.*, ll. 48 ff.)

The interest of the passage is that the desire it names has already been canceled out by the statement made at the onset of the poem. The passion that produces these lines is precisely what has been rejected at the start as the main obstacle to the "liberty" of poetic creation. Before Fanny's presence had put the poet within "the reach of fluttering love," his poetic faculties could grow unimpaired:

> My muse had wings
> And ever ready was to take her course
> Whither I bent her force, . . .
>
> (*Idem.*, ll. 11 ff.)

This belongs to a past that preceded his involvement; the movement toward the future is checked by the awareness of a contradiction that opposes love to poetry as memory is opposed to dream. Contradicting the prayer for her return, the poem concludes by stating a preference for imaginary passion over actual presence:

> Enough! Enough! it is enough for me
> To dream of thee!

It is certainly true that the poem destroys itself in a hopeless conflict between temptation and rejection, between praise and blame, that no language can hope to resolve. What is so revealing, however, is that the contradiction so crudely manifest here is potentially present in the earlier odes as well.

The difference in situation between this late poem and the odes "On a Grecian Urn" and "To a Nightingale" is obvious enough: the urn and the nightingale are general, impersonal entities, endowed with significance by an act of the poet's imagination; Fanny Brawne, on the other hand, is a highly distinct and specific person whose presence awakens in him an acute sense of threatened selfhood. The temptation she incarnates clashes directly with his desire to forget his own self. In the earlier odes, this conflict is avoided by keeping carefully apart what the urn and the nightingale signify for Keats himself, and what they signify for Keats in relation to humanity in general. The poetic effectiveness of the odes depends entirely on the positive temptation that emanates from the symbolic entities: the world to which they give access is a world of happiness and beauty, and it is by the suggestive evocation of this world that beauty enters the poems. This, in turn, allows for the dramatic contrast with the world of actual experience, caught in the destructive power of mutability and described throughout, in the Grecian Urn as well as in the Nightingale Ode, in terms that appeal directly to our moral sympathy:

> Here, where men sit and hear each other groan;
> Where palsy shakes a few, sad, last gray hairs,
> Where youth grows pale, and specter-thin, and dies;
> Where but to think is to be full of sorrow
> And leaden-eyed despairs . . .
> ("Ode to a Nightingale," ll. 24 ff.)

The mixture of emotions, in these texts, is subtle and self-deceiving. On the one hand, the poet's sympathy for the suffering of mankind gives him the kind of moral authority that allows him to call authoritatively for a lucid acceptance of human limitations. It is this morally responsible voice that warns his fellow men against the danger of giving in to the deceptive quality of poetic symbols: they "tease" and "deceive" in foreshadowing an eternity that is not within our reach; the urn and the nightingale finally act as powers of death and, in that sense, these poems are also written against the objects they set out to praise. But Keats does not remain in the barren, impoverished world of human contingency, the world of gray rocks and stones that is the landscape of Wordsworth's *Prelude*. As a poet, he does not seem to share in the torments of temporality. The youth that "grows pale, and specter-thin, and dies" in Stanza 3 of the Nightingale Ode could not possibly be the same voice that evokes so magnificently the change that comes over the world by losing oneself in the "embalmèd darkness" of the bird's song:

> I cannot see what flowers are at my feet,
>   Nor what soft incense hangs upon the boughs,
> But, in embalmèd darkness, guess each sweet
>   Wherewith the seasonable month endows
> The grass, the thicket, and the fruit-tree wild . . .
> (*Idem.*, ll. 41 ff.)

The richness of these most un-Wordsworthian lines can only come into being because Keats's self is in fact dissociated from the suffering mankind with which he sympathizes. As a humanist, he can lay claim to a good conscience and write poems that have reassured generations of readers, willing to be authoritatively told about the limits of their knowledge ("that is all/Ye know on earth, and all ye need to know"); but as a poet, he can indulge in the wealth of a soaring imagination whose power of metamorphosis knows no limits. The poet of the Grecian Urn would hardly be able to evoke the happy world on the urn if he were himself the creature "lowing at the skies" about to be sacrificed.

We can see, from the poem "To ──" what happens when this distance between the private self and its moral stance vanishes: the late poem is the "Ode to a Nightingale" with the metamorphic power of the imagination destroyed by a sense of real selfhood. This destruction now openly coincides with the appearance of love on the scene, in an overt admission that, up to this point, the moral seriousness of the poems had not, in fact, been founded on love at all:

> How shall I do
> To get anew
> Those molted feathers, and so mount once more
> Above, above
> The reach of fluttering Love
> And make him cower lowly while I soar?
> ("To ──," ll. 18 ff.)

The violence of the feeling is reminiscent of the hostile language in which Endymion refers to solitary self-knowledge. In the experience of love, the self comes to know itself without mask, and when this happens the carefree movement of the poetic imagination falters. Before, as we know from the Nightingale Ode, the intoxication of the imagination, like that of wine, was able to fuse the familiar Keatsian tension between heat and cold into one single sensation:

> O, for a draught of vintage! that hath been
> Cooled a long age in the deep-delved earth,
> Tasting of Flora and the country green,
> Dance, and Provençal song, and sunburned mirth!
> ("Ode to a Nightingale," ll. 11 ff.)

But now, in a world ruled by the law of love, such easy

syntheses are no longer within our power:

> Shall I gulp wine? No, that is vulgarism,
> A heresy and schism,
> Foisted into the canon law of love;—
> No—wine is only sweet to happy men; ...
> ("To ——," ll. 24 ff.)

Consequently, the metamorphosis of the landscape, achieved in Stanza 5 of the Nightingale Ode under the impact of the trancelike song, fails, and we are confronted instead with the bleakness of a totally de-mythologized world:

> That monstrous region, whose dull rivers pour,
> Ever from their sordid urns unto the shore,
> Unowned of any weedy-hairèd gods;
> Whose winds, all zephyrless, hold scourging rods,
> Iced in the great lakes, to afflict mankind;
> Whose rank-grown forests, frosted, black, and blind,
> Would fright a Dryad; whose harsh herbaged meads
> Make lean and lank the starved ox while he feeds;
> There bad flowers have no scent, birds no sweet song,
> And great unerring nature once seems wrong.
> (*Idem.*, ll. 34 ff.)

The landscape, at last, is that of Keats's real self, which he had kept so carefully hidden up till now under poetic myth and moral generosity. It is still an imagined landscape, but rooted this time in an experience that is both intimate and painful: his brother's financial disaster near the very "Great Lakes" here evoked was caused by such a landscape and it is certain that Keats equated his own miseries with the calamitous misadventures of his brother in America.[2] This does not make this landscape less "symbolic" than the world of the nightingale or the Grecian Urn, but it dramatizes the distinction between a symbol rooted in the self and one rooted in an abstract dream.

The power which forces a man to see himself as he

---

[2] Keats's younger brother George emigrated to Illinois, hoping to make a living from land that proved to be untillable; his financial troubles were a constant burden to Keats during the time of his engagement to Fanny Brawne and during his final illness.

really is, is also called "philosophy" in the later Keats; the term receives the same ambiguous value-emphasis as does the word "love." In the same poem "To ——," the previous poetry, written when he was free of the burden of love, is called "unintellectual" and the confining power of self-awareness is stressed again in the rhetorical question:

> What seabird o'er the sea
> Is a philosopher the while he goes
> Winging along where the great water throes?
> (*Idem.*, ll. 15 ff.)

We have come a long way since the early days of *Endymion* when Keats thought of philosophy as a means to help him carry out his generous dream of human redemption. Apollonius, the philosopher in *Lamia,* has all the outward attributes of villainy, yet there can be no doubt that truth is on his side: Lucius is about to mistake the seductiveness of a serpent for real love and it is, after all, his own weakness that is to blame for his inability to survive the revelation of the truth. In this poem, Truth and Beauty are indeed at odds, but one may well conjecture that, as Keats's sense of truth grew, he would have been able to discover a beauty that would have surpassed that of Lamia. Fanny Brawne may well have looked to him more like Moneta than like La Belle Dame sans Merci.

With the development that stood behind him, this final step could only take the violently negative form of his last poems. It is morally consistent that he would have rebelled against a generosity that offered more protection than it cost him. After having acted, in all his dreams of human redemption, as the one who rescues others from their mortal plight, his last poem reverses the parts. Taking off from an innocuous line in *The Fall of Hyperion* ("When this warm scribe my hand is in the grave") he now offers his hand no longer in a gesture of assistance to others, but as the victim who defies another to take away from him the weight of his own death:

> This living hand, now warm and capable
> Of earnest grasping, would, if it were cold
> And in the icy silence of the tomb,
> So haunt thy days and chill thy dreaming nights
> That thou wouldst wish thine own heart dry of blood
> So in my veins red life might stream again,
> And thou be conscience-calmed—see here it is—
> I hold it towards you.
>
> ("This Living Hand," ll. 1-8)

Romantic literature, at its highest moments, encompasses the greatest degree of generality in an experience that never loses contact with the individual self in which it originates. In the *Confessions,* Rousseau tells how an injustice committed at his expense during his youth awakened within him a universal moral sense: "I feel my pulse quicken as I write this; I shall never forget these moments if I live a hundred thousand years. This first experience of violence and injustice remained so deeply engraved on my soul that all ideas related to it take me back to this initial emotion; this experience which, at its origin, existed only for me, has acquired such a strong consistency in itself, and has grown so far away from my own self-interest, that my heart flares up at the sight or at the report of an unjust deed, committed anywhere at anyone's expense, as if it concerned me personally." It is the scope of this generalized passion which makes it possible for Rousseau to be at the same time the poet who wrote *Julie* and the moral philosopher who wrote the *Social Contract*. The same scope is present in Wordsworth and also, at times, in Blake and Coleridge. Nowadays, we are less than ever capable of philosophical generality rooted in genuine self-insight, while our sense of selfhood hardly ever rises above self-justification. Hence that our criticism of romanticism so often misses the mark: for the great romantics, consciousness of self was the first and necessary step toward moral judgment. Keats's last poems reveal that he reached the same insight; the fact that he arrived at it by a negative road may make him all the more significant for us.

INTRODUCTION

The format of this edition made it necessary to establish a selection among Keats's poems. The task was a relatively easy one, the only difficulty being caused by the considerable length of *Endymion*. It seemed preferable to include only complete poems, rather than to offer fragments from a larger number. *Endymion* in its entirety is indispensable for a reader interested in the workings of Keats's mythological imagination. There can be little argument about the inclusion of the other longer texts, nor can one feel too sorry about the absence of *Isabella, Otho the Great, King Stephen* and *The Cap and Bells*. All the odes and a generous selection of the sonnets are included. Although the picture that emerges from this selection is perhaps somewhat more severe than that presented by the complete Keats, it remains faithful in its essential outline.

The order of arrangement of the poems is a more difficult matter. Authoritative editions of the complete poetry follow the practice of printing the three volumes of Keats's poetry that appeared during his lifetime, with the poems arranged in the order suggested or approved by Keats himself (*Poems,* 1817; *Endymion: a Poetic Romance,* 1818; and *Lamia, Isabella,* etc., 1820). This is followed by the posthumous edition that appeared in 1848, edited by Richard Monckton Milnes, and concluded with the texts not included in the Milnes edition: *The Fall of Hyperion* and several shorter poems. In a selected edition, there is no point in following this order. I have preferred to divide the bulk of Keats's poetry in three main parts: the early Keats (until and including *Endymion*), the middle period (until and including the main odes written in May, 1819) and the late Keats, consistent with the thematic outline given in the preface. Within each of these sections, the grouping is roughly chronological. An exact chronological arrangement is impossible: certain dates are unknown or contested, the dates of other works stretch over longer periods and overlap with shorter pieces written during the time of composition of the longer poems. For the sake of symmetry, I have grouped the poems by genre, keeping odes, sonnets and other forms together.

The letters that have been included are chosen for the

light they throw on Keats's poetic and intellectual development, not for biographical reasons. Needless to say, the selection does not begin to do justice to the richness of this correspondence. On the other hand, the exegetic importance of the letters can be exaggerated. The poems are more inclusive, more coherent and further-reaching than the letters; I would not have wanted to sacrifice more of them for the sake of including more letters.

PAUL DE MAN
Cornell University

A General Note on the Text

The overall textual policy for the Signet Classic Poetry Series attempts to strike a balance between the convenience and dependability of total modernization, on the one hand, and the authenticity of an established text on the other. Starting with the Restoration and Augustan poets, the General Editor has set up the following guidelines for the individual editors:

Modern American spelling will be used, although punctuation may be adjusted by the editor of each volume when he finds it advisable. In any case, syllabic final "ed" will be rendered with grave accent to distinguish it from the silent one, which is written out without apostrophe (e.g., "to gild refinèd gold," but "asked" rather than "ask'd"). Archaic words and forms are to be kept, naturally, whenever the meter or the sense may require it.

In the case of poets from earlier periods, the text is more clearly a matter of the individual editor's choice, and the type and degree of modernization has been left to his decision. But in any event, archaic typographical conventions ("i," "j," "u," "v," etc.) have all been normalized in the modern way.

JOHN HOLLANDER

A Note on this Edition

The text of the poems is based on that of *The Poetical Works of John Keats,* edited by H. W. Garrod, second edition (New York and London: Oxford University Press, 1958). In case of important disagreements among editors, a brief note is given. The text of the letters is that of *The Letters of John Keats (1814–1821)* edited by Hyder E. Rollins in two volumes (Cambridge, Mass.: Harvard University Press, 1958). Although spelling has been modernized in the poems, Keats's unique punctuation has been retained in the letters.

Chronology

1795	October 31. Birth of John Keats, first child of Thomas Keats, a livery stable keeper, and Frances Jennings Keats, at Finsbury near London. His two brothers, George and Thomas, were born in 1797 and 1799, his sister Frances in 1803.
1803	Keats is sent to Clarke school in Enfield.
1804	April 16. Death of Keats's father, following a fatal fall from his horse. Keats's mother remarries the following year but the children remain in the care of the Jennings family while still attending the Clarke school.
1810	March. Death of Keats's mother, of tuberculosis. Mrs. Jennings, the only surviving grandmother, makes a will in favor of the three orphaned children and appoints as guardians Abbey and Saudell. Keats's difficulties in obtaining his money from Richard Abbey in later years will be the everlasting bane of his existence.
1811	Summer. Keats is taken out of the Clarke school and apprenticed to become a medical assistant (surgeon, as it was called) at Edmonton.
1814	Keats writes his first poem, an "Imitation of Spenser."
1815	October 1. He registers at Guy's Hospital to continue his apprenticeship. By July, 1816, he

completes his studies and is licensed to practice. He makes his first literary acquaintances and writes several short poems.

1816   May 5. Keats's first published poem, the sonnet "O Solitude," appears in the *Examiner*.

Summer. After completing his studies, goes to Margate and returns to London in September.

October. Writes the sonnet on Chapman's Homer after a visit to Cowden Clarke. Keats meets Leigh Hunt (whose influence preceded the meeting by more than a year), the painter Robert Haydon and John Hamilton Reynolds.

November. The three brothers start living together in Cheapside (London). Keats apprises his guardian Abbey of his decision not to become an apothecary and to choose poetry as a career.

While staying frequently at Hunt's cottage in Hampstead Heath, he expands the formerly begun poem *I Stood Tiptoe* and writes *Sleep and Poetry*.

1817   January–February. While writing several more sonnets, Keats prepares the publication of his first volume of poems.

March 1 or 3. In the company of Haydon and Reynolds, he sees the marbles of the Parthenon brought to England by Lord Elgin.

March 3. Publication of his first volume, entitled *Poems;* it went by nearly unnoticed.

April 14. Keats leaves for the Isle of Wight to start work on *Endymion*. His progress is slow; he moves to Margate, then to Canterbury and finally, in September, goes to stay at Oxford with Benjamin Bailey. He returns to London on October 30 and finishes the poem. This is the period of several important letters, including the letter on "Negative Capability."

December 28. The "immortal dinner" at Haydon's with Wordsworth, Monkhouse, Lamb and Reynolds.

1818   January. Revision of *Endymion;* Keats starts writing again, mostly sonnets.

March 4. Goes to stay in Devon and writes *Isabella.*

George Keats marries and announces his intent to emigrate to the United States.

May 3. Letter to Reynolds on Wordsworth and Milton.

May 4 or 5. Return to London, with Tom Keats increasingly ill.

May 13. *Endymion* appears.

June 24. George leaves from Liverpool to America and Keats departs with Charles Brown on a walking tour through Scotland. After a rainy and tiresome sojourn, he returns to London on August 8 and finds his brother Tom considerably worse.

September. Three violent attacks on *Endymion* appear in *Blackwood's,* the *Quarterly Review* and the *British Critic.*

In spite of Tom's approaching death and his own persistent sore throat, Keats begins *Hyperion.*

November. First meeting with Fanny Brawne though, at that time, Keats is mostly interested in Isabella Jones.

December. Tom Keats dies.

1819   January. Writes *The Eve of St. Agnes.*

February. Writes *The Eve of St. Mark,* broken off on February 17.

March. Keats has a final try at *Hyperion,* then gives it up.

April 21. He writes "La Belle Dame sans Merci."

Late April–May. Writes the main odes, in quick succession: Psyche, Nightingale, Grecian Urn, Melancholy and Indolence.

May 12. George Keats writes from America, asking for money; Keats goes to see Abbey but fails to get any support from him.

June 27. Leaves from Portsmouth to the Isle of Wight, where he starts *Lamia*.
Correspondence with Fanny Brawne.
July 22. Brown arrives at Shanklin (Isle of Wight) to collaborate at *Otho the Great*.
July 25. Keats is working on *The Fall of Hyperion* which he abandons on September 21.
August 12. Moves to Winchester, where, on September 10, he receives another letter from George announcing further financial loss. He makes another unsuccessful visit to Abbey.
September 19. Ode "To Autumn."
October 8 or 9. Returns to London and, after a period of uncertainty, goes back to live at Wentworth Place in Hampstead with Brown. During this period, he writes the last poems addressed to Fanny Brawne and, possibly, the sonnet "Bright Star."
December. Engaged to Fanny Brawne.

1820
January 7–9. George Keats comes to London to try to settle his affairs, with partial success.
February 3. Six days after George's departure to the U. S., Keats has a severe hemorrhage and will be steadily ill from now on.
April 27. Final volume of Keats's poems given to the publishers Taylor and Hessey. He is now mostly living on money borrowed from Brown.
July. At last in competent medical care, Keats is told that he should leave for Italy by the end of the summer.
July 3. His last volume, *Lamia, Isabella, The Eve of St. Agnes and Other Poems,* is published.
September 18. Embarks at Gravesend for Italy in the company of Severn. He will actually go ashore in Naples only on October 31.
November. Keats moves in rooms at the Piazza di Spagna in Rome; his illness gets steadily worse.

1821	February 23. Death of John Keats, buried in Rome on February 26.
1848	Monckton Milnes edits *The Life, Letters and Literary Remains of John Keats*.
1867	*The Life and Letters of John Keats*, edited by Lord Houghton.
1900–01	*The Complete Works of John Keats*, 5 volumes, edited by Harry Buxton Forman.

Selected Bibliography

Editions of the Works

The Poetical Works and Other Writings of John Keats. Harry Buxton Forman (ed.). Revised by Maurice Buxton Forman. 8 volumes. New York and London: Charles Scribner's Sons, 1938–1939.

The Poetical Works of John Keats. H. W. Garrod (ed.). 2nd edition. New York and London: Oxford University Press, 1958.

The Letters of John Keats (1814–1821). Hyder E. Rollins (ed.). 2 volumes. Cambridge, Mass.: Harvard University Press; London: Cambridge University Press; Toronto: S. J. Reginald Saunders & Company, Ltd., 1958.

Biographies

Bate, Walter Jackson. *John Keats.* Cambridge, Mass.: Harvard University Press; London: Oxford University Press; Toronto: S. J. Reginald Saunders & Company, Ltd., 1963.

Brown, Charles Armitage. *Life of John Keats.* Edited by Dorothy Bodurtha and Willard B. Pope. New York and London: Oxford University Press, 1937.

Colvin, Sir Sidney. *John Keats: His Life and Poetry, His Friends, Critics, and After-Fame.* 3rd edition. New York and London: Charles Scribner's Sons, 1925.

Gittings, Robert. *John Keats: The Living Year.* Cambridge, Mass.: Harvard University Press; London: William Heinemann, Ltd., 1954.

Hewlett, Dorothy. *A Life of John Keats*. 2nd edition. London: Hurst & Blackett, Ltd., 1949; New York: Barnes & Noble, Inc., 1950.

Lowell, Amy. *John Keats*. 2 volumes. Boston: Houghton Mifflin Company, 1925.

Rollins, Hyder E. (ed.). *The Keats Circle: Letters and Papers*. 2 volumes. Cambridge, Mass.: Harvard University Press, 1948.

Ward, Aileen. *John Keats: The Making of a Poet*. New York: The Viking Press, Inc.; London: Martin Secker & Warburg, Ltd.; Toronto: The Macmillan Company of Canada, Limited, 1963.

Criticism

Arnold, Matthew. *Essays in Criticism: First Series*. New York and London: The Macmillan Company, 1925.

Bate, Walter Jackson. *The Stylistic Development of Keats*. New York: Modern Language Association of America; London: Oxford University Press, 1945.

Blackstone, Bernard. *The Consecrated Urn: An Interpretation of Keats in Terms of Growth and Form*. New York and Toronto: Longmans, Green & Co., Inc., 1959.

Bloom, Harold. *The Visionary Company*. New York and Toronto: Doubleday & Company, Inc.; London: Faber & Faber, Ltd., 1961.

Bostetter, Edward E. *The Romantic Ventriloquists*. Seattle: University of Washington Press, 1963.

Brooks, Cleanth. *The Well-Wrought Urn*. New York: Harcourt, Brace & Company, Inc.; Toronto: McClelland & Stewart, Ltd., 1947.

Burke, Kenneth. *A Grammar of Motives*. New York: Prentice-Hall, Inc.; London: Dennis Dobson, Ltd.; Toronto: George J. McLeod, Ltd., 1945.

Bush, Douglas. *Mythology and the Romantic Tradition in English Poetry*. Cambridge, Mass.: Harvard University Press; London: Oxford University Press, 1937.

SELECTED BIBLIOGRAPHY

Caldwell, James. *John Keats' Fancy*. Ithaca, N.Y.: Cornell University Press; London: Oxford University Press, 1945.

Empson, William. *The Structure of Complex Words*. Norfolk, Conn.: New Directions; London: Chatto & Windus; Toronto: Clarke, Irwin & Company, Ltd., 1951.

Finney, Claude. *The Evolution of Keats's Poetry*. 2 volumes. Cambridge, Mass.: Harvard University Press; London: Oxford University Press, 1936.

Fogle, Richard H. *The Imagery of Keats and Shelley: A Comparative Study*. Chapel Hill, N.C.: University of North Carolina Press; London: Oxford University Press, 1949.

Ford, Newell F. *The Prefigurative Imagination of John Keats*. Stanford, Calif.: Stanford University Press; London: Oxford University Press, 1951.

Gittings, Robert. *The Mask of Keats*. Cambridge, Mass.: Harvard University Press; London: William Heinemann, Ltd., 1956.

Lyon, Harvey T. (ed.). *Keats' Well-Read Urn*. New York: Henry Holt & Co., Inc., 1958.

MacGillivray, James R. *Keats: A Bibliography and Reference Guide*. London: Oxford University Press; Toronto: University of Toronto Press, 1949.

Muir, Kenneth. "The Meaning of *Hyperion*," *Essays in Criticism*, II (1952), 54–75.

Murry, John Middleton. *Keats*. Revised edition. New York: Noonday Press; London: Jonathan Cape, Ltd.; Toronto: Clarke, Irwin & Company, Ltd., 1955.

Perkins, David. *The Quest for Permanence*. Cambridge, Mass.: Harvard University Press; London: Oxford University Press, 1959.

Pettet, Ernest Charles. *On the Poetry of Keats*. London: Cambridge University Press, 1957.

Thorpe, Clarence. "Keats and Hazlitt," *Publications of the Modern Language Association*, LXXII (1947), 487–502.

Thorpe, Clarence. *The Mind of John Keats*. London: Oxford University Press, 1926.

Wasserman, Earl. *The Finer Tone: Keats' Major Poems.* Baltimore: Johns Hopkins Press; London: Oxford University Press; Toronto: Burns and MacEachern, 1953.

———. *The Subtler Language.* Baltimore: Johns Hopkins Press; London: Oxford University Press; Toronto: Burns & MacEachern, 1959.

Wicker, Brian. "The Disputed Lines in *The Fall of Hyperion,*" *Essays in Criticism,* VII (1957), 28–41.

I. The Early Keats

EPISTLES

To George Felton Mathew°

'Among the rest a shepheard (though but young
'Yet hartned to his pipe) with all the skill
'His few yeeres could, began to fit his quill.'
     Britannia's Pastorals.—BROWNE.

Sweet are the pleasures that to verse belong,
And doubly sweet a brotherhood in song;
Nor can remembrance, Mathew! bring to view
A fate more pleasing, a delight more true
Than that in which the brother Poets joyed,   5
Who with combined powers, their wit employed
To raise a trophy to the drama's muses.
The thought of this great partnership diffuses
Over the genius-loving heart, a feeling
Of all that's high, and great, and good, and healing. 10

---

0 **To George Felton Mathew** written in November, 1815, the first of three Epistles in the manner of Michael Drayton (1563–1631). George Felton Mathew was a friend of Keats's during the latter's stay at Guy Hospital as an apprentice surgeon. A very mediocre poet, he was nevertheless generously admired by the young Keats. They later drifted apart.

Too partial friend! Fain would I follow thee
Past each horizon of fine poesy;
Fain would I echo back each pleasant note
As o'er Sicilian seas, clear anthems float
15 'Mong the light skimming gondolas far parted,
Just when the sun his farewell beam has darted:
But 'tis impossible; far different cares
Beckon me sternly from soft "Lydian airs,"
And hold my faculties so long in thrall,
20 That I am oft in doubt whether at all
I shall again see Phœbus in the morning:
Or flushed Aurora in the roseate dawning!
Or a white Naiad in a rippling stream;
Or a rapt seraph in a moonlight beam;
25 Or again witness what with thee I've seen,
The dew by fairy feet swept from the green,
After a night of some quaint jubilee
Which every elf and fay° had come to see:
When bright processions took their airy march
30 Beneath the curvèd moon's triumphal arch.

But might I now each passing moment give
To the coy muse, with me she would not live
In this dark city, nor would condescend
'Mid contradictions her delights to lend.
35 Should e'er the fine-eyed maid to me be kind,
Ah! surely it must be whene'er I find
Some flowery spot, sequestered, wild, romantic,
That often must have seen a poet frantic;
Where oaks, that erst the Druid knew, are growing,
40 And flowers, the glory of one day, are blowing;
Where the dark-leaved laburnum's drooping clusters
Reflect athwart the stream their yellow lusters,
And intertwined the cassia's arms unite,
With its own drooping buds, but very white;
45 Where on one side are covert branches hung,
'Mong which the nightingales have always sung

---

28 **elf and fay** in the manner of Wieland's *Oberon*, which Keats and Mathews had read together in the translation by William Sotheby.

TO GEORGE FELTON MATHEW

In leafy quiet: where to pry, aloof,
Atween the pillars of the sylvan roof,
Would be to find where violet beds were nestling,
And where the bee with cowslip bells was wrestling.   50
There must be too a ruin dark, and gloomy,
To say "joy not too much in all that's bloomy."

Yet this is vain—O Mathew lend thy aid
To find a place where I may greet the maid—
Where we may soft humanity put on,   55
And sit, and rhyme and think on Chatterton;°
And that warm-hearted Shakespeare sent to meet him
Four laureled spirits, heavenward to intreat him.
With reverence would we speak of all the sages
Who have left streaks of light athwart their ages: 60
And thou shouldst moralize on Milton's blindness,
And mourn the fearful dearth of human kindness
To those who strove with the bright golden wing
Of genius, to flap away each sting
Thrown by the pitiless world. We next could tell   65
Of those who in the cause of freedom fell;
Of our own Alfred,° of Helvetian Tell;
Of him whose name to ev'ry heart's a solace,
High-minded and unbending William Wallace.°
While to the rugged north our musing turns   70
We well might drop a tear for him, and Burns.°

Felton! without incitements such as these,
How vain for me the niggard Muse to tease:
For thee, she will thy every dwelling grace,
And make "a sunshine in a shady place":   75

---

56 Chatterton the unfortunate author of the spurious Rowley poems, whose suicide in 1770, when he was 18 years old, became a universal romantic myth. *Endymion* is dedicated to Chatterton, and there exists a very early sonnet by Keats "To Chatterton." **67 Alfred** Alfred the Great (848–899), who defeated the Danes and conquered England, frequently appears, with Wilhelm Tell or some other national hero, among Keats's emblems of liberal patriotism. **69 William Wallace** (1272–1305), the popular hero of the Scottish national liberation. **71 Burns** Robert Burns (1759–1796), the famous Scottish poet, for whom Keats always had a considerable admiration. See the two sonnets on Burns on pp. 259, 260.

For thou wast once a flowret blooming wild,
Close to the source,° bright, pure, and undefiled,
Whence gush the streams of song: in happy hour
Came chaste Diana° from her shady bower,
80 Just as the sun was from the east uprising;
And, as for him some gift she was devising,
Beheld thee, plucked thee, cast thee in the stream
To meet her glorious brother's greeting beam.
I marvel much that thou hast never told
85 How, from a flower, into a fish of gold
Apollo changed thee; how thou next didst seem
A black-eyed swan upon the widening stream;
And when thou first didst in that mirror trace
The placid features of a human face:
90 That thou hast never told thy travels strange,
And all the wonders of the mazy range
O'er pebbly crystal, and o'er golden sands;
Kissing thy daily food from Naiad's pearly hands.

To My Brother George°

Full many a dreary hour° have I past,
My brain bewildered, and my mind o'ercast
With heaviness; in seasons when I've thought
No spherey strains by me could e'er be caught
5 From the blue dome, though I to dimness gaze
On the far depth where sheeted lightning plays;

---

77 **source** the Pierian Spring of the Muses, where all poetic song originates. 79 **Diana** one of the first mentions of the moon goddess, who will play such a prominent part in Keats's mythology. 0 **To My Brother George** George Keats, born on February 28, 1797, sixteen months younger than John Keats, remained very close to the poet throughout his life. When George emigrated to America in 1818, some of Keats's most important letters were addressed to him and to his wife Georgiana. This poem was written in August, 1816, from the seaside resort of Margate, where Keats had gone on a short vacation after taking his examinations. 1 **dreary hour** Keats had left for Margate in the hope of finding easy inspiration for his poetry and discovered, with some despair, that his main experience was the difficulty of writing.

TO MY BROTHER GEORGE 55

Or, on the wavy grass outstretched supinely,
Pry 'mong the stars, to strive to think divinely:
That I should never hear Apollo's song,
Though feathery clouds were floating all along   10
The purple west, and, two bright streaks between,
The golden lyre itself were dimly seen:
That the still murmur of the honey bee
Would never teach a rural song to me:
That the bright glance from beauty's eyelids slanting 15
Would never make a lay of mine enchanting,
Or warm my breast with ardor to unfold
Some tale of love and arms in time of old.

But there are times, when those that love the bay,
Fly from all sorrowing far, far away;   20
A sudden glow comes on them, naught they see
In water, earth, or air, but poesy.
It has been said, dear George, and true I hold it,
(For knightly Spenser to Libertas° told it,)
That when a Poet is in such a trance,   25
In air he sees white coursers paw, and prance,
Bestridden of gay knights, in gay apparel,
Who at each other tilt in playful quarrel,
And what we, ignorantly, sheet-lightning call,
Is the swift opening of their wide portal,   30
When the bright warder blows his trumpet clear,
Whose tones reach naught on earth but Poet's ear.
When these enchanted portals open wide,
And through the light the horsemen swiftly glide,
The Poet's eye can reach those golden halls,   35
And view the glory of their festivals:
Their ladies fair, that in the distance seem
Fit for the silv'ring of a seraph's dream;
Their rich-brimmed goblets, that incessant run
Like the bright spots that move about the sun;   40
And, when upheld, the wine from each bright jar

---

24 **Libertas** pseudonym for Leigh Hunt, in reference to his liberal political convictions (see also Epistle to C. C. Clarke, line 44). Hunt's poetic manner was a latter-day imitation of Spenser.

Pours with the luster of a falling star.
Yet further off, are dimly seen their bowers,
Of which, no mortal eye can reach the flowers;
And 'tis right just, for well Apollo knows
'Twould make the Poet quarrel with the rose.
All that's revealed from that far seat of blisses,
Is, the clear fountains' interchanging kisses,
As gracefully descending, light and thin,
Like silver streaks across a dolphin's fin,
When he upswimmeth from the coral caves,
And sports with half his tail above the waves.

These wonders strange he sees, and many more,
Whose head is pregnant with poetic lore.
Should he upon an evening ramble fare
With forehead to the soothing breezes bare,
Would he naught see but the dark, silent blue
With all its diamonds trembling through and through?
Or the coy moon, when in the waviness
Of whitest clouds she does her beauty dress,
And staidly paces higher up, and higher,
Like a sweet nun in holy-day attire?
Ah, yes! much more would start into his sight—
The revelries, and mysteries of night:
And should I ever see them, I will tell you
Such tales as needs must with amazement spell you.

These are the living pleasures of the bard:
But richer far posterity's award.
What does he murmur with his latest breath,
While his proud eye looks through the film of death?
"What though I leave this dull, and earthly mold,
Yet shall my spirit lofty converse hold
With after times.—The patriot shall feel
My stern alarum, and unsheath his steel;
Or, in the senate thunder out my numbers
To startle princes from their easy slumbers.
The sage will mingle with each moral theme
My happy thought sententious; he will teem
With lofty periods when my verses fire him,

TO MY BROTHER GEORGE

And then I'll stoop from heaven to inspire him.
Lays have I left of such a dear delight
That maids will sing them on their bridal night.
Gay villagers, upon a morn of May,
When they have tired their gentle limbs with play,
And formed a snowy circle on the grass,
And placed in midst of all that lovely lass
Who chosen is their queen,—with her fine head
Crownèd with flowers purple, white, and red:
For there the lily, and the musk-rose, sighing,
Are emblems true of hapless lovers dying:
Between her breasts, that never yet felt trouble,
A bunch of violets full blown, and double,
Serenely sleep:—she from a casket takes
A little book—and then a joy awakes
About each youthful heart—with stifled cries,
And rubbing of white hands, and sparkling eyes:
For she's to read a tale of hopes, and fears;
One that I fostered in my youthful years:
The pearls, that on each glist'ning circlet sleep,
Gush ever and anon with silent creep,
Lured by the innocent dimples. To sweet rest
Shall the dear babe, upon its mother's breast,
Be lulled with songs of mine. Fair world, adieu!
Thy dales, and hills, are fading from my view:
Swiftly I mount, upon wide spreading pinions,
Far from the narrow bounds of thy dominions.
Full joy I feel, while thus I cleave the air,
That my soft verse will charm thy daughters fair,
And warm thy sons!" Ah, my dear friend and brother,
Could I, at once, my mad ambition smother,
For tasting joys like these, sure I should be
Happier, and dearer to society.
At times, 'tis true, I've felt relief from pain
When some bright thought has darted through my brain:
Through all that day I've felt a greater pleasure
Than if I'd brought to light a hidden treasure.
As to my sonnets, though none else should heed them,
I feel delighted, still, that you should read them.
Of late, too, I have had much calm enjoyment,

Stretched on the grass at my best loved employment
Of scribbling lines for you. These things I thought
While, in my face, the freshest breeze I caught.
E'en now I'm pillowed on a bed of flowers
That crowns a lofty clift, which proudly towers
Above the ocean waves. The stalks, and blades,
Checker my tablet with their quivering shades.
On one side is a field of drooping oats,
Through which the poppies show their scarlet coats;
So pert and useless, that they bring to mind
The scarlet coats° that pester humankind.
And on the other side, outspread, is seen
Ocean's blue mantle streaked with purple, and green.
Now 'tis I see a canvassed ship, and now
Mark the bright silver curling round her prow.
I see the lark down-dropping to his nest,
And the broad winged sea gull never at rest;
For when no more he spreads his feathers free,
His breast is dancing on the restless sea.
Now I direct my eyes into the west,
Which at this moment is in sunbeams dressed:
Why westward turn? 'Twas but to say adieu!
'Twas but to kiss my hand, dear George, to you!

To Charles Cowden Clarke°

Off have you seen a swan superbly frowning,
And with proud breast his own white shadow crowning;
He slants his neck beneath the waters bright

---

130 **scarlet coats** political allusion, in the manner of Leigh Hunt, to the oppressive regime of the King and his Army. 0 **To Charles Cowden Clarke** The poem is dated from September, 1816. Charles Cowden Clarke was the son of John Clarke, the director of the school at Enfield where Keats was a student from 1803 to 1811. Though eight years older than John Keats, their friendship, based on common literary interests, was close and long-lasting. Clarke's recollections of Keats's early boyhood are the main source of information on Keats's youth.

TO CHARLES COWDEN CLARKE

So silently, it seems a beam of light
Come from the Galaxy: anon he sports—
With outspread wings the Naiad Zephyr courts,
Or ruffles all the surface of the lake
In striving from its crystal face to take
Some diamond water drops, and them to treasure
In milky nest, and sip them off at leisure.
But not a moment can he there insure them,
Nor to such downy rest can he allure them;
For down they rush as though they would be free,
And drop like hours into eternity.
Just like that bird am I in loss of time,
Whene'er I venture on the stream of rhyme;
With shattered boat, oar snapped, and canvas rent,
I slowly sail, scarce knowing my intent;
Still scooping up the water with my fingers,
In which a trembling diamond never lingers.

By this, friend Charles, you may full plainly see
Why I have never penned a line to thee:
Because my thoughts were never free, and clear,
And little fit to please a classic ear;
Because my wine was of too poor a savor
For one whose palate gladdens in the flavor
Of sparkling Helicon:°—small good it were
To take him to a desert rude, and bare,
Who had on Baiæ's° shore reclined at ease,
While Tasso's page was floating in a breeze
That gave soft music from Armida's° bowers,
Mingled with fragrance from her rarest flowers:
Small good to one who had by Mulla's° stream
Fondled the maidens with the breasts of cream;°
Who had beheld Belphœbe° in a brook,
And lovely Una° in a leafy nook,

---

27 **Helicon** the mountain of the Muses. Clarke was one of the first to introduce Keats to classical poetry. 29 **Baiæ** city of ancient Italy, near Naples, here symbolizing Roman and Italian poetry. 31 **Armida** one of the heroines of Tasso's poem *Jerusalem Delivered*. 33 **Mulla** a river near Spenser's first home, frequently alluded to in his poetry. Clarke had introduced Keats to the work of Spenser. 34 **breasts of cream** a Keatsian version of a line in Spenser's *Epithalamion* (l. 175). 35–36 **Belphœbe, Una,** the main characters in Books I and II of Spenser's *Faerie Queene*.

TO CHARLES COWDEN CLARKE

And Archimago° leaning o'er his book:
Who had of all that's sweet tasted, and seen,
From silv'ry ripple, up to beauty's queen;
From the sequester'd haunts of gay Titania,°
To the blue dwelling of divine Urania:°
One, who, of late, had ta'en sweet forest walks
With him who elegantly chats, and talks—
The wrongèd Libertas,°—who has told you stories
Of laurel chaplets, and Apollo's glories;
Of troops chivalrous prancing through a city,
And tearful ladies made for love, and pity:
With many else which I have never known.

Thus have I thought; and days on days have flown
Slowly, or rapidly—unwilling still
For you to try my dull, unlearnèd quill.
Nor should I now, but that I've known you long;
That you first taught me all the sweets of song:
The grand, the sweet, the terse, the free, the fine;
What swelled with pathos, and what right divine:
Spenserian vowels that elope with ease,
And float along like birds o'er summer seas;
Miltonian storms, and more, Miltonian tenderness;
Michael in arms, and more, meek Eve's fair slenderness.
Who read for me the sonnet swelling loudly
Up to its climax and then dying proudly?
Who found for me the grandeur of the ode,
Growing, like Atlas, stronger from its load?
Who let me taste that more than cordial dram,
The sharp, the rapier-pointed epigram?
Showed me that epic was of all the king,
Round, vast, and spanning all like Saturn's ring?
You too upheld the veil from Clio's° beauty,
And pointed out the patriot's stern duty;

---

37 **Archimago** the villainous wizard in the *Faerie Queene*. 40 **Titania** Queen of the Fairies in Shakespeare's *A Midsummer Night's Dream*. 41 **Urania** the sky. 44 **Libertas** the poet Leigh Hunt, to whom Clarke later introduced Keats. He is "wronged" because he has been jailed for his liberal political leanings. 68 **Clio** Muse of History.

TO CHARLES COWDEN CLARKE

The might of Alfred,° and the shaft of Tell; 70
The hand of Brutus,° that so grandly fell
Upon a tyrant's head. Ah! had I never seen,
Or known your kindness, what might I have been?
What my enjoyments in my youthful years,
Bereft of all that now my life endears? 75
And can I e'er these benefits forget?
And can I e'er repay the friendly debt?
No, doubly no;—yet should these rhymings please,
I shall roll on the grass with twofold ease:
For I have long time been my fancy feeding 80
With hopes that you would one day think the reading
Of my rough verses not an hour misspent;
Should it e'er be so, what a rich content!

Some weeks have passed since last I saw the spires
In lucent Thames reflected:—warm desires 85
To see the sun o'er-peep the eastern dimness,
And morning shadows streaking into slimness
Across the lawny fields, and pebbly water;
To mark the time as they grow broad, and shorter;
To feel the air that plays about the hills, 90
And sips its freshness from the little rills;
To see high, golden corn wave in the light
When Cynthia° smiles upon a summer's night,
And peers among the cloudlet's jet and white,
As though she were reclining in a bed 95
Of bean blossoms, in heaven freshly shed—
No sooner had I stepped into these pleasures
Than I began to think of rhymes and measures:
The air that floated by me seemed to say
"Write! thou wilt never have a better day." 100
And so I did. When many lines I'd written,
Though with their grace I was not oversmitten,
Yet, as my hand was warm, I thought I'd better
Trust to my feelings, and write you a letter.

70 **Alfred** See note to line 67 of the *Epistle to Mathew*. 71 **Brutus** As the consul who instituted the Roman Republic, Brutus is one of Keats's symbols for political liberalism. 93 **Cynthia** another name for Diana, the moon goddess. She reappears under this name in *En-*

TO CHARLES COWDEN CLARKE

¹⁰⁵ Such an attempt required an inspiration
Of peculiar sort—a consummation—
Which, had I felt, these scribblings might have been
Verses from which the soul would never wean:
But many days have past since last my heart
¹¹⁰ Was warmed luxuriously by divine Mozart;
By Arne° delighted, or by Handel maddened;
Or by the song of Erin pierced and saddened:
What time you were before the music sitting,
And the rich notes to each sensation fitting;
¹¹⁵ Since I have walked with you through shady lanes
That freshly terminate in open plains,
And reveled in a chat that ceasèd not
When at nightfall among your books we got:
No, nor when supper came, nor after that—
¹²⁰ Nor when reluctantly I took my hat;
No, nor till cordially you shook my hand
Midway between our homes:—your accents bland
Still sounded in my ears, when I no more
Could hear your footsteps touch the grav'ly floor.
¹²⁵ Sometimes I lost them, and then found again;
You changed the footpath for the grassy plain.
In those still moments I have wished you joys
That well you know to honor:—"Life's very toys
With him," said I, "will take a pleasant charm;
¹³⁰ It cannot be that ought will work him harm."
These thoughts now come o'er me with all their might:—
Again I shake your hand—friend Charles, good night.

---

dymion. 111 **Arne** Thomas A. Arne (1710–1778) English composer of operas, masques, and incidental music for plays, notably Shakespeare's.

I STOOD TIPTOE°

> Places of nestling green for Poets made.
> STORY OF RIMINI.°

I stood tiptoe upon a little hill,
The air was cooling, and so very still,
That the sweet buds which with a modest pride
Pull droopingly, in slanting curve aside,
Their scantly leaved, and finely tapering stems,   5
Had not yet lost those starry diadems
Caught from the early sobbing of the morn.
The clouds were pure and white as flocks new shorn,
And fresh from the clear brook; sweetly they slept
On the blue fields of heaven, and then there crept   10
A little noiseless noise among the leaves,
Born of the very sigh that silence heaves:
For not the faintest motion could be seen
Of all the shades that slanted o'er the green.
There was wide wand'ring for the greediest eye,   15
To peer about upon variety;
Far round the horizon's crystal air to skim,
And trace the dwindled edgings of its brim;
To picture out the quaint, and curious bending
Of a fresh woodland alley, never ending;   20
Or by the bowery clefts, and leafy shelves,
Guess where the jaunty streams refresh themselves.
I gazed awhile, and felt as light, and free
As though the fanning wings of Mercury
Had played upon my heels: I was light-hearted,   25
And many pleasures to my vision started;
So I straightway began to pluck a posy
Of luxuries bright, milky, soft and rosy.

0 **I Stood Tiptoe** is now generally used as the title of the poem; it was originally entitled *Endymion*. Begun before July, 1817, it was completed in December, 1817.   0 **Story of Rimini** a romance published in February, 1816, by Leigh Hunt, Keats's closest friend and master at the time of writing this poem.

63

A bush of May flowers with the bees about them;
30 Ah, sure no tasteful nook would be without them;
And let a lush laburnum oversweep them,
And let long grass grow round the roots to keep them
Moist, cool and green; and shade the violets,
That they may bind the moss in leafy nets.

35 A filbert hedge with wild brier overtwined,
And clumps of woodbine taking the soft wind
Upon their summer thrones; there too should be
The frequent checker of a youngling tree,
That with a score of light green brethren shoots
40 From the quaint mossiness of agèd roots:
Round which is heard a spring-head of clear waters
Babbling so wildly of its lovely daughters
The spreading blue bells: it may haply mourn
That such fair clusters should be rudely torn
45 From their fresh beds, and scattered thoughtlessly
By infant hands, left on the path to die.

Open afresh your round of starry folds,
Ye ardent marigolds!
Dry up the moisture from your golden lids,
50 For great Apollo bids
That in these days your praises should be sung
On many harps, which he has lately strung;
And when again your dewiness he kisses,
Tell him, I have you in my world of blisses:
55 So haply when I rove in some far vale,
His mighty voice may come upon the gale.

Here are sweet peas, on tiptoe for a flight:
With wings of gentle flush o'er delicate white,
And taper fingers catching at all things,
60 To bind them all about with tiny rings.

Linger awhile upon some bending planks
That lean against a streamlet's rushy banks,
And watch intently Nature's gentle doings:
They will be found softer than ring-dove's cooings.
65 How silent comes the water round that bend;

I STOOD TIPTOE

Not the minutest whisper does it send
To the o'erhanging sallows: blades of grass
Slowly across the checkered shadows pass.

Why, you might read two sonnets, ere they reach
To where the hurrying freshnesses aye preach
A natural sermon o'er their pebbly beds;
Where swarms of minnows show their little heads,
Staying their wavy bodies 'gainst the streams,
To taste the luxury of sunny beams
Tempered with coolness. How they ever wrestle
With their own sweet delight, and ever nestle
Their silver bellies on the pebbly sand.
If you but scantily hold out the hand,
That very instant not one will remain;
But turn your eye, and they are there again.
The ripples seem right glad to reach those cresses,
And cool themselves among the em'rald tresses;
The while they cool themselves, they freshness give,
And moisture, that the bowery green may live:
So keeping up an interchange of favors,
Like good men in the truth of their behaviors.
Sometimes goldfinches one by one will drop
From low hung branches; little space they stop;
But sip, and twitter, and their feathers sleek;
Then off at once, as in a wanton freak:
Or perhaps, to show their black, and golden wings,
Pausing upon their yellow flutterings.
Were I in such a place, I sure should pray
That nought less sweet might call my thoughts away,
Than the soft rustle of a maiden's gown
Fanning away the dandelion's down;
Than the light music of her nimble toes
Patting against the sorrel as she goes.
How she would start, and blush, thus to be caught
Playing in all her innocence of thought.
O let me lead her gently o'er the brook,
Watch her half-smiling lips, and downward look;
O let me for one moment touch her wrist;
Let me one moment to her breathing list;
And as she leaves me may she often turn

Her fair eyes looking through her locks aubùrne.
What next? A tuft of evening primroses,
O'er which the mind may hover till it dozes;
O'er which it well might take a pleasant sleep,
110 But that 'tis ever startled by the leap
Of buds into ripe flowers; or by the flitting
Of diverse moths, that aye their rest are quitting;
Or by the moon lifting her silver rim
Above a cloud, and with a gradual swim
115 Coming into the blue with all her light,
O Maker of sweet poets, dear delight
Of this fair world, and all its gentle livers;
Spangler of clouds, halo of crystal rivers,
Mingler with leaves, and dew and tumbling streams,
120 Closer of lovely eyes to lovely dreams,
Lover of loneliness, and wandering,
Of upcast eye, and tender pondering!
Thee must I praise above all other glories
That smile us on to tell delightful stories.
125 For what has made the sage or poet write
But the fair paradise of Nature's light?
In the calm grandeur of a sober line,
We see the waving of the mountain pine;
And when a tale is beautifully staid,
130 We feel the safety of a hawthorn glade:
When it is moving on luxurious wings,
The soul is lost in pleasant smotherings:
Fair dewy roses brush against our faces,
And flowering laurels spring from diamond vases;
135 O'er head we see the jasmine and sweet brier,
And bloomy grapes laughing from green attire;
While at our feet, the voice of crystal bubbles
Charms us at once away from all our troubles:
So that we feel uplifted from the world,
140 Walking upon the white clouds wreathed and curled.
So felt he, who first told, how Psyche° went

141 **Psyche** The Latin writer Apuleius (second century A.D.) tells the story of the love between Cupid (Eros) and Psyche. Keats knows the myth from Adlington's translation of Apuleius (1566), from Lemprière's *Classical Dictionary* and from Mary Tighe's eighteenth-century poem *Psyche*.

I STOOD TIPTOE

On the smooth wind to realms of wonderment;
What Psyche felt, and Love, when their full lips
First touched; what amorous, and fondling nips
They gave each other's cheeks; with all their sighs,   145
And how they kissed each other's tremulous eyes:
The silver lamp—the ravishment—the wonder—
The darkness—loneliness—the fearful thunder;
Their woes gone by, and both to heaven upflown,
To bow for gratitude before Jove's throne.°   150
So did he feel, who pulled the boughs aside,
That we might look into a forest wide,
To catch a glimpse of fawns, and dryads
Coming with softest rustle through the trees;
And garlands woven of flowers wild, and sweet,   155
Upheld on ivory wrists, or sporting feet:
Telling us how fair, trembling Syrinx fled
Arcadian Pan,° with such a fearful dread.
Poor nymph—poor Pan—how he did weep to find,
Nought but a lovely sighing of the wind   160
Along the reedy stream; a half-heard strain,
Full of sweet desolation—balmy pain.

What first inspired a bard of old to sing
Narcissus° pining o'er the untainted spring?
In some delicious ramble, he had found   165
A little space, with boughs all woven round;
And in the midst of all, a clearer pool
Than e'er reflected in its pleasant cool
The blue sky here, and there, serenely peeping
Through tendril wreaths fantastically creeping.   170
And on the bank a lonely flower he spied,

---

150 **Jove's throne** After many tribulations, the mortal Psyche was finally made immortal by Jove himself and allowed to dwell on Olympus with Eros. Various details in the story are alluded to in the preceding lines: Psyche was never allowed to see her huband, and betrayed his confidence by watching him by the light of a silver lamp. Keats will use the myth again in the later "Ode to Psyche."   158 **Pan** The story of Pan's pursuit of the nymph Syrinx, changed by her sisters into a marsh reed, is told in Ovid (I, ll. 701 ff.) Pan reappears in *Endymion* and implicitly in other poems.   164 **Narcissus** Ovid (III, ll. 345 ff.) tells at length the story of Narcissus, who fell in love with his own reflected image. This passage is one of Keats's only explicit references to this famous myth.

A meek and forlorn flower, with naught of pride,
Drooping its beauty o'er the watery clearness,
To woo its own sad image into nearness:
175 Deaf to light Zephyrus it would not move;
But still would seem to droop, to pine, to love
So while the poet stood in this sweet spot,
Some fainter gleamings o'er his fancy shot;
Nor was it long ere he had told the tale
180 Of young Narcissus, and sad Echo's bale.
Where had he been, from whose warm head outflew
That sweetest of all songs, that ever new,
That aye refreshing, pure deliciousness,
Coming ever to bless
185 The wanderer by moonlight? to him bringing
Shapes from the invisible world, unearthly singing
From out the middle air, from flowery nests,
And from the pillowy silkiness that rests
Full in the speculation of the stars.
190 Ah! surely he had burst our mortal bars;
Into some wondrous region he had gone,
To search for thee, divine Endymion!

He was a poet, sure a lover too,
Who stood on Latmus' top, what time there blew
195 Soft breezes from the myrtle-vale below;
And brought in faintness solemn, sweet, and slow
A hymn from Dian's temple; while upswelling,
The incense went to her own starry dwelling.
But though her face was clear as infant's eyes,
200 Though she stood smiling o'er the sacrifice,
The poet wept at her so piteous fate,
Wept that such beauty should be desolate:
So in fine wrath some golden sounds he won,
And gave meek Cynthia her Endymion.°

205 Queen of the wide air; thou most lovely queen

204 **Endymion** The story of the Latmian shepherd who pined for the moon goddess Diana (Artemis) appears in several versions in English poetry. Keats probably met it first in *The Man in the Moon* by Michael Drayton (1563–1631). Cynthia is another name for Diana, after the mountain Cynthus in her birthplace Delos.

I STOOD TIPTOE

Of all the brightness that mine eyes have seen!
As thou exceedest all things in thy shine,
So every tale, does this sweet tale of thine.
O for three words of honey, that I might
Tell but one wonder of thy bridal night! 210

Where distant ships do seem to show their keels,
Phœbus awhile delayed his mighty wheels,
And turned to smile upon thy bashful eyes,
Ere he his unseen pomp would solemnize.
The evening weather was so bright, and clear, 215
That men of health were of unusual cheer;
Stepping like Homer at the trumpet's call,
Or young Apollo on the pedestal:°
And lovely women were as fair and warm,
As Venus looking sideways in alarm. 220
The breezes were ethereal, and pure,
And crept through half-closed lattices to cure
The languid sick; it cooled their fevered sleep,
And soothed them into slumbers full and deep.
Soon they awoke clear-eyed: nor burnt with thirsting, 225
Nor with hot fingers, nor with temples bursting:
And springing up, they met the wond'ring sight
Of their dear friends, nigh foolish with delight;
Who feel their arms, and breasts, and kiss and stare,
And on their placid foreheads part the hair. 230
Young men, and maidens at each other gazed
With hands held back, and motionless, amazed
To see the brightness in each other's eyes;
And so they stood, filled with a sweet surprise,
Until their tongues were loosed in poesy. 235
Therefore no lover did of anguish die:
But the soft numbers, in that moment spoken,
Made silken ties, that never may be broken.

---

218 **Stepping . . . pedestal** "The best explanation is that Keats had in mind an anecdote of the youthful Homer told by Chapman in the preface to his translation of the *Iliad*. . . . In the following line Keats is thinking of a statue of Apollo which suggests motion." (Douglas Bush, *Mythology and the Romantic Tradition in English Poetry*, p. 86)

Cynthia! I cannot tell the greater blisses,
240 That followed thine, and thy dear shepherd's kisses:
Was there a poet born?—but now no more,
My wand'ring spirit must no further soar.—

SLEEP AND POETRY°

> As I lay in my bed slepe full unmete
> Was unto me, but why that I ne might
> Rest I ne wist, for there n'as erthly wight
> [As I suppose] had more of hertis ese
> Than I, for I n'ad sicknesse nor disease.
>   CHAUCER.

What is more gentle than a wind in summer?
What is more soothing than the pretty hummer
That stays one moment in an open flower,
And buzzes cheerily from bower to bower?
5 What is more tranquil than a musk rose blowing
In a green island, far from all men's knowing?
More healthful than the leafiness
More secret than a nest of nightingales?
More serene than Cordelia's° countenance?
10 More full of visions than a high romance?
What, but thee Sleep? Soft closer of our eyes!
Low murmurer of tender lullabies!
Light hoverer around our happy pillows!
Wreather of poppy buds, and weeping willows!
15 Silent entangler of a beauty's tresses!
Most happy listener! when the morning blesses
Thee for enlivening all the cheerful eyes
That glance so brightly at the new sunrise.

But what is higher beyond thought than thee?
20 Fresher than berries of a mountain tree?

---

0 **Sleep and Poetry** written in late summer and winter 1816, when the influence of Leigh Hunt was at its height. 9 **Cordelia** in Shakespeare's *King Lear*.

SLEEP AND POETRY

More strange, more beautiful, more smooth, more
   regal,
Than wings of swans, than doves, than dim-seen
   eagle?
What is it? And to what shall I compare it?
It has a glory, and nought else can share it:
The thought thereof is awful, sweet, and holy, 25
Chasing away all worldliness and folly;
Coming sometimes like fearful claps of thunder,
Or the low rumblings earth's regions under;
And sometimes like a gentle whispering
Of all the secrets of some wondrous thing 30
That breathes about us in the vacant air;
So that we look around with prying stare,
Perhaps to see shapes of light, aerial limning,
And catch soft floatings from a faint-heard hymning;
To see the laurel wreath, on high suspended, 35
That is to crown our name when life is ended.
Sometimes it gives a glory to the voice,
And from the heart upsprings "Rejoice! rejoice!"
Sounds which will reach the Framer of all things,
And die away in ardent mutterings. 40

No one who once the glorious sun has seen,
And all the clouds, and felt his bosom clean
For his great Maker's presence, but must know
What 'tis I mean, and feel his being glow:
Therefore no insult will I give his spirit, 45
By telling what he sees from native merit.

O Poesy! for thee I hold my pen
That am not yet a glorious denizen
Of thy wide heaven—Should I rather kneel
Upon some mountaintop until I feel 50
A glowing splendor round about me hung,
And echo back the voice of thine own tongue?
O Poesy! for thee I grasp my pen
That am not yet a glorious denizen
Of thy wide heaven; yet, to my ardent prayer, 55
Yield from thy sanctuary some clear air,

Smoothed for intoxication by the breath
Of flowering bays, that I may die a death
Of luxury, and my young spirit follow
60 The morning sunbeams to the great Apollo
Like a fresh sacrifice; or, if I can bear
The o'erwhelming sweets, 'twill bring to me the fair
Visions of all places: a bowery nook
Will be Elysium—an eternal book
65 Whence I may copy many a lovely saying
About the leaves, and flowers—about the playing
Of nymphs in woods, and fountains; and the shade
Keeping a silence round a sleeping maid;
And many a verse from so strange influence
70 That we must ever wonder how, and whence
It came. Also imaginings will hover
Round my fireside, and haply there discover
Vistas of solemn beauty, where I'd wander
In happy silence, like the clear meander
75 Through its lone vales; and where I found a spot
Of awfuller shade, or an enchanted grot,
Or a green hill o'erspread with checkered dress
Of flowers, and fearful from its loveliness,
Write on my tablets all that was permitted,
80 All that was for our human senses fitted.
Then the events of this wide world I'd seize
Like a strong giant, and my spirit tease
Till at its shoulders it should proudly see
Wings to find out an immortality.

85 Stop and consider! life is but a day;
A fragile dewdrop on its perilous way
From a tree's summit; a poor Indian's sleep
While his boat hastens to the monstrous steep
Of Montmorency. Why so sad a moan?
90 Life is the rose's hope while yet unblown;
The reading of an ever-changing tale;
The light uplifting of a maiden's veil;
A pigeon tumbling in clear summer air;
A laughing schoolboy, without grief or care,
95 Riding the springy branches of an elm.

SLEEP AND POETRY

O for ten years, that I may overwhelm
Myself in poesy; so I may do the deed
That my own soul has to itself decreed.
Then will I pass the countries that I see
In long perspective, and continually 100
Taste their pure fountains. First the realm I'll pass
Of Flora, and old Pan: sleep in the grass,
Feed upon apples red, and strawberries,
And choose each pleasure that my fancy sees;
Catch the white-handed nymphs in shady places, 105
To woo sweet kisses from averted faces—
Play with their fingers, touch their shoulders white
Into a pretty shrinking with a bite
As hard as lips can make it: till agreed,
A lovely tale of human life we'll read. 110
And one will teach a tame dove how it best
May fan the cool air gently o'er my rest;
Another, bending o'er her nimble tread,
Will set a green robe floating round her head,
And still will dance with ever varied ease, 115
Smiling upon the flowers and the trees:
Another will entice me on, and on
Through almond blossoms and rich cinnamon;
Till in the bosom of a leafy world
We rest in silence, like two gems upcurled 120
In the recesses of a pearly shell.

And can I ever bid these joys farewell?
Yes, I must pass them for a nobler life,
Where I may find the agonies, the strife
Of human hearts: for lo! I see afar, 125
O'er-sailing the blue cragginess, a car
And steeds with streamy manes—the charioteer
Looks out upon the winds with glorious fear:
And now the numerous tramplings quiver lightly
Along a huge cloud's ridge; and now with sprightly 130
Wheel downward come they into fresher skies,
Tipped round with silver from the sun's bright eyes.
Still downward with capacious whirl they glide;
And now I see them on a green hill's side

SLEEP AND POETRY

135 In breezy rest among the nodding stalks.
The charioteer with wondrous gesture talks
To the trees and mountains; and there soon appear
Shapes of delight, of mystery, and fear,
Passing along before a dusky space
140 Made by some mighty oaks: as they would chase
Some ever-fleeting music on they sweep.
Lo! how they murmur, laugh, and smile, and weep:
Some with upholden hand and mouth severe;
Some with their faces muffled to the ear
145 Between their arms; some, clear in youthful bloom,
Go glad and smilingly athwart the gloom;
Some looking back, and some with upward gaze;
Yes, thousands in a thousand different ways
Flit onward—now a lovely wreath of girls
150 Dancing their sleek hair into tangled curls;
And now broad wings. Most awfully intent
The driver of those steeds is forward bent,
And seems to listen: O that I might know
All that he writes with such a hurrying glow.

155 The visions all are fled—the car is fled
Into the light of heaven, and in their stead
A sense of real things comes doubly strong,
And, like a muddy stream, would bear along
My soul to nothingness: but I will strive
160 Against all doubtings, and will keep alive
The thought of that same chariot, and the strange
Journey it went.

    Is there so small a range
In the present strength of manhood, that the high
Imagination cannot freely fly
165 As she was wont of old? prepare her steeds,
Paw up against the light, and do strange deeds
Upon the clouds? Has she not shown us all?
From the clear space of ether, to the small
Breath of new buds unfolding? From the meaning
170 Of Jove's large eyebrow, to the tender greening
Of April meadows? Here her altar shone,
E'en in this isle; and who could paragon

SLEEP AND POETRY

The fervid choir° that lifted up a noise
Of harmony, to where it aye will poise
Its mighty self of convoluting sound,   175
Huge as a planet, and like that roll round,
Eternally around a dizzy void?
Ay, in those days the Muses were nigh cloyed
With honors; nor had any other care
Than to sing out and soothe their wavy hair.   180

Could all this be forgotten? Yes, a schism
Nurtured by foppery and barbarism,
Made great Apollo blush for this his land.
Men were thought wise who could not understand
His glories: with a puling infant's force   185
They swayed about upon a rocking horse,
And thought it Pegasus.° Ah dismal souled!
The winds of heaven blew, the ocean rolled
Its gathering waves—ye felt it not. The blue
Bared its eternal bosom, and the dew   190
Of summer nights collected still to make
The morning precious: beauty was awake!
Why were ye not awake? But ye were dead
To things ye knew not of—were closely wed
To musty laws lined out with wretched rule   195
And compass vile: so that ye taught a school
Of dolts to smooth, inlay, and clip, and fit,
Till, like the certain wands of Jacob's wit,
Their verses tallied. Easy was the task:
A thousand handicraftsmen wore the mask   200
Of Poesy. Ill-fated, impious race!
That blasphemed the bright lyrist to his face,
And did not know it—no, they went about,
Holding a poor, decrepit standard out
Marked with most flimsy mottoes, and in large   205
The name of one Boileau!

---

173 fervid choir alludes to the past grandeur of English poetry and would primarily consist of Spenser, Shakespeare and Milton. **181–187 Could all this ... Pegasus** In accordance with the militant attitude of Leigh Hunt (a. o. in the preface to the *Story of Rimini*) Keats is attacking what was considered mechanical versification in Pope and the Augustan poets.

                              O ye whose charge
It is to hover round our pleasant hills!
Whose congregated majesty so fills
My boundly reverence, that I cannot trace
210 Your hallowed names, in this unholy place,
So near those common folk; did not their shames
Affright you? Did our old lamenting Thames
Delight you? Did ye never cluster round
Delicious Avon, with a mournful sound,
215 And weep? Or did ye wholly bid adieu
To regions where no more the laurel grew?
Or did ye stay to give a welcoming
To some lone spirits who could proudly sing
Their youth away, and die?° 'Twas even so:
220 But let me think away those times of woe:
Now 'tis a fairer season; ye have breathed
Rich benedictions o'er us; ye have wreathed
Fresh garlands: for sweet music has been heard
In many places;—some has been upstirred
225 From out its crystal dwelling in a lake,
By a swan's ebon bill;° from a thick brake,
Nested and quiet in a valley mild,
Bubbles a pipe;° fine sounds are floating wild
About the earth: happy are ye and glad.

230 These things are doubtless: yet in truth we've had
Strange thunders from the potency of song;
Mingled indeed with what is sweet and strong,
From majesty: but in clear truth the themes
Are ugly clubs, the poets Polyphemes
235 Disturbing the grand sea.° A drainless shower
Of light is poesy; 'tis the supreme of power;

---

219 **die** alludes to Chatterton, who killed himself in 1770 and to whom *Endymion* is dedicated. 224–226 **some . . . bill** alludes to Wordsworth. 226–228 **from . . . pipe** alludes to Leigh Hunt. 233–235 **but . . . sea** The allusion is by no means clear. Harold Bloom (*The Visionary Company*, p. 357) glosses the passage convincingly as follows: "Keats . . . here repudiates what he takes to be tendentiouness, the use of poetry to teach a moral doctrine or aggrandize a personality. The *themes* are ugly clubs; they are so many blind Cyclopses enragingly throwing stones at an elusive Odysseus out on the immensity of water, and merely disturbing it."

SLEEP AND POETRY

'Tis might half slumb'ring on its own right arm.
The very archings of her eyelids charm
A thousand willing agents to obey,
And still she governs with the mildest sway:
But strength alone though of the Muses born
Is like a fallen angel:° trees uptorn,
Darkness, and worms, and shrouds, and sepulchers
Delight it; for it feeds upon the burrs
And thorns of life; forgetting the great end
Of poesy, that it should be a friend
To soothe the cares, and lift the thoughts of man.

Yet I rejoice: a myrtle fairer than
E'er grew in Paphos,° from the bitter weeds
Lifts its sweet head into the air, and feeds
A silent space with ever-sprouting green.
All tenderest birds there find a pleasant screen,
Creep through the shade with jaunty fluttering,
Nibble the little cuppèd flowers and sing.
Then let us clear away the choking thorns
From round its gentle stem; let the young fawns,
Yeaned in after-times, when we are flown,
Find a fresh sward beneath it, overgrown
With simple flowers: let there nothing be
More boisterous than a lover's bended knee;
Nought more ungentle than the placid look
Of one who leans upon a closèd book;
Nought more untranquil than the grassy slopes
Between two hills. All hail delightful hopes!
As she was wont, th' imagination
Into most lovely labyrinths will be gone,
And they shall be accounted poet kings
Who simply tell the most heart-easing things.
O may these joys be ripe before I die.

Will not some say that I presumptuously

---

242 **fallen angel** identifies the specific allusion as being to Byron's *Manfred*, although more general references may also be present in the background.   249 **Paphos** is the island of Venus.

Have spoken? that from hastening disgrace
'Twere better far to hide my foolish face?
That whining boyhood should with reverence bow
Ere the dread thunderbolt could reach? How!
275 If I do hide myself, it sure shall be
In the very fane, the light of Poesy:
If I do fall, at least I will be laid
Beneath the silence of a poplar shade;
And over me the grass shall be smooth shaven;
280 And there shall be a kind memorial graven.
But off, Despondence! miserable bane!
They should not know thee, who athirst to gain
A noble end, are thirsty every hour.
What though I am not wealthy in the dower
285 Of spanning wisdom; though I do not know
The shiftings of the mighty winds that blow
Hither and thither all the changing thoughts
Of man: though no great minist'ring reason sorts
Out the dark mysteries of human souls
290 To clear conceiving: yet there ever rolls
A vast idea before me, and I glean
Therefrom my liberty; thence too I've seen
The end and aim of Poesy. 'Tis clear
As any thing most true; as that the year
295 Is made of the four seasons—manifest
As a large cross, some old cathedral's crest,
Lifted to the white clouds. Therefore should I
Be but the essence of deformity,
A coward, did my very eyelids wink
300 At speaking out what I have dared to think.
Ah! rather let me like a madman run
Over some precipice; let the hot sun
Melt my Dedalian wings, and drive me down
Convulsed and headlong! Stay! an inward frown
305 Of conscience bids me be more calm awhile.
An ocean dim, sprinkled with many an isle,
Spreads awfully before me. How much toil!
How many days! what desperate turmoil!
Ere I can have explored its widenesses.
310 Ah, what a task! upon my bended knees,

SLEEP AND POETRY

I could unsay those—no, impossible!
Impossible!

        For sweet relief I'll dwell
On humbler thoughts, and let this strange assay
Begun in gentleness die so away.
E'en now all tumult from my bosom fades:
I turn full-hearted to the friendly aids
That smooth the path of honor; brotherhood,
And friendliness the nurse of mutual good.
The hearty grasp that sends a pleasant sonnet
Into the brain ere one can think upon it;
The silence when some rhymes are coming out;
And when they're come, the very pleasant rout:
The message certain to be done tomorrow—
'Tis perhaps as well that it should be to borrow
Some precious book from out its snug retreat,
To cluster round it when we next shall meet.
Scarce can I scribble on; for lovely airs
Are fluttering round the room like doves in pairs;
Many delights of that glad day recalling,
When first my senses caught their tender falling.
And with these airs come forms of elegance
Stooping their shoulders o'er a horse's prance,
Careless, and grand—fingers soft and round
Parting luxuriant curls;—and the swift bound
Of Bacchus from his chariot, when his eye
Made Ariadne's cheek look blushingly.
Thus I remember all the pleasant flow
Of words at opening a portfolio.

Things such as these are ever harbingers
To trains of peaceful images: the stirs
Of a swan's neck unseen among the rushes:
A linnet starting all about the bushes:
A butterfly, with golden wings broad-parted,
Nestling a rose, convulsed as though it smarted
With over pleasure—many, many more,
Might I indulge at large in all my store
Of luxuries: yet I must not forget
Sleep, quiet with his poppy coronet:

For what there may be worthy in these rhymes
I partly owe to him—and thus: The chimes
Of friendly voices had just given place
To as sweet a silence, when I 'gan retrace
The pleasant day, upon a couch at ease.
It was a poet's house° who keeps the keys
Of Pleasure's temple. Round about were hung
The glorious features of the bards who sung
In other ages—cold and sacred busts
Smiled at each other. Happy he who trusts
To clear Futurity his darling fame!
Then there were Fauns and Satyrs taking aim
At swelling apples with a frisky leap
And reaching fingers, 'mid a luscious heap
Of vine leaves. Then there rose to view a fane
Of liny marble, and thereto a train
Of nymphs approaching fairly o'er the sward:
One, loveliest, holding her white hand toward
The dazzling sunrise: two sisters sweet,
Bending their graceful figures till they meet
Over the trippings of a little child:
And some are hearing, eagerly, the wild
Thrilling liquidity of dewy piping.
See, in another picture, nymphs are wiping
Cherishingly Diana's timorous limbs;—
A fold of lawny mantle dabbling swims
At the bath's edge, and keeps a gentle motion
With the subsiding crystal: as when ocean
Heaves calmly its broad swelling smoothness o'er
Its rocky marge, and balances once more
The patient weeds; that now unshent by foam
Feel all about their undulating home.

Sappho's meek head was there half smiling down
At nothing; just as though the earnest frown
Of over thinking had that moment gone
From off her brow, and left her all alone.

---

354 **house** The ensuing catalog lists several objects found in the library of Hunt's cottage, where Keats frequently stayed at the time.

SLEEP AND POETRY

Great Alfred's° too, with anxious, pitying eyes, 385
As if he always listened to the sighs
Of the goaded world; and Kosciusko's° worn
By horrid suffrance—mightily forlorn.

Petrarch, outstepping from the shady green,
Starts at the sight of Laura; nor can wean 390
His eyes from her sweet face. Most happy they!
For over them was seen a free display
Of outspread wings, and from between them shone
The face of Poesy: from off her throne
She overlooked things that I scarce could tell. 395
The very sense of where I was might well
Keep Sleep aloof: but more than that there came
Thought after thought to nourish up the flame
Within my breast; so that the morning light
Surprised me even from a sleepless night; 400
And up I rose refreshed, and glad, and gay,
Resolving to begin that very day
These lines; and howsoever they be done,
I leave them as a father does his son.

---

385 **Alfred** Alfred the Great (848–899), the Saxon king who defended England against the Danes. The founder of Oxford, he was a symbol of enlightened rule. 387 **Kosciusko** (1746–1817), a Polish general identified with the national liberation of his country and an idol of political liberalism. The listing of Alfred the Great with Kosciusko recurs in the early Keats sonnet "To Kosciusko."

SONNETS

O Solitude°

O Solitude! If I must with thee dwell,
  Let it not be among the jumbled heap
  Of murky buildings; climb with me the steep—
Nature's observatory—whence the dell,
     Its flowery slopes, its river's crystal swell,
  May seem a span; let me thy vigils keep
  'Mongst boughs pavilioned, where the deer's swift leap
Startles the wild bee from the foxglove bell.
But though I'll gladly trace these scenes with thee,
     Yet the sweet converse of an innocent mind,
Whose words are images of thoughts refined,
  Is my soul's pleasure; and it sure must be
Almost the highest bliss of humankind,
  When to thy haunts two kindred spirits flee.

How Many Bards°

How many bards gild the lapses of time!
  A few of them have ever been the food
  Of my delighted fancy—I could brood
Over their beauties, earthly, or sublime:
     And often, when I sit me down to rhyme,
  These will in throngs before my mind intrude:
  But no confusion, no disturbance rude
Do they occasion; 'tis a pleasing chime.

0 **O Solitude** Keats's first published poem, printed by Hunt in the *Examiner*, May 5, 1816. 0 **How Many Bards** The poem, in praise of the poets of the past, dates from March, 1816.

So the unnumbered sounds that evening store;
  The songs of birds—the whisp'ring of the leaves—   10
The voice of waters—the great bell that heaves
  With solemn sound—and thousand others more,
That distance of recognizance bereaves,
  Make pleasing music, and not wild uproar.

Written on the Day that Mr. Leigh Hunt Left Prison°

What though, for showing truth to flattered state,
  Kind Hunt was shut in prison, yet has he,
  In his immortal spirit, been as free
As the sky-searching lark, and as elate.
Minion of grandeur! think you he did wait?   5
  Think you he nought but prison walls did see,
  Till, so unwilling, thou unturn'dst the key?
Ah, no! far happier, nobler was his fate!
In Spenser's halls he strayed, and bowers fair,
  Culling enchanted flowers; and he flew   10
With daring Milton through the fields of air:
  To regions of his own his genius true
Took happy flights. Who shall his fame impair
  When thou art dead, and all thy wretched crew?

To One Long in City Pent

To one who has been long in city pent,°
  'Tis very sweet to look into the fair
  And open face of heaven—to breathe a prayer

---

0 **Prison** Hunt was released from prison, where he had been confined for political reasons, on February 2, 1815. 1 **To ... pent** cf. "As one who long in populous city pent . . ." (*Paradise Lost*, IX, ll. 445).

    Full in the smile of the blue firmament.
5   Who is more happy, when, with heart's content,
        Fatigued he sinks into some pleasant lair
        Of wavy grass, and reads a debonair
    And gentle tale° of love and languishment?
    Returning home at evening, with an ear
10   Catching the notes of Philomel°—an eye
    Watching the sailing cloudlet's bright career,
        He mourns that day so soon has glided by:
    E'en like the passage of an angel's tear
        That falls through the clear ether silently.

On First Looking into Chapman's Homer°

    Much have I traveled in the realms of gold,
        And many goodly states and kingdoms seen;
        Round many western islands have I been
    Which bards in fealty to Apollo hold.
5   Oft of one wide expanse had I been told
        That deep-browed Homer ruled as his demesne;
        Yet did I never breathe its pure serene
    Till I heard Chapman speak out loud and bold:
    Then felt I like some watcher of the skies
10   When a new planet swims into his ken;
    Or like stout Cortez when with eagle eyes
        He stared at the Pacific—and all his men
    Looked at each other with a wild surmise—
        Silent, upon a peak in Darien.

---

8 **tale** presumably Hunt's "Story of Rimini."   10 **Philomel** the nightingale.   0 **On First . . . Homer** This famous sonnet was written on October, 1816, very quickly, after returning from an evening spent with Cowden Clarke. Clarke had read to Keats from Chapman's Elizabethan translation of the *Odyssey*. Keats had read about the conquest of America in Robertson's *History of America* and other books; at school in Enfield, he had received a prize book (Bonnycastle's *Introduction to Astronomy*) that contains a description of Herschel's discovery of Uranus.

Keen, Fitful Gusts°

Keen, fitful gusts are whisp'ring here and there
   Among the bushes half leafless, and dry;
   The stars look very cold about the sky,
And I have many miles on foot to fare.
Yet feel I little of the cool bleak air,
   Or of the dead leaves rustling drearily,
   Or of those silver lamps that burn on high,
Or of the distance from home's pleasant lair:
For I am brim-full of the friendliness
   That in a little cottage I have found;
Of fair-haired Milton's eloquent distress,
   And all his love for gentle Lycid drowned;
Of lovely Laura in her light green dress,
   And faithful Petrarch gloriously crowned.

On Leaving Some Friend at an Early Hour°

Give me a golden pen, and let me lean
   On heaped-up flowers, in regions clear, and far;
   Bring me a tablet whiter than a star,
Or hand of hymning angel, when 'tis seen
The silver strings of heavenly harp atween:
   And let there glide by many a pearly car,
   Pink robes, and wavy hair, and diamond jar,
And half-discovered wings, and glances keen.
The while let music wander round my ears,
   And as it reaches each delicious ending,

0 **Keen, Fitful Gusts** written in November, 1816, after a visit to Hunt's cottage in Hampstead. 0 **On Leaving ... Hour** companion piece to the previous sonnet, written on the same occasion, November, 1816.

Let me write down a line of glorious tone,
And full of many wonders of the spheres:
    For what a height my spirit is contending!
    'Tis not content so soon to be alone.

To My Brothers°

Small, busy flames play through the fresh-laid coals,
    And their faint cracklings o'er our silence creep
    Like whispers of the household gods that keep
A gentle empire o'er fraternal souls.
And while, for rhymes, I search around the poles,
    Your eyes are fixed, as in poetic sleep,
    Upon the lore so voluble and deep,
That aye at fall of night our care condoles.
This is your birthday, Tom, and I rejoice
    That thus it passes smoothly, quietly.
Many such eves of gently whisp'ring noise
    May we together pass, and calmly try
What are this world's true joys—ere the great voice,
    From its fair face, shall bid our spirits fly.

Addressed to Haydon°

Highmindedness, a jealousy for good,
    A loving-kindness for the great man's fame,

---

0 **To My Brothers** written on the occasion of the birthday of Keats's younger brother Tom, who was to die two years later. 0 **Addressed to Haydon** dates from November 20, 1816. Benjamin Robert Haydon (1786–1846) was, next to Hunt, the main artistic admiration of the young Keats. He was a grandiloquent painter, as large in spirit as his canvases were large in size. He was instrumental in having the Parthenon sculptures brought to England by Lord Elgin for purchase by the English government.

Dwells here and there with people of no name,
In noisome alley, and in pathless wood:
And where we think the truth least understood,
  Oft may be found a "singleness of aim,"
  That ought to frighten into hooded shame
A money-mong'ring, pitiable brood.
How glorious this affection for the cause
  Of steadfast genius, toiling gallantly!
What when a stout unbending champion awes
  Envy, and Malice to their native sty?
Unnumbered souls breathe out a still applause,
  Proud to behold him in his country's eye.

Addressed to the Same°

Great spirits now on earth are sojourning;
  He of the cloud, the cataract, the lake,
Who on Helvellyn's summit, wide awake,
Catches his freshness from archangel's wing:
He of the rose, the violet, the spring,
  The social smile, the chain for freedom's sake:
  And lo!—whose steadfastness would never take
A meaner sound than Raphael's whispering.
And other spirits there are standing apart
  Upon the forehead of the age to come;
These, these will give the world another heart,
  And other pulses. Hear ye not the hum
Of mighty workings?——
  Listen awhile ye nations, and be dumb.

---

0 **Addressed to the Same** companion piece to the previous sonnet. The allusions are, in turn, to Wordsworth (ll. 2–4), to Hunt (ll. 5–7) and to Haydon himself.

Written in Disgust of Vulgar Superstition°

The church bells toll a melancholy round,
   Calling the people to some other prayers,
   Some other gloominess, more dreadful cares,
More hearkening to the sermon's horrid sound.
Surely the mind of man is closely bound
   In some black spell; seeing that each one tears
   Himself from fireside joys, and Lydian airs,
And converse high of those with glory crowned.
Still, still they toll, and I should feel a damp
   A chill as from a tomb, did I not know
That they are dying like an outburned lamp;
   That 'tis their sighing, wailing ere they go
   Into oblivion;—that fresh flowers will grow,
And many glories of immortal stamp.

On the Grasshopper and Cricket°

The poetry of earth is never dead:
   When all the birds are faint with the hot sun,
   And hide in cooling trees, a voice will run
From hedge to hedge about the new-mown mead;
That is the grasshopper's—he takes the lead
   In summer luxury—he has never done
   With his delights; for when tired out with fun
He rests at ease beneath some pleasant weed.
The poetry of earth is ceasing never:
   On a lone winter evening, when the frost

---

0 **Written ... Superstition** written on December 23, 1816, "in fifteen minutes" according to Tom Keats. 0 **On the ... Cricket** written at an impromptu contest between Keats and Hunt, composing on the given theme. Hunt's poem can be found a. o. in W. J. Bate's *Keats* (p. 121).

Has wrought a silence, from the stove there shrills
The cricket's song, in warmth increasing ever,
　　And seems to one in drowsiness half lost,
　　　The grasshopper's among some grassy hills.

After Dark Vapors°

After dark vapors have oppressed our plains
　　For a long dreary season, comes a day
　　Born of the gentle South, and clears away
From the sick heavens all unseemly stains.
The anxious month, relieving from its pains,
　　Takes as a long-lost right the feel of May,
　　The eyelids with the passing coolness play,
Like rose leaves with the drip of summer rains.
The calmest thoughts come round us—as of leaves
　　Budding—fruit ripening in stillness—autumn suns
Smiling at eve upon the quiet sheaves—
Sweet Sappho's cheek—a sleeping infant's breath—
　　The gradual sand that through an hourglass runs—
A woodland rivulet—a poet's death.

On Seeing the Elgin Marbles°

My spirit is too weak—mortality
　　Weighs heavily on me like unwilling sleep,
　　And each imagined pinnacle and steep
Of godlike hardship tells me I must die
Like a sick eagle looking at the sky.
　　Yet 'tis a gentle luxury to weep
　　That I have not the cloudy winds to keep
Fresh for the opening of the morning's eye.

0 **After Dark Vapors** written on January 31, 1817.　0 **Elgin Marbles**
See note on the sonnet "Addressed to Haydon."

Such dim-conceivèd glories of the brain
10 Bring round the heart an undescribable feud;
So do these wonders a most dizzy pain,
   That mingles Grecian grandeur with the rude
Wasting of old time—with a billowy main—
   A sun—a shadow of a magnitude.

To B. R. Haydon, with the Foregoing Sonnet on the Elgin Marbles

Haydon! forgive me that I cannot speak
   Definitively on these mighty things;
   Forgive me that I have not eagle's wings—
That what I want I know not where to seek:
5 And think that I would not be over meek
   In rolling out upfollowed thunderings,
   Even to the steep of Heliconian springs,
Were I of ample strength for such a freak—
Think too, that all those numbers should be thine;
10   Whose else? In this who touch thy vesture's hem?
For when men stared at what was most divine
   With browless idiotism—o'erwise phlegm—
Thou hadst beheld the Hesperian shine
   Of their star in the east, and gone to worship them.

On the Sea°

It keeps eternal whisperings around
   Desolate shores, and with its mighty swell
   Gluts twice ten thousand caverns, till the spell
Of Hecate° leaves them their old shadowy sound.
5 Often 'tis in such gentle temper found,
   That scarcely will the very smallest shell

---

0 **On the Sea** Written on April 17, 1817. 4 **Hecate** here refers to Artemis, the moon goddess. "The spell/Of Hecate" then means the tides.

Be moved for days from where it sometime fell,
When last the winds of heaven were unbound.
Oh ye! who have your eyeballs vexed and tired,
    Feast them upon the wideness of the sea;
       Oh ye! whose ears are dinned with uproar rude,
  Or fed too much with cloying melody—
       Sit ye near some old cavern's mouth, and brood
Until ye start, as if the sea nymphs quired!

ENDYMION - A POETIC ROMANCE

"The Stretched Meter of an Antique Song"

Inscribed to the Memory of Thomas Chatterton.

Preface

Knowing within myself the manner in which this poem has been produced,° it is not without a feeling of regret that I make it public.

What manner I mean will be quite clear to the reader, who must soon perceive great inexperience, immaturity, and every error denoting a feverish attempt, rather than a deed accomplished. The two first books, and indeed the two last, I feel sensible are not of such completion as to warrant their passing the press; nor should they if I thought a year's castigation would do them any good;—it will not: the foundations are too sandy. It is just that this youngster should die away: a sad thought for me, if I had not

---

2 **produced** *Endymion* was written between April and November, 1817. Keats deliberately set himself the task of writing a narrative poem of 4,000 lines and retreated to the Isle of Wight to work in privacy. Most of the poem was written during a later visit to Oxford, where he stayed with B. Bailey. He completed the poem in London in November.

some hope that while it is dwindling I may be plotting, and fitting myself for verses fit to live.

This may be speaking too presumptuously, and may deserve a punishment: but no feeling man will be forward to inflict it: he will leave me alone, with the conviction that there is not a fiercer hell than the failure in a great object. This is not written with the least atom of purpose to forestall criticisms of course, but from the desire I have to conciliate men who are competent to look, and who do look with a zealous eye, to the honor of English literature.

The imagination of a boy is healthy, and the mature imagination of a man is healthy; but there is a space of life between, in which the soul is in a ferment, the character undecided, the way of life uncertain, the ambition thick-sighted: thence proceeds mawkishness, and all the thousand bitters which those men I speak of must necessarily taste in going over the following pages.

I hope I have not in too late a day touched the beautiful mythology of Greece, and dulled its brightness: for I wish to try once more,° before I bid it farewell.

Teignmouth, April 10, 1818

Book I°

A thing of beauty is a joy forever:
Its loveliness increases; it will never
Pass into nothingness; but still will keep
A bower quiet for us, and a sleep

---

35 **once more** alludes to *Hyperion*. 0 **Book I** The sources of *Endymion* have been extensively studied. Sandys' translation of Ovid provided many of the mythological details, but the story of Endymion itself does not appear in Ovid. Michael Drayton's poem *The Man in the Moone* and, possibly, his *Endimion and Phoebe* (1595) are likely sources, but there are several others. At least as important as the historical sources is Keats's deliberate intent to write a counterpart to his contemporary Shelley's poem *Alastor*.

Full of sweet dreams, and health, and quiet breathing. 5
Therefore, on every morrow, are we wreathing
A flowery band to bind us to the earth,
Spite of despondence, of the inhuman dearth
Of noble natures, of the gloomy days,
Of all the unhealthy and o'er darkened ways 10
Made for our searching: yes, in spite of all,
Some shape of beauty moves away the pall
From our dark spirits. Such the sun, the moon,
Trees old, and young sprouting a shady boon
For simple sheep; and such are daffodils 15
With the green world they live in; and clear rills
That for themselves a cooling covert make
'Gainst the hot season; the mid forest brake,
Rich with a sprinkling of fair musk rose blooms:
And such too is the grandeur of the dooms 20
We have imagined for the mighty dead;
All lovely tales that we have heard or read:
An endless fountain of immortal drink,
Pouring unto us from the heaven's brink.

Nor do we merely feel these essences 25
For one short hour; no, even as the trees
That whisper round a temple become soon
Dear as the temple's self, so does the moon,
The passion poesy, glories infinite,
Haunt us till they become a cheering light 30
Unto our souls, and bound to us so fast,
That, whether there be shine, or gloom o'ercast,
They alway must be with us, or we die.

Therefore, 'tis with full happiness that I
Will trace the story of Endymion. 35
The very music of the name has gone
Into my being, and each pleasant scene
Is growing fresh before me as the green
Of our own valleys: so I will begin
Now while I cannot hear the city's din;° 40

40 **din** indicates that the poem was begun in the spring and on the Isle of Wight.

Now while the early budders are just new,
And run in mazes of the youngest hue
About old forests; while the willow trails
Its delicate amber; and the dairy pails
45 Bring home increase of milk. And, as the year
Grows lush in juicy stalks, I'll smoothly steer
My little boat, for many quiet hours,
With streams that deepen freshly into bowers.
Many and many a verse I hope to write,
50 Before the daisies, vermeil rimmed and white,
Hide in deep herbage; and ere yet the bees
Hum about globes of clover and sweet peas,
I must be near the middle of my story.
O may no wintry season, bare and hoary,
55 See it half finished: but let autumn bold,
With universal tinge of sober gold,
Be all about me when I make an end.°
And now at once, adventuresome, I send
My herald thought into a wilderness:
60 There let its trumpet blow, and quickly dress
My uncertain path with green, that I may speed
Easily onward, through flowers and weed.

Upon the sides of Latmos was outspread
A mighty forest; for the moist earth fed
65 So plenteously all weed-hidden roots
Into o'er-hanging boughs, and precious fruits.
And it had gloomy shades, sequestered deep,
Where no man went; and if from shepherd's keep
A lamb strayed far a-down those inmost glens,
70 Never again saw he the happy pens
Whither his brethren, bleating with content,
Over the hills at every nightfall went.
Among the shepherds, 'twas believèd ever,
That not one fleecy lamb which thus did sever
75 From the white flock, but passed unworried
By angry wolf, or pard with prying head,
Until it came to some unfooted plains

57 **end** Keats kept to this timetable and finished in the fall.

ENDYMION

Where fed the herds of Pan: ay great his gains
Who thus one lamb did lose. Paths there were many,
Winding through palmy fern, and rushes fenny,
And ivy banks; all leading pleasantly
To a wide lawn, whence one could only see
Stems thronging all around between the swell
Of turf and slanting branches: who could tell
The freshness of the space of heaven above,
Edged round with dark treetops? through which a dove
Would often beat its wings, and often too
A little cloud would move across the blue.

Full in the middle of this pleasantness
There stood a marble altar, with a tress
Of flowers budded newly; and the dew
Had taken fairy fantasies to strew
Daisies upon the sacred sward last eve,
And so the dawnèd light in pomp receive.
For 'twas the morn: Apollo's upward fire
Made every eastern cloud a silvery pyre
Of brightness so unsullied, that therein
A melancholy spirit well might win
Oblivion, and melt out his essence fine
Into the winds: rain-scented eglantine
Gave temperate sweets to that well-wooing sun;
The lark was lost in him; cold springs had run
To warm their chilliest bubbles in the grass;
Man's voice was on the mountains; and the mass
Of nature's lives and wonders pulsed tenfold,
To feel this sunrise and its glories old.

Now while the silent workings of the dawn
Were busiest, into that self-same lawn
All suddenly, with joyful cries, there sped
A troop of little children garlanded;
Who, gathering round the altar, seemed to pry
Earnestly round as wishing to espy
Some folk of holiday: nor had they waited
For many moments, ere their ears were sated

115 With a faint breath of music, which ev'n then
Filled out its voice, and died away again.
Within a little space again it gave
Its airy swellings, with a gentle wave,
To light-hung leaves, in smoothest echoes breaking
Through copse-clad valleys—ere their death, o'ertak-
120 ing
The surgy murmurs of the lonely sea.

And now, as deep into the wood as we
Might mark a lynx's eye, there glimmered light
Fair faces and a rush of garments white,
125 Plainer and plainer showing, till at last
Into the widest alley they all past,
Making directly for the woodland altar.
O kindly muse! let not my weak tongue falter
In telling of this goodly company,
130 Of their old piety, and of their glee:
But let a portion of ethereal dew
Fall on my head, and presently unmew
My soul; that I may dare, in wayfaring,
To stammer where old Chaucer used to sing.

135   Leading the way, young damsels danced along,
Bearing the burden of a shepherd song;
Each having a white wicker overbrimmed
With April's tender younglings: next, well trimmed,
A crowd of shepherds with as sunburned looks
140 As may be read of in Arcadian books;
Such as sat listening round Apollo's pipe,
When the great deity, for earth too ripe,
Let his divinity o'er-flowing die
In music, through the vales of Thessaly:
145 Some idly trailed their sheep hooks on the ground,
And some kept up a shrilly mellow sound
With ebon-tippèd flutes: close after these,
Now coming from beneath the forest trees,
A venerable priest full soberly,
150 Begirt with minist'ring looks: alway his eye
Steadfast upon the matted turf he kept,

ENDYMION

And after him his sacred vestments swept.
From his right hand there swung a vase, milk-white,
Of mingled wine, outsparkling generous light;
And in his left he held a basket full   155
Of all sweet herbs that searching eye could cull:
Wild thyme, and valley-lilies whiter still
Than Leda's love,° and cresses from the rill.
His agèd head, crownèd with beechen wreath,
Seemed like a poll of ivy in the teeth   160
Of winter hoar. Then came another crowd
Of shepherds, lifting in due time aloud
Their share of the ditty. After them appeared,
Upfollowed by a multitude that reared
Their voices to the clouds, a fair-wrought car,   165
Easily rolling so as scarce to mar
The freedom of three steeds of dapple brown:
Who stood therein did seem of great renown
Among the throng. His youth was fully blown,
Showing like Ganymede to manhood grown;   170
And, for those simple times, his garments were
A chieftain king's: beneath his breast, half bare,
Was hung a silver bugle, and between
His nervy knees there lay a boar-spear keen.
A smile was on his countenance; he seemed,   175
To common lookers-on, like one who dreamed
Of idleness in groves Elysian:
But there were some who feelingly could scan
A lurking trouble in his nether lip,
And see that oftentimes the reins would slip   180
Through his forgotten hands: then would they sigh,
And think of yellow leaves, of owlet's cry,
Of logs piled solemnly.—Ah, well-a-day,
Why should our young Endymion pine away!

   Soon the assembly, in a circle ranged,   185
Stood silent round the shrine: each look was changed
To sudden veneration: women meek
Beckoned their sons to silence; while each cheek

---

158 **Leda's love** Zeus in the shape of a swan.

Of virgin bloom paled gently for slight fear.
190 Endymion too, without a forest peer,
Stood wan, and pale, and with an awèd face,
Among his brothers of the mountain chase.
In midst of all, the venerable priest
Eyed them with joy from greatest to the least,
195 And, after lifting up his agèd hands,
Thus spake he: "Men of Latmos! shepherd bands!
Whose care it is to guard a thousand flocks:
Whether descended from beneath the rocks
That overtop your mountains; whether come
200 From valleys where the pipe is never dumb;
Or from your swelling downs, where sweet air stirs
Blue harebells lightly, and where prickly furze
Buds lavish gold; or ye, whose precious charge
Nibble their fill at ocean's very marge,
205 Whose mellow reeds are touched with sounds forlorn
By the dim echoes of old Triton's horn:°
Mothers and wives! who day by day prepare
The scrip, with needments, for the mountain air;
And all ye gentle girls who foster up
210 Udderless lambs, and in a little cup
Will put choice honey for a favored youth:
Yea, every one attend! for in good truth
Our vows are wanting to our great god Pan.
Are not our lowing heifers sleeker than
215 Night-swollen mushrooms? Are not our wide plains
Speckled with countless fleeces? Have not rains
Greened over April's lap? No howling sad
Sickens our fearful ewes; and we have had
Great bounty from Endymion our lord.
220 The earth is glad: the merry lark has poured
His early song against yon breezy sky,
That spreads so clear o'er our solemnity."

Thus ending, on the shrine he heaped a spire
Of teeming sweets, enkindling sacred fire;
225 Anon he stained the thick and spongy sod

---

206 **Triton's horn** Son of Poseidon and Amphitrite, Triton is the trumpeter of the sea.

With wine, in honor of the shepherd god.
Now while the earth was drinking it, and while
Bay leaves were crackling in the fragrant pile,
And gummy frankincense was sparkling bright
'Neath smothering parsley, and a hazy light
Spread grayly eastward, thus a chorus sang:

"O thou, whose mighty palace roof doth hang
From jagged trunks, and overshadoweth
Eternal whispers, glooms, the birth, life, death
Of unseen flowers in heavy peacefulness;
Who lov'st to see the hamadryads dress
Their ruffled locks where meeting hazels darken;
And through whole solemn hours dost sit, and hearken
The dreary melody of bedded reeds—
In desolate places, where dank moisture breeds
The pipy hemlock to strange overgrowth;
Bethinking thee, how melancholy loth
Thou wast to lose fair Syrinx°—do thou now,
By thy love's milky brow!
By all the trembling mazes that she ran,
Hear us, great Pan!

"O thou, for whose soul-soothing quiet, turtles
Passion their voices cooingly 'mong myrtles,
What time thou wanderest at eventide
Through sunny meadows, that outskirt the side
Of thine enmossed realms: O thou, to whom
Broad-leaved fig trees even now foredoom
Their ripened fruitage; yellow-girted bees
Their golden honeycombs; our village leas
Their fairest blossomed beans and poppied corn;
The chuckling linnet its five young unborn,
To sing for thee; low creeping strawberries
Their summer coolness; pent up butterflies
Their freckled wings; yea, the fresh budding year
All its completions—be quickly near,

---

243 **Syrinx** The pursuit of Syrinx by Pan is told in Ovid (I, ll. 701 ff.).

By every wind that nods the mountain pine,
O forester divine!

"Thou, to whom every faun and satyr flies
For willing service; whether to surprise
The squatted hare while in half-sleeping fit;
Or upward ragged precipices flit
To save poor lambkins from the eagle's maw;
Or by mysterious enticement draw
Bewildered shepherds to their path again;
Or to tread breathless round the frothy main,
And gather up all fancifulest shells
For thee to tumble into Naiads' cells,
And, being hidden, laugh at their outpeeping;
Or to delight thee with fantastic leaping,
The while they pelt each other on the crown
With silvery oak apples, and fir cones brown—
By all the echoes that about thee ring,
Hear us, O satyr king!

"O Hearkener to the loud clapping shears,
While ever and anon to his shorn peers
A ram goes bleating: Winder of the horn,
When snoutèd wild boars routing tender corn
Anger our huntsmen: Breather round our farms,
To keep off mildews, and all weather harms:
Strange ministrant of undescribèd sounds,
That come a-swooning over hollow grounds,
And wither drearily on barren moors:
Dread opener of the mysterious doors
Leading to universal knowledge—see,
Great son of Dryope,°
The many that are come to pay their vows
With leaves about their brows!

"Be still the unimaginable lodge
For solitary thinkings; such as dodge

---

290 **Dryope** is not usually considered to be the mother of Pan; she is the mother of Amphissus by Apollo.

ENDYMION

Conception° to the very bourn of heaven, 295
Then leave the naked brain: be still the leaven,
That spreading in this dull and clodded earth
Gives it a touch ethereal—a new birth:
Be still a symbol of immensity;
A firmament reflected in a sea; 300
An element filling the space between;
An unknown—but no more: we humbly screen
With uplift hands our foreheads, lowly bending,
And giving out a shout most heaven rending,
Conjure thee to receive our humble Pæan, 305
Upon thy Mount Lycean!"

Even while they brought the burden to a close,
A shout from the whole multitude arose,
That lingered in the air like dying rolls
Of abrupt thunder, when Ionian shoals 310
Of dolphins bob their noses through the brine.
Meantime, on shady levels, mossy fine,
Young companies nimbly began dancing
To the swift treble pipe, and humming string.
Aye, those fair living forms swam heavenly 315
To tunes forgotten—out of memory:
Fair creatures! whose young childrens' children bred
Thermopylæ its heroes—not yet dead,
But in old marbles ever beautiful.
High genitors, unconscious did they cull 320
Time's sweet first-fruits—they danced to weariness,
And then in quiet circles did they press
The hillock turf, and caught the latter end
Of some strange history, potent to send
A young mind from its bodily tenement. 325
Or they might watch the quoit pitchers, intent
On either side; pitying the sad death

---

295 **conception** is presumably used in a negative sense here: dogmatic, systematic, and mechanical wisdom, as opposed to "solitary thinkings" that manage to ascend to great heights without having recourse to systems, and issue from a brain that has been left pure, uncluttered ("naked"), unencumbered by dead knowledge.

ENDYMION

Of Hyacinthus,° when the cruel breath
Of Zephyr slew him—Zephyr penitent,
Who now, ere Phœbus mounts the firmament, 330
Fondles the flower amid the sobbing rain.
The archers too, upon a wider plain,
Beside the feathery whizzing of the shaft,
And the dull twanging bowstring, and the raft
Branch down sweeping from a tall ash top, 335
Called up a thousand thoughts to envelope
Those who would watch. Perhaps, the trembling knee
And frantic gape of lonely Niobe,
Poor, lonely Niobe!° when her lovely young
Were dead and gone, and her caressing tongue 340
Lay a lost thing upon her paly lip,
And very, very deadliness did nip
Her motherly cheeks. Aroused from this sad mood
By one, who at a distance loud hallooed,
Uplifting his strong bow into the air, 345
Many might after brighter visions stare:
After the Argonauts,° in blind amaze
Tossing about on Neptune's restless ways,
Until, from the horizon's vaulted side,
There shot a golden splendor far and wide, 350
Spangling those million poutings of the brine
With quivering ore: 'twas even an awful shine
From the exaltation of Apollo's bow;
A heavenly beacon in their dreary woe.
Who thus were ripe for high contemplating, 355
Might turn their steps towards the sober ring
Where sat Endymion and the agèd priest
'Mong shepherds gone in eld, whose looks increased
The silvery setting of their mortal star.
There they discoursed upon the fragile bar 360

328 **Hyacinthus** The story is told in Ovid (X, ll. 160 ff.). The youthful Hyacinth was accidentally killed by Apollo at a game of quoits. 339 **Niobe** insulted the goddess Latona by boasting of her good fortune in giving birth to seven sons and seven daughters. Her children were killed and, in her grief, she was changed into a rock (Ovid, VI, ll. 165 ff.). 347 **Argonauts** sailed to Colchis in quest of the Golden Fleece. It is not easy to find a unifying principle that gives meaning to this particular catalog of myths (Hyacinth, Niobe, and the Argonauts).

ENDYMION

That keeps us from our homes ethereal;
And what our duties there: to nightly call
Vesper, the beauty-crest of summer weather;
To summon all the downiest clouds together
For the sun's purple couch; to emulate 365
In minist'ring the potent rule of fate
With speed of fire-tailed exhalations;
To tint her pallid cheek with bloom, who cons
Sweet poesy by moonlight: besides these,
A world of other unguessed offices. 370
Anon they wandered, by divine converse,
Into Elysium; vying to rehearse
Each one his own anticipated bliss.
One felt heart-certain that he could not miss
His quick gone love, among fair blossomed boughs, 375
Where every zephyr-sigh pouts, and endows
Her lips with music for the welcoming.
Another wished, mid that eternal spring,
To meet his rosy child, with feathery sails,
Sweeping, eye-earnestly, through almond vales: 380
Who, suddenly, should stoop through the smooth wind,
And with the balmiest leaves his temples bind;
And, ever after, through those regions be
His messenger, his little Mercury.
Some were athirst in soul to see again 385
Their fellow huntsmen o'er the wide champain
In times long past; to sit with them, and talk
Of all the chances in their earthly walk;
Comparing, joyfully, their plenteous stores
Of happiness, to when upon the moors, 390
Benighted, close they huddled from the cold,
And shared their famished scrips. Thus all out-told
Their fond imaginations—saving him
Whose eyelids curtained up their jewels dim,
Endymion: yet hourly had he striven 395
To hide the cankering venom, that had riven
His fainting recollections. Now indeed
His senses had swooned off: he did not heed
The sudden silence, or the whispers low,
Or the old eyes dissolving at his woe, 400

Or anxious calls, or close of trembling palms,
Or maiden's sigh, that grief itself embalms:
But in the self-same fixèd trance he kept,
Like one who on the earth had never stepped.
Aye, even as dead-still as a marble man,
Frozen in that old tale Arabian.

Who whispers him so pantingly and close?
Peona, his sweet sister: of all those,
His friends, the dearest. Hushing signs she made,
And breathed a sister's sorrow to persuade
A yielding up, a cradling on her care.
Her eloquence did breathe away the curse:
She led him, like some midnight spirit nurse
Of happy changes in emphatic dreams,
Along a path between two little streams—
Guarding his forehead, with her round elbow,
From low-grown branches, and his footsteps slow
From stumbling over stumps and hillocks small;
Until they came to where these streamlets fall,
With mingled bubblings and a gentle rush,
Into a river, clear, brim full, and flush
With crystal mocking of the trees and sky.
A little shallop, floating there hard by,
Pointed its beak over the fringèd bank;
And soon it lightly dipped, and rose, and sank,
And dipped again, with the young couple's weight—
Peona guiding, through the water straight,
Towards a bowery island opposite;
Which gaining presently, she steerèd light
Into a shady, fresh, and ripply cove,
Where nested was an arbor, overwove
By many a summer's silent fingering;
To whose cool bosom she was used to bring
Her playmates, with their needle broidery,
And minstrel memories of times gone by.

So she was gently glad to see him laid
Under her favorite bower's quiet shade,
On her own couch, new made of flower leaves,

ENDYMION

Dried carefully on the cooler side of sheaves
When last the sun his autumn tresses shook,
And the tanned harvesters rich armfuls took.
Soon was he quieted to slumbrous rest:
But, ere it crept upon him, he had pressed
Peona's busy hand against his lips,
And still, a-sleeping, held her fingertips
In tender pressure. And as a willow keeps
A patient watch over the stream that creeps
Windingly by it, so the quiet maid
Held her in peace: so that a whispering blade
Of grass, a wailful gnat, a bee bustling
Down in the bluebells, or a wren light rustling
Among sere leaves and twigs, might all be heard.

   O magic sleep! O comfortable bird
That broodest o'er the troubled sea of the mind
Till it is hushed and smooth! O unconfined
Restraint! imprisoned liberty! great key
To golden palaces, strange minstrelsy,
Fountains grotesque, new trees, bespangled caves,
Echoing grottoes, full of tumbling waves
And moonlight; aye, to all the mazy world
Of silvery enchantment!—who, upfurled
Beneath thy drowsy wing a triple hour,
But renovates and lives?—Thus, in the bower,
Endymion was calmed to life again.
Opening his eyelids with a healthier brain,
He said: "I feel this thine endearing love
All through my bosom: thou art as a dove
Trembling its closèd eyes and sleekèd wings
About me; and the pearliest dew not brings
Such morning incense from the fields of May,
As do those brighter drops that twinkling stray
From those kind eyes—the very home and haunt
Of sisterly affection. Can I want
Aught else, aught nearer heaven, than such tears?
Yet dry them up, in bidding hence all fears
That, any longer, I will pass my days
Alone and sad. No, I will once more raise

My voice upon the mountain heights; once more
Make my horn parley from their foreheads hoar:
480 Again my trooping hounds their tongues shall loll
Around the breathèd boar: again I'll poll
The fair-grown yew tree, for a chosen bow:
And, when the pleasant sun is getting low,
Again I'll linger in a sloping mead
485 To hear the speckled thrushes, and see feed
Our idle sheep. So be thou cheerèd, sweet,
And, if thy lute is here, softly intreat
My soul to keep in its resolvèd course."

Hereat Peona, in their silver source,
490 Shut her pure sorrow drops with glad exclaim,
And took a lute, from which there pulsing came
A lively prelude, fashioning the way
In which her voice should wander. 'Twas a lay
More subtle cadencèd, more forest wild
495 Than Dryope's° lone lulling of her child;
And nothing since has floated in the air
So mournful strange. Surely some influence rare
Went, spiritual, through the damsel's hand;
For still, with Delphic emphasis, she spanned
500 The quick invisible strings, even though she saw
Endymion's spirit melt away and thaw
Before the deep intoxication.
But soon she came, with sudden burst, upon
Her self-possession—swung the lute aside,
505 And earnestly said: "Brother, 'tis vain to hide
That thou dost know of things mysterious,
Immortal, starry; such alone could thus
Weigh down thy nature. Hast thou sinned in aught
Offensive to the heavenly powers? Caught
510 A Paphian dove upon a message sent?
Thy deathful bow against some dear-head bent,
Sacred to Dian? Haply, thou hast seen
Her naked limbs among the alders green;

---

495 **Dryope** The reference is to Ovid's Dryope, who carried her infant with her when she was changed into a tree.

ENDYMION

And that, alas! is death. No, I can trace
Something more high-perplexing in thy face!"

Endymion looked at her, and pressed her hand,
And said, "Art thou so pale, who wast so bland
And merry in our meadows? How is this?
Tell me thine ailment: tell me all amiss!—
Ah! thou hast been unhappy at the change
Wrought suddenly in me. What indeed more strange?
Or more complete to overwhelm surmise?
Ambition is no sluggard: 'tis no prize,
That toiling years would put within my grasp,
That I have sighed for: with so deadly gasp
No man e'er panted for a mortal love.
So all have set my heavier grief above
These things which happen. Rightly have they done:
I, who still saw the horizontal sun
Heave his broad shoulder o'er the edge of the world,
Outfacing Lucifer, and then had hurled
My spear aloft, as signal for the chase—
I, who, for very sport of heart, would race
With my own steed from Araby; pluck down
A vulture from his towery perching; frown
A lion into growling, loth retire—
To lose, at once, all my toil breeding fire,
And sink thus low! but I will ease my breast
Of secret grief, here in this bowery nest.

"This river does not see the naked sky,
Till it begins to progress silverly
Around the western border of the wood,
Whence, from a certain spot, its winding flood
Seems at the distance like a crescent moon:
And in that nook, the very pride of June,
Had I been used to pass my weary eves;
The rather for the sun unwilling leaves
So dear a picture of his sovereign power,
And I could witness his most kingly hour,
When he doth tighten up the golden reins,
And paces leisurely down amber plains

His snorting four. Now when his chariot last
Its beam against the zodiac-lion cast,
There blossomed suddenly a magic bed
Of sacred ditamy, and poppies red:
At which I wondered greatly, knowing well
That but one night had wrought this flowery spell;
And, sitting down close by, began to muse
What it might mean. Perhaps, thought I, Morpheus,
In passing here, his owlet pinions shook;
Or, it may be, ere matron Night uptook
Her ebon urn, young Mercury, by stealth,
Had dipped his rod in it: such garland wealth
Came not by common growth. Thus on I thought,
Until my head was dizzy and distraught.
Moreover, through the dancing poppies stole
A breeze, most softly lulling to my soul;
And shaping visions all about my sight
Of colors, wings, and bursts of spangly light;
The which became more strange, and strange, and dim,
And then were gulfed in a tumultuous swim:
And then I fell asleep. Ah, can I tell
The enchantment that afterwards befell?
Yet it was but a dream: yet such a dream
That never tongue, although it overteem
With mellow utterance, like a cavern spring,
Could figure out and to conception bring
All I beheld and felt. Methought I lay
Watching the zenith, where the milky way
Among the stars in virgin splendor pours;
And traveling my eye, until the doors
Of heaven appeared to open for my flight,
I became loth and fearful to alight
From such high soaring by a downward glance:
So kept me steadfast in that airy trance,
Spreading imaginary pinions wide.
When, presently, the stars began to glide,
And faint away, before my eager view:
At which I sighed that I could not pursue,
And dropped my vision to the horizon's verge;

ENDYMION

And lo! from the opening clouds, I saw emerge
The loveliest moon, that ever silvered o'er
A shell for Neptune's goblet: she did soar
So passionately bright, my dazzled soul
Commingling with her argent spheres did roll   595
Through clear and cloudy, even when she went
At last into a dark and vapory tent—
Whereat, methought, the lidless-eyèd train
Of planets all were in the blue again.
To commune with those orbs, once more I raised   600
My sight right upward: but it was quite dazed
By a bright something, sailing down apace,
Making me quickly veil my eyes and face:
Again I looked, and, O ye deities,
Who from Olympus watch our destinies!   605
Whence that completed form of all completeness?
Whence came that high perfection of all sweetness?
Speak, stubborn earth, and tell me where, O where
Hast thou a symbol of her golden hair?
Not oat sheaves drooping in the western sun;   610
Not—thy soft hand, fair sister! let me shun
Such follying before thee—yet she had,
Indeed, locks bright enough to make me mad;
And they were simply gordianed up and braided,
Leaving, in naked comeliness, unshaded,   615
Her pearl round ears, white neck, and orbèd brow;
The which were blended in, I know not how,
With such a paradise of lips and eyes,
Blush-tinted cheeks, half smiles, and faintest sighs,
That, when I think thereon, my spirit clings   620
And plays about its fancy, till the stings
Of human neighborhood envenom all.
Unto what awful power shall I call?
To what high fane?—Ah! see her hovering feet,
More bluely veined, more soft, more whitely sweet 625
Than those of sea-born Venus, when she rose
From out her cradle shell. The wind outblows
Her scarf into a fluttering pavilion;
'Tis blue, and over-spangled with a million

630 Of little eyes, as though thou wert to shed,
    Over the darkest, lushest bluebell bed,
    Handfuls of daisies."—"Endymion, how strange!
    Dream within dream!"—"She took an airy range,
    And then, towards me, like a very maid,
635 Came blushing, waning, willing, and afraid,
    And pressed me by the hand: Ah! 'twas too much;
    Methought I fainted at the charmèd touch,
    Yet held my recollection, even as one
    Who dives three fathoms where the waters run
640 Gurgling in beds of coral: for anon,
    I felt upmounted in that region
    Where falling stars dart their artillery forth,
    And eagles struggle with the buffeting north
    That balances the heavy meteor stone;—
645 Felt too, I was not fearful, nor alone,
    But lapped and lulled along the dangerous sky.
    Soon, as it seemed, we left our journeying high,
    And straightway into frightful eddies swooped;
    Such as aye muster where gray time has scooped
650 Huge dens and caverns in a mountain's side:
    There hollow sounds aroused me, and I sighed
    To faint once more by looking on my bliss—
    I was distracted; madly did I kiss
    The wooing arms which held me, and did give
655 My eyes at once to death: but 'twas to live,
    To take in draughts of life from the gold fount
    Of kind and passionate looks; to count, and count
    The moments, by some greedy help that seemed
    A second self, that each might be redeemed
660 And plundered of its load of blessedness.
    Ah, desperate mortal! I even dared to press
    Her very cheek against my crownèd lip,
    And at that moment, felt my body dip
    Into a warmer air: a moment more
665 Our feet were soft in flowers. There was store
    Of newest joys upon that alp. Sometimes
    A scent of violets, and blossoming limes,
    Loitered around us; then of honey cells,
    Made delicate from all white-flower bells;

And once, above the edges of our nest,
An arch face peeped—an Oread as I guessed.

"Why did I dream that sleep o'er-powered me
In midst of all this heaven? Why not see,
Far off, the shadows of his pinions dark,
And stare them from me? But no, like a spark
That needs must die, although its little beam
Reflects upon a diamond, my sweet dream
Fell into nothing—into stupid sleep.
And so it was, until a gentle creep,
A careful moving caught my waking ears,
And up I started: Ah! my sighs, my tears,
My clenchèd hands;—for lo! the poppies hung
Dew-dabbled on their stalks, the ouzel sung
A heavy ditty, and the sullen day
Had chidden herald Hesperus away,
With leaden looks: the solitary breeze
Blustered, and slept, and its wild self did tease
With wayward melancholy; and I thought,
Mark me, Peona! that sometimes it brought
Faint fare-thee-wells, and sigh-shrilled adieus!—
Away I wandered—all the pleasant hues
Of heaven and earth had faded: deepest shades
Were deepest dungeons; heaths and sunny glades
Were full of pestilent light; our taintless rills
Seemed sooty, and o'er-spread with upturned gills
Of dying fish; the vermeil rose had blown
In frightful scarlet, and its thorns outgrown
Like spikèd aloe. If an innocent bird
Before my heedless footsteps stirred, and stirred
In little journeys, I beheld in it
A disguised demon, missionèd to knit
My soul with under darkness; to entice
My stumblings down some monstrous precipice:
Therefore I eager followed, and did curse
The disappointment. Time, that agèd nurse,
Rocked me to patience. Now, thank gentle heaven!
These things, with all their comfortings, are given
To my down-sunken hours, and with thee,

         Sweet sister, help to stem the ebbing sea
         Of weary life."

710   Thus ended he, and both
         Sat silent: for the maid was very loth
         To answer; feeling well that breathèd words
         Would all be lost, unheard, and vain as swords
         Against the enchasèd crocodile, or leaps
715   Of grasshoppers against the sun. She weeps,
         And wonders; struggles to devise some blame;
         To put on such a look as would say, *Shame
         On this poor weakness!* but, for all her strife,
         She could as soon have crushed away the life
720   From a sick dove. At length, to break the pause,
         She said with trembling chance: "Is this the cause?
         This all? Yet it is strange, and sad, alas!
         That one who through this middle earth should pass
         Most like a sojourning demigod, and leave
725   His name upon the harpstring, should achieve
         No higher bard than simple maidenhood,
         Singing alone, and fearfully—how the blood
         Left his young cheek; and how he used to stray
         He knew not where; and how he would say, *nay,
730   If any said 'twas love*: and yet 'twas love;
         What could it be but love? How a ringdove
         Let fall a sprig of yew tree in his path;
         And how he died: and then, that love doth scathe
         The gentle heart, as northern blasts do roses;
735   And then the ballad of his sad life closes
         With sighs, and an alas!—Endymion!
         Be rather in the trumpet's mouth—anon
         Among the winds at large—that all may hearken!
         Although, before the crystal heavens darken,
740   I watch and dote upon the silver lakes
         Pictured in western cloudiness, that takes
         The semblance of gold rocks and bright gold sands,
         Islands, and creeks, and amber-fretted strands
         With horses prancing o'er them, palaces
745   And towers of amethyst—would I so tease
         My pleasant days, because I could not mount

ENDYMION 113

Into those regions? The Morphean fount
Of that fine element that visions, dreams,
And fitful whims of sleep are made of, streams
Into its airy channels with so subtle, 750
So thin a breathing, not the spider's shuttle,
Circled a million times within the space
Of a swallow's nest door, could delay a trace,
A tinting of its quality: how light
Must dreams themselves be; seeing they're more slight 755
Than the mere nothing that engenders them!
Then wherefore sully the entrusted gem
Of high and noble life with thoughts so sick?
Why pierce high-fronted honor to the quick
For nothing but a dream?" Hereat the youth 760
Looked up: a conflicting of shame and ruth
Was in his plaited brow: yet, his eyelids
Widened a little, as when Zephyr bids
A little breeze to creep between the fans
Of careless butterflies: amid his pains 765
He seemed to taste a drop of manna dew,
Full palatable; and a color grew
Upon his cheek, while thus he lifeful spake.

"Peona! ever have I longed to slake
My thirst for the world's praises: nothing base, 770
No merely slumberous phantasm, could unlace
The stubborn canvas for my voyage prepared—
Though now 'tis tattered; leaving my bark bared
And sullenly drifting: yet my higher hope
Is of too wide, too rainbow-large a scope, 775
To fret at myriads of earthly wrecks.
Wherein lies happiness? In that which becks
Our ready minds to fellowship divine,
A fellowship with essence; till we shine,
Full alchemized, and free of space. Behold 780
The clear religion of heaven!° Fold

777–781 **Wherein . . . heaven** This passage was added on January 30, 1818, when *Endymion* was finished and going to press. The expression "fellowship with essence" has been at the root of most of the discussions on the interpretation of the poem.

A rose leaf round thy finger's taperness,
And soothe thy lips: hist, when the airy stress
Of music's kiss impregnates the free winds,
785 And with a sympathetic touch unbinds
Eolian magic from their lucid wombs:
Then old songs waken from enclouded tombs;
Old ditties sigh above their father's grave;
Ghosts of melodious prophecyings rave
790 Round every spot where trod Apollo's foot;
Bronze clarions awake, and faintly bruit,
Where long ago a giant battle was;
And, from the turf, a lullaby doth pass
In every place where infant Orpheus slept.
795 Feel we these things?—that moment have we stepped
Into a sort of oneness, and our state
Is like a floating spirit's. But there are
Richer entanglements, enthrallments far
More self-destroying, leading, by degrees,
800 To the chief intensity: the crown of these
Is made of love and friendship, and sits high
Upon the forehead of humanity.
All its more ponderous and bulky worth
Is friendship, whence there ever issues forth
805 A steady splendor; but at the tip-top,
There hangs by unseen film, an orbèd drop
Of light, and that is love: its influence,
Thrown in our eyes, genders a novel sense,
At which we start and fret; till in the end,
810 Melting into its radiance, we blend,
Mingle, and so become a part of it—
Nor with aught else can our souls interknit
So wingedly: when we combine therewith,
Life's self is nourished by its proper pith,
815 And we are nurtured like a pelican brood.
Aye, so delicious is the unsating food,
That men, who might have towered in the van
Of all the congregated world, to fan
And winnow from the coming step of time
820 All chaff of custom, wipe away all slime
Left by men-slugs and human serpentry,

ENDYMION 115

Have been content to let occasion die,
Whilst they did sleep in love's Elysium.
And, truly, I would rather be struck dumb,
Than speak against this ardent listlessness: 825
For I have ever thought that it might bless
The world with benefits unknowingly;
As does the nightingale, upperchèd high,
And cloistered among cool and bunchèd leaves—
She sings but to her love, nor e'er conceives 830
How tiptoe Night holds back her dark-gray hood.
Just so may love, although 'tis understood
The mere commingling of passionate breath,
Produce more than our searching witnesseth:
What I know not: but who, of men, can tell 835
That flowers would bloom, or that green fruit would swell
To melting pulp, that fish would have bright mail,
The earth its dower of river, wood, and vale,
The meadows runnels, runnels pebble-stones,
The seed its harvest, or the lute its tones, 840
Tones ravishment, or ravishment its sweet,
If human souls did never kiss and greet?

"Now, if this earthly love has power to make
Men's being mortal, immortal; to shake
Ambition from their memories, and brim 845
Their measure of content; what merest whim,
Seems all this poor endeavor after fame,
To one, who keeps within his steadfast aim
A love immortal, an immortal too.
Look not so wildered; for these things are true, 850
And never can be born of atomies
That buzz about our slumbers, like brain-flies,
Leaving us fancy-sick. No, no, I'm sure,
My restless spirit never could endure
To brood so long upon one luxury, 855
Unless it did, though fearfully, espy
A hope beyond the shadow of a dream.
My sayings will the less obscurèd seem,
When I have told thee how my waking sight

860 Has made me scruple whether that same night
Was passed in dreaming. Hearken, sweet Peona!
Beyond the matron temple of Latona,
Which we should see but for these darkening boughs,
Lies a deep hollow, from whose ragged brows
865 Bushes and trees do lean all round athwart,
And meet so nearly, that with wings outraught,
And spreaded tail, a vulture could not glide
Past them, but he must brush on every side.
Some mouldered steps lead into this cool cell,
870 Far as the slabbèd margin of a well,
Whose patient level peeps its crystal eye
Right upward, through the bushes, to the sky.
Oft have I brought thee flowers, on their stalks set
Like vestal primroses, but dark velvet
875 Edges them round, and they have golden pits:
'Twas there I got them, from the gaps and slits
In a mossy stone, that sometimes was my seat,
When all above was faint with midday heat.
And there in strife no burning thoughts to heed,
880 I'd bubble up the water through a reed;
So reaching back to boyhood: make me ships
Of molted feathers, touchwood, alder chips,
With leaves stuck in them; and the Neptune be
Of their petty ocean. Oftener, heavily,
885 When lovelorn hours had left me less a child,
I sat contemplating the figures wild
Of o'er-head clouds melting the mirror through.
Upon a day, while thus I watched, by flew
A cloudy Cupid, with his bow and quiver;
890 So plainly charactered, no breeze would shiver
The happy chance: so happy, I was fain
To follow it upon the open plain,
And, therefore, was just going; when, behold!
A wonder, fair as any I have told—
895 The same bright face I tasted in my sleep,
Smiling in the clear well. My heart did leap
Through the cool depth.—It moved as if to flee—
I started up, when lo! refreshfully,
There came upon my face, in plenteous showers,

ENDYMION

Dewdrops, and dewy buds, and leaves, and flowers, 900
Wrapping all objects from my smothered sight,
Bathing my spirit in a new delight.
Aye, such a breathless honey-feel of bliss
Alone preserved me from the drear abyss
Of death, for the fair form had gone again. 905
Pleasure is oft a visitant; but pain
Clings cruelly to us, like the gnawing sloth
On the deer's tender haunches: late, and loth,
'Tis scared away by slow returning pleasure.
How sickening, how dark the dreadful leisure 910
Of weary days, made deeper exquisite,
By a foreknowledge of unslumb'rous night!
Like sorrow came upon me, heavier still,
Than when I wandered from the poppy hill:
And a whole age of lingering moments crept 915
Sluggishly by, ere more contentment swept
Away at once the deadly yellow spleen.
Yes, thrice have I this fair enchantment seen;
Once more been tortured with renewèd life.
When last the wintry gusts gave over strife 920
With the conquering sun of spring, and left the skies
Warm and serene, but yet with moistened eyes
In pity of the shattered infant buds—
That time thou didst adorn, with amber studs,
My hunting cap, because I laughed and smiled, 925
Chatted with thee, and many days exiled
All torment from my breast;—'twas even then,
Straying about, yet, cooped up in the den
Of helpless discontent—hurling my lance
From place to place, and following at chance, 930
At last, by hap, through some young trees it struck,
And, plashing among bedded pebbles, stuck
In the middle of a brook—whose silver ramble
Down twenty little falls, through reeds and bramble,
Tracing along, it brought me to a cave, 935
Whence it ran brightly forth, and white did lave
The nether sides of mossy stones and rock—
'Mong which it gurgled blithe adieus, to mock
Its own sweet grief at parting. Overhead,

Hung a lush screen of drooping weeds, and spread
Thick, as to curtain up some wood nymph's home.
'Ah! impious mortal, whither do I roam?'
Said I, low voiced: 'Ah, whither! 'Tis the grot
Of Proserpine,° when Hell, obscure and hot,
Doth her resign; and where her tender hands
She dabbles, on the cool and sluicy sands:
Or 'tis the cell of Echo,° where she sits,
And babbles thorough silence, till her wits
Are gone in tender madness, and anon,
Faints into sleep, with many a dying tone
Of sadness. O that she would take my vows,
And breathe them sighingly among the boughs,
To sue her gentle ears for whose fair head,
Daily, I pluck sweet flowerets from their bed,
And weave them dyingly—send honey-whispers
Round every leaf, that all those gentle lispers
May sigh my love unto her pitying!
O charitable Echo! hear, and sing
This ditty to her!—tell her'—so I stayed
My foolish tongue, and listening, half afraid,
Stood stupefied with my own empty folly,
And blushing for the freaks of melancholy.
Salt tears were coming, when I heard my name
Most fondly lipped, and then these accents came:
'Endymion! the cave is secreter
Than the isle of Delos. Echo hence shall stir
No sighs but sigh-warm kisses, or light noise
Of thy combing hand, the while it traveling cloys
And trembles through my labyrinthine hair.'
At that oppressed I hurried in.—Ah! where
Are those swift moments? Whither are they fled?
I'll smile no more, Peona; nor will wed
Sorrow the way to death; but patiently
Bear up against it: so farewell, sad sigh;
And come instead demurest meditation,

944 **Proserpine** queen of Hell.   947 **Echo** the reference to the myth of Narcissus is altogether unlike that in Ovid since the element of self-love is entirely lacking: the reflection is Cynthia's, and Echo is used as a messenger to woo her.

ENDYMION

To occupy me wholly, and to fashion
My pilgrimage for the world's dusky brink.
No more will I count over, link by link,
My chain of grief: no longer strive to find
A half-forgetfulness in mountain wind
Blustering about my ears: aye, thou shalt see,
Dearest of sisters, what my life shall be;
What a calm round of hours shall make my days.
There is a paly flame of hope that plays
Where'er I look: but yet, I'll say 'tis naught—
And here I bid it die. Have not I caught,
Already, a more healthy countenance?
By this the sun is setting; we may chance
Meet some of our near-dwellers with my car."

This said, he rose, faint-smiling like a star
Through autumn mists, and took Peona's hand:
They stepped into the boat, and launched from land.

Book II

O sovereign power of love! O grief! O balm!
All records, saving thine, come cool, and calm,
And shadowy, through the mist of passèd years:
For others, good or bad, hatred and tears
Have become indolent; but touching thine,
One sigh doth echo, one poor sob doth pine,
One kiss brings honey-dew from buried days.
The woes of Troy, towers smothering o'er their blaze,
Stiff-holden shields, far-piercing spears, keen blades,
Struggling, and blood, and shrieks—all dimly fades
Into some backward corner of the brain;
Yet, in our very souls, we feel amain
The close of Troilus and Cressid sweet.
Hence, pageant history! hence, gilded cheat!
Swart planet in the universe of deeds!
Wide sea, that one continuous murmur breeds
Along the pebbled shore of memory!
Many old rotten-timbered boats there be

Upon thy vaporous bosom, magnified
To goodly vessels; many a sail of pride,
And golden keeled, is left unlaunched and dry.
But wherefore this? What care, though owl did fly
About the great Athenian admiral's° mast?
What care, though striding Alexander past
The Indus with his Macedonian numbers?
Though old Ulysses tortured from his slumbers
The glutted Cyclops, what care?—Juliet leaning
Amid her window flowers—sighing—weaning
Tenderly her fancy from its maiden snow,
Doth more avail than these: the silver flow
Of Hero's° tears, the swoon of Imogen,
Fair Pastorella° in the bandit's den,
Are things to brood on with more ardency
Than the death-day of empires. Fearfully
Must such conviction come upon his head,
Who, thus far, discontent, has dared to tread,
Without one muse's smile, or kind behest,
The path of love and poesy. But rest,
In chafing restlessness, is yet more drear
Than to be crushed, in striving to uprear
Love's standard on the battlements of song.
So once more days and nights aid me along,
Like legioned soldiers.

      Brain-sick shepherd-prince,
What promise hast thou faithful guarded since
The day of sacrifice? Or, have new sorrows
Come with the constant dawn upon thy morrows?
Alas! 'tis his old grief. For many days,
Has he been wandering in uncertain ways:
Through wilderness, and woods of mossèd oaks;
Counting his woe-worn minutes, by the strokes
Of the lone woodcutter; and listening still,

---

23 **admiral** Themistocles at the battle of Salamis. 31 **Hero** The love of Hero and Leander is the subject of a famous poem by Marlowe. Hero, priestess of Aphrodite, killed herself when Leander drowned trying to join her. 32 **Pastorella** The story of her capture is told in Spenser's *Faerie Queene* (Book VI, Cantos x and xi).

ENDYMION

Hour after hour, to each lush-leaved rill.
Now he is sitting by a shady spring,
And elbow-deep with feverous fingering
Stems the upbursting cold: a wild rose tree
Pavilions him in bloom, and he doth see
A bud which snares his fancy: lo! but now
He plucks it, dips its stalk in the water: how!
It swells, it buds, it flowers beneath his sight;
And, in the middle, there is softly pight
A golden butterfly; upon whose wings
There must be surely charactered strange things,
For with wide eye he wonders, and smiles oft.

Lightly this little herald flew aloft,
Followed by glad Endymion's claspèd hands:
Onward it flies. From languor's sullen bands
His limbs are loosed, and eager, on he hies
Dazzled to trace it in the sunny skies.
It seemed he flew, the way so easy was;
And like a newborn spirit did he pass
Through the green evening quiet in the sun,
O'er many a heath, through many a woodland dun,
Through buried paths, where sleepy twilight dreams
The summer time away. One track unseams
A wooded cleft, and, far away, the blue
Of ocean fades upon him; then, anew,
He sinks adown a solitary glen,
Where there was never sound of mortal men,
Saving, perhaps, some snow-light cadences
Melting to silence, when upon the breeze
Some holy bark let forth an anthem sweet,
To cheer itself to Delphi. Still his feet
Went swift beneath the merry-wingèd guide,
Until it reached a splashing fountain's side
That, near a cavern's mouth, forever poured
Unto the temperate air: then high it soared,
And, downward, suddenly began to dip,
As if, athirst with so much toil, 'twould sip
The crystal spout-head: so it did, with touch
Most delicate, as though afraid to smutch

Even with mealy gold the waters clear.
But, at that very touch, to disappear
So fairy-quick, was strange! Bewilderèd,
Endymion sought around, and shook each bed
95 Of covert flowers in vain; and then he flung
Himself along the grass. What gentle tongue,
What whisperer disturbed his gloomy rest?
It was a nymph uprisen to the breast
In the fountain's pebbly margin, and she stood
100 'Mong lilies, like the youngest of the brood.
To him her dripping hand she softly kissed,
And anxiously began to plait and twist
Her ringlets round her fingers, saying: "Youth!
Too long, alas, hast thou starved on the ruth,
105 The bitterness of love: too long indeed,
Seeing thou art so gentle. Could I weed
Thy soul of care, by heavens, I would offer
All the bright riches of my crystal coffer
To Amphitrite;° all my clear-eyed fish,
110 Golden, or rainbow-sided, or purplish,
Vermilion-tailed, or finned with silvery gauze;
Yea, or my veinèd pebble-floor, that draws
A virgin light to the deep; my grotto-sands
Tawny and gold, oozed slowly from far lands
115 By my diligent springs; my level lilies, shells,
My charming rod, my potent river spells;
Yes, everything, even to the pearly cup
Meander gave me—for I bubbled up
To fainting creatures in a desert wild.
120 But woe is me, I am but as a child
To gladden thee; and all I dare to say,
Is, that I pity thee; that on this day
I've been thy guide; that thou must wander far
In other regions, past the scanty bar
125 To mortal steps, before thou canst be ta'en
From every wasting sigh, from every pain,
Into the gentle bosom of thy love.
Why it is thus, one knows in heaven above:

---

109 **Amphitrite** Poseidon's (Neptune's) wife.

ENDYMION

But, a poor Naiad, I guess not. Farewell!
I have a ditty for my hollow cell."

Hereat, she vanished from Endymion's gaze,
Who brooded o'er the water in amaze:
The dashing fount poured on, and where its pool
Lay, half asleep, in grass and rushes cool,
Quick waterflies and gnats were sporting still,
And fish were dimpling, as if good nor ill
Had fallen out that hour. The wanderer,
Holding his forehead, to keep off the burr
Of smothering fancies, patiently sat down;
And, while beneath the evening's sleepy frown
Glowworms began to trim their starry lamps,
Thus breathed he to himself: "Whoso encamps
To take a fancied city of delight,
O what a wretch is he! and when 'tis his,
After long toil and traveling, to miss
The kernel of his hopes, how more than vile:
Yet, for him there's refreshment even in toil;
Another city doth he set about,
Free from the smallest pebble-bead of doubt
That he will seize on trickling honeycombs:
Alas, he finds them dry; and then he foams,
And onward to another city speeds.
But this is human life: the war, the deeds,
The disappointment, the anxiety,
Imagination's struggles, far and nigh,
All human; bearing in themselves this good,
That they are still the air, the subtle food,
To make us feel existence, and to show
How quiet death is. Where soil is, men grow,
Whether to weeds or flowers; but for me,
There is no depth to strike in: I can see
Nought earthly worth my compassing; so stand
Upon a misty, jutting head of land—
Alone? No, no; and by the Orphean lute,
When mad Eurydice is listening to 't;
I'd rather stand upon this misty peak,
With not a thing to sigh for, or to seek,

But the soft shadow of my thrice-seen love,
Than be—I care not what. O meekest dove
170 Of heaven! O Cynthia,° ten times bright and fair!
From thy blue throne, now filling all the air,
Glance but one little beam of tempered light
Into my bosom, that the dreadful might
And tyranny of love be somewhat scared!
175 Yet do not so, sweet queen; one torment spared,
Would give a pang to jealous misery,
Worse than the torment's self: but rather tie
Large wings upon my shoulders, and point out
My love's far dwelling. Though the playful rout
180 Of Cupids shun thee, too divine art thou,
Too keen in beauty, for thy silver prow
Not to have dipped in love's most gentle stream.
O be propitious, nor severely deem
My madness impious; for, by all the stars
185 That tend thy bidding, I do think the bars
That kept my spirit in are burst—that I
Am sailing with thee through the dizzy sky!
How beautiful thou art! The world how deep!
How tremulous-dazzlingly the wheels sweep
190 Around their axle! Then these gleaming reins,
How lithe! When this thy chariot attains
Its airy goal, haply some bower veils
Those twilight eyes? Those eyes!—my spirit fails—
Dear goddess, help! or the wide-gaping air
195 Will gulf me—help!"—At this with maddened stare,
And lifted hands, and trembling lips he stood;
Like old Deucalion° mountained o'er the flood,
Or blind Orion° hungry for the morn.
And, but from the deep cavern there was borne
200 A voice, he had been froze to senseless stone;
Nor sigh of his, nor plaint, nor passioned moan

170 **Cynthia** epithet for Diana. Endymion evokes the moon goddess, not knowing at this point that his "thrice-seen love" is Diana. 197 **Deucalion** was the only man saved, together with his wife, from the flood.   198 **Orion** is represented in a famous painting by Poussin as, blinded, he sets out in quest of the place where the sun rises. The myth is to the point here (more than Deucalion's) since, in the Poussin painting, Orion is guided by Diana.

Had more been heard. Thus swelled it forth: "Descend,
Young mountaineer! descend where alleys bend
Into the sparry hollows of the world!
Oft hast thou seen bolts of the thunder hurled 205
As from thy threshold; day by day hast been
A little lower than the chilly sheen
Of icy pinnacles, and dipp'dst thine arms
Into the deadening ether that still charms
Their marble being: now, as deep profound 210
As those are high, descend! He ne'er is crowned
With immortality, who fears to follow
Where airy voices lead: so through the hollow,
The silent mysteries of earth, descend!"

He heard but the last words, nor could contend 215
One moment in reflection: for he fled
Into the fearful deep, to hide his head
From the clear moon, the trees, and coming madness.

'Twas far too strange, and wonderful for sadness;
Sharpening, by degrees, his appetite 220
To dive into the deepest. Dark, nor light,
The region; nor bright, nor somber wholly,
But mingled up; a gleaming melancholy;
A dusky empire and its diadems;
One faint eternal eventide of gems. 225
Aye, millions sparkled on a vein of gold,
Along whose track the prince quick footsteps told,
With all its lines abrupt and angular:
Outshooting sometimes, like a meteor star,
Through a vast antre; then the metal woof, 230
Like Vulcan's rainbow, with some monstrous roof
Curves hugely: now, far in the deep abyss,
It seems an angry lightning, and doth hiss
Fancy into belief: anon it leads
Through winding passages, where sameness breeds 235
Vexing conceptions of some sudden change;
Whether to silver grots, or giant range
Of sapphire columns, or fantastic bridge
Athwart a flood of crystal. On a ridge

ENDYMION

240 Now fareth he, that o'er the vast beneath
Towers like an ocean cliff, and whence he seeth
A hundred waterfalls, whose voices come
But as the murmuring surge. Chilly and numb
His bosom grew, when first he, far away,
245 Descried an orbèd diamond, set to fray
Old darkness from his throne: 'twas like the sun
Uprisen o'er chaos: and with such a stun
Came the amazement, that, absorbed in it,
He saw not fiercer wonders—past the wit
250 Of any spirit to tell, but one of those
Who, when this planet's sphering time doth close,
Will be its high remembrancers: who they?
The mighty ones° who have made eternal day
For Greece and England. While astonishment
255 With deep-drawn sighs was quieting, he went
Into a marble gallery, passing through
A mimic temple, so complete and true
In sacred custom, that he well nigh feared
To search it inwards; whence far off appeared,
260 Through a long pillared vista, a fair shrine,
And, just beyond, on light tiptoe divine,
A quivered Dian.° Stepping awfully,
The youth approached; oft turning his veiled eye
Down sidelong aisles, and into niches old.
265 And when, more near against the marble cold
He had touched his forehead, he began to thread
All courts and passages, where silence dead
Roused by his whispering footsteps murmured faint:
And long he traversed to and fro, to acquaint
270 Himself with every mystery, and awe;
Till, weary, he sat down before the maw
Of a wide outlet, fathomless and dim,
To wild uncertainty and shadows grim.
There, when new wonders ceased to float before,
275 And thoughts of self came on, how crude and sore

253 **The mighty ones** Homer and Virgil (both of whom described descents into the underworld), Spenser and Milton. Keats read Dante later. 262 **Dian** Endymion does not recognize Diana, but returns to the temple later (l. 300).

The journey homeward to habitual self!
A mad-pursuing of the fog-born elf,
Whose flitting lantern, through rude nettle-brier,
Cheats us into a swamp, into a fire,
Into the bosom of a hated thing.

What misery most drowningly doth sing
In lone Endymion's ear, now he has raught
The goal of consciousness? Ah, 'tis the thought,
The deadly feel of solitude: for lo!
He cannot see the heavens, nor the flow
Of rivers, nor hill flowers running wild
In pink and purple checker, nor, up-piled,
The cloudy rack slow journeying in the west,
Like herded elephants; nor felt, nor pressed
Cool grass, nor tasted the fresh slumberous air;
But far from such companionship to wear
An unknown time, surcharged with grief, away,
Was now his lot. And must he patient stay,
Tracing fantastic figures with his spear?
"No!" exclaimed he, "why should I tarry here?"
No! loudly echoed times innumerable.
At which he straightway started, and 'gan tell
His paces back into the temple's chief;
Warming and glowing strong in the belief
Of help from Dian: so that when again
He caught her airy form, thus did he plain,
Moving more near the while. "O Haunter chaste
Of river sides, and woods, and heathy waste,
Where with thy silver bow and arrows keen
Art thou now forested? O woodland Queen,
What smoothest air thy smoother forehead woos?
Where dost thou listen to the wide halloos
Of thy disparted nymphs? Through what dark tree
Glimmers thy crescent? Wheresoe'er it be,
'Tis in the breath of heaven: thou dost taste
Freedom as none can taste it, nor dost waste
Thy loveliness in dismal elements;
But, finding in our green earth sweet contents,
There livest blissfully. Ah, if to thee

315 It feels Elysian, how rich to me,
An exiled mortal, sounds its pleasant name!
Within my breast there lives a choking flame—
O let me cool it the zephyr boughs among!
A homeward fever parches up my tongue—
320 O let me slake it at the running springs!
Upon my ear a noisy nothing rings—
O let me once more hear the linnet's note!
Before mine eyes thick films and shadows float—
O let me 'noint them with the heaven's light!
325 Dost thou now lave thy feet and ankles white?
O think how sweet to me the freshening sluice!
Dost thou now please thy thirst with berry juice?
O think how this dry palate would rejoice!
If in soft slumber thou dost hear my voice,
330 O think how I should love a bed of flowers!—
Young goddess! let me see my native bowers!
Deliver me from this rapacious deep!"

Thus ending loudly, as he would o'er-leap
His destiny, alert he stood: but when
335 Obstinate silence came heavily again,
Feeling about for its old couch of space
And airy cradle, lowly bowed his face
Desponding, o'er the marble floor's cold thrill.
But 'twas not long; for, sweeter than the rill
340 To its cold channel, or a swollen tide
To margin sallows, were the leaves he spied,
And flowers, and wreaths, and ready myrtle crowns
Up heaping through the slab: refreshment drowns
Itself, and strives its own delights to hide—
345 Nor in one spot alone; the floral pride
In a long whispering birth enchanted grew
Before his footsteps; as when heaved anew
Old ocean rolls a lengthened wave to the shore,
Down whose green back the short-lived foam, all hoar,
350 Bursts gradual, with a wayward indolence.

Increasing still in heart, and pleasant sense,
Upon his fairy journey on he hastes;

ENDYMION

So anxious for the end, he scarcely wastes
One moment with his hand among the sweets:
Onward he goes—he stops—his bosom beats
As plainly in his ear, as the faint charm
Of which the throbs were born. This still alarm,
This sleepy music, forced him walk tiptoe:
For it came more softly than the east could blow
Arion's° magic to the Atlantic isles;
Or than the west, made jealous by the smiles
Of thronèd Apollo, could breathe back the lyre
To seas Ionian and Tyrian.

O did he ever live, that lonely man,
Who loved—and music slew not? 'Tis the pest
Of love, that fairest joys give most unrest;
That things of delicate and tenderest worth
Are swallowed all, and made a searèd dearth,
By one consuming flame: it doth immerse
And suffocate true blessings in a curse.
Half-happy, by comparison of bliss,
Is miserable. 'Twas even so with this
Dew-dropping melody, in the Carian's ear;
First heaven, then hell, and then forgotten clear,
Vanished in elemental passion.

And down some swart abysm he had gone,
Had not a heavenly guide benignant led
To where thick myrtle branches, 'gainst his head
Brushing, awakened: then the sounds again
Went noiseless as a passing noontide rain
Over a bower, where little space he stood;
For as the sunset peeps into a wood
So saw he panting light, and towards it went
Through winding alleys; and lo, wonderment!
Upon soft verdure saw, one here, one there,
Cupids aslumbering on their pinions fair.

---

360 **Arion** Spenser, *Faerie Queene* (IV, ii. 1. 23). Arion's song enraptured the dolphins who bore him back to the island of Taenarus.

After a thousand mazes overgone,
At last, with sudden step, he came upon
A chamber, myrtle walled, embowered high,
390 Full of light, incense, tender minstrelsy,
And more of beautiful and strange beside:
For on a silken couch of rosy pride,
In midst of all, there lay a sleeping youth
Of fondest beauty; fonder, in fair sooth,
395 Than sighs could fathom, or contentment reach:
And coverlids gold-tinted like the peach,
Or ripe October's faded marigolds,
Fell sleek about him in a thousand folds—
Not hiding up an Apollonian curve
400 Of neck and shoulder, nor the tenting swerve
Of knee from knee, nor ankles pointing light;
But rather, giving them to the filled sight
Officiously. Sideway his face reposed
On one white arm, and tenderly unclosed,
405 By tenderest pressure, a faint damask mouth
To slumbery pout; just as the morning south
Disparts a dew-lipped rose. Above his head,
Four lily stalks did their white honors wed
To make a coronal; and round him grew
410 All tendrils green, of every bloom and hue,
Together intertwined and trammeled fresh:
The vine of glossy sprout; the ivy mesh,
Shading its Ethiop berries; and woodbine,
Of velvet leaves and bugle-blooms divine;
415 Convolvulus in streakèd vases flush;
The creeper, mellowing for an autumn blush;
And virgin's bower, trailing airily;
With others of the sisterhood. Hard by,
Stood serene Cupids watching silently.
420 One, kneeling to a lyre, touched the strings,
Muffling to death the pathos with his wings;
And, ever and anon, uprose to look
At the youth's slumber; while another took
A willow bough, distilling odorous dew,
425 And shook it on his hair; another flew

ENDYMION

In through the woven roof, and fluttering-wise
Rained violets upon his sleeping eyes.

At these enchantments, and yet many more,
The breathless Latmian wondered o'er and o'er;
Until, impatient in embarrassment, 430
He forthright passed, and lightly treading went
To that same feathered lyrist,° who straightway,
Smiling, thus whispered: "Though from upper day
Thou art a wanderer, and thy presence here
Might seem unholy, be of happy cheer! 435
For 'tis the nicest touch of human honor,
When some ethereal and high-favoring donor
Presents immortal bowers to mortal sense;
As now 'tis done to thee, Endymion. Hence
Was I in no wise startled. So recline 440
Upon these living flowers. Here is wine,
Alive with sparkles—never, I aver,
Since Ariadne° was a vintager,
So cool a purple: taste these juicy pears,
Sent me by sad Vertumnus,° when his fears 445
Were high about Pomona: here is cream,
Deepening to richness from a snowy gleam;
Sweeter than that Nurse Amalthea° skimmed
For the boy Jupiter: and here, undimmed
By any touch, a bunch of blooming plums 450
Ready to melt between an infant's gums:
And here is manna picked from Syrian trees,
In starlight, by the three Hesperides.
Feast on, and meanwhile I will let thee know
Of all these things around us." He did so, 455
Still brooding o'er the cadence of his lyre;
And thus: "I need not any hearing tire
By telling how the sea-born goddess pined
For a mortal youth, and how she strove to bind

---

432 **feathered lyrist** the Cupid mentioned in line 420.   443 **Ariadne** was loved by Bacchus, the wine god.   445 **Vertumnus** wooed Pomona in disguise by offering her fruit.   448 **Amalthea** was the nymph who fed Zeus goat's milk.

132   ENDYMION

460 Him all in all unto her doting self.
    Who would not be so imprisoned? but, fond elf,
    He was content to let her amorous plea
    Faint through his careless arms; content to see
    An unseized heaven dying at his feet;
465 Content, O fool! to make a cold retreat,
    When on the pleasant grass such love, lovelorn,
    Lay sorrowing; when every tear was born
    Of diverse passion; when her lips and eyes
    Were closed in sullen moisture, and quick sighs
470 Came vexed and pettish through her nostrils small.
    Hush! no exclaim—yet, justly mightst thou call
    Curses upon his head.—I was half glad,
    But my poor mistress went distract and mad,
    When the boar tusked him: so away she flew
475 To Jove's high throne, and by her plainings drew
    Immortal teardrops down the thunderer's beard;
    Whereon, it was decreed he should be reared
    Each summer time to life. Lo! this is he,
    That same Adonis,° safe in the privacy
480 Of this still region all his winter sleep.
    Aye, sleep; for when our love-sick queen did weep
    Over his waned corse, the tremulous shower
    Healed up the wound, and, with a balmy power,
    Medicined death to a lengthened drowsiness:
485 The which she fills with visions, and doth dress
    In all this quiet luxury; and hath set
    Us young immortals, without any let,
    To watch his slumber through. 'Tis well nigh passed,
    Even to a moment's filling up, and fast
490 She scuds with summer breezes, to pant through
    The first long kiss, warm firstling, to renew
    Embowered sports in Cytherea's isle.
    Look! how those winged listeners all this while
    Stand anxious: see! behold!"—This clamant word
495 Broke through the careful silence; for they heard
    A rustling noise of leaves, and out there fluttered

---

479 **Adonis** The story of Venus and Adonis is told with elements from Ovid (X, ll. 524 ff.), Shakespeare and, most of all, Spenser (*Faerie Queene*, III, vi).

Pigeons and doves: Adonis something muttered,
The while one hand, that erst upon his thigh
Lay dormant, moved convulsed and gradually
Up to his forehead. Then there was a hum   500
Of sudden voices, echoing, "Come! come!
Arise! awake! Clear summer has forth walked
Unto the clover-sward, and she has talked
Full soothingly to every nested finch:
Rise, Cupids! or we'll give the bluebell pinch   505
To your dimpled arms. Once more sweet life begin!"
At this, from every side they hurried in,
Rubbing their sleepy eyes with lazy wrists,
And doubling over head their little fists
In backward yawns. But all were soon alive: 510
For as delicious wine doth, sparkling, dive
In nectared clouds and curls through water fair,
So from the arbor roof down swelled an air
Odorous and enlivening; making all
To laugh, and play, and sing, and loudly call   515
For their sweet queen: when lo! the wreathèd green
Disparted, and far upward could be seen
Blue heaven, and a silver car, air-borne,
Whose silent wheels, fresh wet from clouds of morn,
Spun off a drizzling dew—which falling chill   520
On soft Adonis' shoulders, made him still
Nestle and turn uneasily about.
Soon were the white doves plain, with necks stretched out,
And silken traces tightened in descent;
And soon, returning from love's banishment,   525
Queen Venus leaning downward open-armed:
Her shadow fell upon his breast, and charmed
A tumult to his heart, and a new life
Into his eyes. Ah, miserable strife,
But for her comforting! unhappy sight,   530
But meeting her blue orbs! Who, who can write
Of these first minutes? The unchariest muse
To embracements warm as theirs makes coy excuse.

   O it has ruffled every spirit there,

535 Saving love's self, who stands superb to share
The general gladness: awfully he stands;
A sovereign quell is in his waving hands;
No sight can bear the lightning of his bow;
His quiver is mysterious, none can know
540 What themselves think of it; from forth his eyes
There darts strange light of varied hues and dyes:
A scowl is sometimes on his brow, but who
Look full upon it feel anon the blue
Of his fair eyes run liquid through their souls.
545 Endymion feels it, and no more controls
The burning prayer within him; so, bent low,
He had begun a plaining of his woe.
But Venus, bending forward, said: "My child,
Favor this gentle youth; his days are wild
550 With love—he—but alas! too well I see
Thou know'st the deepness of his misery.
Ah, smile not so, my son: I tell thee true,
That when through heavy hours I used to rue
The endless sleep of this newborn Adon',
555 This stranger ay I pitied. For upon
A dreary morning once I fled away
Into the breezy clouds, to weep and pray
For this my love: for vexing Mars had teased
Me even to tears: thence, when a little eased
560 Down-looking, vacant, through a hazy wood,
I saw this youth as he despairing stood:
Those same dark curls blown vagrant in the wind;
Those same full fringèd lids a constant blind
Over his sullen eyes: I saw him throw
565 Himself on withered leaves, even as though
Death had come sudden; for no jot he moved,
Yet muttered wildly. I could hear he loved
Some fair immortal, and that his embrace
Had zoned her through the night. There is no trace
570 Of this in heaven: I have marked each cheek,
And find it is the vainest thing to seek;
And that of all things 'tis kept secretest.
Endymion! one day thou wilt be blessed:
So still obey the guiding hand that fends

ENDYMION

Thee safely through these wonders for sweet ends. 575
'Tis a concealment needful in extreme;
And if I guessed not so, the sunny beam
Thou shouldst mount up to with me. Now adieu!
Here must we leave thee."—At these words up flew
The impatient doves, up rose the floating car, 580
Up went the hum celestial. High afar
The Latmian saw them minish into nought;
And, when all were clear vanished, still he caught
A vivid lightning from that dreadful bow.
When all was darkened, with Etnean throe 585
The earth closed—gave a solitary moan—
And left him once again in twilight lone.

He did not rave, he did not stare aghast,
For all those visions were o'er-gone, and past,
And he in loneliness: he felt assured 590
Of happy times, when all he had endured
Would seem a feather to the mighty prize.
So, with unusual gladness, on he hies
Through caves, and palaces of mottled ore,
Gold dome, and crystal wall, and turquois floor, 595
Black polished porticos of awful shade,
And, at the last, a diamond balustrade,
Leading afar past wild magnificence,
Spiral through ruggedest loopholes, and thence
Stretching across a void, then guiding o'er 600
Enormous chasms, where, all foam and roar,
Streams subterranean tease their granite beds;
Then heightened just above the silvery heads
Of a thousand fountains, so that he could dash
The waters with his spear; but at the splash, 605
Done heedlessly, those spouting columns rose
Sudden a poplar's height, and 'gan to enclose
His diamond path with fretwork, streaming round
Alive, and dazzling cool, and with a sound,
Haply, like dolphin tumults, when sweet shells 610
Welcome the float of Thetis. Long he dwells
On this delight; for, every minute's space,
The streams with changed magic interlace:

Sometimes like delicatest lattices,
Covered with crystal vines; then weeping trees,
Moving about as in a gentle wind,
Which, in a wink, to watery gauze refined,
Poured into shapes of curtained canopies,
Spangled, and rich with liquid broideries
Of flowers, peacocks, swans, and naiads fair.
Swifter than lightning went these wonders rare;
And then the water, into stubborn streams
Collecting, mimicked the wrought oaken beams,
Pillars, and frieze, and high fantastic roof,
Of those dusk places in times far aloof
Cathedrals called. He bade a loth farewell
To these founts Protean, passing gulf, and dell,
And torrent, and ten thousand jutting shapes,
Half seen through deepest gloom, and grisly gapes,
Blackening on every side, and overhead
A vaulted dome like heaven's, far bespread
With starlight gems: aye, all so huge and strange,
The solitary felt a hurried change
Working within him into something dreary—
Vexed like a morning eagle, lost, and weary,
And purblind amid foggy, midnight wolds.
But he revives at once: for who beholds
New sudden things, nor casts his mental slough?
Forth from a rugged arch, in the dusk below,
Came mother Cybele!° alone—alone—
In somber chariot; dark foldings thrown
About her majesty, and front death-pale,
With turrets crowned. Four manèd lions hale
The sluggish wheels; solemn their toothèd maws,
Their surly eyes brow-hidden, heavy paws
Uplifted drowsily, and nervy tails
Cowering their tawny brushes. Silent sails
This shadowy queen athwart, and faints away
In another gloomy arch.

---

640 **Cybele** The forlorn appearance of the mother of the gods, somewhat surprising at this moment of the action, seems to be derived from a note in Sandys' Ovid.

                    Wherefore delay,
Young traveler, in such a mournful place?
Art thou wayworn, or canst not further trace
The diamond path? And does it indeed end
Abrupt in middle air? Yet earthward bend
Thy forehead, and to Jupiter cloud-borne
Call ardently! He was indeed wayworn;
Abrupt, in middle air, his way was lost;
To cloud-borne Jove he bowed, and there crossed
Towards him a large eagle, 'twixt whose wings,
Without one impious word, himself he flings,
Committed to the darkness and the gloom:
Down, down, uncertain to what pleasant doom,
Swift as a fathoming plummet down he fell
Through unknown things; till exhaled asphodel,
And rose, with spicy fannings interbreathed,
Came swelling forth where little caves were wreathed
So thick with leaves and mosses, that they seemed
Large honeycombs of green, and freshly teemed
With airs delicious. In the greenest nook
The eagle landed him, and farewell took.

    It was a jasmine bower, all bestrown
With golden moss. His every sense had grown
Ethereal for pleasure; 'bove his head
Flew a delight half-graspable; his tread
Was Hesperean; to his capable ears
Silence was music from the holy spheres;
A dewy luxury was in his eyes;
The little flowers felt his pleasant sighs
And stirred them faintly. Verdant cave and cell
He wandered through, oft wondering at such swell
Of sudden exaltation: but, "Alas!"
Said he, "will all this gush of feeling pass
Away in solitude? And must they wane,
Like melodies upon a sandy plain,
Without an echo? Then shall I be left
So sad, so melancholy, so bereft!
Yet still I feel immortal! O my love,
My breath of life, where art thou? High above,

ENDYMION

Dancing before the morning gates of heaven?
Or keeping watch among those starry seven,
690 Old Atlas' children? Art a maid of the waters,
One of shell-winding Triton's bright-haired daughters?
Or art, impossible! a nymph of Dian's,
Weaving a coronal of tender scions
For very idleness? Where'er thou art,
695 Methinks it now is at my will to start
Into thine arms; to scare Aurora's train,
And snatch thee from the morning; o'er the main
To scud like a wild bird, and take thee off
From thy sea-foamy cradle; or to doff
700 Thy shepherd vest, and woo thee mid fresh leaves.
No, no, too eagerly my soul deceives
Its powerless self: I know this cannot be.
O let me then by some sweet dreaming flee
To her entrancements: hither, Sleep, awhile!
705 Hither, most gentle Sleep! and soothing foil
For some few hours the coming solitude."

Thus spake he, and that moment felt endued
With power to dream deliciously; so wound
Through a dim passage, searching till he found
710 The smoothest mossy bed and deepest, where
He threw himself, and just into the air
Stretching his indolent arms, he took, O bliss!
A naked waist: "Fair Cupid, whence is this?"
A well-known voice sighed, "Sweetest, here am I!"
715 At which soft ravishment, with doting cry
They trembled to each other.—Helicon!
O fountained hill! Old Homer's Helicon!
That thou wouldst spout a little streamlet o'er
These sorry pages; then the verse would soar
720 And sing above this gentle pair, like lark
Over his nested young: but all is dark
Around thine aged top, and thy clear fount
Exhales in mists to heaven. Aye, the count
Of mighty poets is made up; the scroll
725 Is folded by the Muses; the bright roll
Is in Apollo's hand: our dazed eyes

ENDYMION 139

Have seen a new tinge in the western skies:
The world has done its duty. Yet, oh yet,
Although the sun of Poesy is set,
These lovers did embrace, and we must weep 730
That there is no old power left to steep
A quill immortal in their joyous tears.
Long time in silence did their anxious fears
Question that thus it was; long time they lay
Fondling and kissing every doubt away; 735
Long time ere soft caressing sobs began
To mellow into words, and then there ran
Two bubbling springs of talk from their sweet lips.
"O known Unknown! from whom my being sips
Such darling essence, wherefore may I not 740
Be ever in these arms? in this sweet spot
Pillow my chin forever? ever press
These toying hands and kiss their smooth excess?
Why not forever and forever feel
That breath about my eyes? Ah, thou wilt steal 745
Away from me again, indeed, indeed—
Thou wilt be gone away, and wilt not heed
My lonely madness. Speak, delicious fair!
Is it to be so? No! for who will dare
To pluck thee from me? And, of thine own will, 750
Full well I feel thou wouldst not leave me. Still
Let me entwine thee surer, surer—now
How can we part? Elysium! who art thou?
Who, that thou canst not be forever here,
Or lift me with thee to some starry sphere? 755
Enchantress! tell me by this soft embrace,
By the most soft completion of thy face,
Those lips, O slippery blisses, twinkling eyes,
And by these tenderest, milky sovereignties—
These tenderest, and by the nectar wine, 760
The passion"——"O doved Ida the divine!
Endymion! dearest! Ah, unhappy me!
His soul will 'scape us—O felicity!
How he does love me! His poor temples beat
To the very tune of love—how sweet, sweet, sweet. 765
Revive, dear youth, or I shall faint and die;

Revive, or these soft hours will hurry by
In trancèd dullness; speak, and let that spell
Affright this lethargy! I cannot quell
Its heavy pressure, and will press at least
My lips to thine, that they may richly feast
Until we taste the life of love again.
What! dost thou move? dost kiss? O bliss! O pain!
I love thee, youth, more than I can conceive;
And so long absence from thee doth bereave
My soul of any rest: yet must I hence:
Yet, can I not to starry eminence
Uplift thee; nor for very shame can own
Myself to thee. Ah, dearest, do not groan
Or thou wilt force me from this secrecy,
And I must blush in heaven. O that I
Had done 't already; that the dreadful smiles
At my lost brightness, my impassioned wiles,
Had wanèd from Olympus' solemn height,
And from all serious gods; that our delight
Was quite forgotten, save of us alone!
And wherefore so ashamed? 'Tis but to atone
For endless pleasure, by some coward blushes:
Yet must I be a coward!—Horror rushes
Too palpable before me—the sad look
Of Jove—Minerva's start—no bosom shook
With awe of purity—no Cupid pinion
In reverence veiled—my crystalline dominion
Half lost, and all old hymns made nullity!
But what is this to love? O I could fly
With thee into the ken of heavenly powers,
So thou wouldst thus, for many sequent hours,
Press me so sweetly. Now I swear at once
That I am wise, that Pallas is a dunce—
Perhaps her love like mine is but unknown—
O I do think that I have been alone
In chastity: yes, Pallas has been sighing,
While every eve saw me my hair uptying
With fingers cool as aspen leaves. Sweet love,
I was as vague as solitary dove,
Nor knew that nests were built. Now a soft kiss—

ENDYMION

Aye, by that kiss, I vow an endless bliss,
An immortality of passion's thine:
Ere long I will exalt thee to the shine
Of heaven ambrosial; and we will shade
Ourselves whole summers by a river glade;
And I will tell thee stories of the sky,
And breathe thee whispers of its minstrelsy.
My happy love will overwing all bounds!
O let me melt into thee; let the sounds
Of our close voices marry at their birth;
Let us entwine hoveringly—O dearth
Of human words! roughness of mortal speech!
Lispings empyrean will I sometime teach
Thine honeyed tongue—lute-breathings, which I gasp
To have thee understand, now while I clasp
Thee thus, and weep for fondness—I am pained,
Endymion: woe! woe! is grief contained
In the very deeps of pleasure, my sole life?"
Hereat, with many sobs, her gentle strife
Melted into a languor. He returned
Entrancèd vows and tears.

                    Ye who have yearned
With too much passion, will here stay and pity,
For the mere sake of truth; as 'tis a ditty
Not of these days, but long ago 'twas told
By a cavern wind unto a forest old;
And then the forest told it in a dream
To a sleeping lake, whose cool and level gleam
A poet caught as he was journeying
To Phœbus' shrine; and in it he did fling
His weary limbs, bathing an hour's space,
And, after straight, in that inspirèd place
He sang the story up into the air,
Giving it universal freedom. There
Has it been ever sounding for those ears
Whose tips are glowing hot. The legend cheers
Yon sentinel stars; and he who listens to it
Must surely be self-doomed or he will rue it:
For quenchless burnings come upon the heart,

ENDYMION

845 Made fiercer by a fear lest any part
Should be engulfèd in the eddying wind.
As much as here is penned doth always find
A resting place, thus much comes clear and plain;
Anon the strange voice is upon the wane—
850 And 'tis but echoed from departing sound,
That the fair visitant at last unwound
Her gentle limbs, and left the youth asleep.—
Thus the tradition of the gusty deep.

Now turn we to our former chroniclers.—
855 Endymion awoke, that grief of hers
Sweet-paining on his ear: he sickly guessed
How lone he was once more, and sadly pressed
His empty arms together, hung his head,
And most forlorn upon that widowed bed
860 Sat silently. Love's madness he had known:
Often with more than tortured lion's groan
Moanings had burst from him; but now that rage
Had passed away: no longer did he wage
A rough-voiced war against the dooming stars.
865 No, he had felt too much for such harsh jars:
The lyre of his soul Eolian tuned
Forgot all violence, and but communed
With melancholy thought: O he had swooned
Drunken from Pleasure's nipple; and his love
870 Henceforth was dove-like.—Loth was he to move
From the imprinted couch, and when he did,
'Twas with slow, languid paces, and face hid
In muffling hands. So tempered, out he strayed
Half seeing visions that might have dismayed
875 Alecto's° serpents; ravishments more keen
Than Hermes' pipe, when anxious he did lean
Over eclipsing eyes: and at the last
It was a sounding grotto, vaulted vast,
O'er studded with a thousand, thousand pearls,
880 And crimson-mouthèd shells with stubborn curls,
Of every shape and size, even to the bulk

---

875 **Alecto** one of the Furies.

ENDYMION 143

In which whales arbor close, to brood and sulk
Against an endless storm. Moreover too,
Fish semblances, of green and azure hue,
Ready to snort their streams. In this cool wonder   885
Endymion sat down, and 'gan to ponder
On all his life: his youth, up to the day
When 'mid acclaim, and feasts, and garlands gay,
He stepped upon his shepherd throne: the look
Of his white palace in wild forest nook,   890
And all the revels he had lorded there:
Each tender maiden whom he once thought fair,
With every friend and fellow woodlander—
Passed like a dream before him. Then the spur
Of the old bards to mighty deeds: his plans   895
To nurse the golden age 'mong shepherd clans:
That wondrous night: the great Pan-festival:
His sister's sorrow; and his wanderings all,
Until into the earth's deep maw he rushed:
Then all its buried magic, till it flushed   900
High with excessive love. "And now," thought he,
"How long must I remain in jeopardy
Of blank amazements that amaze no more?
Now I have tasted her sweet soul to the core
All other depths are shallow: essences,   905
Once spiritual, are like muddy lees,
Meant but to fertilize my earthly root,
And make my branches lift a golden fruit
Into the bloom of heaven: other light,
Though it be quick and sharp enough to blight   910
The Olympian eagle's vision, is dark,
Dark as the parentage of chaos. Hark!
My silent thoughts are echoing from these shells;
Or they are but the ghosts, the dying swells
Of noises far away?—list!"—Hereupon   915
He kept an anxious ear. The humming tone
Came louder, and behold, there as he lay,
On either side outgushed, with misty spray,
A copious spring; and both together dashed
Swift, mad, fantastic round the rocks, and lashed   920
Among the conches and shells of the lofty grot,

144   ENDYMION

Leaving a trickling dew. At last they shot
Down from the ceiling's height, pouring a noise
As of some breathless racers whose hopes poise
925 Upon the last few steps, and with spent force
Along the ground they took a winding course.
Endymion followed—for it seemed that one
Ever pursued, the other strove to shun—
Followed their languid mazes, till well nigh
930 He had left thinking of the mystery—
And was now rapt in tender hoverings
Over the vanished bliss. Ah! what is it sings
His dream away? What melodies are these?
They sound as through the whispering of trees,
935 Not native in such barren vaults. Give ear!

"O Arethusa,° peerless nymph! why fear
Such tenderness as mine? Great Dian, why,
Why didst thou hear her prayer? O that I
Were rippling round her dainty fairness now,
940 Circling about her waist, and striving how
To entice her to a dive! then stealing in
Between her luscious lips and eyelids thin.
O that her shining hair was in the sun,
And I distilling from it thence to run
945 In amorous rillets down her shrinking form!
To linger on her lily shoulders, warm
Between her kissing breasts, and every charm
Touch raptured!—See how painfully I flow:
Fair maid, be pitiful to my great woe.
950 Stay, stay thy weary course, and let me lead,
A happy wooer, to the flowery mead

936 **Arethusa** The story of Alpheus and Arethusa is told in Ovid (V, ll. 572 ff.). She was an attendant of Diana; the river god Alpheus fell in love with her when she bathed in the pool that bears his name, and pursued her; Diana encircled her in an impenetrable cloud of mist. While Alpheus stayed to watch, she was changed into a stream of water. Keats sentimentalizes Ovid's version by stressing Arethusa's love for Alpheus and making Diana the obstacle to their union. This allows for the ironic dramatic effect of stressing Diana's own humanity (ll. 984 ff.), since she is now a victim of the same passion. By interceding in favor of Arethusa, Endymion further narrows the gap between his human and her divine nature.

ENDYMION

Where all that beauty snared me."—"Cruel god,
Desist! or my offended mistress' nod
Will stagnate all thy fountains:—tease me not
With Siren words—Ah, have I really got
Such power to madden thee? And is it true—
Away, away, or I shall dearly rue
My very thoughts: in mercy then away,
Kindest Alpheus, for should I obey
My own dear will, 'twould be a deadly bane.—
O, Oread-queen! would that thou hadst a pain
Like this of mine, then would I fearless turn
And be a criminal.—Alas, I burn,
I shudder—gentle river, get thee hence.
Alpheus! thou enchanter! every sense
Of mine was once made perfect in these woods.
Fresh breezes, bowery lawns, and innocent floods,
Ripe fruits, and lonely couch, contentment gave;
But ever since I heedlessly did lave
In thy deceitful stream, a panting glow
Grew strong within me: wherefore serve me so,
And call it love? Alas, 'twas cruelty.
Not once more did I close my happy eye
Amid the thrushes' song. Away! Avaunt!
O 'twas a cruel thing."—"Now thou dost taunt
So softly, Arethusa, that I think
If thou wast playing on my shady brink,
Thou wouldst bathe once again. Innocent maid!
Stifle thine heart no more;—nor be afraid
Of angry powers: there are deities
Will shade us with their wings. Those fitful sighs
'Tis almost death to hear: O let me pour
A dewy balm upon them!—fear no more,
Sweet Arethusa! Dian's self must feel
Sometimes these very pangs. Dear maiden, steal
Blushing into my soul, and let us fly
These dreary caverns for the open sky.
I will delight thee all my winding course,
From the green sea up to my hidden source
About Arcadian forests; and will show
The channels where my coolest waters flow

Through mossy rocks; where, 'mid exuberant green,
I roam in pleasant darkness, more unseen
Than Saturn in his exile; where I brim
Round flowery islands, and take thence a skim
Of mealy sweets, which myriads of bees
Buzz from their honeyed wings: and thou shouldst please
Thyself to choose the richest, where we might
Be incense-pillowed every summer night.
Doff all sad fears, thou white deliciousness,
And let us be thus comforted; unless
Thou couldst rejoice to see my hopeless stream
Hurry distracted from Sol's temperate beam,
And pour to death along some hungry sands."—
"What can I do, Alpheus? Dian stands
Severe before me: persecuting fate!
Unhappy Arethusa! thou wast late
A huntress free in"—At this, sudden fell
Those two sad streams adown a fearful dell.
The Latmian listened, but he heard no more,
Save echo, faint repeating o'er and o'er
The name of Arethusa. On the verge
Of that dark gulf he wept, and said: "I urge
Thee, gentle Goddess of my pilgrimage,
By our eternal hopes, to soothe, to assuage,
If thou art powerful, these lovers' pains;
And make them happy in some happy plains."

He turned—there was a whelming sound—he stepped,
There was a cooler light; and so he kept
Towards it by a sandy path, and lo!
More suddenly than doth a moment go,
The visions of the earth were gone and fled—
He saw the giant sea above his head.

Book III

There are who lord it o'er their fellow-men

With most prevailing tinsel: who unpen
Their baaing vanities, to browse away
The comfortable green and juicy hay
From human pastures; or, O torturing fact!
Who, through an idiot blink, will see unpacked
Fire-branded foxes to sear up and singe
Our gold and ripe-eared hopes. With not one tinge
Of sanctuary splendor, not a sight
Able to face an owl's they still are dight
By the blear-eyed nations in empurpled vests,
And crowns, and turbans. With unladen breasts,
Save of blown self-applause, they proudly mount
To their spirit's perch, their being's high account,
Their tiptop nothings, their dull skies, their thrones—
Amid the fierce intoxicating tones
Of trumpets, shoutings, and belabored drums,
And sudden cannon. Ah! how all this hums,
In wakeful ears, like uproar past and gone—
Like thunder clouds that spake to Babylon,
And set those old Chaldeans to their tasks.—
Are then regalities all gilded masks?
No, there are thronèd seats unscalable
But by a patient wing, a constant spell,
Or by ethereal things that, unconfined,
Can make a ladder of the eternal wind,
And poise about in cloudy thunder-tents
To watch the abysm-birth of elements.
Aye, 'bove the withering of old-lipped fate
A thousand Powers keep religious state,
In water, fiery realm, and airy bourn;
And, silent as a consecrated urn,
Hold sphery sessions for a season due.
Yet few of these far majesties, ah, few!
Have bared their operations to this globe—
Few, who with gorgeous pageantry enrobe
Our piece of heaven—whose benevolence
Shakes hand with our own Ceres; every sense
Filling with spiritual sweets to plenitude,
As bees gorge full their cells. And, by the feud
'Twixt Nothing and Creation, I here swear,

Eterne Apollo! that thy sister fair
Is of all these° the gentlier-mightiest,
When thy gold breath is misting in the west,
45 She unobservèd steals unto her throne,
And there she sits most meek and most alone;
As if she had not pomp subservient;
As if thine eye, high poet! was not bent
Towards her with the Muses in thine heart;
50 As if the minist'ring stars kept not apart,
Waiting for silver-footed messages.
O Moon! the oldest shades 'mong oldest trees
Feel palpitations when thou lookest in:
O Moon! old boughs lisp forth a holier din
55 The while they feel thine airy fellowship
Thou dost bless everywhere, with silver lip
Kissing dead things to life. The sleeping kine,
Couched in thy brightness, dream of fields divine:
Innumerable mountains rise, and rise,
60 Ambitious for the hallowing of thine eyes;
And yet thy benediction passeth not
One obscure hiding place, one little spot
Where pleasure may be sent: the nested wren
Has thy fair face within its tranquil ken,
65 And from beneath a sheltering ivy leaf
Takes glimpses of thee; thou art a relief
To the poor patient oyster, where it sleeps
Within its pearly house.—The mighty deeps,
The monstrous sea is thine—the myriad sea!
70 O Moon! far-spooming Ocean bows to thee,
And Tellus° feels his forehead's cumbrous load.

Cynthia! where art thou now? What far abode
Of green or silvery bower doth enshrine
Such utmost beauty? Alas, thou dost pine
75 For one as sorrowful: thy cheek is pale
For one whose cheek is pale: thou dost bewail

43 **these** refers to the gods, the "far majesties" of line 34, and makes the transition from the passage on the relationships between gods and men to the hymn to Apollo's sister, Diana, the moon goddess.
71 **Tellus** the earth.

His tears, who weeps for thee. Where dost thou sigh?
Ah! surely that light peeps from Vesper's eye,
Or what a thing is love! 'Tis she, but lo!
How changed, how full of ache, how gone in woe!　　80
She dies at the thinnest cloud; her loveliness
Is wan on Neptune's blue: yet there's a stress
Of love-spangles, just off yon cape of trees,
Dancing upon the waves, as if to please
The curly foam with amorous influence.　　85
O, not so idle: for down-glancing thence
She fathoms eddies, and runs wild about
O'erwhelming watercourses; scaring out
The thorny sharks from hiding holes, and fright'ning
Their savage eyes with unaccustomed lightning.　　90
Where will the splendor be content to reach?
O Love! how potent hast thou been to teach
Strange journeyings! Wherever beauty dwells,
In gulf or aerie, mountains or deep dells,
In light, in gloom, in star or blazing sun,　　95
Thou pointest out the way, and straight 'tis won.
Amid his toil thou gav'st Leander° breath;
Thou leddest Orpheus through the gleams of death;
Thou madest Pluto bear thin element;
And now, O winged chieftain! thou has sent　　100
A moonbeam to the deep, deep water-world,
To find Endymion.

　　　　　　　　On gold sand impearled
With lily shells, and pebbles milky white,
Poor Cynthia greeted him, and soothed her light
Against his pallid face: he felt the charm　　105
To breathlessness, and suddenly a warm
Of his heart's blood: 'twas very sweet; he stayed
His wandering steps, and half-entrancèd laid
His head upon a tuft of straggling weeds,
To taste the gentle moon, and freshening beads,　　110
Lashed from the crystal roof by fishes' tails.
And so he kept, until the rosy veils

97 **Leander** had to swim across the Hellespont every night to join Hero.

ENDYMION

Mantling the east, by Aurora's peering hand
Were lifted from the water's breast, and fanned
115 Into sweet air; and sobered morning came
Meekly through billows:—when like taper-flame
Left sudden by a dallying breath of air,
He rose in silence, and once more 'gan fare
Along his fated way.

     Far had he roamed,
120 With nothing save the hollow vast, that foamed
Above, around, and at his feet; save things
More dead than Morpheus' imaginings;
Old rusted anchors, helmets, breastplates large
Of gone sea warriors; brazen beaks and targe;
125 Rudders that for a hundred years had lost
The sway of human hand; gold vase embossed
With long-forgotten story, and wherein
No reveler had ever dipped a chin
But those of Saturn's vintage;° moldering scrolls,
130 Writ in the tongue of heaven, by those souls
Who first were on the earth; and sculptures rude
In ponderous stone, developing the mood
Of ancient Nox;°—then skeletons of man,
Of beast, behemoth, and leviathan,
135 And elephant, and eagle, and huge jaw
Of nameless monster. A cold, leaden awe
These secrets struck into him; and unless
Dian had chased away that heaviness,
He might have died: but now, with cheerèd feel,
140 He onward kept; wooing these thoughts to steal
About the labyrinth in his soul of love.

"What is there in thee, Moon! that thou shouldst move
My heart so potently? When yet a child
I oft have dried my tears when thou hast smiled.
145 Thou seem'dst my sister: hand in hand we went

---

129 **Saturn's vintage** i.e., so old that only the Titans, the older gods, would have known them. 133 **Nox** goddess of night, daughter of Chaos.

ENDYMION

From eve to morn across the firmament.
No apples would I gather from the tree,
Till thou hadst cooled their cheeks deliciously:
No tumbling water ever spake romance,
But when my eyes with thine thereon could dance: 150
No woods were green enough, no bower divine,
Until thou liftedst up thine eyelids fine:
In sowing time ne'er would I dibble take,
Or drop a seed, till thou wast wide awake;
And, in the summer tide of blossoming, 155
No one but thee hath heard me blithely sing
And mesh my dewy flowers all the night.
No melody was like a passing spright
If it went not to solemnize thy reign.
Yes, in my boyhood, every joy and pain 160
By thee were fashioned to the self-same end;
And as I grew in years, still didst thou blend
With all my ardors: thou wast the deep glen;
Thou wast the mountaintop—the sage's pen—
The poet's harp—the voice of friends—the sun; 165
Thou wast the river—thou wast glory won;
Thou wast my clarion's blast—thou wast my steed—
My goblet full of wine—my topmost deed:—
Thou wast the charm of women, lovely Moon!
O what a wild and harmonizèd tune 170
My spirit struck from all the beautiful!
On some bright essence could I lean, and lull
Myself to immortality: I pressed
Nature's soft pillow in a wakeful rest.
But, gentle Orb! there came a nearer bliss— 175
My strange love came—Felicity's abyss!
She came, and thou didst fade, and fade away°—
Yet not entirely; no, thy starry sway
Has been an under-passion to this hour.
Now I begin to feel thine orby power 180
Is coming fresh upon me: O be kind,
Keep back thine influence, and do not blind

177 **fade away** Endymion's ignorance of Cynthia's real identity is
continually used for dramatic effect and prepares the conflicts and
the conclusion of the last book.

My sovereign vision.—Dearest love, forgive
That I can think away from thee and live!—
185 Pardon me, airy planet, that I prize
One thought beyond thine argent luxuries!
How far beyond!" At this a surprised start
Frosted the springing verdure of his heart;
For as he lifted up his eyes to swear
190 How his own goddess was past all things fair,
He saw far in the concave green of the sea
An old man sitting calm and peacefully.
Upon a weeded rock this old man sat,
And his white hair was awful, and a mat
195 Of weeds were cold beneath his cold thin feet;
And, ample as the largest winding-sheet,
A cloak of blue wrapped up his agèd bones,
O'er-wrought with symbols by the deepest groans
Of ambitious magic: every ocean form
200 Was woven in with black distinctness; storm,
And calm, and whispering, and hideous roar,
Quicksand, and whirlpool, and deserted shore
Were emblemed in the woof; with every shape
That skims, or dives, or sleeps, 'twixt cape and cape.
205 The gulfing whale was like a dot in the spell,
Yet look upon it, and 'twould size and swell
To its huge self; and the minutest fish
Would pass the very hardest gazer's wish,
And show his little eye's anatomy.
210 Then there was pictured the regality
Of Neptune; and the sea nymphs round his state,
In beauteous vassalage, look up and wait.
Beside this old man lay a pearly wand,
And in his lap a book, the which he conned
215 So steadfastly, that the new denizen
Had time to keep him in amazèd ken,
To mark these shadowings, and stand in awe.

The old man raised his hoary head and saw
The wildered stranger—seeming not to see,
220 His features were so lifeless. Suddenly
He woke as from a trance; his snow-white brows

Went arching up, and like two magic plows
Furrowed deep wrinkles in his forehead large,
Which kept as fixedly as rocky marge,
Till round his withered lips had gone a smile.
Then up he rose, like one whose tedious toil
Had watched for years in forlorn hermitage,
Who had not from mid-life to utmost age
Eased in one accent his o'er-burdened soul,
Even to the trees. He rose: he grasped his stole,
With convulsed clenches waving it abroad,
And in a voice of solemn joy, that awed
Echo into oblivion, he said:—

"Thou art the man! Now shall I lay my head
In peace upon my watery pillow: now
Sleep will come smoothly to my weary brow.
O Jove! I shall be young again, be young!
O shell-borne Neptune, I am pierced and stung
With newborn life! What shall I do? Where go,
When I have cast this serpent-skin of woe?—
I'll swim to the sirens, and one moment listen
Their melodies, and see their long hair glisten;
Anon upon that giant's arm I'll be,
That writhes about the roots of Sicily:
To northern seas I'll in a twinkling sail,
And mount upon the snortings of a whale
To some black cloud; thence down I'll madly sweep
On forkèd lightning, to the deepest deep,
Where through some sucking pool I will be hurled
With rapture to the other side of the world!
O, I am full of gladness! Sisters three,
I bow full-hearted to your old decree!
Yes, every god be thanked, and power benign,
For I no more shall wither, droop, and pine.
Thou art the man!" Endymion started back
Dismayed; and, like a wretch from whom the rack
Tortures hot breath, and speech of agony,
Muttered: "What lonely death am I to die
In this cold region! Will he let me freeze,
And float my brittle limbs o'er polar seas?

Or will he touch me with his searing hand,
And leave a black memorial on the sand?
Or tear me piecemeal with a bony saw,
And keep me as a chosen food to draw
265 His magian fish through hated fire and flame?
O misery of hell! resistless, tame,
Am I to be burned up? No, I will shout,
Until the gods through heaven's blue look out!—
O Tartarus! but some few days agone
270 Her soft arms were entwining me, and on
Her voice I hung like fruit among green leaves:
Her lips were all my own, and—ah, ripe sheaves
Of happiness! ye on the stubble droop,
But never may be garnered. I must stoop
275 My head, and kiss death's foot. Love! love, farewell!
Is there no hope from thee? This horrid spell
Would melt at thy sweet breath.—By Dian's hind
Feeding from her white fingers, on the wind
I see the streaming hair! and now, by Pan,
280 I care not for this old mysterious man!"

He spake, and walking to that agèd form,
Looked high defiance. Lo! his heart 'gan warm
With pity, for the gray-haired creature wept.
Had he then wronged a heart where sorrow kept?
285 Had he, though blindly contumelious, brought
Rheum to kind eyes, a sting to humane thought,
Convulsion to a mouth of many years?
He had in truth; and he was ripe for tears.
The penitent shower fell, as down he knelt
290 Before that care-worn sage, who trembling felt
About his large dark locks, and faltering spake:

"Arise, good youth, for sacred Phœbus' sake!
I know thine inmost bosom, and I feel
A very brother's yearning for thee steal
295 Into mine own: for why? thou openest
The prison gates that have so long oppressed
My weary watching. Though thou know'st it not,
Thou art commissioned to this fated spot

ENDYMION

For great enfranchisement. O weep no more;
I am a friend to love, to loves of yore:
Aye, hadst thou never loved an unknown power,
I had been grieving at this joyous hour.
But even now most miserable old,
I saw thee, and my blood no longer cold
Gave mighty pulses: in this tottering case
Grew a new heart, which at this moment plays
As dancingly as thine. Be not afraid,
For thou shalt hear this secret all displayed,
Now as we speed towards our joyous task."

So saying, this young soul in age's mask
Went forward with the Carian side by side:
Resuming quickly thus; while ocean's tide
Hung swollen at their backs, and jeweled sands
Took silently their footprints.

      "My soul stands
Now past the midway from mortality,
And so I can prepare without a sigh
To tell thee briefly all my joy and pain.
I was a fisher once, upon this main,
And my boat danced in every creek and bay;
Rough billows were my home by night and day—
The seagulls not more constant; for I had
No housing from the storm and tempests mad,
But hollow rocks—and they were palaces
Of silent happiness, of slumberous ease:
Long years of misery have told me so.
Aye, thus it was one thousand years ago.
One thousand years!—Is it then possible
To look so plainly through them? to dispel
A thousand years with backward glance sublime?
To breathe away as 'twere all scummy slime
From off a crystal pool, to see its deep,
And one's own image from the bottom peep?
Yes: now I am no longer wretched thrall,
My long captivity and moanings all
Are but a slime, a thin-pervading scum,

The which I breathe away, and thronging come
Like things of yesterday my youthful pleasures.

"I touched no lute, I sang not, trod no measures:
I was a lonely youth on desert shores.
My sports were lonely, 'mid continuous roars,
And craggy isles, and sea-mew's plaintive cry
Plaining discrepant between sea and sky.
Dolphins were still my playmates; shapes unseen
Would let me feel their scales of gold and green,
Nor be my desolation; and, full oft,
When a dread waterspout had reared aloft
Its hungry hugeness, seeming ready ripe
To burst with hoarsest thunderings, and wipe
My life away like a vast sponge of fate,
Some friendly monster, pitying my sad state,
Has dived to its foundations, gulfed it down,
And left me tossing safely. But the crown
Of all my life was utmost quietude:
More did I love to lie in cavern rude,
Keeping in wait whole days for Neptune's voice,
And if it came at last, hark, and rejoice!
There blushed no summer eve but I would steer
My skiff along green shelving coasts, to hear
The shepherd's pipe coming clear from aery steep,
Mingled with ceaseless bleatings of his sheep:
And never was a day of summer shine,
But I beheld its birth upon the brine:
For I would watch all night to see unfold
Heaven's gates, and Æthon snort his morning gold
Wide o'er the swelling streams: and constantly
At brim of day tide, on some grassy lea,
My nets would be spread out, and I at rest.
The poor folk of the sea country I blessed
With daily boon of fish most delicate:
They knew not whence this bounty, and elate
Would strew sweet flowers on a sterile beach.

"Why was I not contented? Wherefore reach
At things which, but for thee, O Latmian!

Had been my dreary death? Fool! I began
To feel distempered longings: to desire 375
The utmost privilege that ocean's sire
Could grant in benediction: to be free
Of all his kingdom. Long in misery
I wasted, ere in one extremest fit
I plunged for life or death. To interknit 380
One's senses with so dense a breathing stuff
Might seem a work of pain; so not enough
Can I admire how crystal-smooth it felt,
And buoyant round my limbs. At first I dwelt
Whole days and days in sheer astonishment; 385
Forgetful utterly of self-intent;
Moving but with the mighty ebb and flow.
Then, like a new fledged bird that first doth show
His spreaded feathers to the morrow chill,
I tried in fear the pinions of my will. 390
'Twas freedom! and at once I visited
The ceaseless wonders of this ocean bed.
No need to tell thee of them, for I see
That thou has been a witness—it must be—
For these I know thou canst not feel a drouth, 395
By the melancholy corners of that mouth.
So I will in my story straightway pass
To more immediate matter. Woe, alas!
That love should be my bane! Ah, Scylla fair!
Why did poor Glaucus° ever—ever dare 400
To sue thee to his heart? Kind stranger-youth!
I loved her to the very white of truth,
And she would not conceive it. Timid thing!
She fled me swift as seabird on the wing,
Round every isle, and point, and promontory, 405
From where large Hercules wound up his story
Far as Egyptian Nile. My passion grew
The more, the more I saw her dainty hue
Gleam delicately through the azure clear:
Until 'twas too fierce agony to bear; 410
And in that agony, across my grief

---

400 **Glaucus'** story is told in Ovid (XIII, ll. 906 ff. and XIV, ll. 9 ff.).

It flashed, that Circe might find some relief—
Cruel enchantress! So above the water
I reared my head, and looked for Phœbus' daughter.
415 Æa's isle was wondering at the moon:—
It seemed to whirl around me, and a swoon
Left me dead-drifting to that fatal power.

"When I awoke, 'twas in a twilight bower;
Just when the light of morn, with hum of bees,
420 Stole through its verdurous matting of fresh trees.
How sweet, and sweeter! for I heard a lyre,
And over it a sighing voice expire.
It ceased—I caught light footsteps; and anon
The fairest face that morn e'er looked upon
425 Pushed through a screen of roses. Starry Jove!
With tears, and smiles, and honey words she wove
A net whose thralldom was more bliss than all
The range of flowered Elysium. Thus did fall
The dew of her rich speech: 'Ah! Art awake?
430 O let me hear thee speak, for Cupid's sake!
I am so oppressed with joy! Why, I have shed
An urn of tears, as though thou wert cold dead;
And now I find thee living, I will pour
From these devoted eyes their silver store,
435 Until exhausted of the latest drop,
So it will pleasure thee, and force thee stop
Here, that I too may live: but if beyond
Such cool and sorrowful offerings, thou art fond
Of soothing warmth, of dalliance supreme;
440 If thou art ripe to taste a long love dream;
If smiles, if dimples, tongues for ardor mute,
Hang in thy vision like a tempting fruit,
O let me pluck it for thee.' Thus she linked
Her charming syllables, till indistinct
445 Their music came to my o'er-sweetened soul;
And then she hovered over me, and stole
So near, that if no nearer it had been
This furrowed visage thou hadst never seen.

"Young man of Latmos! thus particular

ENDYMION

Am I, that thou may'st plainly see how far 450
This fierce temptation went: and thou may'st not
Exclaim, How then, was Scylla quite forgot?°

"Who could resist? Who in this universe?
She did so breathe ambrosia; so immerse
My fine existence in a golden clime. 455
She took me like a child of suckling time,
And cradled me in roses. Thus condemned,
The current of my former life was stemmed,
And to this arbitrary queen of sense
I bowed a trancèd vassal: nor would thence 460
Have moved, even though Amphion's° harp had wooed
Me back to Scylla o'er the billows rude.
For as Apollo each eve doth devise
A new appareling for western skies;
So every eve, nay every spendthrift hour 465
Shed balmy consciousness within that bower.
And I was free of haunts umbrageous;
Could wander in the mazy forest house
Of squirrels, foxes shy, and antlered deer,
And birds from coverts innermost and drear 470
Warbling for very joy mellifluous sorrow—
To me newborn delights!

      "Now let me borrow,
For moments few, a temperament as stern
As Pluto's scepter, that my words not burn
These uttering lips, while I in calm speech tell 475
How specious heaven was changèd to real hell.

"One morn she left me sleeping: half awake
I sought for her smooth arms and lips, to slake

---

452 **forgot** Glaucus' unfaithfulness to Scylla is Keats's invention; in Ovid he haughtily rejects Circe's advances and thus brings down her ire on Scylla.
461 **Amphion** Son of Zeus and husband of Niobe, Amphion was such an accomplished musician that the heaviest stones would move at the sound of his lyre.

My greedy thirst with nectarous camel-draughts;
480 But she was gone. Whereat the barbèd shafts
Of disappointment stuck in me so sore,
That out I ran and searched the forest o'er.
Wandering about in pine and cedar gloom
Damp awe assailed me; for there 'gan to boom
485 A sound of moan, an agony of sound,
Sepulchral from the distance all round
Then came a conquering earth thunder, and rumbled
That fierce complain to silence: while I stumbled
Down a precipitous path, as if impelled.
490 I came to a dark valley.—Groanings swelled
Poisonous about my ears, and louder grew,
The nearer I approached a flame's gaunt blue,
That glared before me through a thorny brake.
This fire, like the eye of gordian snake,
495 Bewitched me towards; and I soon was near
A sight too fearful for the feel of fear:
In thicket hid I cursed the haggard scene—
The banquet of my arms, my arbor queen,
Seated upon an uptorn forest root;
500 And all around her shapes, wizard and brute,
Laughing, and wailing, groveling, serpenting,
Showing tooth, tusk, and venom bag, and sting!
O such deformities! Old Charon's self,
Should he give up awhile his penny pelf,
505 And take a dream 'mong rushes Stygian,
It could not be so fantasied. Fierce, wan,
And tyrannizing was the lady's look,
As over them a gnarled staff she shook.
Oft-times upon the sudden she laughed out,
510 And from a basket emptied to the rout
Clusters of grapes, the which they ravened quick
And roared for more; with many a hungry lick
About their shaggy jaws. Avenging, slow,
Anon she took a branch of mistletoe,
515 And emptied on't a black dull-gurgling phial:
Groaned one and all, as if some piercing trial
Was sharpening for their pitiable bones.
She lifted up the charm: appealing groans

From their poor breasts went suing to her ear
In vain; remorseless as an infant's bier   520
She whisked against their eyes the sooty oil.
Whereat was heard a noise of painful toil,
Increasing gradual to a tempest rage,
Shrieks, yells, and groans of torture pilgrimage;
Until their grievèd bodies 'gan to bloat   525
And puff from the tail's end to stifled throat:
Then was appalling silence: then a sight
More wildering than all that hoarse affright;
For the whole herd, as by a whirlwind writhen,
Went through the dismal air like one huge Python   530
Antagonizing Boreas—and so vanished.
Yet there was not a breath of wind: she banished
These phantoms with a nod. Lo! from the dark
Came waggish fauns, and nymphs, and satyrs stark,
With dancing and loud revelry—and went   535
Swifter than centaurs after rapine bent.—
Sighing an elephant appeared and bowed
Before the fierce witch, speaking thus aloud
In human accent: 'Potent goddess! chief
Of pains resistless! make my being brief,   540
Or let me from this heavy prison fly:
Or give me to the air, or let me die!
I sue not for my happy crown again;
I sue not for my phalanx on the plain;
I sue not for my lone, my widowed wife;   545
I sue not for my ruddy drops of life,
My children fair, my lovely girls and boys
I will forget them; I will pass these joys;
Ask nought so heavenward, so too—too high:
Only I pray, as fairest boon, to die,   550
Or be delivered from this cumbrous flesh,
From this gross, detestable, filthy mesh,
And merely given to the cold bleak air.
Have mercy, goddess! Circe, feel my prayer!'

"That cursed magician's name fell icy numb   555
Upon my wild conjecturing: truth had come
Naked and saber-like against my heart.

                I saw a fury whetting a death dart;
                And my slain spirit, overwrought with fright,
    560   Fainted away in that dark lair of night.
                Think, my deliverer, how desolate
                My waking must have been! disgust, and hate,
                And terrors manifold divided me
                A spoil amongst them. I prepared to flee
    565   Into the dungeon core of that wild wood:
                I fled three days—when lo! before me stood
                Glaring the angry witch. O Dis, even now,
                A clammy dew is beading on my brow,
                At mere remembering her pale laugh, and curse.
    570   'Ha! ha! Sir Dainty! there must be a nurse
                Made of rose leaves and thistledown, express,
                To cradle thee my sweet, and lull thee: yes,
                I am too flinty-hard for thy nice touch:
                My tenderest squeeze is but a giant's clutch.
    575   So, fairy-thing, it shall have lullabies
                Unheard of yet; and it shall still its cries
                Upon some breast more lily-feminine.
                Oh, no—it shall not pine, and pine, and pine
                More than one pretty, trifling thousand years;
    580   And then 'twere pity, but fate's gentle shears
                Cut short its immortality. Sea-flirt!
                Young dove of the waters! truly I'll not hurt
                One hair of thine: see how I weep and sigh,
                That our heartbroken parting is so nigh.
    585   And must we part? Ah, yes, it must be so.
                Yet ere thou leavest me in utter woe,
                Let me sob over thee my last adieus,
                And speak a blessing: Mark me! thou hast thews
                Immortal, for thou art of heavenly race:°
    590   But such a love is mine, that here I chase
                Eternally away from thee all bloom
                Of youth, and destine thee towards a tomb.
                Hence shalt thou quickly to the watery vast;
                And there, ere many days be overpast,

---

589 **race** This trait is taken from Ovid (XIV, ll. 39–40) who, unlike Keats, has made the deification of the mortal Glaucus the main theme of the first part of his story.

ENDYMION   163

Disabled age shall seize thee; and even then   595
Thou shalt not go the way of agèd men;
But live and wither, cripple and still breathe
Ten hundred years: which gone, I then bequeath
Thy fragile bones to unknown burial.
Adieu, sweet love, adieu!'—As shot stars fall,   600
She fled ere I could groan for mercy. Stung
And poisoned was my spirit: despair sung
A war song of defiance 'gainst all hell.
A hand was at my shoulder to compel
My sullen steps; another 'fore my eyes   605
Moved on with pointed finger. In this guise
Enforced, at the last by ocean's foam
I found me; by my fresh, my native home.
Its tempering coolness, to my life akin,
Came salutary as I waded in;   610
And, with a blind voluptuous rage, I gave
Battle to the swollen billow ridge, and drave
Large froth before me, while there yet remained
Hale strength, nor from my bones all marrow drained.

"Young lover, I must weep—such hellish spite   615
With dry cheek who can tell? While thus my might
Proving upon this element, dismayed,
Upon a dead thing's face my hand I laid;
I looked—'twas Scylla! Cursèd, cursèd Circe!
O vulture witch, hast never heard of mercy?   620
Could not thy harshest vengeance be content,
But thou must nip this tender innocent
Because I loved her?—Cold, O cold indeed
Were her fair limbs, and like a common weed
The sea swell took her hair. Dead as she was   625
I clung about her waist, nor ceased to pass
Fleet as an arrow through unfathomed brine,
Until there shone a fabric crystalline,
Ribbed and inlaid with coral, pebble, and pearl.
Headlong I darted; at one eager swirl   630
Gained its bright portal, entered, and behold!
'Twas vast, and desolate, and icy-cold;
And all around—But wherefore this to thee

ENDYMION

Who in few minutes more thyself shalt see?—
I left poor Scylla in a niche and fled.
My fevered parchings up, my scathing dread
Met palsy half way: soon these limbs became
Gaunt, withered, sapless, feeble, cramped, and lame.

"Now let me pass a cruel, cruel space,
Without one hope, without one faintest trace
Of mitigation, or redeeming bubble
Of colored phantasy; for I fear 'twould trouble
Thy brain to loss of reason: and next tell
How a restoring chance came down to quell
One half of the witch in me.

"On a day,°
Sitting upon a rock above the spray,
I saw grow up from the horizon's brink
A gallant vessel: soon she seemed to sink
Away from me again, as though her course
Had been resumed in spite of hindering force—
So vanished: and not long before arose
Dark clouds, and mutterings of winds morose.
Old Æolus would stifle his mad spleen,
But could not: therefore all the billows green
Tossed up the silver spume against the clouds.
The tempest came: I saw that vessel's shrouds
In perilous bustle; while upon the deck
Stood trembling creatures. I beheld the wreck;
The final gulfing; the poor struggling souls:
I heard their cries amid loud thunder rolls.
O they had all been saved but crazèd eld
Annulled my vigorous cravings: and thus quelled
And curbed, think on't, O Latmian! did I sit
Writhing with pity, and a cursing fit
Against that hell-born Circe. The crew had gone,
By one and one, to pale oblivion;
And I was gazing on the surges prone,
With many a scalding tear and many a groan,

---

645 **day** This entire development of the story is Keats's own invention.

When at my feet emerged an old man's hand,
Grasping this scroll, and this same slender wand.
I knelt with pain—reached out my hand—had grasped
These treasures—touched the knuckles—they unclasped—
I caught a finger: but the downward weight
O'er-powered me—it sank. Then 'gan abate
The storm, and through chill aguish gloom outburst
The comfortable sun. I was athirst
To search the book, and in the warming air
Parted its dripping leaves with eager care.
Strange matters did it treat of, and drew on
My soul page after page, till well-nigh won
Into forgetfulness; when, stupefied,
I read these words, and read again, and tried
My eyes against the heavens, and read again.
O what a load of misery and pain
Each Atlas-line bore off!—a shrine of hope
Came gold around me, cheering me to cope
Strenuous with hellish tyranny. Attend!
For thou hast brought their promise to an end.

"In the wide sea there lives a forlorn wretch,
Doomed with enfeebled carcass to outstretch
His loathed existence through ten centuries,
And then to die alone. Who can devise
A total opposition? No one. So
One million times ocean must ebb and flow,
And he oppressed. Yet he shall not die,
These things accomplished:—If he utterly
Scans all the depth of magic,° and expounds
The meanings of all motions, shapes, and sounds;
If he explores all forms and substances
Straight homeward to their symbol essences;
He shall not die. Moreover, and in chief,

---

697 magic The theme of magic (magic herbs, potions, etc.) figures much more prominently in Ovid's tale than in Keats's. The term is certainly not to be interpreted in an esoteric sense here, but rather seems to designate the knowledge to be gained by a poetic faculty that is not supernatural in substance or intent.

*He must pursue this task of joy and grief
Most piously;—all lovers tempest-tossed,
And in the savage overwhelming lost,*
705 *He shall deposit side by side, until
Time's creeping shall the dreary space fulfill:
Which done, and all these labors ripenèd,
A youth, by heavenly power loved and led,
Shall stand before him; whom he shall direct*
710 *How to consummate all. The youth elect
Must do the thing, or both will be destroyed."—*

"Then," cried the young Endymion, overjoyed,
"We are twin brothers in this destiny!
Say, I entreat thee, what achievement high
715 Is, in this restless world, for me reserved.
What! if from thee my wandering feet had swerved,
Had we both perished?"—"Look!" the sage replied,
"Dost thou not mark a gleaming through the tide,
Of diverse brilliances? 'tis the edifice
720 I told thee of, where lovely Scylla lies;
And where I have enshrinèd piously
All lovers, whom fell storms have doomed to die
Throughout my bondage." Thus discoursing, on
They went till unobscured the porches shone;
725 Which hurryingly they gained, and entered straight.
Sure never since king Neptune held his state
Was seen such wonder underneath the stars.
Turn to some level plain where haughty Mars
Has legioned all his battle; and behold
730 How every soldier, with firm foot doth hold
His even breast: see, many steelèd squares,
And rigid ranks of iron—whence who dares
One step? Imagine further, line by line,
These warrior thousands on the field supine:—
735 So in that crystal place, in silent rows,
Poor lovers lay at rest from joys and woes.—
The stranger from the mountains, breathless, traced
Such thousands of shut eyes in order placed;
Such ranges of white feet, and patient lips
740 All ruddy—for here death no blossom nips.

He marked their brows and foreheads; saw their hair
Put sleekly on one side with nicest care;
And each one's gentle wrists, with reverence,
Put crosswise to its heart.

                "Let us commence,"
Whispered the guide, stuttering with joy, "even now." 745
He spake, and, trembling like an aspen bough,
Began to tear his scroll in pieces small,
Uttering the while some mumblings funeral.
He tore it into pieces small as snow
That drifts unfeathered when bleak northerns blow; 750
And having done it, took his dark blue cloak
And bound it round Endymion: then stroke
His wand against the empty air times nine.—
"What more there is to do, young man, is thine:
But first a little patience; first undo 755
This tangled thread, and wind it to a clue.
Ah, gentle! 'tis as weak as spider's skein;
And shouldst thou break it—What, is it done so clean?
A power overshadows thee! Oh, brave!
The spite of hell is tumbling to its grave. 760
Here is a shell; 'tis pearly blank to me,
Nor marked with any sign or charactery—
Canst thou read aught? O read for pity's sake!
Olympus! we are safe! Now, Carian, break
This wand against yon lyre on the pedestal." 765

'Twas done: and straight with sudden swell and fall
Sweet music breathed her soul away, and sighed
A lullaby to silence.—"Youth! now strew
These mincèd leaves on me, and passing through
Those files of dead, scatter the same around, 770
And thou wilt see the issue."—'Mid the sound
Of flutes and viols, ravishing his heart,
Endymion from Glaucus stood apart,
And scattered in his face some fragments light.
How lightning-swift the change! a youthful wight 775
Smiling beneath a coral diadem,
Outsparkling sudden like an upturned gem,

Appeared, and, stepping to a beauteous corse,
Kneeled down beside it, and with tenderest force
Pressed its cold hand, and wept—and Scylla sighed!
Endymion, with quick hand, the charm applied—
The nymph arose: he left them to their joy,
And onward went upon his high employ,
Showering those powerful fragments on the dead.
And, as he passed, each lifted up its head,
As doth a flower at Apollo's touch.
Death felt it to his inwards; 'twas too much:
Death fell aweeping in his charnel house.
The Latmian persevered along, and thus
All were reanimated. There arose
A noise of harmony, pulses and throes
Of gladness in the air—while many, who
Had died in mutual arms devout and true,
Sprang to each other madly; and the rest
Felt a high certainty of being blessed.
They gazed upon Endymion. Enchantment
Grew drunken, and would have its head and bent.
Delicious symphonies, like airy flowers,
Budded, and swelled, and, full-blown, shed full showers
Of light, soft, unseen leaves of sounds divine.
The two deliverers tasted a pure wine
Of happiness, from fairy-press oozed out.
Speechless they eyed each other, and about
The fair assembly wandered to and fro,
Distracted with the richest overflow
Of joy that ever poured from heaven.

——"Away!"
Shouted the newborn god; "Follow, and pay
Our piety to Neptunus supreme!"—
Then Scylla, blushing sweetly from her dream,
They led on first, bent to her meek surprise,
Through portal columns of a giant size,
Into the vaulted, boundless emerald.
Joyous all followed, as the leader called,
Down marble steps; pouring as easily
As hourglass sand—and fast, as you might see

Swallows obeying the south summer's call,
Or swans upon a gentle waterfall.

    Thus went that beautiful multitude, nor far,
Ere from among some rocks of glittering spar,
Just within ken, they saw descending thick
Another multitude. Whereat more quick
Moved either host. On a wide sand they met,
And of those numbers every eye was wet;
For each their old love found. A murmuring rose,
Like what was never heard in all the throes
Of wind and waters: 'tis past human wit
To tell; 'tis dizziness to think of it.

    This mighty consummation made, the host
Moved on for many a league; and gained, and lost
Huge sea marks; vanward swelling in array,
And from the rear diminishing away—
Till a faint dawn surprised them. Glaucus cried,
"Behold! behold, the palace of his pride!
God Neptune's palaces!" With noise increased,
They shouldered on towards that brightening east.
At every onward step proud domes arose
In prospect—diamond gleams, and golden glows
Of amber 'gainst their faces leveling.
Joyous, and many as the leaves in spring,
Still onward; still the splendor gradual swelled.
Rich opal domes were seen, on high upheld
By jasper pillars, letting through their shafts
A blush of coral. Copious wonder-draughts
Each gazer drank; and deeper drank more near:
For what poor mortals fragment up, as mere
As marble was there lavish, to the vast
Of one fair palace, that far far surpassed,
Even for common bulk, those olden three,
Memphis, and Babylon, and Nineveh.

    As large, as bright, as colored as the bow
Of Iris, when unfading it doth show
Beyond a silvery shower, was the arch

Through which this Paphian army took its march,
Into the outer courts of Neptune's state:
Whence could be seen, direct, a golden gate,
To which the leaders sped; but not half raught
Ere it burst open swift as fairy thought,
And made those dazzled thousands veil their eyes
Like callow eagles at the first sunrise.
Soon with an eagle nativeness their gaze
Ripe from hue-golden swoons took all the blaze,
And then, behold! large Neptune on his throne
Of emerald deep: yet not exalt alone;
At his right hand stood wingèd Love, and on
His left sat smiling Beauty's paragon.

Far as the mariner on highest mast
Can see all round upon the calmèd vast,
So wide was Neptune's hall: and as the blue
Doth vault the waters, so the waters drew
Their doming curtains, high, magnificent,
Awed from the throne aloof;—and when storm-rent
Disclosed the thunder gloomings in Jove's air;
But soothed as now, flashed sudden everywhere,
Noiseless, sub-marine cloudlets, glittering
Death to a human eye: for there did spring
From natural west, and east, and south, and north,
A light as of four sunsets, blazing forth
A gold-green zenith 'bove the Sea God's head.
Of lucid depth the floor, and far outspread
As breezeless lake, on which the slim canoe,
Of feathered Indian darts about, as through
The delicatest air: air verily,
But for the portraiture of clouds and sky:
This palace floor breath-air—but for the amaze
Of deep-seen wonders motionless—and blaze
Of the dome pomp, reflected in extremes,
Globing a golden sphere.

      They stood in dreams
Till Triton blew his horn. The palace rang;
The Nereids danced; the Sirens faintly sang;

And the great Sea King bowed his dripping head. 890
Then Love took wing, and from his pinions shed
On all the multitude a nectarous dew.
The ooze-born Goddess beckoned and drew
Fair Scylla and her guides to conference;
And when they reached the thronèd eminence 895
She kissed the sea-nymph's cheek—who sat her down
Atoying with the doves. Then—"Mighty crown
And scepter of this kingdom!" Venus said,
"Thy vows were on a time to Nais paid:
Behold!"—Two copious teardrops instant fell 900
From the God's large eyes; he smiled delectable,
And over Glaucus held his blessing hands.—
"Endymion!° Ah! still wandering in the bands
Of love? Now this is cruel. Since the hour
I met thee in earth's bosom, all my power 905
Have I put forth to serve thee. What, not yet
Escaped from dull mortality's harsh net?
A little patience, youth! 'twill not be long,
Or I am skilless quite: an idle tongue,
A humid eye, and steps luxurious,
Where these are new and strange, are ominous. 910
Aye, I have seen these signs in one of heaven,
When others were all blind; and were I given
To utter secrets, haply I might say
Some pleasant words:—but Love will have his day. 915
So wait awhile expectant. Prithee soon,
Even in the passing of thine honeymoon,
Visit thou my Cythera: thou wilt find
Cupid well-natured, my Adonis kind;
And pray persuade with thee—Ah, I have done, 920
All blisses be upon thee, my sweet son!"—
Thus the fair goddess: while Endymion
Knelt to receive those accents halcyon.

    Meantime a glorious revelry began 925
Before the Water Monarch. Nectar ran
In courteous fountains to all cups outreached;

---

903 **Endymion** These lines are spoken by Venus, not Neptune.

And plundered vines, teeming exhaustless, pleached
New growth about each shell and pendent lyre;
The which, in disentangling for their fire,
Pulled down fresh foliage and coverture
For dainty toying. Cupid, empire-sure,
Fluttered and laughed, and oft-times through the throng
Made a delighted way. Then dance, and song,
And garlanding grew wild; and pleasure reigned.
In harmless tendril they each other chained,
And strove who should be smothered deepest in
Fresh crush of leaves.

O 'tis a very sin
For one so weak to venture his poor verse
In such a place as this. O do not curse,
High Muses! let him hurry to the ending.

All suddenly were silent. A soft blending
Of dulcet instruments came charmingly;
And then a hymn.

"King of the stormy sea!
Brother of Jove, and co-inheritor
Of elements! Eternally before
Thee the waves awful bow. Fast, stubborn rock,
At thy feared trident shrinking, doth unlock
Its deep foundations, hissing into foam.
All mountain rivers lost in the wide home
Of thy capacious bosom, ever flow.
Thou frownest, and old Æolus thy foe
Skulks to his cavern, 'mid the gruff complaint
Of all his rebel tempests. Dark clouds faint
When, from thy diadem, a silver gleam
Slants over blue dominion. Thy bright team
Gulfs in the morning light, and scuds along
To bring thee nearer to that golden song
Apollo singeth, while his chariot
Waits at the doors of heaven. Thou art not
For scenes like this: an empire stern hast thou;

And it has furrowed that large front: yet now,
As newly come of heaven, dost thou sit
To blend and interknit
Subduèd majesty with this glad time.
O shell-borne King sublime!   965
We lay our hearts before thee evermore—
We sing, and we adore!

  "Breathe softly, flutes;
Be tender of your strings, ye soothing lutes;
Nor be the trumpet heard! O vain, O vain;   970
Not flowers budding in an April rain,
Nor breath of sleeping dove, nor river's flow—
No, nor the Æolian twang of Love's own bow,
Can mingle music fit for the soft ear
Of goddess Cytherea!   975
Yet deign, white Queen of Beauty, thy fair eyes
On our souls' sacrifice.

  "Bright-wingèd Child!°
Who has another care when thou hast smiled?
Unfortunates on earth, we see at last   980
All death shadows, and glooms that overcast
Our spirits, fanned away by thy light pinions.
O sweetest essence! sweetest of all minions!
God of warm pulses, and disheveled hair,
And panting bosoms bare!   985
Dear unseen light in darkness! eclipser
Of light in light! delicious poisoner
Thy venomed goblet will we quaff until
We fill—we fill!
And by thy mother's lips———"

                        Was heard no more   990
For clamor, when the golden palace door
Opened again, and from without, in shone
A new magnificence. On oozy throne

---

978 **Child** Eros.

Smooth-moving came Oceanus the old,
To take a latest glimpse at his sheep fold,
Before he went into his quiet cave
To muse forever—Then a lucid wave,
Scooped from its trembling sisters of mid-sea,
Afloat, and pillowing up the majesty
Of Doris, and the Ægean seer, her spouse—
Next, on a dolphin, clad in laurel boughs,
Theban Amphion leaning on his lute:
His fingers went across it—All were mute
To gaze on Amphitrite, queen of pearls,
And Thetis pearly too.—

                    The palace whirls
Around giddy Endymion; seeing he
Was there far strayèd from mortality.
He could not bear it—shut his eyes in vain;
Imagination gave a dizzier pain.
"O I shall die! sweet Venus, be my stay!
Where is my lovely mistress? Well-away!
I die—I hear her voice—I feel my wing—"
At Neptune's feet he sank. A sudden ring
Of Nereids were about him, in kind strife
To usher back his spirit into life:
But still he slept. At last they interwove
Their cradling arms, and purposed to convey
Towards a crystal bower far away.

Lo! while slow carried through the pitying crowd,
To his inward senses these words spake aloud;
Written in starlight on the dark above:
Dearest Endymion! my entire love!
How have I dwelt in fear of fate: 'tis done—
Immortal bliss for me too hast thou won.
Arise then! for the hen dove shall not hatch
Her ready eggs, before I'll kissing snatch
Thee into endless heaven. Awake! awake!

The youth at once arose: a placid lake
Came quiet to his eyes; and forest green,

ENDYMION

Cooler than all the wonders he had seen, 1030
Lulled with its simple song his fluttering breast.
How happy once again in grassy nest!

Book IV

Muse of my native land! Loftiest Muse!
O first-born on the mountains! by the hues
Of heaven on the spiritual air begot:
Long didst thou sit alone in northern grot,
While yet our England was a wolfish den; 5
Before our forests heard the talk of men;
Before the first of Druids was a child;—
Long didst thou sit amid our regions wild
Rapt in a deep prophetic solitude.
There came an eastern voice° of solemn mood:— 10
Yet wast thou patient. Then sang forth the Nine,
Apollo's garland:°—yet didst thou divine
Such home-bred glory, that they cried in vain,
"Come hither, Sister of the Island!" Plain
Spake fair Ausonia;° and once more she spake 15
A higher summons:—still didst thou betake
Thee to thy native hopes. O thou hast won
A full accomplishment! The thing is done,
Which undone, these our latter days had risen
On barren souls. Great Muse, thou know'st what prison 20
Of flesh and bone curbs, and confines, and frets
Our spirit's wings: despondency besets
Our pillows; and the fresh tomorrow morn
Seems to give forth its light in very scorn
Of our dull, uninspired, snail-paced lives. 25
Long have I said, how happy he who shrives
To thee! But then I thought on poets gone,°
And could not pray:—nor can I now—so on
I move to the end in lowliness of heart.——

10 **eastern voice** refers to the Hebrew poetry of the Old Testament.
12 **Apollo's garland** the literature of Greece. 15 **Ausonia** is a poetic name for Italy; the line presumably refers to Roman poetry.
27 **poets gone** The allusion is to Chatterton, to whom *Endymion* is dedicated.

176   ENDYMION

30 "Ah, woe is me!° that I should fondly part
    From my dear native land! Ah, foolish maid!
    Glad was the hour, when with thee, myriads bade
    Adieu to Ganges and their pleasant fields!
    To one so friendless the clear freshet yields
35 A bitter coolness; the ripe grape is sour:
    Yet I would have, great gods! but one short hour
    Of native air—let me but die at home."

    Endymion to heaven's airy dome
    Was offering up a hecatomb of vows,
40 When these words reached him. Whereupon he bows
    His head through thorny-green entanglement
    Of underwood, and to the sound is bent,
    Anxious as hind towards her hidden fawn.

    "Is no one near to help me? No fair dawn
45 Of life from charitable voice? No sweet saying
    To set my dull and saddened spirit playing?
    No hand to toy with mine? No lips so sweet
    That I may worship them? No eyelids meet
    To twinkle on my bosom? No one dies
50 Before me, till from these enslaving eyes
    Redemption sparkles!—I am sad and lost."

    Thou, Carian lord, hadst better have been tossed
    Into a whirlpool. Vanish into air,
    Warm mountaineer! for canst thou only bear
55 A woman's sigh alone and in distress?
    See not her charms! Is Phœbe passionless?
    Phœbe is fairer far—O gaze no more:—
    Yet if thou wilt behold all beauty's store,
    Behold her panting in the forest grass!
60 Do not those curls of glossy jet surpass
    For tenderness the arms so idly lain
    Amongst them? Feelest not a kindred pain,
    To see such lovely eyes in swimming search
    After some warm delight, that seems to perch

---

30 **woe is me** Without the slightest transition, we are suddenly hearing the lament of an Indian maiden.

ENDYMION

Dove-like in the dim cell lying beyond 65
Their upper lids?—Hist!

              "O for Hermes' wand,
To touch this flower into human shape!
That woodland Hyacinthus could escape
From his green prison, and here kneeling down
Call me his queen, his second life's fair crown! 70
Ah me, how I could love!—My soul doth melt
For the unhappy youth—Love! I have felt
So faint a kindness, such a meek surrender
To what my own full thoughts had made too tender,
That but for tears my life had fled away!— 75
Ye deaf and senseless minutes of the day,
And thou, old forest, hold ye this for true,
There is no lightning, no authentic dew
But in the eye of love: there's not a sound,
Melodious howsoever, can confound 80
The heavens and earth in one to such a death
As doth the voice of love: there's not a breath
Will mingle kindly with the meadow air,
Till it has panted round, and stolen a share
Of passion from the heart!"—

                      Upon a bough 85
He leaned, wretchèd. He surely cannot now
Thirst for another love: O impious,
That he can even dream upon it thus!—
Thought he, "Why am I not as are the dead,
Since to a woe like this I have been led 90
Through the dark earth, and through the wondrous sea?
Goddess! I love thee not the less: from thee
By Juno's smile I turn not—no, no, no—
While the great waters are at ebb and flow.—
I have a triple soul!° O fond pretense— 95

---

95 **triple soul** one third for Cynthia, one third for his unknown visionary love, and one third for the newly arrived maiden. In the next line, Diana seems no longer to be remembered and we go back from three to two.

ENDYMION

For both, for both my love is so immense,
I fell my heart is cut for them in twain."

And so he groaned, as one by beauty slain.
The lady's heart beat quick, and he could see
Her gentle bosom heave tumultuously.
He sprang from his green covert: there she lay,
Sweet as a musk rose upon new-made hay;
With all her limbs on tremble, and her eyes
Shut softly up alive. To speak he tries.
"Fair damsel, pity me! forgive that I
Thus violate thy bower's sanctity!
O pardon me, for I am full of grief—
Grief born of thee, young angel! fairest thief!
Who stolen hast away the wings wherewith
I was to top the heavens. Dear maid, sith
Thou art my executioner, and I feel
Loving and hatred, misery and weal,
Will in a few short hours be nothing to me,
And all my story that much passion slew me;
Do smile upon the evening of my days:
And, for my tortured brain begins to craze,
Be thou my nurse; and let me understand
How dying I shall kiss that lily hand.—
Dost weep for me? Then should I be content.
Scowl on, ye fates! until the firmament
Outblackens Erebus, and the full-caverned earth
Crumbles into itself. By the cloud girth
Of Jove, those tears have given me a thirst
To meet oblivion."—As her heart would burst
The maiden sobbed awhile, and then replied:
"Why must such desolation betide
As that thou speak'st of? Are not these green nooks
Empty of all misfortune? Do the brooks
Utter a gorgon voice? Does yonder thrush,
Schooling its half-fledged little ones to brush
About the dewy forest, whisper tales?—
Speak not of grief, young stranger, or cold snails
Will slime the rose to night. Though if thou wilt,
Methinks 'twould be a guilt—a very guilt—

ENDYMION

Not to companion thee, and sigh away 135
The light—the dusk—the dark—till break of day!"
"Dear lady," said Endymion, " 'tis past:
I love thee! and my days can never last.
That I may pass in patience still speak:
Let me have music dying, and I seek 140
No more delight—I bid adieu to all.
Didst thou not after other climates call,
And murmur about Indian streams?"—Then she,
Sitting beneath the midmost forest tree,
For pity sang this roundelay—— 145

"O Sorrow,
Why dost borrow
The natural hue of health, from vermeil lips?—
To give maiden blushes
To the white rose bushes? 150
Or is't thy dewy hand the daisy tips?

"O Sorrow,
Why dost borrow
The lustrous passion from a falcon eye?—
To give the glowworm light? 155
Or, on a moonless night,
To tinge, on Siren shores, the salt sea-spry?

"O Sorrow,
Why dost borrow
The mellow ditties from a mourning tongue?— 160
To give at evening pale
Unto the nightingale,
That thou mayst listen the cold dews among?

"O Sorrow,
Why dost borrow 165
Heart's lightness from the merriment of May?—
A lover would not tread
A cowslip on the head,
Though he should dance from eve till peep of day—
Nor any drooping flower 170

Held sacred for thy bower,
Wherever he may sport himself and play.

"To Sorrow,
 I bade good morrow,
And thought to leave her far away behind;
 But cheerly, cheerly,
 She loves me dearly;
She is so constant to me, and so kind:
 I would deceive her
 And so leave her,
But ah! she is so constant and so kind.

"Beneath my palm trees, by the river side,
I sat a weeping: in the whole world wide
There was no one to ask me why I wept—
 And so I kept
Brimming the water-lily cups with tears
 Cold as my fears.

"Beneath my palm trees, by the riverside,
I sat aweeping: what enamored bride,
Cheated by shadowy wooer from the clouds,
 But hides and shrouds
Beneath dark palm trees by a river-side?

"And as I sat, over the light blue hills
There came a noise of revelers: the rills
Into the wide stream came of purple hue—
 'Twas Bacchus and his crew!
The earnest trumpet spake, and silver thrills
From kissing cymbals made a merry din—
 'Twas Bacchus and his kin!
Like to a moving vintage down they came,
Crowned with green leaves, and faces all on flame;
All madly dancing through the pleasant valley,
 To scare thee, Melancholy!
O then, O then, thou wast a simple name!
And I forgot thee, as the berried holly
By shepherds is forgotten, when, in June,

Tall chestnuts keep away the sun and moon:—
    I rushed into the folly!

"Within his car, aloft, young Bacchus stood,
Trifling his ivy dart, in dancing mood,
    With sidelong laughing;
And little rills of crimson wine imbrued
His plump white arms, and shoulders, enough white
    For Venus' pearly bite:
And near him rode Silenus on his ass,
Pelted with flowers as he on did pass
    Tipsily quaffing.

"Whence came ye, merry Damsels! whence came ye!
So many, and so many, and such glee?
Why have ye left your bowers desolate,
    Your lutes, and gentler fate?—
'We follow Bacchus! Bacchus on the wing,
    A conquering!
Bacchus, young Bacchus! good or ill betide,
We dance before him through kingdoms wide:—
Come hither, lady fair, and joinèd be
    To our wild minstrelsy!'

"Whence came ye, jolly Satyrs! whence came ye!
So many, and so many, and such glee?
Why have ye left your forest haunts, why left
    Your nuts in oak-tree cleft?—
'For wine, for wine we left our kernel tree;
For wine we left our heath, and yellow brooms,
    And cold mushrooms;
For wine we follow Bacchus through the earth;
Great God of breathless cups and chirping mirth!—
Come hither, lady fair, and joinèd be
    To our mad minstrelsy!'

"Over wide streams and mountains great we went,
And, save when Bacchus kept his ivy tent,
Onward the tiger and the leopard pants,
    With Asian elephants:

Onward these myriads—with song and dance,
With zebras striped, and sleek Arabians' prance,
Web-footed alligators, crocodiles,
Bearing upon their scaly backs, in files,
Plump infant laughters mimicking the coil
Of seamen, and stout galley rowers' toil:
With toying oars and silken sails they glide,
      Nor care for wind and tide.

"Mounted on panthers' furs and lions' manes,
From rear to van they scour about the plains;
A three days' journey in a moment done:
And always, at the rising of the sun,
About the wilds they hunt with spear and horn,
      On spleenful unicorn.

"I saw Osirian Egypt kneel adown
      Before the vine-wreath crown!
I saw parched Abyssinia rouse and sing
      To the silver cymbals' ring!
I saw the whelming vintage hotly pierce
      Old Tartary the fierce!
The kings of Inde their jewel-scepters vail,
And from their treasures scatter pearlèd hail;
Great Brahma from his mystic heaven groans,
      And all his priesthood moans;
Before young Bacchus' eye-wink turning pale.—
Into these regions came I following him,
Sick hearted, weary—so I took a whim
To stray away into these forests drear
      Alone, without a peer:
And I have told thee all thou mayest hear.

      "Young stranger!
      I've been a ranger
In search of pleasure throughout every clime:
      Alas! 'tis not for me!
      Bewitched I sure must be,
To lose in grieving all my maiden prime.

"Come then, Sorrow!
 Sweetest Sorrow!
Like an own babe I nurse thee on my breast:
 I thought to leave thee
 And deceive thee,
But now of all the world I love thee best.

"There is not one,
 No, no, not one
But thee to comfort a poor lonely maid;
 Thou art her mother,
 And her brother,
Her playmate, and her wooer in the shade."

 O what a sigh she gave in finishing,
And look, quite dead to every worldly thing!
Endymion could not speak, but gazed on her;
And listened to the wind that now did stir
About the crispèd oaks full drearily,
Yet with as sweet a softness as might be
Remembered from its velvet summer song.
At last he said: "Poor lady, how thus long
Have I been able to endure that voice?
Fair Melody! kind Siren! I've no choice;
I must be thy sad servant evermore:
I cannot choose but kneel here and adore.
Alas, I must not think—by Phœbe, no!
Let me not think, soft Angel! shall it be so?
Say, beautifullest, shall I never think?
O thou couldst foster me beyond the brink
Of recollection! make my watchful care
Close up its bloodshot eyes, nor see despair!
Do gently murder half my soul, and I
Shall feel the other half so utterly!—
I'm giddy at that cheek so fair and smooth;
O let it blush so ever! let it soothe
My madness! let it mantle rosy-warm
With the tinge of love, panting in safe alarm.—
This cannot be thy hand, and yet it is;

And this is sure thine other softling—this
Thine own fair bosom, and I am so near!
Wilt fall asleep? O let me sip that tear!
And whisper one sweet word that I may know
320 This is this world—sweet dewy blossom!"—*Woe!
Woe! Woe to that Endymion! Where is he?*—
Even these words went echoing dismally
Through the wide forest—a most fearful tone,
Like one repenting in his latest moan;
325 And while it died away a shade passed by,
As of a thunder cloud. When arrows fly
Through the thick branches, poor ringdoves sleek forth
Their timid necks and tremble; so these both
Leaned to each other trembling, and sat so
330 Waiting for some destruction—when lo,
Foot-feathered Mercury appeared sublime
Beyond the tall treetops; and in less time
Than shoots the slanted hailstorm, down he dropped
Towards the ground; but rested not, nor stopped
335 One moment from his home: only the sward
He with his wand light touched, and heavenward
Swifter than sight was gone—even before
The teeming earth a sudden witness bore
Of his swift magic. Diving swans appear
340 Above the crystal circlings white and clear;
And catch the cheated eye in wide surprise,
How they can dive in sight and unseen rise—
So from the turf outsprang two steeds jet-black,
Each with large dark blue wings upon his back.
345 The youth of Caria placed the lovely dame
On one, and felt himself in spleen to tame
The other's fierceness. Through the air they flew,
High as the eagles. Like two drops of dew
Exhaled to Phœbus' lips, away they are gone,
350 Far from the earth away—unseen, alone,
Among cool clouds and winds, but that the free,
The buoyant life of song can floating be
Above their heads, and follow them untired.—
Muse of my native land, am I inspired?
355 This is the giddy air, and I must spread

ENDYMION

Wide pinions to keep here; nor do I dread
Or height, or depth, or width, or any chance
Precipitous: I have beneath my glance
Those towering horses and their mournful freight.
Could I thus sail, and see, and thus await 360
Fearless for power of thought, without thine aid?—

There is a sleepy dusk, an odorous shade
From some approachinng wonder, and behold
Those wingèd steeds, with snorting nostrils bold
Snuff at its faint extreme, and seem to tire, 365
Dying to embers from their native fire!

There curled a purple mist around them; soon,
It seemed as when around the pale new moon
Sad Zephyr droops the clouds like weeping willow:
'Twas Sleep slow journeying with head on pillow. 370
For the first time, since he came nigh dead born
From the old womb of night, his cave forlorn
Had he left more forlorn; for the first time,
He felt aloof the day and morning's prime—
Because into his depth Cimmerian 375
There came a dream, showing how a young man,
Ere a lean bat could plump its wintery skin,
Would at high Jove's empyreal footstool win
An immortality, and how espouse
Jove's daughter, and be reckoned of his house. 380
Now was he slumbering towards heaven's gate,
That he might at the threshold one hour wait
To hear the marriage melodies, and then
Sink downward to his dusky cave again.
His litter of smooth semilucent mist, 385
Diversely tinged with rose and amethyst,
Puzzled those eyes that for the center sought;
And scarcely for one moment could be caught
His sluggish form reposing motionless.
Those two on wingèd steeds, with all the stress 390
Of vision searched for him, as one would look
Athwart the sallows of a river nook
To catch a glance at silver throated eels—

Or from old Skiddaw's° top, when fog conceals
His rugged forehead in a mantle pale,
With an eye-guess towards some pleasant vale
Descry a favorite hamlet faint and far.

These raven horses, though they fostered are
Of earth's splenetic fire, dully drop
Their full-veined ears, nostrils blood wide, and stop;
Upon the spiritless mist have they outspread
Their ample feathers, are in slumber dead—
And on those pinions, level in midair,
Endymion sleepeth and the lady fair.
Slowly they sail, slowly as icy isle
Upon a calm sea drifting: and meanwhile
The mournful wanderer dreams. Behold! he walks
On heaven's pavement; brotherly he talks
To divine powers: from his hand full fain
Juno's proud birds are pecking pearly grain:
He tries the nerve of Phœbus' golden bow,
And asketh where the golden apples grow:
Upon his arm he braces Pallas' shield,
And strives in vain to unsettle and wield
A Jovian thunderbolt: arch Hebe brings
A full-brimmed goblet, dances lightly, sings
And tantalizes long; at last he drinks,
And lost in pleasure at her feet he sinks,
Touching with dazzled lips her starlight hand.
He blows a bugle—an ethereal band
Are visible above: the Seasons four—
Green-kirtled Spring, flush Summer, golden store
In Autumn's sickle, Winter frosty-hoar,
Join dance with shadowy Hours; while still the blast,
In swells unmitigated, still doth last
To sway their floating morris. "Whose is this?
Whose bugle?" he inquires: they smile—"O Dis!
Why is this mortal here? Dost thou not know
Its mistress' lips? Not thou?—'Tis Dian's: lo!
She rises crescented!" He looks, 'tis she,

394 **Skiddaw** a mountain in Scotland.

His very goddess: good-bye earth, and sea,
And air, and pains, and care, and suffering;
Good-bye to all but love! Then doth he spring
Towards her, and awakes—and, strange, o'erhead,
Of those same fragrant exhalations bred, 435
Beheld awake his very dream: the gods
Stood smiling; merry Hebe laughs and nods;
And Phœbe bends towards him crescented.
O state perplexing! On the pinion bed,
Too well awake, he feels the panting side 440
Of his delicious lady. He who died
For soaring too audacious in the sun,
When that same treacherous wax began to run,
Felt not more tongue-tied than Endymion.
His heart leaped up as to its rightful throne, 445
To that fair shadowed passion pulsed its way—
Ah, what perplexity! Ah, well a day!
So fond, so beauteous was his bedfellow,
He could not help but kiss her: then he grew
Awhile forgetful of all beauty save 450
Young Phœbe's, golden haired; and so 'gan crave
Forgiveness: yet he turned once more to look
At the sweet sleeper—all his soul was shook—
She pressed his hand in slumber; so once more
He could not help but kiss her and adore. 455
At this the shadow wept, melting away.
The Latmian started up: "Bright goddess, stay!
Search my most hidden breast! By truth's own tongue,
I have no dædale heart: why is it wrung
To desperation? Is there nought for me, 460
Upon the bourn of bliss, but misery?"

These words awoke the stranger of dark tresses:
Her dawning love-look rapt Endymion blesses
With 'havior soft. Sleep yawned from underneath.
"Thou swan of Ganges, let us no more breathe 465
This murky phantasm! thou contented seem'st
Pillowed in lovely idleness, nor dream'st
What horrors may discomfort thee and me.
Ah, shouldst thou die from my heart-treachery!—

470　Yet did she merely weep—her gentle soul
　　Hath no revenge in it: as it is whole
　　In tenderness, would I were whole in love!
　　Can I prize thee, fair maid, all price above,
　　Even when I feel as true as innocence?
475　I do, I do.—What is this soul then? Whence
　　Came it? It does not seem my own, and I
　　Have no self-passion or identity.
　　Some fearful end must be: where, where is it?
　　By Nemesis, I see my spirit flit
480　Alone about the dark—Forgive me, sweet:
　　Shall we away?" He roused the steeds: they beat
　　Their wings chivalrous into the clear air,
　　Leaving old Sleep within his vapory lair.

　　The good-night blush of eve was waning slow,
485　And Vesper, risen star, began to throe
　　In the dusk heavens silverly, when they
　　Thus sprang direct towards the Galaxy.
　　Nor did speed hinder converse soft and strange—
　　Eternal oaths and vows they interchange,
490　In such wise, in such temper, so aloof
　　Up in the winds, beneath a starry roof,
　　So witless of their doom, that verily
　　'Tis well nigh past man's search their hearts to see;
　　Whether they wept, or laughed, or grieved, or toyed—
495　Most like with joy gone mad, with sorrow cloyed.

　　Full facing their swift flight, from ebon streak,
　　The moon put forth a little diamond peak,
　　No bigger than an unobservèd star,
　　Or tiny point of fairy scimitar;
500　Bright signal that she only stooped to tie
　　Her silver sandals, ere deliciously
　　She bowed into the heavens her timid head.
　　Slowly she rose, as though she would have fled,
　　While to his lady meek the Carian turned,
505　To mark if her dark eyes had yet discerned
　　This beauty in its birth—Despair! despair!
　　He saw her body fading gaunt and spare

ENDYMION

In the cold moonshine. Straight he seized her wrist;
It melted from his grasp: her hand he kissed,
And, horror! kissed his own—he was alone. 510
Her steed a little higher soared, and then
Dropped hawkwise to the earth.

                          There lies a den,
Beyond the seeming confines of the space
Made for the soul to wander in and trace
Its own existence, of remotest glooms. 515
Dark regions are around it, where the tombs
Of buried griefs the spirit sees, but scarce
One hour doth linger weeping, for the pierce
Of newborn woe it feels more inly smart:
And in these regions many a venomed dart 520
At random flies; they are the proper home
Of every ill: the man is yet to come
Who hath not journeyed in this native hell.
But few have ever felt how calm and well
Sleep may be had in that deep den of all. 525
There anguish does not sting; nor pleasure pall:
Woe-hurricanes beat ever at the gate,
Yet all is still within and desolate.
Beset with painful gusts, within ye hear
No sound so loud as when on curtained bier 530
The death-watch tick is stifled. Enter none
Who strive therefore: on the sudden it is won.
Just when the sufferer begins to burn,
Then it is free to him; and from an urn,
Still fed by melting ice, he takes a draught— 535
Young Semele° such richness never quaffed
In her maternal longing! Happy gloom!
Dark paradise! where pale becomes the bloom
Of health by due; where silence dreariest
Is most articulate; where hopes infest; 540
Where those eyes are the brightest far that keep
Their lids shut longest in a dreamless sleep.
O happy spirit-home! O wondrous soul!

536 **Semele** mother of Bacchus, Zeus himself being the father.

Pregnant with such a den to save the whole
545 In thine own depth.° Hail, gentle Carian!
For, never since thy griefs and woes began,
Hast thou felt so content: a grievous feud
Hath led thee to this cave of quietude.
Aye, his lulled soul was there, although upborne
550 With dangerous speed: and so he did not mourn
Because he knew not whither he was going.
So happy was he, not the aerial blowing
Of trumpets at clear parley from the east
Could rouse from that fine relish, that high feast.
555 They stung the feathered horse: with fierce alarm
He flapped towards the sound. Alas, no charm
Could lift Endymion's head, or he had viewed
A skyey mask, a pinioned multitude—
And silvery was its passing: voices sweet
560 Warbling the while as if to lull and greet
The wanderer in his path. Thus warbled they,
While past the vision went in bright array.

"Who, who from Dian's feast would be away?
For all the golden bowers of the day
565 Are empty left? Who, who away would be
From Cynthia's wedding and festivity?
Not Hesperus: lo! upon his silver wings
He leans away for highest heaven and sings,
Snapping his lucid fingers merrily!—
570 Ah, Zephyrus! art here, and Flora too!
Ye tender bibbers of the rain and dew,
Young playmates of the rose and daffodil,
Be careful, ere ye enter in, to fill
    Your baskets high
575 With fennel green, and balm, and golden pines,
Savory, latter-mint, and columbines,
Cool parsley, basil sweet, and sunny thyme;
Yea, every flower and leaf of every clime,
All gathered in the dewy morning: hie

---

545 **thine own depth** Threatened by division, the soul is capable of saving its own integrity because it contains within itself the possibility of retreat into quietude.

ENDYMION

>   Away! fly, fly!—
> Crystalline brother of the belt of heaven,
> Aquarius! to whom king Jove has given
> Two liquid pulse-streams 'stead of feathered wings,
> Two fan-like fountains—thine illuminings
>   For Dian play:
> Dissolve the frozen purity of air;
> Let thy white shoulders silvery and bare
> Show cold through watery pinions; make more bright
> The Star Queen's crescent on her marriage night:
>   Haste, haste away!—
> Castor has tamed the planet Lion, see!
> And of the Bear has Pollux mastery:
> A third is in the race! who is the third,
> Speeding away swift as the eagle bird?
>   The ramping Centaur!
> The Lion's mane's on end: the Bear how fierce!
> The Centaur's arrow ready seems to pierce
> Some enemy: far forth his bow is bent
> Into the blue of heaven. He'll be shent,
>   Pale unrelentor,
> When he shall hear the wedding lutes° aplaying.—
> Andromeda! sweet woman! why delaying
> So timidly among the stars: come hither!
> Join this bright throng, and nimbly follow whither
>   They all are going.
> Danae's son,° before Jove newly bowed,
> Has wept for thee, calling to Jove aloud.
> Thee, gentle lady, did he disenthrall:
> Ye shall forever live and love, for all
>   Thy tears are flowing.—
> By Daphne's fright, behold Apollo!—"
>   More
> Endymion heard not: down his steed him bore,
> Prone to the green head of a misty hill.

---

601 **wedding lutes** The battle of the Centaurs and the Lapithae took place at the wedding of Pirithoüs and Hippodamia (Ovid, XII, ll. 210 ff.).   606 **Danae's son** Perseus, who freed Andromeda from the sea serpent that threatened to devour her.

His first touch of the earth went nigh to kill.
615 "Alas!" said he, "were I but always borne
Through dangerous winds, had but my footsteps worn
A path in hell, forever would I bless
Horrors which nourish an uneasiness
For my own sullen conquering: to him
620 Who lives beyond earth's boundary, grief is dim,
Sorrow is but a shadow: now I see
The grass; I feel the solid ground—Ah, me!
It is thy voice—divinest! Where?—who? who
Left thee so quiet on this bed of dew?
625 Behold upon this happy earth we are;
Let us aye love each other; let us fare
On forest fruits, and never, never go
Among the abodes of mortals here below,
Or be by phantoms duped. O destiny!
630 Into a labyrinth now my soul would fly,
But with thy beauty will I deaden it.
Where didst thou melt to? By thee will I sit
Forever: let our fate stop here—a kid
I on this spot will offer: Pan will bid
635 Us live in peace, in love and peace among
His forest wildernesses. I have clung
To nothing, loved a nothing, nothing seen
Or felt but a great dream! O I have been
Presumptuous against love, against the sky,
640 Against all elements, against the tie
Of mortals each to each, against the blooms
Of flowers, rush of rivers, and the tombs
Of heroes gone! Against his proper glory
Has my own soul conspired: so my story
645 Will I to children utter, and repent.
There never lived a mortal man, who bent
His appetite beyond his natural sphere,
But starved and died. My sweetest Indian, here,
Here will I kneel, for thou redeemèd hast
650 My life from too thin breathing: gone and past
Are cloudy phantasms. Caverns lone, farewell!
And air of visions, and the monstrous swell
Of visionary seas! No, never more

ENDYMION

Shall airy voices cheat me to the shore
Of tangled wonder, breathless and aghast.
Adieu, my daintiest dream! although so vast
My love is still for thee. The hour may come
When we shall meet in pure Elysium.
On earth I may not love thee; and therefore
Doves will I offer up, and sweetest store
All through the teeming year: so thou wilt shine
On me, and on this damsel fair of mine,
And bless our simple lives. My Indian bliss!
My river-lily bud! one human kiss!
One sigh of real breath—one gentle squeeze,
Warm as a dove's nest among summer trees,
And warm with dew at ooze from living blood!
Whither didst melt? Ah, what of that!—all good
We'll talk about—no more of dreaming.—Now,
Where shall our dwelling be? Under the brow
Of some steep mossy hill, where ivy dun
Would hide us up, although spring leaves were none;
And where dark yew trees, as we rustle through,
Will drop their scarlet berry cups of dew?
O thou wouldst joy to live in such a place;
Dusk for our loves, yet light enough to grace
Those gentle limbs on mossy bed reclined:
For by one step the blue sky shouldst thou find,
And by another, in deep dell below,
See, through the trees, a little river go
All in its midday gold and glimmering.
Honey from out the gnarlèd hive I'll bring,
And apples, wan with sweetness, gather thee—
Cresses that grow where no man may them see,
And sorrel untorn by the dew-clawed stag:
Pipes will I fashion of the syrinx flag,
That thou mayest always know whither I roam,
When it shall please thee in our quiet home
To listen and think of love. Still let me speak;
Still let me dive into the joy I seek—
For yet the past doth prison me. The rill,
Thou haply mayst delight in, will I fill
With fairy fishes from the mountain tarn,

And thou shalt feed them from the squirrel's barn.
Its bottom will I strew with amber shells,
And pebbles blue from deep enchanted wells.
Its sides I'll plant with dew-sweet eglantine,
And honeysuckles full of clear bee-wine.
I will entice this crystal rill to trace
Love's silver name upon the meadow's face.
I'll kneel to Vesta, for a flame of fire;
And to god Phœbus, for a golden lyre;
To empress Dian, for a hunting spear;
To Vesper, for a taper silver-clear,
That I may see thy beauty through the night;
To Flora, and a nightingale shall light
Tame on thy finger; to the river gods,
And they shall bring thee taper fishing-rods
Of gold, and lines of naiads' long bright tress.
Heaven shield thee for thine utter loveliness!
Thy mossy footstool shall the altar be
'Fore which I'll bend, bending, dear love, to thee:
Those lips shall be my Delphos, and shall speak
Laws to my footsteps, color to my cheek,
Trembling or steadfastness to this same voice,
And of three sweetest pleasurings the choice:
And that affectionate light, those diamond things,
Those eyes, those passions, those supreme pearl springs,
Shall be my grief, or twinkle me to pleasure.
Say, is not bliss within our perfect seizure?
O that I could not doubt!"

                              The mountaineer
Thus strove by fancies vain and crude to clear
His briered path to some tranquillity.
It gave bright gladness to his lady's eye,
And yet the tears she wept were tears of sorrow;
Answering thus, just as the golden morrow
Beamed upward from the valleys of the east:
"O that the flutter of this heart had ceased,
Or the sweet name of love had passed away.

Young feathered tyrant! by a swift decay 730
Wilt thou devote this body to the earth:
And I do think that at my very birth
I lisped thy blooming titles inwardly;
For at the first, first dawn and thought of thee,
With uplift hands I blessed the stars of heaven. 735
Art thou not cruel? Ever have I striven
To think thee kind, but ah, it will not do!
When yet a child, I heard that kisses drew
Favor from thee, and so I kisses gave
To the void air, bidding them find out love: 740
But when I came to feel how far above
All fancy, pride, and fickle maidenhood,
All earthly pleasure, all imagined good,
Was the warm tremble of a devout kiss—
Even then, that moment, at the thought of this, 745
Fainting I fell into a bed of flowers,
And languished there three days. Ye milder powers,
Am I not cruelly wronged? Believe, believe
Me, dear Endymion, were I to weave
With my own fancies garlands of sweet life, 750
Thou shouldst be one of all. Ah, bitter strife!
I may not be thy love: I am forbidden—
Indeed I am—thwarted, affrighted, chidden,
By things I trembled at, and gorgon wrath.
Twice hast thou asked whither I went: henceforth 755
Ask me no more! I may not utter it,
Nor may I be thy love. We might commit
Ourselves at once to vengeance; we might die;
We might embrace and die: voluptuous thought!
Enlarge not to my hunger, or I'm caught 760
In trammels of perverse deliciousness.
No, no, that shall not be: thee will I bless,
And bid a long adieu."

The Carian

No word returned: both lovelorn, silent, wan,
Into the valleys green together went. 765
Far wandering, they were perforce content

To sit beneath a fair lone beechen tree;
Nor at each other gazed, but heavily
Pored on its hazel cirque of shedded leaves.

770   Endymion! unhappy! it nigh grieves
Me to behold thee thus in last extreme:
Enskyed ere this, but truly that I deem
Truth the best music in a first-born song.
Thy lute-voiced brother° will I sing ere long,
775 And thou shalt aid—hast thou not aided me?
Yes, moonlight emperor! felicity
Has been thy meed for many thousand years;
Yet often have I, on the brink of tears,
Mourned as if yet thou wert a forester;—
Forgetting the old tale.

780   He did not stir
His eyes from the dead leaves, or one small pulse
Of joy he might have felt. The spirit culls
Unfaded amaranth, when wild it strays
Through the old garden-ground of boyish days.
785 A little onward ran the very stream
By which he took his first soft poppy dream;
And on the very bark 'gainst which he leant
A crescent he had carved, and round it spent
His skill in little stars. The teeming tree
790 Had swollen and greened the pious charactery,
But not ta'en out. Why, there was not a slope
Up which he had not feared the antelope;
And not a tree, beneath whose rooty shade
He had not with his tamed leopards played.
795 Nor could an arrow light, or javelin,
Fly in the air where his had never been—
And yet he knew it not.

                            O treachery!
Why does his lady smile, pleasing her eye
With all his sorrowing? He sees her not.

774 **thy lute-voiced brother** announces Keats's next major poem, *Hyperion*.

ENDYMION 197

But who so stares on him? His sister sure!   800
Peona of the woods!—Can she endure—
Impossible—how dearly they embrace!
His lady smiles; delight is in her face;
It is no treachery.

                    "Dear brother mine!
Endymion, weep not so! Why shouldst thou pine   805
When all great Latmos so exalt will be?
Thank the great gods, and look not bitterly;
And speak not one pale word, and sigh no more.
Sure I will not believe thou hast such store
Of grief, to last thee to my kiss again.   810
Thou surely canst not bear a mind in pain,
Come hand in hand with one so beautiful.
Be happy both of you! for I will pull
The flowers of autumn for your coronals.
Pan's holy priest for young Endymion calls   815
And when he is restored, thou, fairest dame,
Shalt be our queen. Now, is it not a shame
To see ye thus—not very, very sad?
Perhaps ye are too happy to be glad:
O feel as if it were a common day;   820
Free-voiced as one who never was away.
No tongue shall ask, whence come ye? but ye shall
Be gods of your own rest imperial.
Not even I, for one whole month, will pry
Into the hours that have passed us by,   825
Since in my arbor I did sing to thee.
O Hermes! on this very night will be
A hymning up to Cynthia, queen of light;
For the soothsayers old saw yesternight
Good visions in the air—whence will befall,   830
As say these sages, health perpetual
To shepherds and their flocks; and furthermore,
In Dian's face they read the gentle lore:
Therefore for her these vesper-carols are.
Our friends will all be there from nigh and far.   835
Many upon thy death have ditties made;
And many, even now, their foreheads shade

With cypress, on a day of sacrifice.
New singing for our maids shalt thou devise,
840 And pluck the sorrow from our huntsmen's brows.
Tell me, my lady queen, how to espouse
This wayward brother to his rightful joys!
His eyes are on thee bent, as thou didst poise
His fate most goddess-like. Help me, I pray,
845 To lure—Endymion! Dear brother, say
What ails thee?" He could bear no more, and so
Bent his soul fiercely like a spiritual bow,
And twanged it inwardly, and calmly said:
"I would have thee my only friend, sweet maid!
850 My only visitor! not ignorant though,
That those deceptions which for pleasure go
'Mong men, are pleasures real as real may be:
But there are higher ones I may not see,
If impiously an earthly realm I take.
855 Since I saw thee, I have been wide awake
Night after night, and day by day, until
Of the empyrean I have drunk my fill.
Let it content thee, sister, seeing me
More happy than betides mortality.
860 A hermit young, I'll live in mossy cave,
Where thou alone shalt come to me, and lave
Thy spirit in the wonders I shall tell.
Through me the shepherd realm shall prosper well;
For to thy tongue will I all health confide.
865 And, for my sake, let this young maid abide
With thee as a dear sister. Thou alone,
Peona, mayst return to me. I own
This may sound strangely: but when, dearest girl,
Thou seest it for my happiness, no pearl
870 Will trespass down those cheeks. Companion fair!
Wilt be content to dwell with her, to share
This sister's love with me?" Like one resigned
And bent by circumstance, and thereby blind
In self-commitment, thus that meek unknown:
875 "Aye, but a buzzing by my ears has flown,
Of jubilee to Dian:—truth I heard?
Well then, I see there is no little bird,

ENDYMION

Tender soever, but is Jove's own care.
Long have I sought for rest, and, unaware,
Behold I find it! so exalted too! 880
So after my own heart! I knew, I knew
There was a place untenanted in it:
In that same void white chastity shall sit,
And monitor me nightly to lone slumber.
With sanest lips I vow me to the number 885
Of Dian's sisterhood; and, kind lady,
With thy good help, this very night shall see
My future days to her fane consecrate."

As feels a dreamer what doth most create
His own particular fright, so these three felt: 890
Or like one who, in after ages, knelt
To Lucifer or Baal, when he'd pine
After a little sleep: or when in mine
Far underground, a sleeper meets his friends
Who know him not. Each diligently bends 895
Towards common thoughts and things for very fear;
Striving their ghastly malady to cheer,
By thinking it a thing of yes and no,
That housewives talk of. But the spirit-blow
Was struck, and all were dreamers. At the last 900
Endymion said: "Are not our fates all cast?
Why stand we here? Adieu, ye tender pair!
Adieu!" Whereat those maidens, with wild stare,
Walked dizzily away. Pained and hot
His eyes went after them, until they got 905
Near to a cypress grove, whose deadly maw,
In one swift moment, would what then he saw
Engulf forever. "Stay!" he cried, "ah, stay!
Turn, damsels! hist! one word I have to say:
Sweet Indian, I would see thee once again. 910
It is a thing I dote on: so I'd fain,
Peona, ye should hand in hand repair
Into those holy groves, that silent are
Behind great Dian's temple. I'll be yon,
At Vesper's earliest twinkle—they are gone— 915
But once, once, once again—" At this he pressed

His hands against his face, and then did rest
His head upon a mossy hillock green,
And so remained as he a corpse had been
920 All the long day; save when he scantly lifted
His eyes abroad, to see how shadows shifted
With the slow move of time—sluggish and weary
Until the poplar tops, in journey dreary,
Had reached the river's brim. Then up he rose,
925 And, slowly as that very river flows,
Walked towards the temple grove with this lament:
"Why such a golden eve? The breeze is sent
Careful and soft, that not a leaf may fall
Before the serene father of them all
930 Bows down his summer head below the west.
Now am I of breath, speech, and speed possessed,
But at the setting I must bid adieu
To her for the last time. Night will strew
On the damp grass myriads of lingering leaves,
935 And with them shall I die; nor much it grieves
To die, when summer dies on the cold sward.
Why, I have been a butterfly, a lord
Of flowers, garlands, love knots, silly posies,
Groves, meadows, melodies, and arbor roses;
940 My kingdom's at its death, and just it is
That I should die with it: so in all this
We miscall grief, bale, sorrow, heartbreak, woe,
What is there to plain of? By Titan's foe
I am but rightly served." So saying, he
945 Tripped lightly on, in sort of deathful glee
Laughing at the clear stream and setting sun,
As though they jests had been: nor had he done
His laugh at nature's holy countenance,
Until that grove appeared, as if perchance,
950 And then his tongue with sober seemlihead
Gave utterance as he entered: "Ha!" I said,
"King of the butterflies; but by this gloom,
And by old Rhadamanthus' tongue of doom,
This dusk religion, pomp of solitude,
955 And the Promethean clay by thief endued,
By old Saturnus' forelock, by his head

ENDYMION

Shook with eternal palsy, I did wed
Myself to things of light from infancy;
And thus to be cast out, thus lorn to die,
Is sure enough to make a mortal man
Grow impious." So he inwardly began
On things for which no wording can be found;
Deeper and deeper sinking, until drowned
Beyond the reach of music: for the choir
Of Cynthia he heard not, though rough brier
Nor muffling thicket interposed to dull
The vesper hymn, far swollen, soft and full,
Through the dark pillars of those sylvan aisles.
He saw not the two maidens, nor their smiles,
Wan as primroses gathered at midnight
By chilly fingered spring. "Unhappy wight!
Endymion!" said Peona, "we are here!
What wouldst thou ere we all are laid on bier?"
Then he embraced her, and his lady's hand
Pressed, saying: "Sister, I would have command,
If it were heaven's will, on our sad fate."
At which that dark-eyed stranger stood elate
And said, in a new voice, but sweet as love,
To Endymion's amaze: "By Cupid's dove,
And so thou shalt! and by the lily truth
Of my own breast thou shalt, belovèd youth!"
And as she spake, into her face there came
Light, as reflected from a silver flame:
Her long black hair swelled ampler, in display
Full golden; in her eyes a brighter day
Dawned blue and full of love. Aye, he beheld
Phœbe, his passion! joyous she upheld
Her lucid bow, continuing thus; "Drear, drear
Has our delaying been; but foolish fear
Withheld me first; and then decrees of fate;
And then 'twas fit that from this mortal state
Thou shouldst, my love, by some unlooked for change
Be spiritualized. Peona, we shall range
These forests, and to thee they safe shall be
As was thy cradle; hither shalt thou flee
To meet us many a time." Next Cynthia bright

Peona kissed, and blessed with fair good night:
Her brother kissed her too, and knelt adown
Before his goddess, in a blissful swoon.
She gave her fair hands to him, and behold,
Before three swiftest kisses he had told,
They vanished far away!—Peona went
Home through the gloomy wood in wonderment.

II. The Middle Period

HYPERION°

A Fragment

Book I

Deep in the shady sadness of a vale
Far sunken from the healthy breath of morn,
Far from the fiery noon, and eve's one star,
Sat gray-haired Saturn, quiet as a stone,
Still as the silence round about his lair; 5
Forest on forest hung above his head
Like cloud on cloud. No stir of air was there,
Not so much life as on a summer's day
Robs not one light seed from the feathered grass,
But where the dead leaf fell, there did it rest. 10

---

0 **Hyperion** The fragment, Keats's unfinished epic, was written between September, 1818, and early spring, 1819, after Keats's return from a walking trip with Charles Brown in Scotland and while nursing his brother Tom, who died on December 1, 1818. The plan to write *Hyperion* goes back to the late summer of 1817 and is referred to in *Endymion*. The story of the war of the Titans is told briefly in Ovid's *Metamorphoses,* in Hesiod's *Works and Days* (translated by Chapman) and his *Theogony*. The main influence in the epic is, of course, that of Milton's *Paradise Lost* from which Keats borrows the blank verse, the general epic mode, the dramatic situation and numberless stylistic and thematic features. The action begins after the Titans have been defeated by the new Olympian gods, with only the sun god Hyperion still free.

A stream went voiceless by, still deadened more
By reason of his fallen divinity
Spreading a shade: the naiad 'mid her reeds
Pressed her cold finger closer to her lips.

15   Along the margin-sand large foot marks went,
No further than to where his feet had strayed,
And slept there since. Upon the sodden ground
His old right hand lay nerveless, listless, dead,
Unsceptered; and his realmless eyes were closed;
20 While his bowed head seemed list'ning to the Earth,
His ancient mother, for some comfort yet.

It seemed no force could wake him from his place;
But there came one, who with a kindred hand
Touched his wide shoulders, after bending low
25 With reverence, though to one who knew it not.
She was a goddess of the infant world;
By her in stature the tall Amazon
Had stood a pygmy's height: she would have ta'en
Achilles by the hair and bent his neck;
30 Or with a finger stayed Ixion's° wheel.
Her face was large as that of Memphian sphinx,°
Pedestaled haply in a palace court,
When sages looked to Egypt for their lore.
But oh! how unlike marble was that face:
35 How beautiful, if sorrow had not made
Sorrow more beautiful than Beauty's self.
There was a listening fear in her regard,
As if calamity had but begun;
As if the vanward clouds of evil days
40 Had spent their malice, and the sullen rear
Was with its stored thunder laboring up.
One hand she pressed upon that aching spot
Where beats the human heart, as if just there,
Though an immortal, she felt cruel pain:

---

30 **Ixion** king of the Lapithae, who was bound to a whirling wheel in the Underworld for having attacked Juno.   31 **sphinx** The Egyptian sources of much decorative detail in *Hyperion* have been studied, a. o. by Helen Darbishire (*RES*, III, January, 1927).

The other upon Saturn's bended neck
She laid, and to the level of his ear
Leaning with parted lips, some words she spake
In solemn tenor and deep organ tone:
Some mourning words, which in our feeble tongue
Would come in these like accents; O how frail
To that large utterance of the early Gods!
"Saturn, look up!—though wherefore, poor old King?
I have no comfort for thee, no not one:
I cannot say, 'O wherefore sleepest thou?'
For heaven is parted from thee, and the earth
Knows thee not, thus afflicted, for a God;
And ocean too, with all its solemn noise,
Has from thy scepter passed; and all the air
Is emptied of thine hoary majesty.
Thy thunder, conscious of the new command,
Rumbles reluctant o'er our fallen house;
And thy sharp lightning in unpracticed hands
Scorches and burns our once serene domain.
O aching time! O moments big as years!
All as ye pass swell out the monstrous truth,
And press it so upon our weary griefs
That unbelief has not a space to breathe.
Saturn, sleep on:—O thoughtless, why did I
Thus violate thy slumbrous solitude?
Why should I ope thy melancholy eyes?
Saturn, sleep on! while at thy feet I weep."

As when, upon a trancèd summer night,
Those green-robed senators of mighty woods,
Tall oaks, branch-charmèd by the earnest stars,
Dream, and so dream all night without a stir,
Save from one gradual solitary gust
Which comes upon the silence, and dies off,
As if the ebbing air had but one wave;
So came these words and went; the while in tears
She touched her fair large forehead to the ground,
Just where her fallen hair might be outspread
A soft and silken mat for Saturn's feet.
One moon, with alteration slow, had shed

Her silver seasons four upon the night,
And still these two were postured motionless,
Like natural sculpture in cathedral cavern;
The frozen God still couchant on the earth,
And the sad Goddess weeping at his feet:
Until at length old Saturn lifted up
His faded eyes, and saw his kingdom gone,
And all the gloom and sorrow of the place,
And that fair kneeling Goddess; and then spake,
As with a palsied tongue, and while his beard
Shook horrid with such aspen-malady:
"O tender spouse of gold Hyperion,
Thea,° I feel thee ere I see thy face;
Look up, and let me see our doom in it;
Look up, and tell me if this feeble shape
Is Saturn's; tell me, if thou hear'st the voice
Of Saturn; tell me, if this wrinkling brow,
Naked and bare of its great diadem,
Peers like the front of Saturn. Who had power
To make me desolate? whence came the strength?
How was it nurtured to such bursting forth,
While fate seemed strangled in my nervous grasp?
But it is so; and I am smothered up,
And buried from all god-like exercise
Of influence benign on planets pale,
Of admonitions to the winds and seas,
Of peaceful sway above man's harvesting,
And all those acts which Deity supreme
Doth ease its heart of love in.—I am gone
Away from my own bosom: I have left
My strong identity, my real self,
Somewhere between the throne, and where I sit
Here on this spot of earth. Search, Thea, search!
Open thine eyes eterne, and sphere them round
Upon all space: space starred, and lorn of light;
Space regioned with life-air; and barren void;
Spaces of fire, and all the yawn of hell.—

---

96 **Thea** wife of Hyperion, presumably the moon. The prominence of her part may be due to Keats's preference for the moon goddess Diana (Artemis).

Search, Thea, search! and tell me, if thou seest
A certain shape or shadow, making way
With wings or chariot fierce to repossess
A heaven he lost erewhile: it must—it must
Be of ripe progress—Saturn must be king. 125
Yes, there must be a golden victory;
There must be Gods thrown down, and trumpets blown
Of triumph calm, and hymns of festival
Upon the gold clouds metropolitan,
Voices of soft proclaim, and silver stir 130
Of strings in hollow shells; and there shall be
Beautiful things made new, for the surprise
Of the sky-children; I will give command:
Thea! Thea! Thea! where is Saturn?"

    This passion lifted him upon his feet, 135
And made his hands to struggle in the air,
His Druid locks to shake and ooze with sweat,
His eyes to fever out, his voice to cease.
He stood, and heard not Thea's sobbing deep;
A little time, and then again he snatched 140
Utterance thus.—"But cannot I create?
Cannot I form? Cannot I fashion forth
Another world, another universe,
To overbear and crumble this to nought?
Where is another Chaos? Where?"—That word 145
Found way unto Olympus, and made quake
The rebel three.°—Thea was startled up,
And in her bearing was a sort of hope,
As thus she quick-voiced spake, yet full of awe.

    "This cheers our fallen house: come to our friends, 150
O Saturn! come away, and give them heart;
I know the covert, for thence came I hither."
Thus brief; then with beseeching eyes she went
With backward footing through the shade a space:
He followed, and she turned to lead the way 155

---

147 **rebel three** the leaders of the new gods, Jupiter, Neptune, and Pluto (Zeus, Poseidon, and Hades).

Through agèd boughs, that yielded like the mist
Which eagles cleave upmounting from their nest.

Meanwhile in other realms big tears were shed,
More sorrow like to this, and such like woe,
Too huge for mortal tongue or pen of scribe:
The Titans fierce, self-hid, or prison-bound,
Groaned for the old allegiance once more,
And listened in sharp pain for Saturn's voice.
But one of the whole mammoth-brood still kept
His sov'reignty, and rule, and majesty;
Blazing Hyperion on his orbèd fire
Still sat, still snuffed the incense, teeming up
From Man to the sun's God; yet unsecure:
For as among us mortals omens drear
Fright and perplex, so also shuddered he—
Not at dog's howl, or gloom-bird's hated screech,
Or the familiar visiting of one
Upon the first toll of his passing-bell,
Or prophesyings of the midnight lamp;
But horrors, portioned to a giant nerve,
Oft made Hyperion ache. His palace bright
Bastioned with pyramids of glowing gold,
And touched with shade of bronzed obelisks,
Glared a blood-red through all its thousand courts,
Arches, and domes, and fiery galleries;
And all its curtains of Aurorian clouds
Flushed angerly: while sometimes eagle's wings,
Unseen before by Gods or wondering men,
Darkened the place; and neighing steeds were heard,
Not heard before by Gods or wondering men.
Also, when he would taste the spicy wreaths
Of incense, breathed aloft from sacred hills,
Instead of sweets, his ample palate took
Savor of poisonous brass and metal sick:
And so, when harbored in the sleepy west,
After the full completion of fair day—
For rest divine upon exalted couch
And slumber in the arms of melody,

He paced away the pleasant hours of ease
With stride colossal, on from hall to hall; 195
While far within each aisle and deep recess,
His wingèd minions in close clusters stood,
Amazed and full of fear; like anxious men
Who on wide plains gather in panting troops,
When earthquakes jar their battlements and towers. 200
Even now, while Saturn, roused from icy trance,
Went step for step with Thea through the woods,
Hyperion, leaving twilight in the rear,
Came slope upon the threshold of the west;
Then, as was wont, his palace door flew ope 205
In smoothest silence, save what solemn tubes,
Blown by the serious Zephyrs, gave of sweet
And wandering sounds, slow-breathèd melodies;
And like a rose in vermeil tint and shape,
In fragrance soft, and coolness to the eye, 210
That inlet to severe magnificence
Stood full blown, for the God to enter in.

He entered, but he entered full of wrath;
His flaming robes streamed out beyond his heels,
And gave a roar, as if of earthly fire, 215
That scared away the meek ethereal Hours
And made their dove-wings tremble. On he flared,
From stately nave to nave, from vault to vault,
Through bowers of fragrant and enwreathèd light,
And diamond-pavèd lustrous long arcades, 220
Until he reached the great main cupola;
There standing fierce beneath, he stamped his foot,
And from the basements deep to the high towers
Jarred his own golden region; and before
The quavering thunder thereupon had ceased, 225
His voice leaped out, despite of god-like curb,
To this result: "O dreams of day and night!
O monstrous form! O effigies of pain!
O specters busy in a cold, cold gloom!
O lank-eared phantoms of black-weeded pools! 230
Why do I know ye? why have I seen ye? why

Is my eternal essence thus distraught
To see and to behold these horrors new?
Saturn is fallen, am I too to fall?
Am I to leave this haven of my rest,
This cradle of my glory, this soft clime,
This calm luxuriance of blissful light,
These crystalline pavilions, and pure fanes,
Of all my lucent empire? It is left
Deserted, void, nor any haunt of mine.
The blaze, the splendor, and the symmetry
I cannot see—but darkness, death and darkness.
Even here, into my center of repose,
The shady visions come to domineer,
Insult, and blind, and stifle up my pomp.—
Fall!—No, by Tellus° and her briny robes!
Over the fiery frontier of my realms
I will advance a terrible right arm
Shall scare that infant thunderer, rebel Jove,
And bid old Saturn take his throne again."—
He spake, and ceased, the while a heavier threat
Held struggle with his throat but came not forth;
For as in theaters of crowded men
Hubbub increases more they call out "Hush!"
So at Hyperion's words the phantoms pale
Bestirred themselves, thrice horrible and cold;
And from the mirrored level where he stood
A mist arose, as from a scummy marsh.
At this, through all his bulk an agony
Crept gradual, from the feet unto the crown,
Like a lithe serpent vast and muscular
Making slow way, with head and neck convulsed
From overstrainèd might. Released, he fled
To the eastern gates, and full six dewy hours
Before the dawn in season due should blush,
He breathed fierce breath against the sleepy portals,
Cleared them of heavy vapors, burst them wide
Suddenly on the ocean's chilly streams.
The planet orb of fire, whereon he rode

246 **Tellus** the earth goddess.

HYPERION

Each day from east to west the heavens through, 270
Spun round in sable curtaining of clouds;
Not therefore veilèd quite, blindfold, and hid,
But ever and anon the glancing spheres,
Circles, and arcs, and broad-belting colure,
Glowed through, and wrought upon the muffling dark 275
Sweet-shaped lightnings from the nadir deep
Up to the zenith—hieroglyphics old,
Which sages and keen-eyed astrologers
Then living on the earth, with laboring thought
Won from the gaze of many centuries: 280
Now lost, save what we find on remnants huge
Of stone, or marble swart; their import gone,
Their wisdom long since fled.—Two wings this orb
Possessed for glory, two fair argent wings,
Ever exalted at the God's approach 285
And now, from forth the gloom their plumes immense
Rose, one by one, till all outspreaded were;
While still the dazzling globe maintained eclipse,
Awaiting for Hyperion's command.
Fain would he have commanded, fain took throne 290
And bid the day begin, if but for change.
He might not.°—No, though a primeval God:
The sacred seasons might not be disturbed.
Therefore the operations of the dawn
Stayed in their birth, even as here 'tis told. 295
Those silver wings expanded sisterly,
Eager to sail their orb; the porches wide
Opened upon the dusk demesnes of night
And the bright Titan, frenzied with new woes,
Unused to bend, by hard compulsion bent 300
His spirit to the sorrow of the time;
And all along a dismal rack of clouds,
Upon the boundaries of day and night,
He stretched himself in grief and radiance faint.
There as he lay, the Heaven with its stars 305
Looked down on him with pity, and the voice

---

292 **He might not** Hyperion tried to make the dawn begin six hours earlier (l. 264), but failed.

Of Cœlus,° from the universal space,
Thus whispered low and solemn in his ear.
"O brightest of my children dear, earth-born
310 And sky-engendered, son of mysteries
All unrevealèd even to the powers
Which met at thy creating; at whose joys
And palpitations sweet, and pleasures soft,
I, Cœlus, wonder, how they came and whence;
315 And at the fruits thereof what shapes they be,
Distinct, and visible; symbols divine,
Manifestations of that beauteous life
Diffused unseen throughout eternal space:
Of these new-formed art thou, oh brightest child!
320 Of these, thy brethren and the Goddesses!
There is sad feud among ye, and rebellion
Of son against his sire. I saw him fall,
I saw my first-born tumbled from his throne!
To me his arms were spread, to me his voice
325 Found way from forth the thunders round his head!
Pale wox I, and in vapors hid my face.
Art thou, too, near such doom? vague fear there is:
For I have seen my sons most unlike Gods.
Divine ye were created, and divine
330 In sad demeanor, solemn, undisturbed,
Unruffled, like high Gods, ye lived and ruled:
Now I behold in you fear, hope, and wrath;
Actions of rage and passion; even as
I see them, on the mortal world beneath,
335 In men who die.—This is the grief, O son!
Sad sign of ruin, sudden dismay, and fall!
Yet do thou strive; as thou art capable,
As thou canst move about, an evident God;

---

307 **Cœlus** the sky, also Uranus. The ensuing passage (ll. 309–319) establishes a distinction between the pure, elemental forces of nature that are diffuse and omnipresent, such as light, and the incarnated world of all earthly forms, natural and human. As one passes from Coelus to Hyperion, from an elemental to a natural world, one may surmise that, from Hyperion to Apollo, one passes from a natural to a human world. A similar hierarchy, from Chaos to Light to Heavens and finally reaching Earth, is set up in Oceanus's speech (II, ll. 191 ff.).

HYPERION   215

And canst oppose to each malignant hour
Ethereal presence:—I am but a voice;   340
My life is but the life of winds and tides,
No more than winds and tides can I avail:—
But thou canst.—Be thou therefore in the van
Of circumstance; yea, seize the arrow's barb
Before the tense string murmur.—To the earth!   345
For there thou wilt find Saturn, and his woes.
Meantime I will keep watch on thy bright sun,
And of thy seasons be a careful nurse."—
Ere half this region-whisper had come down,
Hyperion arose, and on the stars   350
Lifted his curvèd lids, and kept them wide
Until it ceased; and still he kept them wide:
And still they were the same bright, patient stars.
Then with a slow incline of his broad breast,
Like to a diver in the pearly seas,   355
Forward he stooped over the airy shore,
And plunged all noiseless into the deep night.

Book II

Just at the self-same beat of Time's wide wings
Hyperion slid into the rustled air,
And Saturn gained with Thea that sad place
Where Cybele° and the bruised Titans mourned.
It was a den where no insulting light   5
Could glimmer on their tears; where their own groans
They felt, but heard not, for the solid roar
Of thunderous waterfalls and torrents hoarse,
Pouring a constant bulk, uncertain where.
Crag jutting forth to crag, and rocks that seemed   10
Ever as if just rising from a sleep,
Forehead to forehead held their monstrous horns;
And thus in thousand hugest fantasies
Made a fit roofing to this nest of woe.
Instead of thrones, hard flint they sat upon,   15

4 **Cybele** identical here with Rhea, wife of Cronus (Saturn) and mother of the gods.

HYPERION

Couches of rugged stone, and slaty ridge
Stubborned with iron. All were not assembled:
Some chained in torture, and some wandering.
Cœus, and Gyges, and Briareüs,
Typhon, and Dolor, and Porphyrion,° 20
With many more, the brawniest in assault,
Were pent in regions of laborious breath;
Dungeoned in opaque element, to keep
Their clenchèd teeth still clenched, and all their limbs
Locked up like veins of metal, cramped and screwed; 25
Without a motion, save of their big hearts
Heaving in pain, and horribly convulsed
With sanguine feverous boiling gurge of pulse.
Mnemosyne° was straying in the world;
Far from her moon had Phœbe° wandered; 30
And many else were free to roam abroad,
But for the main, here found they covert drear.
Scarce images of life, one here, one there,
Lay vast and edgeways; like a dismal cirque
Of Druid stones, upon a forlorn moor, 35
When the chill rain° begins at shut of eve,
In dull November, and their chancel vault,
The Heaven itself, is blinded throughout night.
Each one kept shroud, nor to his neighbor gave
Or word, or look, or action of despair. 40
Creüs was one; his ponderous iron mace
Lay by him, and a shattered rib of rock
Told of his rage, ere he thus sank and pined.
Iäpetus another; in his grasp,
A serpent's plashy neck; its barbed tongue 45
Squeezed from the gorge, and all its uncurled length

---

20 **Porphyrion** The names attributed to the Titans indicate Keats's mixed sources. They derive from Hesiod's *Theogony* and from Celtic and various other sources. Such mixtures of mythologies are frequent in Milton.   29 **Mnemosyne** Memory, the mother of the Muses, daughter of heaven and earth. No reference is made at this point to the role Mnemosyne will play in Book III as the mentor of Apollo. 30 **Phœbe** a Titan, mother of Leto who, in turn, gave birth to the moon goddess Artemis. Keats amalgamates grandmother and granddaughter into one person.   36 **chill rain** Keats had very recent memories of this "chill rain" from his Scottish tour, during which he hardly ever caught a glimpse of sunshine.

HYPERION   217

Dead; and because the creature could not spit
Its poison in the eyes of conquering Jove.
Next Cottus: prone he lay, chin uppermost,
As though in pain; for still upon the flint   50
He ground severe his skull, with open mouth
And eyes at horrid working. Nearest him
Asia, born of most enormous Caf,
Who cost her mother Tellus keener pangs,
Though feminine, than any of her sons: 55
More thought than woe was in her dusky face,
For she was prophesying of her glory;
And in her wide imagination stood
Palm-shaded temples, and high rival fanes,
By Oxus or in Ganges' sacred isles.   60
Even as Hope upon her anchor leans,
So leaned she, not so fair, upon a tusk
Shed from the broadest of her elephants.
Above her, on a crag's uneasy shelve,
Upon his elbow raised, all prostrate else,   65
Shadowed Enceladus;° once tame and mild
As grazing ox unworried in the meads;
Now tiger-passioned, lion-thoughted, wroth,
He meditated, plotted, and even now
Was hurling mountains in that second war,   70
Not long delayed, that scared the younger gods
To hide themselves in forms of beast and bird.
Not far hence Atlas; and beside him prone
Phorcus, the sire of Gorgons. Neighbored close
Oceanus, and Tethys, in whose lap   75
Sobbed Clymene° among her tangled hair.
In midst of all lay Themis, at the feet
Of Ops° the queen; all clouded round from sight,
No shape distinguishable, more than when
Thick night confounds the pine-tops with the clouds: 80
And many else whose names may not be told.

66 **Enceladus** The identity of the various Titans mentioned in this catalog is a clue to possible sources. Many of the details come from Milton, Sandys, and, in this case, Spenser. 76 **Clymene** who is given a speech later (ll. 252 ff.) is the daughter of Oceanus and Tethys and will be loved by Apollo. 78 **Ops** still another name for the wife of Saturn (Cybele, Rhea).

For when the Muse's wings are air-ward spread,
Who shall delay her flight? And she must chaunt
Of Saturn, and his guide, who now had climbed
85 With damp and slippery footing from a depth
More horrid still. Above a somber cliff
Their heads appeared, and up their stature grew
Till on the level height their steps found ease:
Then Thea° spread abroad her trembling arms
90 Upon the precincts of this nest of pain,
And sidelong fixed her eye on Saturn's face:
There saw she direst strife; the supreme God
At war with all the frailty of grief,
Of rage, of fear, anxiety, revenge,
95 Remorse, spleen, hope, but most of all despair.
Against these plagues he strove in vain; for Fate
Had poured a mortal oil upon his head,
A disanointing poison: so that Thea,
Affrighted, kept her still, and let him pass
100 First onwards in, among the fallen tribe.

As with us mortal men, the laden heart
Is persecuted more, and fevered more,
When it is nighing to the mournful house
Where other hearts are sick of the same bruise;
105 So Saturn, as he walked into the midst,
Felt faint, and would have sunk among the rest,
But that he met Enceladus's eye,
Whose mightiness, and awe of him, at once
Came like an inspiration; and he shouted,
110 "Titans, behold your God!" at which some groaned;
Some started on their feet; some also shouted;
Some wept, some wailed, all bowed with reverence;
And Ops, uplifting her black folded veil,
Showed her pale cheeks, and all her forehead wan,
115 Her eyebrows thin and jet, and hollow eyes.
There is a roaring in the bleak-grown pines
When Winter lifts his voice; there is a noise
Among immortals when a God gives sign,

---

89 **Thea** already appeared in Book I, line 96.

With hushing finger, how he means to load
His tongue with the full weight of utterless thought, 120
With thunder, and with music, and with pomp:
Such noise is like the roar of bleak-grown pines;
Which, when it ceases in this mountained world,
No other sound succeeds; but ceasing here,
Among these fallen, Saturn's voice therefrom 125
Grew up like organ, that begins anew
Its strain, when other harmonies, stopped short,
Leave the dinned air vibrating silverly.
Thus grew it up—"Not in my own sad breast,
Which is its own great judge and searcher out, 130
Can I find reason why ye should be thus:
Not in the legends of the first of days,
Studied from that old spirit-leavèd book
Which starry Uranus with finger bright
Saved from the shores of darkness, when the waves 135
Low-ebbed still hid it up in shallow gloom;—
And the which book ye know I ever kept
For my firm-based footstool:—Ah, infirm!
Not there, nor in sign, symbol, or portent
Of element, earth, water, air, and fire— 140
At war, at peace, or inter-quarreling
One against one, or two, or three, or all
Each several one against the other three,
As fire with air loud warring when rain-floods
Drown both, and press them both against earth's face. 145
Where, finding sulfur, a quadruple wrath
Unhinges the poor world;—not in that strife,
Wherefrom I take strange lore, and read it deep,
Can I find reason why ye should be thus:
No, nowhere can unriddle, though I search, 150
And pore on Nature's universal scroll
Even to swooning, why ye, Divinities,
The first-born of all shaped and palpable Gods,
Should cower beneath what, in comparison,
Is untremendous might. Yet ye are here, 155
O'erwhelmed, and spurned, and battered, ye are here!
O Titans, shall I say 'Arise!'—Ye groan:
Shall I say 'Crouch!'—Ye groan. What can I then?

O Heaven wide! O unseen parent dear!
What can I? Tell me, all ye brethren Gods,
How we can war, how engine our great wrath!
O speak your counsel now, for Saturn's ear
Is all ahungered. Thou, Oceanus,°
Ponderest high and deep; and in thy face
I see, astonied, that severe content
Which comes of thought and musing: give us help!"

So ended Saturn; and the God of the Sea,
Sophist and sage, from no Athenian grove,
But cogitation in his watery shades,
Arose, with locks not oozy, and began,
In murmurs, which his first-endeavoring° tongue
Caught infant-like from the far-foamèd sands.
"O ye, whom wrath consumes! who, passion-stung,
Writhe at defeat, and nurse your agonies!
Shut up your senses, stifle up your ears,
My voice is not a bellows unto ire.
Yet listen, ye who will, whilst I bring proof
How ye, perforce, must be content to stoop:
And in the proof much comfort will I give,
If ye will take that comfort in its truth.
We fall by course of Nature's law, not force
Of thunder, or of Jove. Great Saturn, thou
Hast sifted well the atom-universe;
But for this reason, that thou art the King,
And only blind from sheer supremacy,
One avenue was shaded from thine eyes,
Through which I wandered to eternal truth.
And first, as thou wast not the first of powers,
So art thou not the last; it cannot be:
Thou art not the beginning nor the end.
From Chaos and parental Darkness came
Light, the first fruits of that intestine broil,
That sullen ferment, which for wondrous ends
Was ripening in itself. The ripe hour came,

---

163 **Oceanus** god of the sea, who was the only Titan to refuse to join in the war against the Olympian gods.   171 **first-endeavoring** The wisdom has been his since childhood.

And with it Light, and Light, engendering 195
Upon its own producer, forthwith touched
The whole enormous matter into Life.
Upon that very hour, our parentage,
The Heavens and the Earth, were manifest:
Then thou first-born, and we the giant race, 200
Found ourselves ruling new and beauteous realms.
Now comes the pain of truth, to whom 'tis pain;
O folly! for to bear all naked truths,
And to envisage circumstance, all calm,
That is the top of sovereignty. Mark well! 205
As Heaven and Earth are fairer, fairer far
Than Chaos and blank Darkness, though once chiefs;
And as we show beyond that Heaven and Earth
In form and shape compact and beautiful,
In will, in action free, companionship, 210
And thousand other signs of purer life;
So on our heels a fresh perfection treads,
A power more strong in beauty, born of us
And fated to excel us, as we pass
In glory that old Darkness: nor are we 215
Thereby more conquered, than by us the rule
Of shapeless Chaos. Say, doth the dull soil
Quarrel with the proud forests it hath fed,
And feedeth still, more comely than itself?
Can it deny the chiefdom of green groves? 220
Or shall the tree be envious of the dove
Because it cooeth, and hath snowy wings
To wander wherewithal and find its joys?
We are such forest trees, and our fair boughs
Have bred forth, not pale solitary doves, 225
But eagles golden-feathered, who do tower
Above us in their beauty, and must reign
In right thereof; for 'tis the eternal law
That first in beauty should be first in might:
Yea, by that law, another race may drive 230
Our conquerors to mourn as we do now.
Have ye beheld the young God of the Seas,°

232 **God of the Seas** Neptune.

My dispossessor? Have ye seen his face?
Have ye beheld his chariot, foamed along
By noble wingèd creatures he hath made?
I saw him on the calmed waters scud,
With such a glow of beauty in his eyes,
That it enforced me to bid sad farewell
To all my empire: farewell sad I took,
And hither came, to see how dolorous fate
Had wrought upon ye; and how I might best
Give consolation in this woe extreme.
Receive the truth, and let it be your balm."

Whether through posed conviction, or disdain,
They guarded silence, when Oceanus
Left murmuring, what deepest thought can tell?
But so it was, none answered for a space,
Save one whom none regarded, Clymene;
And yet she answered not, only complained,
With hectic lips, and eyes up-looking mild,
Thus wording timidly among the fierce:
"O Father, I am here the simplest voice,
And all my knowledge is that joy is gone,
And this thing woe crept in among our hearts,
There to remain forever, as I fear:
I would not bode of evil, if I thought
So weak a creature could turn off the help
Which by just right should come of mighty Gods;
Yet let me tell my sorrow, let me tell
Of what I heard, and how it made me weep,
And know that we had parted from all hope.
I stood upon a shore, a pleasant shore,
Where a sweet clime was breathèd from a land
Of fragrance, quietness, and trees, and flowers.
Full of calm joy it was, as I of grief;
Too full of joy and soft delicious warmth;
So that I felt a movement in my heart
To chide, and to reproach that solitude
With songs of misery, music of our woes;
And sat me down, and took a mouthèd shell
And murmured into it, and made melody—

HYPERION

O melody no more! for while I sang,
And with poor skill let pass into the breeze
The dull shell's echo, from a bowery strand
Just opposite, an island of the sea,
There came enchantment with the shifting wind,
That did both drown and keep alive my ears.
I threw my shell away upon the sand,
And a wave filled it, as my sense was filled
With that new blissful golden melody.
A living death was in each gush of sounds,
Each family of rapturous hurried notes,
That fell, one after one, yet all at once,
Like pearl beads dropping sudden from their string:
And then another, then another strain,
Each like a dove leaving its olive perch,
With music winged instead of silent plumes,
To hover round my head, and make me sick
Of joy and grief at once. Grief overcame,
And I was stopping up my frantic ears,
When, past all hindrance of my trembling hands,
A voice came sweeter, sweeter than all tune,
And still it cried, 'Apollo!° young Apollo!
The morning-bright Apollo! young Apollo!'
I fled, it followed me, and cried 'Apollo!'
O Father, and O brethren, had ye felt
Those pains of mine; O Saturn, hadst thou felt,
Ye would not call this too indulgèd tongue
Presumptuous, in thus venturing to be heard."

So far her voice flowed on, like timorous brook
That, lingering along a pebbled coast,
Doth fear to meet the sea: but sea it met,
And shuddered; for the overwhelming voice
Of huge Enceladus swallowed it in wrath:
The ponderous syllables, like sullen waves
In the half-glutted hollows of reef-rocks,
Came booming thus, while still upon his arm

---

293 **Apollo** It is mythologically consistent that Clymene would be the one to describe Apollo in this way, since she was later to marry him; Phaeton is the offspring of their union.

He leaned; not rising, from supreme contempt.
"Or shall we listen to the over-wise,
Or to the over-foolish giant Gods?
Not thunderbolt on thunderbolt, till all
That rebel Jove's whole armory were spent,
Not world on world upon these shoulders piled,
Could agonize me more than baby-words
In midst of this dethronement horrible.
Speak! roar! shout! yell! ye sleepy Titans all.
Do ye forget the blows, the buffets vile?
Are ye not smitten by a youngling arm?
Dost thou forget, sham Monarch of the Waves,
Thy scalding in the seas? What, have I roused
Your spleens with so few simple words as these?
O joy! for now I see ye are not lost:
O joy! for now I see a thousand eyes
Wide-glaring for revenge!"—As this he said,
He lifted up his stature vast, and stood,
Still without intermission speaking thus:
"Now ye are flames, I'll tell you how to burn,
And purge the ether of our enemies;
How to feed fierce the crooked stings of fire,
And singe away the swollen clouds of Jove,
Stifling that puny essence in its tent.
O let him feel the evil he hath done;
For though I scorn Oceanus's lore,
Much pain have I for more than loss of realms:
The days of peace and slumberous calm are fled;
Those days, all innocent of scathing war,
When all the fair Existences of heaven
Came open-eyed to guess what we would speak:—
That was before our brows were taught to frown,
Before our lips knew else but solemn sounds;
That was before we know the wingèd thing,
Victory, might be lost, or might be won.
And be ye mindful that Hyperion,
Our brightest brother, still is undisgraced—
Hyperion, lo! his radiance is here!"

All eyes were on Enceladus's face,

HYPERION

And they beheld, while still Hyperion's name
Flew from his lips up to the vaulted rocks,
A pallid gleam across his features stern:
Not savage, for he saw full many a God
Wroth as himself. He looked upon them all, 350
And in each face he saw a gleam of light,
But splendider in Saturn's, whose hoar locks
Shone like the bubbling foam about a keel
When the prow sweeps into a midnight cove.
In pale and silver silence they remained, 355
Till suddenly a splendor, like the morn,
Pervaded all the beetling gloomy steeps,
All the sad spaces of oblivion,
And every gulf, and every chasm old,
And every height, and every sullen depth, 360
Voiceless, or hoarse with loud tormented streams:
And all the everlasting cataracts,
And all the headlong torrents far and near,
Mantled before in darkness and huge shade,
Now saw the light and made it terrible. 365
It was Hyperion:—a granite peak
His bright feet touched, and there he stayed to view
The misery his brilliance had betrayed
To the most hateful seeing of itself.° 370
Golden his hair of short Numidian curl,
Regal his shape majestic, a vast shade
In midst of his own brightness, like the bulk
Of Memnon's° image at the set of sun
To one who travels from the dusking East: 375
Sighs, too, as mournful as that Memnon's harp
He uttered, while his hands contemplative
He pressed together, and in silence stood.
Despondence seized again the fallen Gods

370 **of itself** The light of the sun has now made visible the dejection of the Titans, first hidden in the dark. 374 **Memnon** son of Aurora, goddess of dawn, and a mortal. He was killed by Achilles before Troy and was described as an Ethiopian (hence the "Numidian curl"). That Hyperion should be associated with this dark and defeated hero, here seen as his black silhouette stands out against the setting sun, may prefigure his future defeat at the hands of Apollo. As son of Aurora, Memnon is aptly associated with the sun symbolism that pervades the poem. The paradoxical combination of light and dark in the figure is primarily derived from the portrait of Satan in *Paradise Lost* (I. 1, 590 ff.)

380 At sight of the dejected King of Day,
And many hid their faces from the light:
But fierce Enceladus sent forth his eyes
Among the brotherhood; and, at their glare,
Uprose Iäpetus, and Creüs too,
385 And Phorcus, sea-born, and together strode
To where he towered on his eminence.
There those four shouted forth old Saturn's name;
Hyperion from the peak loud answered, "Saturn!"
Saturn sat near the Mother of the Gods,
390 In whose face was no joy, though all the Gods
Gave from their hollow throats the name of "Saturn!"

Book III

Thus in alternate uproar and sad peace,
Amazèd were those Titans utterly.
O leave them, Muse! O leave them to their woes;
For thou art weak to sing such tumults dire:
5 A solitary sorrow best befits
Thy lips, and antheming a lonèly grief.
Leave them, O Muse! for thou anon wilt find
Many a fallen old divinity
Wandering in vain about bewildered shores.
10 Meantime touch piously the Delphic harp,
And not a wind of heaven but will breathe
In aid soft warble from the Dorian flute;
For lo! 'tis for the father of all verse.°
Flush every thing that hath a vermeil hue,
15 Let the rose glow intense and warm the air,
And let the clouds of even and of morn
Float in voluptuous fleeces o'er the hills;
Let the red wine within the goblet boil,
Cold as a bubbling well; let faint-lipped shells,
20 On sands, or in great deeps, vermilion turn
Through all their labyrinths; and let the maid
Blush keenly, as with some warm kiss surprised.

13 **Father of all verse** Apollo.

HYPERION

Chief isle of the embowered Cyclades,
Rejoice, O Delos, with thine olives green,
And poplars, and lawn-shading palms, and beech, 25
In which the Zephyr breathes the loudest song,
And hazels thick, dark-stemmed beneath the shade:
Apollo is once more the golden theme!
Where was he, when the giant of the sun
Stood bright, amid the sorrow of his peers? 30
Together had he left his mother fair
And his twin sister° sleeping in their bower,
And in the morning twilight wandered forth
Beside the osiers of a rivulet,
Full ankle-deep in lilies of the vale. 35
The nightingale had ceased, and a few stars
Were lingering in the heavens, while the thrush
Began calm-throated. Throughout all the isle
There was no covert, no retired cave
Unhaunted by the murmurous noise of waves, 40
Though scarcely heard in many a green recess.
He listened, and he wept, and his bright tears
Went trickling down the golden bow he held.
Thus with half-shut suffused eyes he stood,
While from beneath some cumbrous boughs hard by 45
With solemn step an awful Goddess came,
And there was purport in her looks for him,
Which he with eager guess began to read
Perplexed, the while melodiously he said:
"How cam'st thou over the unfooted sea? 50
Or hath that antique mien and robèd form
Moved in these vales invisible till now?
Sure I have heard those vestments sweeping o'er
The fallen leaves, when I have sat alone
In cool mid-forest. Surely I have traced 55
The rustle of those ample skirts about
These grassy solitudes, and seen the flowers
Lift up their heads, as still the whisper passed.
Goddess! I have beheld those eyes before,
And their eternal calm, and all that face, 60

32 **his twin sister** Phoebe, prefigured in the Phoebe of Book II, l. 30.
Keats's first draft occasionally used Phoebus for Apollo.

Or I have dreamed."—"Yes," said the supreme shape,
"Thou hast dreamed of me; and awaking up
Didst find a lyre all golden by thy side,
Whose strings touched by thy fingers, all the vast
65 Unwearied ear of the whole universe
Listened in pain and pleasure at the birth
Of such new tuneful wonder. Is't not strange
That thou shouldst weep, so gifted? Tell me, youth,
What sorrow thou canst feel; for I am sad
70 When thou dost shed a tear: explain thy griefs
To one who in this lonely isle hath been
The watcher of thy sleep and hours of life,
From the young day when first thy infant hand
Plucked witless the weak flowers, till thine arm
75 Could bend that bow heroic to all times.
Show thy heart's secret to an ancient power
Who hath forsaken old and sacred thrones
For prophecies of thee, and for the sake
Of loveliness new born."—Apollo then,
80 With sudden scrutiny and gloomless eyes,
Thus answered, while his white melodious throat
Throbbed with the syllables.—"Mnemosyne!
Thy name is on my tongue, I know not how;
Why should I tell thee what thou so well seest?
85 Why should I strive to show what from thy lips
Would come no mystery? For me, dark, dark,
And painful vile oblivion seals my eyes:
I strive to search wherefore I am so sad,
Until a melancholy numbs my limbs:
90 And then upon the grass I sit, and moan,
Like one who once had wings.—O why should I
Feel cursed and thwarted, when the liegeless air
Yields to my step aspirant? why should I
Spurn the green turf as hateful to my feet?
95 Goddess benign, point forth some unknown thing:
Are there not other regions than this isle?
What are the stars? There is the sun, the sun!
And the most patient brilliance of the moon!
And stars by thousands! Point me out the way
100 To any one particular beauteous star,

And I will flit into it with my lyre,
And make its silvery splendor pant with bliss.
I have heard the cloudy thunder: Where is power?
Whose hand, whose essence, what divinity
Makes this alarum in the elements, 105
While I here idle listen on the shores
In fearless yet in aching ignorance?
O tell me, lonely Goddess, by thy harp,
That waileth every morn and eventide,
Tell me why thus I rave, about these groves! 110
Mute thou remainest—mute! yet I can read
A wondrous lesson in thy silent face:
Knowledge enormous makes a God of me.
Names, deeds, gray legends, dire events, rebellions,
Majesties, sovran voices, agonies, 115
Creations and destroyings, all at once
Pour into the wide hollows of my brain,
And deify me, as if some blithe wine
Or bright elixir peerless I had drunk,
And so become immortal."—Thus the God, 120
While his enkindled eyes, with level glance
Beneath his white soft temples, steadfast kept
Trembling with light upon Mnemosyne.
Soon wild commotions shook him, and made flush
All the immortal fairness of his limbs; 125
Most like the struggle at the gate of death;
Or liker still to one who should take leave
Of pale immortal death, and with a pang
As hot as death's is chill, with fierce convulse
Die into life: so young Apollo anguished: 130
His very hair, his golden tresses famed
Kept undulation round his eager neck.
During the pain Mnemosyne upheld
Her arms as one who prophesied.—At length
Apollo shrieked;—and lo! from all his limbs 135
Celestial° *   *   *   *   *   *
*   *   *   *   *   *   *   *

---

136 **Celestial** the manuscript ends abruptly here, except for a penciled note. "Glory dawned: he was a God—"

THE EVE OF ST. AGNES°

I

St. Agnes' Eve—Ah, bitter chill it was!
The owl, for all his feathers, was a-cold;
The hare limped trembling through the frozen grass,
And silent was the flock in woolly fold:
Numb were the beadsman's fingers, while he told
His rosary, and while his frosted breath,
Like pious incense from a censer old,
Seemed taking flight for heaven, without a death,
Past the sweet Virgin's picture, while his prayer he saith.

II

His prayer he saith, this patient, holy man;
Then takes his lamp, and riseth from his knees,
And back returneth, meager, barefoot, wan,
Along the chapel aisle by slow degrees:
The sculptured dead, on each side, seem to freeze,
Emprisoned in black, purgatorial rails:
Knights, ladies, praying in dumb orat'ries,
He passeth by; and his weak spirit fails
To think how they may ache in icy hoods and mails.

III

Northward he turneth through a little door,
And scarce three steps, ere Music's golden tongue

---

0 **The Eve of St. Agnes** Begun on January 18 or 19 at the suggestion of Isabella Jones, and completed in about nine or ten days. The poem was later much revised. Burton's *Anatomy of Melancholy*, also the source of *Lamia*, has been suggested as a possible source for the tale.

THE EVE OF ST. AGNES

Flattered to tears this agèd man and poor;
But no—already had his deathbell rung;
The joys of all his life were said and sung:
His was harsh penance on St. Agnes' Eve:
Another way he went, and soon among
Rough ashes sat he for his soul's reprieve,
And all night kept awake, for sinners' sake to grieve.

IV

That ancient beadsman heard the prelude soft;
And so it chanced, for many a door was wide,
From hurry to and fro. Soon, up aloft,
The silver, snarling trumpets 'gan to chide:
The level chambers, ready with their pride,
Were glowing to receive a thousand guests:
The carvèd angels, ever eager-eyed,
Stared, where upon their heads the cornice rests,
With hair blown back, and wings put crosswise on their breasts.

V

At length burst in the argent revelry,
With plume, tiara, and all rich array,
Numerous as shadows haunting fairily
The brain, new stuffed, in youth, with triumphs gay
Of old romance. These let us wish away,
And turn, sole-thoughted, to one lady there,
Whose heart had brooded, all that wintry day,
On love, and winged St. Agnes' saintly care,
As she had heard old dames full many times declare.

VI

They told her how, upon St. Agnes' Eve,
Young virgins might have visions of delight,
And soft adorings from their loves receive
Upon the honeyed middle of the night,
If ceremonies due they did aright;
As, supperless to bed they must retire,
And couch supine their beauties, lily white;

THE EVE OF ST. AGNES

Nor look behind, nor sideways, but require
Of Heaven with upward eyes for all that they desire.°

VII

Full of this whim was thoughtful Madeline:
The music, yearning like a God in pain,
She scarcely heard: her maiden eyes divine,
Fixed on the floor, saw many a sweeping train
Pass by—she heeded not at all: in vain
Came many a tiptoe, amorous cavalier,
And back retired; not cooled by high disdain,
But she saw not: her heart was otherwhere:
She sighed for Agnes' dreams, the sweetest of the year.

VIII

She danced along with vague, regardless eyes,
Anxious her lips, her breathing quick and short:
The hallowed hour was near at hand: she sighs
Amid the timbrels, and the thronged resort
Of whisperers in anger, or in sport;
'Mid looks of love, defiance, hate, and scorn,
Hoodwinked with fairy fancy; all amort,
Save to St. Agnes and her lambs unshorn,
And all the bliss to be before tomorrow morn.

IX

So, purposing each moment to retire,
She lingered still. Meantime, across the moors,
Had come young Porphyro, with heart on fire
For Madeline. Beside the portal doors,

---

54 **desire** The following stanza was originally inserted between VI and VII:

> 'Twas said her future lord would there appear
> Offering as sacrifice—all in the dream—
> Delicious food even to her lips brought near:
> Viands and wine and fruit and sugared cream,
> To touch her palate with the fine extreme
> Of relish: then soft music heard; and then
> More pleasure followed in a dizzy stream
> Palpable almost: then to wake again
> Warm in the virgin morn, no weeping Magdalen.

Buttressed from moonlight, stands he, and implores
All saints to give him sight of Madeline,
But for one moment in the tedious hours,
That he might gaze and worship all unseen;
Perchance speak, kneel, touch, kiss—in sooth such things have been.

X

He ventures in: let not buzzed whisper tell:
All eyes be muffled, or a hundred swords
Will storm his heart, Love's fev'rous citadel:
For him, those chambers held barbarian hordes,
Hyena foemen, and hot-blooded lords,
Whose very dogs would execrations howl
Against his lineage: not one breast affords
Him any mercy, in that mansion foul,
Save one old beldame, weak in body and in soul.

XI

Ah, happy chance! the agèd creature came,
Shuffling along with ivory-headed wand,
To where he stood, hid from the torch's flame,
Behind a broad hall-pillar, far beyond
The sound of merriment and chorus bland:
He startled her; but soon she knew his face,
And grasped his fingers in her palsied hand,
Saying, "Mercy, Porphyro! hie thee from this place;
They are all here tonight, the whole blood-thirsty race!

XII

"Get hence! get hence! there's dwarfish Hildebrand;
He had a fever late, and in the fit
He cursèd thee and thine, both house and land:
Then there's that old Lord Maurice, not a whit
More tame for his gray hairs—Alas me! flit!
Flit like a ghost away."—"Ah, Gossip dear,
We're safe enough; here in this armchair sit,
And tell me how"—"Good saints! not here, not here;
Follow me, child, or else these stones will be thy bier."

XIII

He followed through a lowly archèd way,
Brushing the cobwebs with his lofty plume,
And as she muttered "Well-a—well-a-day!"
He found him in a little moonlight room,
Pale, latticed, chill, and silent as a tomb.
"Now tell me where is Madeline," said he,
"O tell me, Angela, by the holy loom
Which none but secret sisterhood may see,
When they St. Agnes' wool are weaving piously."

XIV

"St. Agnes! Ah! it is St. Agnes' Eve—
Yet men will murder upon holy days:
Thou must hold water in a witch's sieve,
And be liege-lord of all the elves and fays,
To venture so: it fills me with amaze
To see thee, Porphyro!—St. Agnes' Eve!
God's help! my lady fair the conjuror plays
This very night: good angels her deceive!
But let me laugh awhile, I've mickle time to grieve."

XV

Feebly she laugheth in the languid moon,
While Porphyro upon her face doth look,
Like puzzled urchin on an agèd crone
Who keepeth closed a wondrous riddle-book,
As spectacled she sits in chimney nook.
But soon his eyes grew brilliant, when she told
His lady's purpose; and he scarce could brook
Tears, at the thought of those enchantments cold
And Madeline asleep in lap of legends old.

XVI

Sudden a thought came like a full-blown rose,
Flushing his brow, and in his painèd heart
Made purple riot: then doth he propose
A stratagem, that makes the beldame start:
"A cruel man and impious thou art:
Sweet lady, let her pray, and sleep, and dream
Alone with her good angels, far apart

From wicked men like thee. Go, go!—I deem
Thou canst not surely be the same that thou didst
    seem."

XVII

"I will not harm her, by all saints I swear," 145
Quoth Porphyro: "O may I ne'er find grace
When my weak voice shall whisper its last prayer,
If one of her soft ringlets I displace,
Or look with ruffian passion in her face:
Good Angela, believe me by these tears; 150
Or I will, even in a moment's space,
Awake, with horrid shout, my foemen's ears,
And beard them, though they be more fanged than
    wolves and bears."

XVIII

"Ah! why wilt thou affright a feeble soul?
A poor, weak, palsy-stricken, churchyard thing, 155
Whose passing-bell may ere the midnight toll;
Whose prayers for thee, each morn and evening,
Were never missed."—Thus plaining, doth she
    bring
A gentler speech from burning Porphyro;
So woeful, and of such deep sorrowing, 160
That Angela gives promise she will do
Whatever he shall wish, betide her weal or woe.

XIX

Which was, to lead him, in close secrecy,
Even to Madeline's chamber, and there hide
Him in a closet, of such privacy 165
That he might see her beauty unespied,
And win perhaps that night a peerless bride,
While legioned fairies paced the coverlet,
And pale enchantment held her sleepy-eyed.
Never on such a night have lovers met, 170
Since Merlin paid his Demon all the monstrous debt.

XX

"It shall be as thou wishest," said the dame:

236   THE EVE OF ST. AGNES
            "All cates and dainties shall be stored there
            Quickly on this feast-night: by the tambour frame
175   Her own lute thou wilt see: no time to spare,
            For I am slow and feeble, and scarce dare
            On such a catering trust my dizzy head.
            Wait here, my child, with patience; kneel in prayer
            The while: Ah! thou must needs the lady wed,
180   Or may I never leave my grave among the dead."

                            XXI

            So saying, she hobbled off with busy fear.
            The lover's endless minutes slowly passed;
            The dame returned, and whispered in his ear
            To follow her; with agèd eyes aghast
185   From fright of dim espial. Safe at last,
            Through many a dusky gallery, they gain
            The maiden's chamber, silken, hushed, and chaste;
            Where Porphyro took covert, pleased amain.
        His poor guide hurried back with agues in her brain.

                            XXII

190   Her falt'ring hand upon the balustrade,
            Old Angela was feeling for the stair,
            When Madeline, St. Agnes' charmèd maid,
            Rose, like a missioned spirit, unaware:
            With silver taper's light, and pious care,
195   She turned, and down the agèd gossip led
            To a safe level matting. Now prepare,
            Young Porphyro, for gazing on that bed;
        She comes, she comes again, like ringdove frayed
            and fled.

                            XXIII

            Out went the taper as she hurried in;
200   Its little smoke, in pallid moonshine, died:
            She closed the door, she panted, all akin
            To spirits of the air, and visions wide:
            No uttered syllable, or, woe betide!
            But to her heart, her heart was voluble,
205   Paining with eloquence her balmy side;

As though a tongueless nightingale should swell
Her throat in vain, and die, heart-stifled, in her dell.

XXIV

A casement high and triple-arched there was,
All garlanded with carven imag'ries
Of fruits, and flowers, and bunches of knot-grass,
And diamonded with panes of quaint device,
Innumerable of stains and splendid dyes,
As are the tiger moth's deep-damasked wings;
And in the midst, 'mong thousand heraldries,
And twilight saints, and dim emblazonings,
A shielded scutcheon blushed with blood of queens
    and kings.

XXV

Full on this casement shone the wintry moon,
And threw warm gules on Madeline's fair breast,
As down she knelt for heaven's grace and boon;
Rose-bloom fell on her hands, together pressed,
And on her silver cross soft amethyst,
And on her hair a glory, like a saint:
She seemed a splendid angel, newly dressed,
Save wings, for heaven:—Porphyro grew faint:
She knelt, so pure a thing, so free from mortal taint.

XXVI

Anon his heart revives: her vespers done,
Of all its wreathèd pearls her hair she frees;
Unclasps her warmèd jewels one by one;
Loosens her fragrant boddice; by degrees
Her rich attire creeps rustling to her knees:
Half-hidden, like a mermaid in seaweed,
Pensive awhile she dreams awake, and sees,
In fancy, fair St. Agnes in her bed,
But dares not look behind, or all the charm is fled.

XXVII

Soon, trembling in her soft and chilly nest,
In sort of wakeful swoon, perplexed she lay,

Until the poppied warmth of sleep oppressed
Her soothèd limbs, and soul fatigued away;
Flown, like a thought, until the morrow-day;
Blissfully havened both from joy and pain;
Clasped like a missal where swart Paynims pray;
Blinded alike from sunshine and from rain,
As though a rose should shut, and be a bud again.

XXVIII

Stolen to this paradise, and so entranced,
Porphyro gazed upon her empty dress,
And listened to her breathing, if it chanced
To wake into a slumberous tenderness;
Which when he heard, that minute did he bless,
And breathed himself: then from the closet crept,
Noiseless as fear in a wide wilderness,
And over the hushed carpet, silent, stepped,
And 'tween the curtains peeped, where, lo!—how fast
   she slept.

XXIX

Then by the bedside, where the faded moon
Made a dim, silver twilight, soft he set
A table, and, half anguished, threw thereon
A cloth of woven crimson, gold, and jet:—
O for some drowsy Morphean amulet!
The boisterous, midnight, festive clarion,
The kettle drum, and far-heard clarionet,
Affray his ears, though but in dying tone:—
The hall door shuts again, and all the noise is gone.

XXX

And still she slept an azure-lidded sleep,
In blanchèd linen, smooth, and lavendered,
While he from forth the closet brought a heap
Of candied apple, quince, and plum, and gourd
With jellies soother than the creamy curd,
And lucent syrups, tinct with cinnamon;
Manna and dates, in argosy transferred

From Fez; and spicèd dainties, every one,
From silken Samarkand to cedared Lebanon.

XXXI

These delicates he heaped with glowing hand
On golden dishes and in baskets bright
Of wreathèd silver: sumptuous they stand
In the retired quiet of the night,
Filling the chilly room with perfume light.—
"And now, my love, my seraph fair, awake!
Thou art my heaven, and I thine eremite:
Open thine eyes, for meek St. Agnes' sake,
Or I shall drowse beside thee, so my soul doth ache."

XXXII

Thus whispering, his warm, unnervèd arm
Sank in her pillow. Shaded was her dream
By the dusk curtains:—'twas a midnight charm
Impossible to melt as icèd stream:
The lustrous salvers in the moonlight gleam;
Broad golden fringe upon the carpet lies:
It seemed he never, never could redeem
From such a steadfast spell his lady's eyes;
So mused awhile, entoiled in woofèd fantasies.

XXXIII

Awakening up, he took her hollow lute—
Tumultuous—and, in chords that tenderest be,
He played an ancient ditty, long since mute,
In Provence called, "La belle dame sans mercy":
Close to her ear touching the melody;—
Wherewith disturbed, she uttered a soft moan:
He ceased—she panted quick—and suddenly
Her blue affrayèd eyes wide open shone:
Upon his knees he sank, pale as smooth-sculptured stone.

XXXIV

Her eyes were open, but she still beheld,

Now wide awake, the vision of her sleep:
There was a painful change, that nigh expelled
The blisses of her dream so pure and deep
At which fair Madeline began to weep,
And moan forth witless words with many a sigh;
While still her gaze on Porphyro would keep;
Who knelt, with joinèd hands and piteous eye,
Fearing to move or speak, she looked so dreamingly.

XXXV

"Ah, Porphyro!" said she, "but even now
Thy voice was at sweet tremble in mine ear,
Made tunable with every sweetest vow;
And those sad eyes were spiritual and clear:
How changed thou art! how pallid, chill, and drear!
Give me that voice again, my Porphyro,
Those looks immortal, those complainings dear!
Oh leave me not in this eternal woe,
For if thou diest, my love, I know not where to go."

XXXVI

Beyond a mortal man impassioned far
At these voluptuous accents, he arose,
Ethereal, flushed, and like a throbbing star
Seen mid the sapphire heaven's deep repose
Into her dream he melted, as the rose
Blendeth its odor with the violet—
Solution sweet: meantime the frost-wind blows
Like Love's alarum pattering the sharp sleet
Against the windowpanes; St. Agnes' moon hath set.

XXXVII

'Tis dark: quick pattereth the flaw-blown sleet:
"This is no dream, my bride, my Madeline!"
'Tis dark: the icèd gusts still rave and beat:
"No dream, alas! alas! and woe is mine!
Porphyro will leave me here to fade and pine.—
Cruel! what traitor could thee hither bring?
I curse not, for my heart is lost in thine

Though thou forsakest a deceivèd thing;—
A dove forlorn and lost with sick unpruned wing."

XXXVIII

"My Madeline! sweet dreamer! lovely bride!
Say, may I be for aye thy vassal blessed?   335
Thy beauty's shield, heart-shaped and vermeil dyed?
Ah, silver shrine, here will I take my rest
After so many hours of toil and quest,
A famished pilgrim—saved by miracle.
Though I have found, I will not rob thy nest   340
  Saving of thy sweet self; if thou think'st well
To trust, fair Madeline, to no rude infidel."

XXXIX

"Hark! 'tis an elfin-storm from fairy land,
Of haggard seeming, but a boon indeed:
Arise—arise! the morning is at hand;—   345
The bloated wassailers will never heed:—
Let us away, my love, with happy speed;
There are no ears to hear, or eyes to see—
Drowned all in Rhenish and the sleepy mead:
Awake! arise! my love, and fearless be,   350
For o'er the southern moors I have a home for thee."

XL

She hurried at his words, beset with fears,
For there were sleeping dragons all around,
At glaring watch, perhaps, with ready spears—
Down the wide stairs a darkling way they found.—   355
In all the house was heard no human sound.
A chain-drooped lamp was flickering by each door;
The arras, rich with horseman, hawk, and hound,
  Fluttered in the besieging wind's uproar;
And the long carpets rose along the gusty floor.   360

XLI

They glide, like phantoms, into the wide hall;
Like phantoms, to the iron porch, they glide;

Where lay the porter, in uneasy sprawl,
With a huge empty flagon by his side:
The wakeful bloodhound rose, and shook his hide,
But his sagacious eye an inmate owns:
By one, and one, the bolts full easy slide:—
The chains lie silent on the footworn stones;—
The key turns, and the door upon its hinges groans.

XLII

And they are gone: ay, ages long ago
These lovers fled away into the storm.
That night the baron dreamt of many a woe,
And all his warrior guests, with shade and form
Of witch, and demon, and large coffin-worm,
Were long be-nightmared. Angela the old
Died palsy-twitched, with meager face deform;
The beadsman, after thousand aves told,
For aye unsought for slept among his ashes cold.

THE EVE OF ST. MARK°

Upon a Sabbath day it fell;
Twice holy was the Sabbath bell,
That called the folk to evening prayer;
The city streets were clean and fair
From wholesome drench of April rains;
And, on the western windowpanes,
The chilly sunset faintly told
Of unmatured green valleys cold,
Of the green thorny bloomless hedge,
Of rivers new with spring-tide sedge,
Of primroses by sheltered rills,
And daisies on the aguish hills.

0 **The Eve of St. Mark** was written on February 13–17, 1819. One can only speculate how it was to continue, for the outline of the story is not clearly to be deduced from the existing fragment. The poem influenced considerably the manner of the later Pre-Raphaelites and was much admired by Rossetti.

THE EVE OF ST. MARK

Twice holy was the Sabbath bell:
The silent streets were crowded well
With staid and pious companies,
Warm from their fireside orat'ries;
And moving, with demurest air,
To evensong, and vesper prayer.
Each archèd porch, and entry low,
Was filled with patient folk and slow,
With whispers hush, and shuffling feet,
While played the organ loud and sweet.

The bells had ceased, the prayers begun,
And Bertha had not yet half done
A curious volume, patched and torn,
That all day long, from earliest morn,
Had taken captive her two eyes,
Among its golden broideries;
Perplexed her with a thousand things—
The stars of Heaven, and angels' wings,
Martyrs in a fiery blaze,
Azure saints in silver rays,
Aaron's breastplate, and the seven
Candlesticks John saw in Heaven,
The wingèd lion of St. Mark,
And the Covenantal Ark,
With its many mysteries,
Cherubim and golden mice.

Bertha was a maiden fair,
Dwelling in the old minster square;
From her fireside she could see,
Sidelong, its rich antiquity,
Far as the Bishop's garden wall;
Where sycamores and elm trees tall,
Full-leaved, the forest had outstripped,
By no sharp north wind ever nipped,
So sheltered by the mighty pile.
Bertha arose, and read awhile,
With forehead 'gainst the windowpane.
Again she tried, and then again,

Until the dusk eve left her dark
Upon the legend of St. Mark.
From plaited lawn-frill, fine and thin,
She lifted up her soft warm chin,
With aching neck and swimming eyes,
And dazed with saintly imag'ries.

All was gloom, and silent all,
Save now and then the still footfall
Of one returning homewards late,
Past the echoing minster gate.

The clamorous daws, that all the day
Above treetops and towers play,
Pair by pair had gone to rest,
Each in its ancient belfry nest,
Where asleep they fall betimes,
To music of the drowsy chimes.

All was silent, all was gloom,
Abroad and in the homely room:
Down she sat, poor cheated soul!
And struck a lamp from the dismal coal;
Leaned forward, with bright drooping hair
And slant book, full against the glare.
Her shadow, in uneasy guise,
Hovered about, a giant size,
On ceiling beam and old oak chair,
The parrot's cage, and panel square;
And the warm angled winter screen,
On which were many monsters seen,
Called doves of Siam, Lima mice,
And legless birds of Paradise,
Macaw, and tender Av'davat,
And silken-furred Angora cat.
Untired she read, her shadow still
Glowered about, as it would fill
The room with wildest forms and shades,
As though some ghostly queen of spades
Had come to mock behind her back,

THE EVE OF ST. MARK

And dance, and ruffle her garments black.
Untired she read the legend page,
Of holy Mark, from youth to age,   90
On land, on sea, in pagan chains,
Rejoicing for his many pains.
Sometimes the learnèd eremite,
With golden star, or dagger bright,
Referred to pious poesies   95
Written in smallest crow-quill size
Beneath the text; and thus the rhyme
Was parceled out from time to time:
"Gif° ye wol stonden hardie wight—   *a*
Amiddes of the blacke night—   *b*
Righte in the churche porch, pardie   *c*
Ye wol behold a companie   *d*
Appouchen thee full dolourouse   *e*
For sooth to sain from everich house   *f*
Be it in City or village   *g*
Wol come the Phantom and image   *h*
Of ilka gent and ilka carle   *i*
Whom coldè Deathè hath in parle   *j*
And wol some day that very year   *k*
Touchen with foulè venìme spear   *l*
And sadly do them all to die—   *m*
Hem all shalt thou see verilie—   *n*
And everichon shall by the[e] pass   *o*
All who must die that year Alas   *p*
——Als writith he of swevenis,
Men han beforne they wake in bliss,   100
Whanne that hir friendes thinke hèm bound
In crimped shroude farre under grounde;
And how a litling child mote be
A saint er its nativitie,
Gif that the modre (God her blese!)   105
Kepen in solitarinesse,
And kissen devoute the holy croce.

98a **Gif** the passage "is in a Middle-English that reminds us of Chatterton's imitations but is a little closer to Chaucer and especially Gower," (W. J. Bate, *Keats*, p. 455).

Of Goddes love, and Sathan's force—
He writith; and thinges many mo:
110 Of swiche thinges I may not show.
Bot I must tellen verilie
Somdel of Saintè Cicilie,
And chieflie what he auctorethe
Of Saintè Markis life and dethe":

115 At length her constant eyelids come
Upon the fervent martyrdom;
Then lastly to his holy shrine,
Exalt amid the tapers' shine
At Venice—

ODE TO MAY°

A Fragment

Mother of Hermes! and still youthful Maia!
    May I sing to thee
As thou wast hymned on the shores of Baiæ?°
    Or may I woo thee
5 In earlier Sicilian? Or thy smiles
Seek as they once were sought, in Grecian isles,
By bards who died content on pleasant sward,
    Leaving great verse unto a little clan?
O, give me their old vigor, and unheard
10   Save of the quiet Primrose, and the span
    Of heaven and few ears,
Rounded by thee, my song should die away
    Content as theirs,
Rich in the simple worship of a day.

---

0 **Ode to May** or Ode to Maia, written on May 1, 1818. Maia, daughter of Atlas, is the mother of Hermes, the messenger of the Gods. 2 **Baiæ** Roman city near Naples, also mentioned in the Epistle to Clarke, line 29. Designates here Roman poetry, as distinguished from the "earlier Sicilian" poetry of Theocritus and the Greeks.

ODE TO PSYCHE°

O goddess! hear these tuneless numbers, wrung
  By sweet enforcement and remembrance dear,
And pardon that thy secrets should be sung
  Even into thine own soft-conchèd ear:
Surely I dreamt today, or did I see   5
  The wingèd Psyche with awakened eyes?
I wandered in a forest thoughtlessly,
  And, on the sudden, fainting with surprise,
Saw two fair creatures, couchèd side by side
  In deepest grass, beneath the whisp'ring roof   10
    Of leaves and trembled blossoms, where there ran
      A brooklet, scarce espied:
'Mid hushed, cool-rooted flowers, fragrant-eyed,
  Blue, silver-white, and budded Tyrian,°

They lay calm-breathing on the bedded grass;   15
  Their arms embraced, and their pinions too;
  Their lips touched not, but had not bid adieu,
As if disjoined by soft-handed slumber,
And ready still past kisses to outnumber
  At tender eye-dawn of aurorean love: 20
    The wingèd boy I knew;

---

0 **Ode to Psyche** The myth of Psyche appears already in *I Stood Tiptoe* (see note on that poem) with details that reveal Keats's knowledge of the myth. It tells of the complex relationship between soul and love in the story of Psyche and Eros. Psyche is allowed to meet her husband at night only, and after having discovered, by breaking her promise, that he is Eros himself, she is left to search for him in endless wanderings. Finally Eros, locked up by Venus, escapes through a window and joins Psyche; at his request, Psyche is made immortal by Zeus.

In sending the poem to his brother George, Keats added the following note: "You must recollect that Psyche was not embodied as a goddess before the time of Apuleius the Platonist who lived after the Augustan Age, and consequently the Goddess was never worshipped or sacrificed to with any of the ancient fervour—and perhaps never thought of in the old religion. I am more orthodox than to let a heathen goddess be so neglected."   14 **Tyrian** purple.

ODE TO PSYCHE

But who wast thou, O happy, happy dove?
  His Psyche true!

O latest born and loveliest vision far
25 Of all Olympus' faded hierarchy!
Fairer than Phœbe's sapphire-regioned star,
  Or Vesper, amorous glowworm of the sky;
Fairer than these, though temple thou hast none,
  Nor altar heaped with flowers;
30 Nor virgin choir to make delicious moan
  Upon the midnight hours;
No voice, no lute, no pipe, no incense sweet
  From chain-swung censer teeming;
No shrine, no grove, no oracle, no heat
35 Of pale-mouthed prophet dreaming.

O brightest! though too late for antique vows,
  Too, too late for the fond believing lyre,
When holy were the haunted forest boughs,
  Holy the air, the water, and the fire;
40 Yet even in these days so far retired
  From happy pieties, thy lucent fans,
  Fluttering among the faint Olympians,
I see, and sing, by my own eyes inspired.
So let me be thy choir, and make a moan
45 Upon the midnight hours;
Thy voice, thy lute, thy pipe, thy incense sweet
  From swingèd censer teeming;
Thy shrine, thy grove, thy oracle, thy heat
  Of pale-mouthed prophet dreaming.

50 Yes, I will be thy priest, and build a fane
  In some untrodden region of my mind,
Where branchèd thoughts, new grown with pleasant pain,
  Instead of pines shall murmur in the wind:
Far, far around shall those dark-clustered trees
55 Fledge the wild-ridged mountains steep by steep;
And there by zephyrs, streams, and birds, and bees,
  The moss-lain Dryads shall be lulled to sleep;

And in the midst of this wide quietness
A rosy sanctuary will I dress
With the wreathed trellis of a working brain, 60
  With buds, and bells, and stars without a name,
With all the gardener Fancy e'er could feign,
  Who breeding flowers, will never breed the same:
And there shall be for thee all soft delight
  That shadowy thought can win, 65
A bright torch, and a casement ope at night,
  To let the warm Love in!

ODE TO A NIGHTINGALE°

1

My heart aches, and a drowsy numbness pains
  My sense, as though of hemlock I had drunk,
Or emptied some dull opiate to the drains
  One minute past, and Lethe-wards had sunk:
'Tis not through envy of thy happy lot, 5
  But being too happy in thine happiness—
    That thou, light-winged Dryad of the trees,
      In some melodious plot
Of beechen green, and shadows numberless,
  Singest of summer in full-throated ease. 10

2

O, for a draught of vintage! that hath been
  Cooled a long age in the deep-delvèd earth,
Tasting of Flora and the country green,
  Dance, and Provençal song, and sunburned mirth!
O for a beaker full of the warm South, 15
  Full of the true, the blushful Hippocrene,°
    With beaded bubbles winking at the brim,

0 **Ode to a Nightingale** was composed with the other great odes in May, 1819. Charles Brown claims it was written in two or three hours and inspired by the song of a nightingale who built his nest near Keats's house. **16 Hippocrene** the fountain of the Muses.

And purple-stainèd mouth;
   That I might drink, and leave the world unseen,
      And with thee fade away into the forest dim:

3

Fade far away, dissolve, and quite forget
   What thou among the leaves hast never known,
The weariness, the fever, and the fret
   Here, where men sit and hear each other groan;
Where palsy shakes a few, sad, last gray hairs,
   Where youth grows pale, and specter-thin, and dies;
      Where but to think is to be full of sorrow
         And leaden-eyed despairs,
   Where Beauty cannot keep her lustrous eyes,
      Or new Love pine at them beyond tomorrow.

4

Away! away! for I will fly to thee,
   Not charioted by Bacchus and his pards,
But on the viewless wings of Poesy,
   Though the dull brain perplexes and retards:
Already with thee! tender is the night,
   And haply the Queen Moon is on her throne,
      Clustered around by all her starry Fays;
         But here there is no light,
   Save what from heaven is with the breezes blown
      Through verdurous glooms and winding mossy ways.

5

I cannot see what flowers are at my feet,
   Nor what soft incense hangs upon the boughs,
But, in embalmèd darkness, guess each sweet
   Wherewith the seasonable month endows
The grass, the thicket, and the fruit-tree wild;
   White hawthorn, and the pastoral eglantine;
      Fast fading violets covered up in leaves;
         And mid-May's eldest child,
   The coming musk rose, full of dewy wine,
      The murmurous haunt of flies on summer eves.

6

Darkling I listen; and, for many a time
 I have been half in love with easeful Death,
Called him soft names in many a musèd rhyme,
 To take into the air my quiet breath;
Now more than ever seems it rich to die,
 To cease upon the midnight with no pain,
  While thou art pouring forth thy soul abroad
   In such an ecstasy!
 Still wouldst thou sing, and I have ears in vain—
  To thy high requiem become a sod.

7

Thou wast not born for death, immortal bird!
 No hungry generations tread thee down;
The voice I hear this passing night was heard
 In ancient days by emperor and clown:
Perhaps the self-same song that found a path
 Through the sad heart of Ruth, when, sick for home,
  She stood in tears amid the alien corn;
   The same that oft-times hath
 Charmed magic casements, opening on the foam
  Of perilous seas, in fairy lands forlorn.

8

Forlorn! the very word is like a bell
 To toll me back from thee to my sole self!
Adieu! the fancy cannot cheat so well
 As she is famed to do, deceiving elf.
Adieu! adieu! thy plaintive anthem fades
 Past the near meadows, over the still stream,
  Up the hillside; and now 'tis buried deep
   In the next valley glades:
 Was it a vision, or a waking dream?
  Fled is that music:—Do I wake or sleep?

ODE ON A GRECIAN URN

1

Thou still unravished bride of quietness,
  Thou foster child of silence and slow time,
Sylvan historian, who canst thus express
  A flowery tale more sweetly than our rhyme:
What leaf-fringed legend haunts about thy shape
  Of deities or mortals, or of both,
    In Tempe° or the dales of Arcady?°
What men or gods are these? What maidens loth?
  What mad pursuit? What struggle to escape?
    What pipes and timbrels? What wild ecstasy?

2

Heard melodies are sweet, but those unheard
  Are sweeter; therefore, ye soft pipes, play on;
Not to the sensual ear, but, more endeared,
  Pipe to the spirit ditties of no tone:
Fair youth, beneath the trees, thou canst not leave
  Thy song, nor ever can those trees be bare;
    Bold lover, never, never canst thou kiss,
Though winning near the goal—yet, do not grieve;
  She cannot fade, though thou hast not thy bliss,
    Forever wilt thou love, and she be fair!

3

Ah, happy, happy boughs! that cannot shed
  Your leaves, nor ever bid the spring adieu;
And, happy melodist, unwearied,
  Forever piping songs forever new;
More happy love! more happy, happy love!
  Forever warm and still to be enjoyed,
    Forever panting, and forever young;
All breathing human passion far above,

---

7 **Tempe** and **Arcady** are the domains of Pan and Apollo, where Ovid describes them pursuing the mortal nymphs Syrinx and Daphne.

ODE ON A GRECIAN URN

>   That leaves a heart high-sorrowful and cloyed,
>   A burning forehead, and a parching tongue.

4

> Who are these coming to the sacrifice?
>   To what green altar, O mysterious priest,
> Lead'st thou that heifer lowing at the skies,
>   And all her silken flanks with garlands dressed?
> What little town by river or sea shore,
>   Or mountain-built with peaceful citadel,
>   Is emptied of this folk, this pious morn?
> And, little town, thy streets for evermore
>   Will silent be; and not a soul to tell
>   Why thou art desolate, can e'er return.

5

> O Attic shape! Fair attitude! with brede
> Of marble men and maidens overwrought,
> With forest branches and the trodden weed;
>   Thou, silent form, dost tease us out of thought
> As doth eternity: Cold Pastoral!
>   When old age shall this generation waste,
>   Thou shalt remain, in midst of other woe
> Than ours, a friend to man, to whom thou say'st,
>   Beauty is truth, truth beauty—that is all°
>   Ye know on earth, and all ye need to know.

---

49 **that is all** H. W. Garrod, the editor of the Oxford Edition of Keats's poetry, prints the line without quotation marks, in conformity with transcripts made by Keats's friends. No copy in Keats's own hand is in existence, but two versions of the ode were printed during his lifetime: an anonymous one in the *Annals of Fine Arts* for 1820 where the line reads:

>   Beauty is Truth, Truth Beauty.—That is all . . .

The other, in the 1820 volume of Keats's poems *Lamia, Isabella and Other Poems,* is printed thus:

>   "Beauty is truth, truth beauty,"—that is all . . .

The transcripts made by his friends read (without quotation marks):

(*Footnote continued on page 254.*)

ODE ON MELANCHOLY

1

No, no, go not to Lethe,° neither twist
    Wolfsbane, tight-rooted, for its poisonous wine;
Nor suffer thy pale forehead to be kissed
    By nightshade, ruby grape of Proserpine;°
Make not your rosary of yew berries,
    Nor let the beetle, nor the death moth be
        Your mournful Psyche, nor the downy owl
A partner in your sorrow's mysteries;
    For shade to shade will come too drowsily,
        And drown the wakeful anguish of the soul.

2

But when the melancholy fit shall fall
    Sudden from heaven like a weeping cloud,
That fosters the droop-headed flowers all,
    And hides the green hill in an April shroud;
Then glut thy sorrow on a morning rose,

        Beauty is truth, truth beauty—that is all . . .
as the line is now given by Garrod.
    Stimulated by the gnomic character of the line and by the textual uncertainty, hundreds of pages have been written on the passage. If one ignores the quotation marks, then the entire statement would be made by the urn, including the following line "that is all ye know on earth and all ye need to know." If one keeps the quotation marks, then the remaining part of the sentence may not be said by the urn; it can either be addressed by Keats to the urn (or the figures on the urn) or, more likely, addressed by Keats to the reader. One can also question, in that case, what the antecedent of "that" would be, since it could refer to the entire sentence beginning with "When old age shall this generation waste. . . ." The matter is fully discussed by A. Whitley, *KSMB,* No. 5 (1954) and J. C. Stillinger, *Publications of the Modern Language Association,* LXXII (1957). Our own comments on the odes in the introduction are not decisively affected by this difficulty. 1 **No, no, go not to Lethe** The beginning picks up another first stanza suppressed in print by Keats. 4 **Proserpine** queen of the Underworld. Several of the images associated with melancholy come from Burton's *Anatomy of Melancholy.*

Or on the rainbow of the salt sand-wave,
    Or on the wealth of globèd peonies;
Or if thy mistress some rich anger shows,
    Emprison her soft hand, and let her rave,
        And feed deep, deep upon her peerless eyes.

3

She dwells with Beauty—Beauty that must die;
    And Joy, whose hand is ever at his lips
Bidding adieu; and aching Pleasure nigh,
    Turning to poison while the bee-mouth sips:
Ay, in the very temple of Delight
    Veiled Melancholy has her sovran shrine,
        Though seen of none save him whose strenuous tongue
Can burst Joy's grape against his palate fine;
    His soul shall taste the sadness of her might,
        And be among her cloudy trophies hung.

ODE ON INDOLENCE

"They toil not, neither do they spin."

1

One morn before me were three figures seen,
    With bowèd necks, and joinèd hands, side-faced;
And one behind the other stepped serene,
    In placid sandals, and in white robes graced;
They passed, like figures on a marble urn,
    When shifted round to see the other side;
        They came again; as when the urn once more
Is shifted round, the first seen shades return;
    And they were strange to me, as may betide
        With vases, to one deep in Phidian lore.

2

How is it, Shadows! that I knew ye not?

ODE ON INDOLENCE

How came ye muffled in so hush a mask?
Was it a silent deep-disguisèd plot
  To steal away, and leave without a task
My idle days? Ripe was the drowsy hour;
  The blissful cloud of summer indolence
    Benumbed my eyes; my pulse grew less and less;
Pain had no sting, and pleasure's wreath no flower:
  O, why did ye not melt, and leave my sense
    Unhaunted quite of all but—nothingness?

3

A third time came they by;—alas! wherefore?
  My sleep had been embroidered with dim dreams;
My soul had been a lawn besprinkled o'er
  With flowers, and stirring shades, and baffled beams:
The morn was clouded, but no shower fell,
  Tho' in her lids hung the sweet tears of May;
    The open casement pressed a new-leaved vine,
Let in the budding warmth and throstle's lay;
  O Shadows! 'twas a time to bid farewell!
    Upon your skirts had fallen no tears of mine.

4

A third time passed they by, and, passing, turned
  Each one the face a moment whiles to me;
Then faded, and to follow them I burned
  And ached for wings because I knew the three;
The first was a fair maid, and Love her name;
  The second was Ambition, pale of cheek,
    And ever watchful with fatiguèd eye;
The last, whom I love more, the more of blame
  Is heaped upon her, maiden most unmeek—
    I knew to be my demon Poesy.

5

They faded, and, forsooth! I wanted wings:
  O folly! What is Love! and where is it?
And for that poor Ambition—it springs
  From a man's little heart's short fever-fit;

For Poesy!—no—she has not a joy— 45
  At least for me—so sweet as drowsy noons,
    And evenings steeped in honeyed indolence;
O, for an age so sheltered from annoy,
  That I may never know how change the moons,
    Or hear the voice of busy common sense! 50

6

So, ye three Ghosts, adieu! Ye cannot raise
  My head cool-bedded in the flowery grass;
For I would not be dieted with praise,
  A pet lamb in a sentimental farce!
Fade softly from my eyes, and be once more 55
  In mask-like figures on the dreamy urn;
    Farewell! I yet have visions for the night,
And for the day faint visions there is store;
  Vanish, ye Phantoms! from my idle sprite,
    Into the clouds, and never more return! 60

SONNETS

On Sitting Down to Read King Lear Once Again°

O golden-tongued Romance,° with serene lute!
  Fair plumed Siren, Queen of far-away!
  Leave melodizing on this wintry day,
Shut up thine olden pages, and be mute:
Adieu! for, once again, the fierce dispute 5

---

0 **On Sitting Down ... Again** composed on January 22, 1818, shortly before writing the "Wherein lies happiness" passage from Book I of *Endymion*. 1 **Romance** refers to *Endymion*, which he was copying while he composed this poem.

258   TO A LADY SEEN ... AT VAUXHALL

    Betwixt damnation and impassioned clay
    Must I burn through; once more humbly assay
The bittersweet of this Shakespearian fruit:
Chief poet! and ye clouds of Albion,
10   Begetters of our deep eternal theme!
When through the old oak forest° I am gone,
    Let me not wander in a barren dream,
But, when I am consumèd in the fire
Give me new phœnix wings to fly at my desire.

When I Have Fears°

When I have fears that I may cease to be
    Before my pen has gleaned my teeming brain,
Before high-pilèd books, in charact'ry,
    Hold like rich garners the full-ripened grain;
5 When I behold, upon the night's starred face,
    Huge cloudy symbols of a high romance,
And think that I may never live to trace
    Their shadows, with the magic hand of chance;
And when I feel, fair creature of an hour!
10   That I shall never look upon thee more,
Never have relish in the fairy power
    Of unreflecting love!—then on the shore
Of the wide world I stand alone, and think
Till love and fame to nothingness do sink.

To a Lady Seen for a Few Moments at Vauxhall°

Time's sea hath been five years at its slow ebb;
    Long hours have to and fro let creep the sand;

---

11 old oak forest of romance. 0 **When I Have Fears** written in February, 1818. 0 **To a Lady Seen for a Few Moments at Vauxhall** dates from February 4, 1818.

Since I was tangled in thy beauty's web,
  And snared by the ungloving of thine hand.
And yet I never look on midnight sky,
  But I behold thine eyes' well-memoried light;
I cannot look upon the rose's dye,
  But to thy cheek my soul doth take its flight;
I cannot look on any budding flower,
  But my fond ear, in fancy at thy lips,
And harkening for a love-sound, doth devour
  Its sweets in the wrong sense: Thou dost eclipse
Every delight with sweet remembering,
And grief unto my darling joys dost bring.

On Visiting the Tomb of Burns°

The town, the churchyard, and the setting sun,
  The clouds, the trees, the rounded hills all seem,
  Though beautiful, cold—strange—as in a dream,
I dreamed long ago, now new begun.
The short-lived, paly summer is but won
  From winter's ague, for one hour's gleam;
  Though sapphire-warm, their stars do never beam:
All is cold beauty; pain is never done:
For who has mind to relish, Minos-wise,°
  The real of beauty, free from that dead hue
    Sickly imagination and sick pride
Cast wan upon it? Burns! with honor due
  I oft have honored thee. Great shadow, hide
Thy face; I sin against thy native skies.

0 **On Visiting the Tomb of Burns** written on July 1, 1818, during Keats's walking tour with Brown through Scotland. The poet Burns (1759–1796) is mentioned with admiration in the Epistle to G. F. Mathew (l. 71). 9 **Minos-wise** Minos, the son of Europa, passes final judgment on the souls in the underworld. The meaning seems to be: with detached judgment, seeing things as they are.

Written in the Cottage Where Burns Was Born°

This mortal body of a thousand days
   Now fills, O Burns, a space in thine own room,
Where thou didst dream alone on budded bays,
   Happy and thoughtless of thy day of doom!
My pulse is warm with thine old Barley-bree,
   My head is light with pledging a great soul,
My eyes are wandering, and I cannot see,
   Fancy is dead and drunken at its goal;
Yet can I stamp my foot upon thy floor,
   Yet can I ope thy window sash to find
The meadow thou hast tramped o'er and o'er—
   Yet can I think of thee till thought is blind—
Yet can I gulp a bumper to thy name—
O smile among the shades, for this is fame!

Read Me a Lesson, Muse

Read me a lesson, Muse, and speak it loud
   Upon the top of Nevis, blind in mist!
I look into the chasms, and a shroud
   Vaporous doth hide them—just so much I wist
Mankind do know of hell; I look o'erhead,
   And there is sullen mist—even so much
Mankind can tell of heaven; mist is spread
   Before the earth, beneath me—even such,
Even so vague is man's sight of himself!
   Here are the craggy stones beneath my feet—
Thus much I know that, a poor witless elf,

° **Written in the Cottage Where Burns was Born** written on July 12–13, 1818, during the same Scottish tour. ° **Read Me a Lesson, Muse** written on August 3, 1818, on top of the Scottish mountain Ben Nevis, after a difficult and lengthy climb in bad weather.

I tread on them—that all my eye doth meet
Is mist and crag, not only on this height,
But in the world of thought and mental might!

To Homer

Standing aloof in giant ignorance,
  Of thee I hear and of the Cyclades,
As one who sits ashore and longs perchance
  To visit dolphin-coral in deep seas.
So thou wast blind!—but then the veil was rent,
  For Jove uncurtained Heaven to let thee live,
And Neptune made for thee a spumy tent,
  And Pan made sing for thee his forest hive;
Aye, on the shores of darkness there is light,
  And precipices show untrodden green;
There is a budding morrow in midnight;
  There is a triple sight in blindness keen;
Such seeing hadst thou, as it once befell
To Dian, Queen of Earth, and Heaven, and Hell.

Why Did I Laugh?°

Why did I laugh tonight? No voice will tell:
  No God, no Demon of severe response,
Deigns to reply from Heaven or from Hell.
  Then to my human heart I turn at once.
Heart! Thou and I are here sad and alone;
  I say, why did I laugh? O mortal pain!
O Darkness! Darkness! ever must I moan,
  To question Heaven and Hell and heart in vain.
Why did I laugh? I know this being's lease,

° **Why Did I Laugh** The sonnet was written on March 19, 1818, at a time when Keats had no particular reason to fear for his health.

10 My fancy to its utmost blisses spreads;
Yet would I on this very midnight cease,
    And the world's gaudy ensigns see in shreds;
Verse, fame, and beauty are intense indeed,
But death intenser—death is life's high meed.

To Sleep

O soft embalmer of the still midnight,
    Shutting, with careful fingers and benign,
Our gloom-pleased eyes, embowered from the light,
    Enshaded in forgetfulness divine;
5 O soothest Sleep! if so it please thee, close,
    In midst of this thine hymn, my willing eyes,
Or wait the amen, ere thy poppy throws
    Around my bed its lulling charities;
Then save me, or the passèd day will shine
10 Upon my pillow, breeding many woes;
    Save me from curious conscience, that still lords
Its strength for darkness, burrowing like a mole;
    Turn the key deftly in the oilèd wards,
And seal the hushed casket of my soul.

On Fame, I

Fame, like a wayward girl, will still be coy
    To those who woo her with too slavish knees,
But makes surrender to some thoughtless boy,
    And dotes the more upon a heart at ease;
5 She is a gypsy, will not speak to those
    Who have not learned to be content without her;
A jilt, whose ear was never whispered close,

ON A DREAM

Who thinks they scandal her who talk about her;
A very gypsy is she, Nilus-born,°
 Sister-in-law to jealous Potiphar;°
Ye love-sick bards! repay her scorn for scorn;
 Ye artists lovelorn! madmen that ye are!
Make your best bow to her and bid adieu,
Then, if she likes it, she will follow you.

On Fame, II

You cannot eat your cake and have it too.—Proverb.

How fevered is the man, who cannot look
 Upon his mortal days with temperate blood,
Who vexes all the leaves of his life's book,
 And robs his fair name of its maidenhood;
It is as if the rose should pluck herself,
 Or the ripe plum finger its misty bloom,
As if a Naiad, like a meddling elf,
 Should darken her pure grot with muddy gloom:
But the rose leaves herself upon the brier,
 For winds to kiss and grateful bees to feed;
And the ripe plum still wears its dim attire,
 The undisturbèd lake has crystal space;
 Why then should man, teasing the world for grace,
Spoil his salvation for a fierce miscreed?

On a Dream

As Hermes once took to his feathers light,
 When lullèd Argus, baffled, swooned and slept,
So on a Delphic reed, my idle sprite
 So played, so charmed, so conquered, so bereft

---

9 **Nilus-born** born of the Nile.   10 **Potiphar** whose wife tried to seduce Joseph.

5 The dragon world of all its hundred eyes;°
   And, seeing it asleep, so fled away,
Not to pure Ida° with its snow-cold skies,
   Nor unto Tempe, where Jove grieved that day;
But to that second circle of sad hell,°
10   Where in the gust, the whirlwind, and the flaw
Of rain and hailstones, lovers need not tell
Their sorrows—pale were the sweet lips I saw,
Pale were the lips I kissed, and fair the form
I floated with, about that melancholy storm.

On the Sonnet

If by dull rhymes° our English must be chained,
And, like Andromeda,° the sonnet sweet
Fettered, in spite of painèd loveliness;
Let us find out, if we must be constrained,
5 Sandals more interwoven° and complete
To fit the naked foot of poesy:
Let us inspect the lyre, and weigh the stress
Of every chord, and see what may be gained
By ear industrious, and attention meet;
10 Misers of sound and syllable, no less
Than Midas° of his coinage, let us be
Jealous of dead leaves in the bay wreath crown;
So, if we may not let the Muse be free,
She will be bound with garlands of her own.

5 **hundred eyes** Ovid (I, ll. 317 ff.) tells of how Mercury (Hermes) lulled the hundred-eyed monster Argus to sleep by playing on a reed, and then beheaded it. 7 **Ida** mountain near Troy. 9 **second circle of hell** alludes to Paolo and Francesca in Dante. 1 **dull rhymes** Keats experiments with the sonnet form, in this poem and also in "To Sleep" and "On Fame, II," by departing both from the Petrarchan and the Shakespearean sonnet rhyme scheme. 2 **Andromeda** was chained to a rock and exposed to a sea monster to atone for her mother's (Cassiopeia's) sins. She was rescued by Perseus. 5 **sandals more interwoven** refers to the rhyme scheme of this sonnet: abc/abd/cab/cde/de. 11 **Midas** When granted a wish by Bacchus, he wished that all he touched might turn to gold.

O Thou Whose Face

O thou whose face hath felt the winter's wind,
 Whose eye has seen the snow clouds hung in mist,
 And the black elm tops 'mong the freezing stars,
 To thee the spring will be a harvest-time.
O thou, whose only book has been the light 5
 Of supreme darkness which thou feddest on
 Night after night when Phœbus was away,
 To thee the spring shall be a triple morn.
O fret not after knowledge—I have none,
 And yet my song comes native with the warmth. 10
O fret not after knowledge—I have none,
 And yet the evening listens. He who saddens
At thought of idleness cannot be idle,
And he's awake who thinks himself asleep.°

TO J. H. REYNOLDS, ESQ.°

Dear Reynolds, as last night I lay in bed,
There came before my eyes that wonted thread
Of shapes, and shadows and remembrances,
That every other minute vex and please:
Things all disjointed come from north and south, 5
Two witch's eyes above a cherub's mouth,
Voltaire with casque and shield and Habergeon,°

1–14 **O thou ... asleep** Keats wrote to Reynolds on February 20, 1818: "I was led into these thoughts ... by the beauty of the morning operating on a sense of Idleness—I have not read any Books—the Morning said I was right—I had no Idea but of the Morning and the Thrush said I was right...."
0 **To J. H. Reynolds, Esq.** dates from March 25, 1818. J. H. Reynolds was one of Keats's closest friends, to whom several memorable letters were written. He was one year older than Keats. After rather humble beginnings as a poet, he turned to the law and an obscure life of relative failure.   7 **Habergeon** a short mail coat.

266   TO J. H. REYNOLDS, ESQ.

And Alexander with his nightcap on—
Old Socrates atying his cravat;
10 And Hazlitt° playing with Miss Edgeworth's° cat;
And Junius Brutus° pretty well so, so,°
Making the best of's way towards Soho.
  Few are there who escape these visitings—
P'erhaps one or two, whose lives have patent wings;
15 And through whose curtains peeps no hellish nose,
No wild boar tushes, and no Mermaid's toes:
But flowers bursting out with lusty pride;
And young Æolian harps personified,
Some, Titian colors touched into real life.
20 The sacrifice° goes on; the pontiff knife
Gleams in the sun, the milk-white heifer lows,
The pipes go shrilly, the libation flows:
A white sail shows above the green-head cliff
Moves round the point, and throws her anchor stiff.
25 The mariners join hymn with those on land.
  You know the Enchanted Castle° it doth stand
Upon a rock on the border of a lake
Nested in trees, which all do seem to shake
From some old magic like Urganda's° sword.
30 O Phœbus, that I had thy sacred word
To show this castle in fair dreaming wise
Unto my friend, while sick and ill° he lies.
  You know it well enough, where it doth seem
A mossy place, a Merlin's Hall, a dream.
35 You know the clear lake, and the little isles,

10 **Hazlitt** (1778–1830). The famous essayist and critic was an important influence on Keats.   10 **Miss Edgeworth** Maria Edgeworth (1767–1849) was the prolific author of several novels (*Castle Rackrent, Belinda, The Modern Griselda*, etc. She was also a notorious bluestocking.   11 **Junius Brutus** The founder of the Roman Republic is mentioned in the Epistle to Clarke, line 71. According to W. J. Bate, the allusion here is to Junius Brutus Booth, a leading Shakespearean actor in Keats's days.   11 **so, so** tipsy.   20 **sacrifice** After the grotesque opening, the dream visions continue in a different mood. The passage is revealing as a prefiguration of the famous fourth stanza of the "Ode on a Grecian Urn."   26 **Enchanted Castle** a painting by Claude Lorrain. The subsequent details of the poem are derived from this painting.   29 **Urganda** a beneficial spirit in medieval romances, protector of knights.   32 **sick and ill** The epistle was originally written to divert Reynolds, who was ill at the time.

The mountains blue, and cold near neighbor rills—
All which elsewhere are but half animate
Here do they look alive to love and hate;
To smiles and frowns; they seem a lifted mound
Above some giant, pulsing underground.

Part of the building was a chosen See
Built by a banished Santon° of Chaldee:
The other part two thousand years from him
Was built by Cuthbert de Saint Aldebrim;
Then there's a little wing, far from the sun,
Built by a Lapland Witch° turned Maudlin nun—
And many other juts of agèd stone
Founded with many a mason-devil's groan.

The doors all look as if they oped themselves,
The windows as if latched by fays and elves—
And from them comes a silver flash of light
As from the westward of a summer's night;
Or like a beauteous woman's large blue eyes
Gone mad through olden songs and poesies—
  See what is coming from the distance dim!
A golden galley all in silken trim!
Three rows of oars are lightening moment-whiles
Into the verdurous bosoms of those isles.
Towards the shade under the castle wall
It comes in silence—now 'tis hidden all.
The clarion sounds; and from a postern grate
An echo of sweet music doth create
A fear in the poor herdsman who doth bring
His beasts to trouble the enchanted spring:
He tells of the sweet music and the spot
To all his friends, and they believe him not.

  O that our dreamings all of sleep or wake
Would all their colors from the sunset take:
From something of material sublime,°

---

42 **Santon** a Moslem religious ascetic.   46 **Lapland Witch** refers to a passage in *Paradise Lost* in which a vision of Hell is described (II, 662–666).   67–69 **O that . . . sublime** Cf. W. Wordsworth, "Tintern Abbey": "A sense sublime/Of something far more deeply interfused/ Whose dwelling is the light of setting suns." The entire passage, until the end of the poem, is rich in prefigurations of themes that will recur in the Odes, although this text precedes them by more than a year.

70 Rather than shadow our own soul's daytime
   In the dark void of night. For in the world
   We jostle—but my flag is not unfurled
   On the Admiral staff—and to philosophize
   I dare not yet!—Oh never will the prize,
75 High reason, and the lore of good and ill
   Be my award. Things cannot to the will
   Be settled, but they tease us out of thought.
   Or is it that imagination brought
   Beyond its proper bound, yet still confined—
80 Lost in a sort of Purgatory blind,
   Cannot refer to any standard law
   Of either earth or heaven?—It is a flaw
   In happiness to see beyond our bourn—
   It forces us in summer skies to mourn:
85 It spoils the singing of the nightingale.
   Dear Reynolds, I have a mysterious tale
   And cannot speak it. The first page I read
   Upon a lampit rock of green seaweed
   Among the breakers—'Twas a quiet eve;
90 The rocks were silent—the wide sea did weave
   An untumultuous fringe of silver foam
   Along the flat brown sand. I was at home,
   And should have been most happy—but I saw
   Too far into the sea; where every maw
95 The greater on the less feeds evermore:
   But I saw too distinct into the core
   Of an eternal fierce destruction,
   And so from happiness I far was gone.
   Still am I sick of it: and though today
100 I've gathered young spring leaves, and flowers gay
   Of Periwinkle and wild strawberry,
   Still do I that most fierce destruction see,
   The shark at savage prey—the hawk at pounce,
   The gentle robin, like a pard or ounce,
105 Ravening a worm—Away ye horrid moods,
   Moods of one's mind! You know I hate them well,
   You know I'd sooner be a clapping bell
   To some Kamschatkan missionary church,
   Than with these horrid moods be left in lurch—

Do you get health—and Tom the same—I'll dance, 110
And from detested moods in new romance
Take refuge—Of bad lines a Centaine dose
Is sure enough—and so "here follows prose"—

LINES ON SEEING A LOCK OF MILTON'S HAIR°

Chief of organic numbers!
   Old scholar of the spheres!
Thy spirit never slumbers,
   But rolls about our ears,
Forever, and forever! 5
O what a mad endeavor
     Worketh he,
Who to thy sacred and ennobled hearse
Would offer a burnt sacrifice of verse
     And melody. 10

How heavenward thou soundest,
   Live temple of sweet noise,
And discord unconfoundest,
   Giving delight new joys,
And pleasure nobler pinions! 15
O, where are thy dominions?
     Lend thine ear
To a young Delian oath—aye, by thy soul,
By all that from thy mortal lips did roll,
And by the kernel of thine earthly love, 20
Beauty, in things on earth, and things above
     (I swear!)

When every childish fashion

° **Lines on . . . Milton's Hair** The poem was written on January 21, 1818, in response to a challenge by Hunt to compose upon a piece he had just acquired for his collection of mementos.

           Has vanished from my rhyme,
25   Will I, gray-gone in passion,
         Leave to an after-time
            Hymning and harmony
Of thee, and of thy works, and of thy life;
But vain is now the burning and the strife,
30 Pangs are in vain, until I grow high-rife
            With old philosophy,
And mad with glimpses of futurity!

For many years my offerings must be hushed;
   When I do speak, I'll think upon this hour,
35 Because I feel my forehead hot and flushed,
   Even at the simplest vassal of thy power—
      A lock of thy bright hair—
      Sudden it came,
And I was startled, when I caught thy name
40   Coupled so unaware;
   Yet, at the moment, temperate was my blood.
I thought I had beheld it from the flood.

WHERE'S THE POET°

Where's the Poet? show him! show him,
   Muses nine! that I may know him!
'Tis the man who with a man
   Is an equal, be he king,
5 Or poorest of the beggar clan,
   Or any other wondrous thing
A man may be 'twixt ape and Plato;
'Tis the man who with a bird,
Wren or eagle, finds his way to
10   All its instincts; he hath heard
The lion's roaring, and can tell
   What his horny throat expresseth,
And to him the tiger's yell

0 **Where's the Poet** dates from 1818.

Comes articulate and presseth
On his ear like mother tongue; . . .

WELCOME JOY . . .°

"Under the flag
Of each his faction, they to battle bring
Their embryon atoms."—MILTON

Welcome joy, and welcome sorrow,
   Lethe's weed and Hermes' feather;
Come today, and come tomorrow,
   I do love you both together!
   I love to mark sad faces in fair weather;
And hear a merry laugh amid the thunder;
   Fair and foul I love together.
Meadows sweet where flames burn under,
And a giggle at a wonder;
Visage sage at pantomime;
Funeral, and steeple chime;
Infant playing with a skull;
Morning fair, and stormwrecked hull;
Nightshade with the woodbine kissing;
Serpents in red roses hissing;
Cleopatra regal-dressed
With the aspic at her breast;
Dancing music, music sad,
Both together, sane and mad;
Muses bright and muses pale;
Somber Saturn, Momus hale;—
Laugh and sigh, and laugh again;
Oh the sweetness of the pain!
Muses bright, and muses pale,
Bare your faces of the veil;
Let me see; and let me write
Of the day, and of the night—

0 **Welcome Joy** . . . dates from 1818. ° **Milton** a quotation from memory of *Paradise Lost* (II, 899–901).

Both together:—let me slake
All my thirst for sweet heartache!
30 Let my bower be of yew,
Interwreathed with myrtles new;
Pines and lime trees full in bloom,
And my couch a low grass tomb.

STANZAS:° IN A DREAR-NIGHTED DECEMBER

I

In a drear-nighted December,
    Too happy, happy tree,
Thy branches ne'er remember
    Their green felicity:
5   The north cannot undo them,
With a sleety whistle through them;
Nor frozen thawings glue them
    From budding at the prime.

II

In a drear-nighted December,
10   Too happy, happy brook,
Thy bubblings ne'er remember
    Apollo's summer look;
But with a sweet forgetting,
They stay their crystal fretting,
15 Never, never petting
    About the frozen time.

III

Ah! would 'twere so with many
    A gentle girl and boy!
But were there ever any
20   Writhed not at passèd joy?
The feel of not to feel it,

° **Stanzas** dates from October or November, **1818.**

When there is none to heal it
Nor numbèd sense to steal it,
    Was never said in rhyme.

FANCY

Ever let the Fancy roam,
Pleasure never is at home:
At a touch sweet Pleasure melteth,
Like to bubbles when rain pelteth;
Then let wingèd Fancy wander
Through the thought still spread beyond her:
Open wide the mind's cage door,
She'll dart forth, and cloudward soar.
O sweet Fancy! let her loose;
Summer's joys are spoiled by use,
And the enjoying of the spring
Fades as does its blossoming;
Autumn's red-lipped fruitage too,
Blushing through the mist and dew,
Cloys with tasting: What do then?
Sit thee by the ingle, when
The sear faggot blazes bright,
Spirit of a winter's night;
When the soundless earth is muffled,
And the cakèd snow is shuffled
From the plowboy's heavy shoon;
When the Night doth meet the Noon
In a dark conspiracy
To banish Even from her sky.
Sit thee there, and send abroad,
With a mind self-overawed,
Fancy, high-commissioned:—send her!
She has vassals to attend her:
She will bring, in spite of frost,
Beauties that the earth hath lost;
She will bring thee, all together,

All delights of summer weather;
All the buds and bells of May,
From dewy sward or thorny spray
35 All the heapèd autumn's wealth,
With a still, mysterious stealth:
She will mix these pleasures up
Like three fit wines in a cup,
And thou shalt quaff it:—thou shalt hear
40 Distant harvest carols clear;
Rustle of the reapèd corn;
Sweet birds antheming the morn:
And, in the same moment— hark!
'Tis the early April lark,
45 Or the rooks, with busy caw,
Foraging for sticks and straw.
Thou shalt, at one glance, behold
The daisy and the marigold;
White-plumed lilies, and the first
50 Hedge-grown primrose that hath burst;
Shaded hyacinth, alway
Sapphire queen of the mid-May;
And every leaf, and every flower
Pearlèd with the self-same shower.
55 Thou shalt see the field mouse peep
Meager from its cellèd sleep;
And the snake all winter-thin
Cast on sunny bank its skin;
Freckled nest eggs thou shalt see
60 Hatching in the hawthorn tree,
When the hen bird's wing doth rest
Quiet on her mossy nest;
Then the hurry and alarm
When the bee hive casts its swarm;
65 Acorns ripe down-pattering,
While the autumn breezes sing.

Oh, sweet Fancy! let her loose;
Everything is spoiled by use:
Where's the cheek that doth not fade,
70 Too much gazed at? Where's the maid

Whose lip mature is ever new?
Where's the eye, however blue,
Doth not weary? Where's the face
One would meet in every place?
Where's the voice, however soft, 75
One would hear so very oft?
At a touch sweet Pleasure melteth
Like to bubbles when rain pelteth.
Let, then, wingèd Fancy find
Thee a mistress to thy mind: 80
Dulcet-eyed as Ceres' daughter,°
Ere the God of Torment taught her
How to frown and how to chide;
With a waist and with a side
White as Hebe's,° when her zone 85
Slipped its golden clasp, and down
Fell her kirtle to her feet,
While she held the goblet sweet,
And Jove grew languid.—Break the mesh
Of the Fancy's silken leash; 90
Quickly break her prison string
And such joys as these she'll bring.—
Let the wingèd Fancy roam
Pleasure never is at home.

---

81 **Ceres' daughter** Proserpine, carried away by Pluto, god of the Underworld.   85 **Hebe** served as cupbearer to the gods and later married Hercules.

LA BELLE DAME SANS MERCI°

A Ballad

I

O what can ail thee, knight-at-arms,
　　Alone and palely loitering?
The sedge has withered from the lake,
　　And no birds sing.

II

O what can ail thee, knight-at-arms,
　　So haggard and so woebegone?
The squirrel's granary is full,
　　And the harvest's done.

III

I see a lily on thy brow,
　　With anguish moist and fever dew,
And on thy cheeks a fading rose
　　Fast withereth too.

IV

I met a lady in the meads,
　　Full beautiful—a fairy's child,
Her hair was long, her foot was light,
　　And her eyes were wild.

V

I made a garland for her head,

° **La Belle Dame sans Merci** dates from April 21, 1819. The title of the poem is taken from the French fifteenth-century poem by Alain Chartier, but the main sources are from Spenser and William Browne.

   And bracelets too, and fragrant zone;
She looked at me as she did love,
   And made sweet moan.

VI

I set her on my pacing steed,
   And nothing else saw all day long,
For sidelong would she bend, and sing
   A fairy's song.

VII

She found me roots of relish sweet,
   And honey wild, and manna dew,
And sure in language strange she said—
   "I love thee true."

VIII

She took me to her elfin grot,
   And there she wept, and sighed full sore,
And there I shut her wild wild eyes
   With kisses four.

IX

And there she lullèd me asleep,
   And there I dreamed—Ah! woe betide!
The latest dream I ever dreamed
   On the cold hillside.

X

I saw pale kings and princes too,
   Pale warriors, death-pale were they all;
They cried—"La Belle Dame sans Merci
   Hath thee in thrall!"

XI

I saw their starved lips in the gloom,
   With horrid warning gapèd wide,
And I awoke and found me here,
   On the cold hill's side.

XII

And this is why I sojourn here,
   Alone and palely loitering,
Though the sedge has withered from the lake,
   And no birds sing.

III. The Late Keats

LAMIA°

Part I

Upon a time, before the fairy broods
Drove Nymph and Satyr from the prosperous woods,

---

0 **Lamia** was begun in early July, 1819, and finished in September of the same year. Keats himself revealed the source by appending the following text from Burton's *Anatomy* to the edition of the poem:

Philostratus, in his fourth book *de Vita Apollonii*, hath a memorable instance in this kind, which I may not omit, of one Menippus Lycius, a young man twenty-five years of age, that going betwixt Cenchreas and Corinth, met such a phantasm in the habit of a fair gentlewoman, which taking him by the hand, carried him home to her house, in the suburbs of Corinth, and told him she was a Phœnician by birth, and if he would tarry with her, he should hear her sing and play, and drink such wine as never any drank, and no man should molest him; but she, being fair and lovely, would live and die with him, that was fair and lovely to behold. The young man, a philosopher, otherwise staid and discreet, able to moderate his passions, though not this of love, tarried with her a while to his great content, and at last married her, to whose wedding, amongst other guests, came Apollonius; who, by some probable conjectures, found her out to be a serpent, a lamia; and that all her furniture was, like Tantalus' gold, described by Homer, no substance but mere illusions. When she saw herself descried, she wept, and desired Apollonius to be silent, but he would not be moved, and thereupon she, plate, house, and all that was in it, vanished in an instant: many thousands took notice of this fact, for it was done in the midst of Greece.
                                      Burton's *Anatomy of Melancholy*. Part 3. Sect. 2.
                                                  Memb. 1. Subs. 1.

LAMIA

  Before King Oberon's bright diadem,
Scepter, and mantle, clasped with dewy gem,
Frighted away the Dryads and the Fauns
From rushes green, and brakes, and cowslipped lawns,
The ever-smitten Hermes empty left
His golden throne, bent warm on amorous theft:
From high Olympus had he stolen light,
On this side of Jove's clouds, to escape the sight
Of his great summoner, and made retreat
Into a forest on the shores of Crete.
For somewhere in that sacred island dwelt
A nymph, to whom all hoofèd Satyrs knelt;
At whose white feet the languid Tritons poured
Pearls, while on land they withered and adored.
Fast by the springs where she to bathe was wont,
And in those meads where sometime she might haunt,
Were strewn rich gifts, unknown to any Muse,
Though Fancy's casket were unlocked to choose.
Ah, what a world of love was at her feet!
So Hermes thought, and a celestial heat
Burnt from his wingèd heels to either ear,
That from a whiteness, as the lily clear,
Blushed into roses 'mid his golden hair,
Fallen in jealous curls about his shoulders bare.
From vale to vale, from wood to wood, he flew,
Breathing upon the flowers his passion new,
And wound with many a river to its head,
To find where this sweet nymph prepared her secret
  bed:
In vain; the sweet nymph might nowhere be found,
And so he rested, on the lonely ground,
Pensive, and full of painful jealousies
Of the Wood Gods, and even the very trees.
There as he stood, he heard a mournful voice,
Such as once heard, in gentle heart, destroys
All pain but pity: thus the lone voice spake:
"When from this wreathèd tomb shall I awake!
When move in a sweet body fit for life,
And love, and pleasure, and the ruddy strife
Of hearts and lips! Ah, miserable me!"

LAMIA

The God, dove-footed, glided silently
Round bush and tree, soft-brushing, in his speed,
The taller grasses and full-flowering weed,
Until he found a palpitating snake, 45
Bright, and cirque-couchant in a dusky brake.

She was a gordian shape of dazzling hue,
Vermilion-spotted, golden, green, and blue;
Striped like a zebra, freckled like a pard,
Eyed like a peacock, and all crimson barred; 50
And full of silver moons, that, as she breathed,
Dissolved, or brighter shone, or interwreathed
Their lusters with the gloomier tapestries—
So rainbow-sided, touched with miseries,
She seemed, at once, some penanced lady elf, 55
Some demon's mistress, or the demon's self.
Upon her crest she wore a wannish fire
Sprinkled with stars, like Ariadne's° tiar:
Her head was serpent, but ah, bitter-sweet!
She had a woman's mouth with all its pearls complete: 60
And for her eyes: what could such eyes do there
But weep, and weep, that they were born so fair?
As Proserpine still weeps for her Sicilian air.
Her throat was serpent, but the words she spake
Came, as through bubbling honey, for love's sake, 65
And thus; while Hermes on his pinions lay,
Like a stooped falcon ere he takes his prey.

"Fair Hermes, crowned with feathers, fluttering light,
I had a splendid dream of thee last night:
I saw thee sitting, on a throne of gold, 70
Among the Gods, upon Olympus old,
The only sad one; for thou didst not hear
The soft, lute-fingered Muses chaunting clear,
Nor even Apollo when he sang alone,

---

58 **Ariadne** daughter of Minos, who lead Theseus out of the labyrinth. The allusion, according to Clarence Thorpe, is to a painting by Titian in which a circlet of stars appears above Ariadne's head.

Deaf to his throbbing throat's long, long melodious moan.
I dreamt I saw thee, robed in purple flakes,
Break amorous through the clouds, as morning breaks,
And, swiftly as a bright Phœbean dart,
Strike for the Cretan isle; and here thou art!
Too gentle Hermes, hast thou found the maid?"
Whereat the star of Lethe not delayed
His rosy eloquence, and thus inquired:
"Thou smooth-lipped serpent, surely high inspired!
Thou beauteous wreath, with melancholy eyes,
Possess whatever bliss thou canst devise,
Telling me only where my nymph is fled—
Where she doth breathe!" "Bright planet, thou hast said,"
Returned the snake, "but seal with oaths, fair God!"
"I swear," said Hermes, "by my serpent rod,
And by thine eyes, and by thy starry crown!"
Light flew his earnest words, among the blossoms blown.
Then thus again the brilliance feminine:
"Too frail of heart! for this lost nymph of thine,
Free as the air, invisibly, she strays
About these thornless wilds; her pleasant days
She tastes unseen; unseen her nimble feet
Leave traces in the grass and flowers sweet;
From weary tendrils, and bowed branches green,
She plucks the fruit unseen, she bathes unseen:
And by my power is her beauty veiled
To keep it unaffronted, unassailed
By the love glances of unlovely eyes,
Of Satyrs, Fauns, and bleared Silenus' sighs.
Pale grew her immortality, for woe
Of all these lovers, and she grievèd so
I took compassion on her, bade her steep
Her hair in weird syrops, that would keep
Her loveliness invisible, yet free
To wander as she loves, in liberty.
Thou shalt behold her, Hermes, thou alone,

LAMIA

If thou wilt, as thou swearest, grant my boon!"
Then, once again, the charmèd God began
An oath, and through the serpent's ears it ran
Warm, tremulous, devout, psalterian.
Ravished, she lifted her Circean head, 115
Blushed a live damask, and swift-lisping said,
"I was a woman, let me have once more
A woman's shape, and charming as before.
I love a youth of Corinth—O the bliss!
Give me my woman's form, and place me where he is. 120
Stoop, Hermes, let me breathe upon thy brow,
And thou shalt see thy sweet nymph even now."
The god on half-shut feathers sank serene,
She breathed upon his eyes, and swift was seen
Of both the guarded nymph near-smiling on the
   green. 125
It was no dream; or say a dream it was,
Real are the dreams of gods, and smoothly pass
Their pleasures in a long immortal dream.
One warm, flushed moment, hovering, it might seem
Dashed by the wood-nymph's beauty, so he burned; 130
Then, lighting on the printless verdure, turned
To the swooned serpent, and with languid arm,
Delicate, put to proof the lythe Caducean charm.
So done, upon the nymph his eyes he bent
Full of adoring tears and blandishment, 135
And towards her stepped: she, like a moon in wane,
Faded before him, cowered, nor could restrain
Her fearful sobs, self-folding like a flower
That faints into itself at evening hour:
But the god fostering her chillèd hand, 140
She felt the warmth, her eyelids opened bland,
And, like new flowers at morning song of bees,
Bloomed, and gave up her honey to the lees.
Into the green-recessèd woods they flew;
Nor grew they pale, as mortal lovers do. 145

Left to herself, the serpent now began
To change; her elfin blood in madness ran,
Her mouth foamed, and the grass, therewith besprent,

Withered at dew so sweet and virulent;
150 Her eyes in torture fixed, and anguish drear,
Hot, glazed, and wide, with lid-lashes all sear,
Flashed phosphor and sharp sparks, without one cooling tear.
The colors all inflamed throughout her train,
She writhed about, convulsed with scarlet pain:
155 A deep volcanian yellow took the place
Of all her milder-moonèd body's grace;
And, as the lava ravishes the mead,
Spoiled all her silver mail, and golden brede,
Made gloom of all her frecklings, streaks and bars,
160 Eclipsed her crescents, and licked up her stars:
So that, in moments few, she was undressed
Of all her sapphires, greens, and amethyst,
And rubious-argent: of all these bereft,
Nothing but pain and ugliness were left.
165 Still shone her crown; that vanished, also she
Melted and disappeared as suddenly;
And in the air, her new voice luting soft,
Cried, "Lycius! gentle Lycius!"—Borne aloft
With the bright mists about the mountains hoar
170 These words dissolved: Crete's forests heard no more.

Whither fled Lamia, now a lady bright,
A full-born beauty new and exquisite?
She fled into that valley they pass o'er
Who go to Corinth from Cenchreas' shore;
175 And rested at the foot of those wild hills,
The rugged founts of the Peræan rills,
And of that other ridge whose barren back
Stretches, with all its mist and cloudy rack,
Southwestward to Cleone. There she stood
180 About a young bird's flutter from a wood,
Fair, on a sloping green of mossy tread,
By a clear pool, wherein she passioned
To see herself escaped from so sore ills,
While her robes flaunted with the daffodils.

185 Ah, happy Lycius!—for she was a maid

More beautiful than ever twisted braid,
Or sighed, or blushed, or on spring-flowered lea
Spread a green kirtle to the minstrelsy:
A virgin purest lipped, yet in the lore
Of love deep learnèd to the red heart's core: 190
Not one hour old, yet of sciential brain
To unperplex bliss from its neighbor pain;
Define their pettish limits, and estrange
Their points of contact, and swift counterchange;
Intrigue with the specious chaos, and dispart 195
Its most ambiguous atoms with sure art;
As though in Cupid's college she had spent
Sweet days a lovely graduate, still unshent,
And kept his rosy terms in idle languishment.

   Why this fair creature chose so fairly 200
By the wayside to linger, we shall see;
But first 'tis fit to tell how she could muse
And dream, when in the serpent prison-house,
Of all she list, strange or magnificent:
How, ever, where she willed, her spirit went; 205
Whether to faint Elysium, or where
Down through tress-lifting waves the Nereids fair
Wind into Thetis' bower by many a pearly stair;
Or where God Bacchus drains his cups divine,
Stretched out, at ease, beneath a glutinous pine; 210
Or where in Pluto's gardens palatine
Mulciber's° columns gleam in far piazzian line.
And sometimes into cities she would send
Her dream, with feast and rioting to blend;
And once, while among mortals dreaming thus, 215
She saw the young Corinthian Lycius
Charioting foremost in the envious race,
Like a young Jove with calm uneager face,
And fell into a swooning love of him.
Now on the moth-time of that evening dim 220
He would return that way, as well she knew,
To Corinth from the shore; for freshly blew

---

212 **Mulciber** the god of fire, Hephaestus or Vulcan who in *Paradise Lost* is said to have "built in Hell" (I. ll. 740 ff.).

The eastern soft wind, and his galley now
Grated the quaystones with her brazen prow
In port Cenchreas, from Egina isle
Fresh anchored; whither he had been awhile
To sacrifice to Jove, whose temple there
Waits with high marble doors for blood and incense
    rare.
Jove heard his vows, and bettered his desire;
For by some freakful chance he made retire
From his companions, and set forth to walk,
Perhaps grown wearied of their Corinth talk:
Over the solitary hills he fared,
Thoughtless at first, but ere eve's star appeared
His fantasy was lost, where reason fades,
In the calmed twilight of Platonic shades.
Lamia beheld him coming, near, more near—
Close to her passing, in indifference drear,
His silent sandals swept the mossy green;
So neighbored to him, and yet so unseen
She stood: he passed, shut up in mysteries,
His mind wrapped like his mantle, while her eyes
Followed his steps, and her neck regal white
Turned—syllabling thus, "Ah, Lycius bright,
And will you leave me on the hills alone?
Lycius, look back! and be some pity shown."
He did; not with cold wonder fearingly,
But Orpheus-like at an Eurydice;
For so delicious were the words she sung,
It seemed he had loved them a whole summer long:
And soon his eyes had drunk her beauty up,
Leaving no drop in the bewildering cup,
And still the cup was full—while he, afraid
Lest she should vanish ere his lip had paid
Due adoration, thus began to adore;
Her soft look growing coy, she saw his chain so sure:
"Leave thee alone! Look back! Ah, Goddess, see
Whether my eyes can ever turn from thee!
For pity do not this sad heart belie—
Even as thou vanishest so I shall die.
Stay! though a Naiad of the rivers, stay!

To thy far wishes will thy streams obey:
Stay! though the greenest woods be thy domain,
Alone they can drink up the morning rain:
Though a descended Pleiad, will not one
Of thine harmonious sisters keep in tune
Thy spheres, and as thy silver proxy shine?
So sweetly to these ravished ears of mine
Came thy sweet greeting, that if thou shouldst fade
Thy memory will waste me to a shade:—
For pity do not melt!"—"If I should stay,"
Said Lamia, "here, upon this floor of clay,
And pain my steps upon these flowers too rough,
What canst thou say or do of charm enough
To dull the nice remembrance of my home?
Thou canst not ask me with thee here to roam
Over these hills and vales, where no joy is—
Empty of immortality and bliss!
Thou art a scholar, Lycius, and must know
That finer spirits cannot breathe below
In human climes, and live: Alas! poor youth,
What taste of purer air hast thou to soothe
My essence? What serener palaces,
Where I may all my many senses please,
And by mysterious sleights a hundred thirsts appease?
It cannot be—Adieu!" So said, she rose
Tiptoe with white arms spread. He, sick to lose
The amorous promise of her lone complain,
Swooned, murmuring of love, and pale with pain.
The cruel lady, without any show
Of sorrow for her tender favorite's woe,
But rather, if her eyes could brighter be,
With brighter eyes and slow amenity,
Put her new lips to his, and gave afresh
The life she had so tangled in her mesh:
And as he from one trance was wakening
Into another, she began to sing,
Happy in beauty, life, and love, and every thing,
A song of love, too sweet for earthly lyres,
While, like held breath, the stars drew in their panting
    fires.

And then she whispered in such trembling tone,
As those who, safe together met alone
For the first time through many anguished days,
Use other speech than looks; bidding him raise
His drooping head, and clear his soul of doubt,
For that she was a woman, and without
Any more subtle fluid in her veins
Than throbbing blood, and that the self-same pains
Inhabited her frail-strung heart as his.
And next she wondered how his eyes could miss
Her face so long in Corinth, where, she said,
She dwelt but half retired, and there had led
Days happy as the gold coin could invent
Without the aid of love; yet in content
Till she saw him, as once she passed him by,
Where 'gainst a column he leant thoughtfully
At Venus' temple porch, 'mid baskets heaped
Of amorous herbs and flowers, newly reaped
Late on that eve, as 'twas the night before
The Adonian feast; whereof she saw no more,
But wept alone those days, for why should she adore?
Lycius from death awoke into amaze,
To see her still, and singing so sweet lays;
Then from amaze into delight he fell
To hear her whisper woman's lore so well;
And every word she spake enticed him on
To unperplexed delight and pleasure known.
Let the mad poets say whate'er they please
Of the sweets of Fairies, Peris, Goddesses,
There is not such a treat among them all,
Haunters of cavern, lake, and waterfall,
As a real woman, lineal indeed
From Pyrrha's° pebbles or old Adam's seed.
Thus gentle Lamia judged, and judged aright,
That Lycius could not love in half a fright,
So threw the goddess off, and won his heart
More pleasantly by playing woman's part,
With no more awe than what her beauty gave,

333 **Pyrrha** After the flood, Pyrrha dispersed pebbles, out of which grew a new generation of men.

LAMIA

That, while it smote, still guaranteed to save.
Lycius to all made eloquent reply, 340
Marrying to every word a twinborn sigh;
And last, pointing to Corinth, asked her sweet,
If 'twas too far that night for her soft feet.
The way was short, for Lamia's eagerness
Made, by a spell, the triple league decrease 345
To a few paces; not at all surmised
By blinded Lycius, so in her comprised.
 They passed the city gates, he knew not how,
So noiseless, and he never thought to know.

 As men talk in a dream, so Corinth all, 350
Throughout her palaces imperial,
And all her populous streets and temples lewd,
Muttered, like tempest in the distance brewed,
To the wide-spread night above her towers.
Men, women, rich and poor, in the cool hours, 355
Shuffled their sandals o'er the pavement white,
Companioned or alone; while many a light
Flared, here and there, from wealthy festivals,
And threw their moving shadows on the walls,
Or found them clustered in the corniced shade 360
Of some arched temple door, or dusky colonnade.

 Muffling his face, of greeting friends in fear,
Her fingers he pressed hard, as one came near
With curled gray beard, sharp eyes, and smooth bald crown,
Slow-stepped, and robed in philosophic gown: 365
Lycius shrank closer, as they met and passed,
Into his mantle, adding wings to haste,
While hurried Lamia trembled: "Ah," said he,
"Why do you shudder, love, so ruefully?
Why does your tender palm dissolve in dew?"— 370
"I'm wearied," said fair Lamia: "tell me who
Is that old man? I cannot bring to mind
His features:—Lycius! wherefore did you blind
Yourself from his quick eyes?" Lycius replied,
" 'Tis Apollonius sage, my trusty guide 375

And good instructor; but tonight he seems
The ghost of folly haunting my sweet dreams."

While yet he spake they had arrived before
A pillared porch, with lofty portal door,
Where hung a silver lamp, whose phosphor glow
Reflected in the slabbèd steps below,
Mild as a star in water; for so new,
And so unsullied was the marble hue,
So through the crystal polish, liquid fine,
Ran the dark veins, that none but feet divine
Could e'er have touched there. Sounds Æolian
Breathed from the hinges, as the ample span
Of the wide doors disclosed a place unknown
Some time to any, but those two alone,
And a few Persian mutes, who that same year
Were seen about the markets: none knew where
They could inhabit; the most curious
Were foiled, who watched to trace them to their house:
And but the flitter-wingèd verse must tell
For truth's sake, what woe afterwards befell,
'Twould humor many a heart to leave them thus,
Shut from the busy world of more incredulous.

Part II

Love in a hut, with water and a crust,
Is—Love, forgive us!—cinders, ashes, dust;
Love in a palace is perhaps at last
More grievous torment than a hermit's fast:—
That is a doubtful tale from fairy land,
Hard for the non-elect to understand.
Had Lycius lived to hand his story down,
He might have given the moral a fresh frown,
Or clenched it quite: but too short was their bliss
To breed distrust and hate, that make the soft voice hiss.
Besides, there, nightly, with terrific glare,
Love, jealous grown of so complete a pair,

LAMIA

Hovered and buzzed his wings, with fearful roar,
Above the lintel of their chamber door,
And down the passage cast a glow upon the floor.

   For all this came a ruin: side by side
They were enthronèd, in the even tide,
Upon a couch, near to a curtaining
Whose airy texture, from a golden string,
Floated into the room, and let appear
Unveiled the summer heaven, blue and clear,
Betwixt two marble shafts:—there they reposed,
Where use had made it sweet, with eyelids closed,
Saving a tythe which love still open kept,
That they might see each other while they almost
    slept;
When from the slope side of a suburb hill,
Deafening the swallow's twitter, came a thrill
Of trumpets—Lycius started—the sounds fled,
But left a thought a-buzzing in his head.
For the first time, since first he harbored in
That purple-linèd palace of sweet sin,
His spirit passed beyond its golden bourn
Into the noisy world almost forsworn.
The lady, ever watchful, penetrant,
Saw this with pain, so arguing a want
Of something more, more than her empery
Of joys; and she began to moan and sigh
Because he mused beyond her, knowing well
That but a moment's thought is passion's passing bell.
"Why do you sigh, fair creature?" whispered he:
"Why do you think?" returned she tenderly:
"You have deserted me;—where am I now?
Not in your heart while care weighs on your brow:
No, no, you have dismissed me; and I go
From your breast houseless: ay, it must be so."
He answered, bending to her open eyes,
Where he was mirrored small in paradise,
"My silver planet, both of eve and morn!
Why will you plead yourself so sad forlorn,
While I am striving how to fill my heart

With deeper crimson, and a double smart?
How to entangle, trammel up and snare
Your soul in mine, and labyrinth you there
Like the hid scent in an unbudded rose?
Ay, a sweet kiss—you see your mighty woes.
My thoughts! shall I unveil them? Listen then!
What mortal hath a prize, that other men
May be confounded and abashed withal,
But lets it sometimes pace abroad majestical,
And triumph, as in thee I should rejoice
Amid the hoarse alarm of Corinth's voice.
Let my foes choke, and my friends shout afar,
While through the throngèd streets your bridal car
Wheels round its dazzling spokes."—The lady's cheek
Trembled; she nothing said, but, pale and meek,
Arose and knelt before him, wept a rain
Of sorrows at his words; at last with pain
Beseeching him, the while his hand she wrung,
To change his purpose. He thereat was stung,
Perverse, with stronger fancy to reclaim
Her wild and timid nature to his aim:
Besides, for all his love, in self despite
Against his better self, he took delight
Luxurious in her sorrows, soft and new.
His passion, cruel grown, took on a hue
Fierce and sanguineous as 'twas possible
In one whose brow had no dark veins to swell.
Fine was the mitigated fury, like
Apollo's presence when in act to strike
The serpent—Ha, the serpent! certes, she
Was none. She burned, she loved the tyranny,
And, all subdued, consented to the hour
When to the bridal he should lead his paramour.
Whispering in midnight silence, said the youth,
"Sure some sweet name thou hast, though, by my truth,
I have not asked it, ever thinking thee
Not mortal, but of heavenly progeny,
As still I do. Hast any mortal name,
Fit appellation for this dazzling frame?

LAMIA

Or friends or kinfolk on the citied earth, 90
To share our marriage feast and nuptial mirth?"
"I have no friends," said Lamia, "no, not one;
My presence in wide Corinth hardly known:
My parents' bones are in their dusty urns
Sepulchered, where no kindled incense burns, 95
Seeing all their luckless race are dead, save me,
And I neglect the holy rite for thee.
Even as you list invite your many guests;
But if, as now it seems, your vision rests
With any pleasure on me, do not bid 100
Old Apollonius—from him keep me hid."
Lycius, perplexed at words so blind and blank,
Made close inquiry; from whose touch she shrank, 105
Feigning a sleep; and he to the dull shade
Of deep sleep in a moment was betrayed.

It was the custom then to bring away
The bride from home at blushing shut of day,
Veiled, in a chariot, heralded along
By strewn flowers, torches, and a marriage song,
With other pageants: but this fair unknown 110
Had not a friend. So being left alone,
(Lycius was gone to summon all his kin)
And knowing surely she could never win
His foolish heart from its mad pompousness,
She set herself, high-thoughted, how to dress 115
The misery in fit magnificence.
She did so, but 'tis doubtful how and whence
Came, and who were her subtle servitors.
About the halls, and to and from the doors,
There was a noise of wings, till in short space 120
The glowing banquet room shone with wide-arched grace.
A haunting music, sole perhaps and lone
Supportress of the fairy roof, made moan
Throughout, as fearful the whole charm might fade.
Fresh carvèd cedar, mimicking a glade 125
Of palm and plantain, met from either side,
High in the midst, in honor of the bride:

Two palms and then two plantains, and so on,
From either side their stems branched one to one
130 All down the aislèd place; and beneath all
There ran a stream of lamps straight on from wall to wall.
So canopied, lay an untasted feast
Teeming with odors. Lamia, regal dressed,
Silently paced about, and as she went,
135 In pale contented sort of discontent,
Missioned her viewless servants to enrich
The fretted splendor of each nook and niche.
Between the tree stems, marbled plain at first,
Came jasper panels; then, anon, there burst
140 Forth creeping imagery of slighter trees,
And with the larger wove in small intricacies.
Approving all, she faded at self-will,
And shut the chamber up, close, hushed and still.
Complete and ready for the revels rude,
When dreadful guests would come to spoil her
145   solitude.

The day appeared, and all the gossip rout.
O senseless Lycius! Madman! wherefore flout
The silent-blessing fate, warm cloistered hours,
And show to common eyes these secret bowers?
150 The herd approached; each guest, with busy brain,
Arriving at the portal, gazed amain,
And entered marveling: for they knew the street,
Remembered it from childhood all complete
Without a gap, yet ne'er before had seen
155 That royal porch, that high-built fair demesne;
So in they hurried all, mazed, curious and keen:
Save one, who looked thereon with eye severe,
And with calm-planted steps walked in austere;
'Twas Apollonius: something too he laughed,
160 As though some knotty problem, that had daft
His patient thought, had now begun to thaw,
And solve and melt:—'twas just as he foresaw.

He met within the murmurous vestibule

LAMIA

His young disciple. " 'Tis no common rule,
Lycius," said he, "for uninvited guest
To force himself upon you, and infest
With an unbidden presence the bright throng
Of younger friends; yet must I do this wrong,
And you forgive me." Lycius blushed, and led
The old man through the inner doors broad-spread;
With reconciling words and courteous mien
Turning into sweet milk the sophist's spleen.

Of wealthy luster was the banquet room,
Filled with pervading brilliance and perfume:
Before each lucid panel fuming stood
A censer fed with myrrh and spicèd wood,
Each by a sacred tripod held aloft,
Whose slender feet wide-swerved upon the soft
Wool-woofèd carpets: fifty wreaths of smoke
From fifty censers their light voyage took
To the high roof, still mimicked as they rose
Along the mirrored walls by twin clouds odorous.
Twelve spherèd tables, by silk seats insphered,
High as the level of a man's breast reared
On libbard's paws, upheld the heavy gold
Of cups and goblets, and the store thrice told
Of Ceres' horn, and, in huge vessels, wine
Come from the gloomy tun with merry shine.
Thus loaded with a feast the tables stood,
Each shrining in the midst the image of a God.

When in an antechamber every guest
Had felt the cold full sponge to pleasure pressed,
By minist'ring slaves, upon his hands and feet,
And fragrant oils with ceremony meet
Poured on his hair, they all moved to the feast
In white robes, and themselves in order placed
Around the silken couches, wondering
Whence all this mighty cost and blaze of wealth could
    spring.

Soft went the music the soft air along,

200 While fluent Greek a voweled undersong
     Kept up among the guests, discoursing low
     At first, for scarcely was the wine at flow;
     But when the happy vintage touched their brains,
     Louder they talk, and louder come the strains
205 Of powerful instruments:—the gorgeous dyes,
     The space, the splendor of the draperies,
     The roof of awful richness, nectarous cheer,
     Beautiful slaves, and Lamia's self, appear,
     Now, when the wine has done its rosy deed,
210 And every soul from human trammels freed,
     No more so strange; for merry wine, sweet wine,
     Will make Elysian shades not too fair, too divine.
     Soon was God Bacchus at meridian height;
     Flushed were their cheeks, and bright eyes double bright:
215 Garlands of every green, and every scent
     From vales deflowered, or forest trees branch-rent,
     In baskets of bright osiered gold were brought
     High as the handles heaped, to suit the thought
     Of every guest; that each, as he did please,
220 Might fancy-fit his brows, silk-pillowed at his ease.

     What wreath for Lamia? What for Lycius?
     What for the sage, old Apollonius?
     Upon her aching forehead be there hung
     The leaves of willow and of adder's tongue;
225 And for the youth, quick, let us strip for him
     The thyrsus, that his watching eyes may swim
     Into forgetfulness; and, for the sage,
     Let spear grass and the spiteful thistle wage
     War on his temples. Do not all charms fly
230 At the mere touch of cold philosophy?
     There was an awful rainbow once in heaven:
     We know her woof, her texture; she is given
     In the dull catalog of common things.
     Philosophy will clip an angel's wings,
235 Conquer all mysteries by rule and line,
     Empty the haunted air, and gnomed mine—

Unweave a rainbow, as it erewhile made
The tender-personed Lamia melt into a shade.

By her glad Lycius sitting, in chief place,
Scarce saw in all the room another face, 240
Till, checking his love trance, a cup he took
Full brimmed, and opposite sent forth a look
'Cross the broad table, to beseech a glance
From his old teacher's wrinkled countenance,
And pledge him. The bald-head philosopher 245
Had fixed his eye, without a twinkle or stir
Full on the alarmèd beauty of the bride,
Brow-beating her fair form, and troubling her sweet
  pride.
Lycius then presed her hand, with devout touch,
As pale it lay upon the rosy couch: 250
'Twas icy, and the cold ran through his veins;
Then sudden it grew hot, and all the pains
Of an unnatural heat shot to his heart.
"Lamia, what means this? Wherefore dost thou start?
Know'st thou that man?" Poor Lamia answered not. 255
He gazed into her eyes, and not a jot
Owned they the lovelorn piteous appeal:
More, more he gazed: his human senses reel:
Some hungry spell that loveliness absorbs;
There was no recognition in those orbs. 260
"Lamia!" he cried—and no soft-toned reply.
The many heard, and the loud revelry
Grew hush; the stately music no more breathes;
The myrtle sickened in a thousand wreaths.
By faint degrees, voice, lute, and pleasure ceased; 265
A deadly silence step by step increased,
Until it seemed a horrid presence there,
And not a man but felt the terror in his hair.
"Lamia!" he shrieked; and nothing but the shriek
With its sad echo did the silence break. 270
"Begone, foul dream!" he cried, gazing again
In the bride's face, where now no azure vein
Wandered on fair-spaced temples; no soft bloom

Misted the cheek; no passion to illume
The deep-recessèd vision:—all was blight;
Lamia, no longer fair, there sat a deadly white.
"Shut, shut those juggling eyes, thou ruthless man!
Turn them aside, wretch! or the righteous ban
Of all the Gods, whose dreadful images
Here represent their shadowy presences,
May pierce them on the sudden with the thorn
Of painful blindness; leaving thee forlorn,
In trembling dotage to the feeblest fright
Of conscience, for their long offended might,
For all thine impious proud-heart sophistries,
Unlawful magic, and enticing lies.
Corinthians! look upon that gray-beard wretch!
Mark how, possessed, his lashless eyelids stretch
Around his demon eyes! Corinthians, see!
My sweet bride withers at their potency."
"Fool!" said the sophist, in an undertone
Gruff with contempt; which a death-nighing moan
From Lycius answered, as heart-struck and lost,
He sank supine beside the aching ghost.
"Fool! Fool!" repeated he, while his eyes still
Relented not, nor moved; "from every ill
Of life have I preserved thee to this day,
And shall I see thee made a serpent's prey?"
Then Lamia breathed death breath; the sophist's eye,
Like a sharp spear, went through her utterly,
Keen, cruel, perceant, stinging: she, as well
As her weak hand could any meaning tell,
Motioned him to be silent; vainly so,
He looked and looked again a level—No!
"A serpent!" echoed he; no sooner said,
Than with a frightful scream she vanished:
And Lycius' arms were empty of delight,
As were his limbs of life, from that same night.
On the high couch he lay!—his friends came round—
Supported him—no pulse, or breath they found,
And, in its marriage robe, the heavy body wound.

THE FALL OF HYPERION

A Dream

Canto I

Fanatics have their dreams, wherewith they weave
A paradise for a sect; the savage too
From forth the loftiest fashion of his sleep
Guesses at Heaven: pity these have not
Traced upon vellum or wild Indian leaf   5
The shadows of melodious utterance.
But bare of laurel they live, dream and die;
For Poesy alone can tell her dreams,
With the fine spell of words alone can save
Imagination from the sable charm   10
And dumb enchantment. Who alive can say
"Thou art no poet; mayst not tell thy dreams"?
Since every man whose soul is not a clod
Hath visions, and would speak, if he had loved
And been well nurtured in his mother tongue   15
Whether the dream now purposed to rehearse
Be poet's or fanatic's will be known
When this warm scribe my hand is in the grave.

   Methought I stood where trees of every clime,
Palm, myrtle, oak, and sycamore, and beech,   20
With plantain, and spice blossoms, made a screen;
In neighborhood of fountains, by the noise
Soft-showering in mine ears; and, by the touch
Of scent, not far from roses. Turning round,
I saw an arbor with a drooping roof   25
Of trellis vines, and bells, and larger blooms,

---

0 **The Fall of Hyperion** The new version of the unfinished epic poem was begun in late July, 1819, and continued till September 21, when Keats left it unfinished.

Like floral censers swinging light in air;
Before its wreathèd doorway, on a mound
Of moss, was spread a feast of summer fruits,
Which nearer seen, seemed refuse of a meal
By angel tasted, or our mother Eve;
For empty shells were scattered on the grass,
And grape stalks but half bare, and remnants more,
Sweet smelling, whose pure kinds I could not know.
Still was more plenty than the fabled horn°
Thrice emptied could pour forth, at banqueting
For Proserpine returned to her own fields,
Where the white heifers low. And appetite
More yearning than on earth I ever felt
Growing within, I ate deliciously;
And, after not long, thirsted, for thereby
Stood a cool vessel of transparent juice,
Sipped by the wandered bee, the which I took,
And, pledging all the mortals of the world,
And all the dead whose names are in our lips,
Drank. That full draught is parent of my theme.
No Asian poppy, nor elixir fine
Of the soon-fading, jealous Caliphat;
No poison gendered in close monkish cell
To thin the scarlet conclave of old men,
Could so have rapt unwilling life away.
Amongst the fragrant husks and berries crushed,
Upon the grass I struggled hard against
The domineering potion; but in vain:
The cloudy swoon came on, and down I sunk
Like a Silenus on an antique vase.
How long I slumbered 'tis a chance to guess.
When sense of life returned, I started up
As if with wings; but the fair trees were gone,
The mossy mound and arbor were no more;
I looked around upon the carved sides
Of an old sanctuary with roof august,
Builded so high, it seemed that filmèd clouds
Might spread beneath, as o'er the stars of heaven;

35 **fabled horn** Amalthea's horn of plenty.

THE FALL OF HYPERION

So old the place was, I remembered none 65
The like upon the earth: what I had seen
Of gray cathedrals, buttressed walls, rent towers,
The superannuations of sunk realms,
Or Nature's rocks toiled hard in waves and winds,
Seemed but the faulture of decrepit things 70
To that eternal domèd monument.
Upon the marble at my feet there lay
Store of strange vessels, and large draperies,
Which needs had been of dyed asbestos wove,
Or in that place the moth could not corrupt, 75
So white the linen; so, in some, distinct
Ran imageries from a somber loom.
All in a mingled heap confused there lay
Robes, golden tongs, censer, and chafing dish,
Girdles, and chains, and holy jewelries— 80
   Turning from these with awe, once more I raised
My eyes to fathom the space every way;
The embossed roof, the silent massy range
Of columns north and south, ending in mist
Of nothing; then to eastward, where black gates 85
Were shut against the sunrise evermore.
Then to the west I looked, and saw far off
An image, huge of feature as a cloud,
At level of whose feet an altar slept,
To be approached on either side by steps, 90
And marble balustrade, and patient travail
To count with toil the innumerable degrees.
Towards the altar sober-paced I went,
Repressing haste, as too unholy there;
And, coming nearer, saw beside the shrine 95
One minist'ring; and there arose a flame.
When in mid-May the sickening east wind
Shifts sudden to the south, the small warm rain
Melts out the frozen incense from all flowers,
And fills the air with so much pleasant health 100
That even the dying man forgets his shroud;
Even so that lofty sacrificial fire,
Sending forth Maian incense, spread around

Forgetfulness of everything but bliss,
105 And clouded all the altar with soft smoke,
From whose white fragrant curtains thus I heard
Language pronounced. "If thou canst not ascend
These steps, die on that marble where thou art.
Thy flesh, near cousin to the common dust,
110 Will parch for lack of nutriment—thy bones
Will wither in few years, and vanish so
That not the quickest eye could find a grain
Of what thou now art on that pavement cold.
The sands of thy short life are spent this hour,
115 And no hand in the universe can turn
Thy hourglass, if these gummed leaves be burned
Ere thou canst mount up these immortal steps."
I heard, I looked: two senses both at once
So fine, so subtle, felt the tyranny
120 Of that fierce threat, and the hard task proposed.
Prodigious seemed the toil, the leaves were yet
Burning—when suddenly a palsied chill
Struck from the pavèd level up my limbs,
And was ascending quick to put cold grasp
125 Upon those streams that pulse beside the throat:
I shrieked; and the sharp anguish of my shriek
Stung my own ears—I strove hard to escape
The numbness; strove to gain the lowest step.
Slow, heavy, deadly was my pace: the cold
130 Grew stifling, suffocating, at the heart;
And when I clasped my hands I felt them not.
One minute before death, my iced foot touched
The lowest stair; and as it touched, life seemed
To pour in at the toes: I mounted up,
135 As once fair angels on a ladder flew
From the green turf to heaven.—"Holy Power,"
Cried I, approaching near the hornèd shrine,
"What am I that should so be saved from death?
What am I that another death come not
140 To choak my utterance sacrilegious here?"
Then said the veilèd shadow—"Thou hast felt
What 'tis to die and live again before
Thy fated hour. That thou hadst power to do so

THE FALL OF HYPERION

Is thy own safety; thou hast dated on
Thy doom." "High Prophetess," said I, "purge off
Benign, if so it please thee, my mind's film—"
"None can usurp this height," returned that shade,
"But those to whom the miseries of the world
Are misery, and will not let them rest.
All else who find a haven in the world,
Where they may thoughtless sleep away their days,
If by a chance into this fane they come,
Rot on the pavement where thou rotted'st half.—"
"Are there not thousands in the world," said I,
Encouraged by the sooth voice of the shade,
"Who love their fellows even to the death;
Who feel the giant agony of the world;
And more, like slaves to poor humanity,
Labor for mortal good? I sure should see
Other men here: but I am here alone."
"They whom thou spak'st of are no vision'ries,"
Rejoined that voice—"they are no dreamers weak,
They seek no wonder but the human face;
No music but a happy-noted voice—
They come not here, they have no thought to come—
And thou art here, for thou art less than they—
What benefit canst thou do, or all thy tribe,
To the great world? Thou art a dreaming thing;
A fever of thyself—think of the Earth;
What bliss even in hope is there for thee?
What haven? every creature hath its home;
Every sole man hath days of joy and pain,
Whether his labors be sublime or low—
The pain alone; the joy alone; distinct:
Only the dreamer venoms all his days,
Bearing more woe than all his sins deserve.
Therefore, that happiness be somewhat shared,
Such things as thou art are admitted oft
Into like gardens thou didst pass erewhile,
And suffered in these temples; for that cause
Thou standest safe beneath this statue's knees."
"That I am favored for unworthiness,
By such propitious parley medicined

In sickness not ignoble, I rejoice,
185   Aye, and could weep for love of such award."
       So answered I, continuing, "If it please,
       Majestic shadow, tell me: sure not all
       Those melodies sung into the world's ear
       Are useless: sure a poet is a sage;
190   A humanist, physician to all men.
       That I am none I feel, as vultures feel
       They are no birds when eagles are abroad.
       What am I then? Thou spakest of my tribe:
       What tribe?"—The tall shade veiled in drooping white
195   Then spake, so much more earnest, that the breath
       Moved the thin linen folds that drooping hung
       About a golden censer from the hand
       Pendent.—"Art thou not of the dreamer tribe?
       The poet and the dreamer are distinct,
200   Diverse, sheer opposite, antipodes.
       The one pours out a balm upon the world,
       The other vexes it." Then shouted I
       Spite of myself, and with a Pythia's spleen,
       "Apollo! faded, farflown Apollo!
205   Where is thy misty pestilence to creep
       Into the dwellings, thro' the door crannies,
       Of all mock lyrists, large self-worshipers,
       And careless Hectorers in proud bad verse.
       Tho' I breathe death with them it will be life
210   To see them sprawl before me into graves.°
       Majestic shadow, tell me where I am,
       Whose altar this; for whom this incense curls:
       What image this, whose face I cannot see,
       For the broad marble knees; and who thou art,
215   Of accent feminine, so courteous."
       Then the tall shade, in drooping linens veiled,

186-210 **If it please ... graves** Richard Woodhouse, the legal adviser to Keats's publishers who made numerous copies of Keats's manuscripts, has indicated that Keats intended to delete these lines from the final version of the poem. Some editors (e.g., Middleton Murry) have followed this suggestion but several commentators consider the lines necessary in the progression of the exchange between Moneta and the poet.

THE FALL OF HYPERION

Spake out, so much more earnest, that her breath
Stirred the thin folds of gauze that drooping hung
About a golden censer from her hand
Pendent; and by her voice I knew she shed   220
Long-treasured tears. "This temple sad and lone
Is all spared from the thunder of a war
Foughten long since by giant hierarchy
Against rebellion: this old image here,
Whose carvèd features wrinkled as he fell,   225
Is Saturn's; I, Moneta,° left supreme
Sole priestess of his desolation."—
I had no words to answer; for my tongue,
Useless, could find about its roofèd home
No syllable of a fit majesty   230
To make rejoinder to Moneta's mourn.
There was a silence while the altar's blaze
Was fainting for sweet food: I looked thereon,
And on the pavèd floor, where nigh were piled
Faggots of cinnamon, and many heaps   235
Of other crispèd spicewood—then again
I looked upon the altar and its horns
Whitened with ashes, and its lang'rous flame,
And then upon the offerings again;
And so by turns—till sad Moneta cried,   240
"The sacrifice is done, but not the less,
Will I be kind to thee for thy goodwill.
My power which to me is still a curse,
Shall be to thee a wonder; for the scenes
Still swooning vivid through my globèd brain   245
With an electral changing misery
Thou shalt with those dull mortal eyes behold,
Free from all pain, if wonder pain thee not."
As near as an immortal's sphered words
Could to a mother's soften, were these last: 250
But yet I had a terror of her robes,
And chiefly of the veils, that from her brow
Hung pale, and curtained her in mysteries

---

226 **Moneta** Roman name of Mnemosyne, who appears in the first version.

That made my heart too small to hold its blood.
This saw that Goddess, and with sacred hand
Parted the veils. Then saw I a wan face,
Not pined by human sorrows, but bright blanched
By an immortal sickness which kills not;
It works a constant change, which happy death
Can put no end to; deathwards progressing
To no death was that visage; it had passed
The lily and the snow; and beyond these
I must not think now, though I saw that face—
But for her eyes I should have fled away.
They held me back, with a benignant light,
Soft-mitigated by divinest lids
Half closed, and visionless entire they seemed
Of all external things—they saw me not,
But in blank splendor beamed like the mild moon,
Who comforts those she sees not, who knows not
What eyes are upward cast. As I had found
A grain of gold upon a mountain's side,
And twinged with avarice strained out my eyes
To search its sullen entrails rich with ore,
So at the view of sad Moneta's brow,
I ached to see what things the hollow brain
Behind enwombed: what high tragedy
In the dark secret chambers of her skull
Was acting, that could give so dread a stress
To her cold lips, and fill with such a light
Her planetary eyes; and touch her voice
With such a sorrow—"Shade of memory!"
Cried I, with act adorant at her feet,
"By all the gloom hung round thy fallen house,
By this last temple, by the golden age,
By great Apollo, thy dear foster child,
And by thyself, forlorn divinity,
The pale Omega of a withered race,
Let me behold, according as thou said'st,
What in thy brain so ferments to and fro."—
No sooner had this conjuration passed
My devout lips; than side by side we stood,
(Like a stunt bramble by a solemn pine)

THE FALL OF HYPERION

Deep in the shady sadness° of a vale,
Far sunken from the healthy breath of morn,
Far from the fiery noon and Eve's one star.
Onward I looked beneath the gloomy boughs,
And saw, what first I thought an image huge,
Like to the image pedestaled so high
In Saturn's temple. Then Moneta's voice
Came brief upon mine ear—"So Saturn sat
When he had lost his realms"—Whereon there grew
A power within me of enormous ken,
To see as a God sees, and take the depth
Of things as nimbly as the outward eye
Can size and shape pervade. The lofty theme
At those few words hung vast before my mind,
With half unraveled web. I set myself
Upon an eagle's watch, that I might see,
And seeing ne'er forget. No stir of life
Was in this shrouded vale, not so much air
As in the zoning of a summer's day
Robs not one light seed from the feathered grass,
But where the dead leaf fell there did it rest.
A stream went voiceless by, still deadened more
By reason of the fallen divinity
Spreading more shade: the Naiad 'mid her reeds
Pressed her cold finger closer to her lips.
Along the margin sand large footmarks went
No farther than to where old Saturn's feet
Had rested, and there slept, how long a sleep!
Degraded, cold, upon the sodden ground
His old right hand lay nerveless, listless, dead,
Unsceptered; and his realmless eyes were closed,
While his bowed head seemed listening to the Earth,
His ancient mother, for some comfort yet.

  It seemed no force could wake him from his place;
But there came one with a kindred hand
Touched his wide shoulders, after bending low
With reverence, though to one who knew it not.
Then came the grieved voice of Mnemosyne,

294 **Deep in the shady sadness** returns to the original version of *Hyperion*, though often with important changes.

And grieved I hearkened. "That divinity
Whom thou saw'st step from yon forlornest wood,
And with slow pace approach our fallen King,
335 Is Thea, softest-natured of our brood."
I marked the goddess in fair statuary
Surpassing wan Moneta by the head,
And in her sorrow nearer woman's tears.
There was a listening fear in her regard,
340 As if calamity had but begun;
As if the vanward clouds of evil days
Had spent their malice, and the sullen rear
Was with its stored thunder laboring up.
One hand she pressed upon that aching spot
345 Where beats the human heart; as if just there
Though an immortal, she felt cruel pain;
The other upon Saturn's bended neck
She laid, and to the level of his hollow ear
Leaning, with parted lips, some words she spoke
350 In solemn tenor and deep organ tune;
Some mourning words, which in our feeble tongue
Would come in this-like accenting; how frail
To that large utterance of the early gods!—
"Saturn! look up—and for what, poor lost king?
355 I have no comfort for thee, no—not one;
I cannot cry, *Wherefore thus sleepest thou:*
For heaven is parted from thee, and the earth
Knows thee not, so afflicted, for a God;
The ocean too, with all its solemn noise,
360 Has from thy scepter passed; and all the air
Is emptied of thine hoary majesty.
Thy thunder, captious at the new command,
Rumbles reluctant o'er our fallen house;
And thy sharp lightning in unpracticed hands
365 Scorches and burns our once serene domain.
With such remorseless speed still come new woes
That unbelief has not a space to breathe.
Saturn, sleep on: Me thoughtless, why should I
Thus violate thy slumbrous solitude?
370 Why should I ope thy melancholy eyes?
Saturn, sleep on, while at thy feet I weep."—

THE FALL OF HYPERION

As when, upon a trancèd summer night,
Forests, branch-charmèd by the earnest stars,
Dream, and so dream all night, without a noise,
Save from one gradual solitary gust, 375
Swelling upon the silence; dying off;
As if the ebbing air had but one wave;
So came these words, and went; the while in tears
She pressed her fair large forehead to the earth,
Just where her fallen hair might spread in curls, 380
A soft and silken mat for Saturn's feet.
Long, long, those two were postured motionless,
Like sculpture builded up upon the grave
Of their own power. A long awful time
I looked upon them; still they were the same; 385
The frozen God still bending to the Earth,
And the sad Goddess weeping at his feet.
Moneta silent. Without stay or prop
But my own weak mortality, I bore
The load of this eternal quietude, 390
The unchanging gloom, and the three fixed shapes
Ponderous upon my senses a whole moon.
For by my burning brain I measured sure
Her silver seasons shedded on the night
And ever day by day methought I grew 395
More gaunt and ghostly—Oftentimes I prayed
Intense, that death would take me from the vale
And all its burthens—Gasping with despair
Of change, hour after hour I cursed myself:
Until old Saturn raised his faded eyes, 400
And looked around and saw his kingdom gone,
And all the gloom and sorrow of the place,
And that fair kneeling Goddess at his feet.
As the moist scent of flowers, and grass, and leaves
Fills forest dells with a pervading air, 405
Known to the woodland nostril, so the words
Of Saturn filled the mossy glooms around,
Even to the hollows of time-eaten oaks,
And to the winding in the foxes' holes,
With sad low tones, while thus he spake, and sent 410
Strange musings to the solitary Pan.

"Moan, brethren, moan; for we are swallowed up
And buried from all godlike exercise
Of influence benign on planets pale,
And peaceful sway above man's harvesting,
And all those acts which Deity supreme
Doth ease its heart of love in. Moan and wail.
Moan, brethren, moan; for lo! the rebel spheres
Spin round, the stars their ancient courses keep,
Clouds still with shadowy moisture haunt the earth,
Still suck their fill of light from sun and moon,
Still buds the tree, and still the seashores murmur.
There is no death in all the universe
No smell of death—there shall be death—moan, moan,
Moan, Cybele, moan, for thy pernicious babes
Have changed a God into a shaking palsy.
Moan, brethren, moan, for I have no strength left,
Weak as the reed—weak—feeble as my voice—
O, O, the pain, the pain of feebleness.
Moan, moan; for still I thaw—or give me help:
Throw down those imps, and give me victory.
Let me hear other groans; and trumpets blown
Of triumph calm, and hymns of festival
From the gold peaks of heaven's high piled clouds;
Voices of soft proclaim, and silver stir
Of strings in hollow shells; and let there be
Beautiful things made new, for the surprise
Of the sky-children"—So he feebly ceased,
With such a poor and sickly sounding pause,
Methought I heard some old man of the earth
Bewailing earthly loss; nor could my eyes
And ears act with that pleasant unison of sense
Which marries sweet sound with the grace of form,
And dolorous accent from a tragic harp
With large-limbed visions. More I scrutinized:
Still fixed he sat beneath the sable trees,
Whose arms spread straggling in wild serpent forms,
With leaves all hushed: his awful presence there
(Now all was silent) gave a deadly lie
To what I erewhile heard: only his lips

THE FALL OF HYPERION

Trembled amid the white curls of his beard.
They told the truth, though, round, the snowy locks
Hung nobly, as upon the face of heaven
A midday fleece of clouds. Thea arose,
And stretched her white arm through the hollow dark, 455
Pointing some whither: whereat he too rose
Like a vast giant seen by men at sea
To grow pale from the waves at dull midnight.
They melted from my sight into the woods:
Ere I could turn, Moneta cried—"These twain 460
Are speeding to the families of grief,
Where roofed in by black rocks they waste in pain
And darkness for no hope."—And she spake on,
As ye may read who can unwearied pass
Onward from the antechamber of this dream, 465
Where even at the open doors awhile
I must delay, and glean my memory
Of her high phrase:—perhaps no further dare.

Canto II

"Mortal, that thou mayst understand aright,
I humanize my sayings to thine ear,
Making comparisons of earthly things;
Or thou might'st better listen to the wind,
Whose language is to thee a barren noise, 5
Though it blows legend-laden through the trees—
In melancholy realms big tears are shed,
More sorrow like to this, and such-like woe,
Too huge for mortal tongue, or pen of scribe.
The Titans fierce, self-hid, or prison-bound, 10
Groan for the old allegiance once more,
Listening in their doom for Saturn's voice.
But one of our whole eagle-brood still keeps
His sov'reignty, and rule, and majesty;
Blazing Hyperion on his orbèd fire 15
Still sits, still snuffs the incense teeming up
From man to the sun's God: yet unsecure,

For as upon the Earth dire prodigies
Fright and perplex, so also shudders he:
20 Nor at dog's howl, or gloom-bird's even screech,
Or the familiar visitings of one
Upon the first toll of his passing bell:
But horrors, portioned to a giant nerve,
Make great Hyperion ache. His palace bright,
25 Bastioned with pyramids of glowing gold,
And touched with shade of bronzèd obelisks,
Glares a blood red through all the thousand courts,
Arches, and domes, and fiery galleries;
And all its curtains of Aurorian clouds
30 Flush angerly: when he would taste the wreaths
Of incense breathed aloft from sacred hills,
Instead of sweets, his ample palate takes
Savor of poisonous brass and metals sick.
Wherefore when harbored in the sleepy west,
35 After the full completion of fair day,
For rest divine upon exalted couch
And slumber in the arms of melody,
He paces through the pleasant hours of ease,
With strides colossal, on from hall to hall;
40 While, far within each aisle and deep recess,
His wingèd minions in close clusters stand
Amazed, and full of fear; like anxious men
Who on a wide plain gather in sad troops,
When earthquakes jar their battlements and towers.
45 Even now, while Saturn, roused from icy trance
Goes, step for step, with Thea from yon woods,
Hyperion, leaving twilight in the rear,
Is sloping to the threshold of the west.—
Thither we tend."—Now in clear light I stood,
50 Relieved from the dusk vale. Mnemosyne
Was sitting on a square-edged polished stone,
That in its lucid depth reflected pure
Her priestess garments. My quick eyes ran on
From stately nave to nave, from vault to vault,
55 Thro' bowers of fragrant and enwreathèd light,
And diamond-pavèd lustrous long arcades.
Anon rushed by the bright Hyperion;

His flaming robes streamed out beyond his heels,
And gave a roar, as if of earthly fire,
That scared away the meek ethereal hours
And made their dove wings tremble: on he flared ...

TO AUTUMN°

1

Season of mists and mellow fruitfulness,
   Close bosom-friend of the maturing sun;
Conspiring with him how to load and bless
   With fruit the vines that round the thatch eves run;
To bend with apples the mossed cottage trees,
   And fill all fruit with ripeness to the core;
      To swell the gourd, and plump the hazel shells
With a sweet kernel; to set budding more,
   And still more, later flowers for the bees,
   Until they think warm days will never cease,
      For summer has o'er-brimmed their clammy cells.

2

Who hath not seen thee oft amid thy store?
   Sometimes whoever seeks abroad may find
Thee sitting careless on a granary floor,
   Thy hair soft-lifted by the winnowing wind;
Or on a half-reaped furrow sound asleep,
   Drowsed with the fume of poppies, while thy hook
      Spares the next swath and all its twinèd flowers:
And sometimes like a gleaner thou dost keep
   Steady thy laden head across a brook;
   Or by a cider press, with patient look,
      Thou watchest the last oozings hours by hours.

3

Where are the songs of spring? Ay, where are they?

---

0 **To Autumn** dates from September 19, 1819.

Think not of them, thou hast thy music too—
25 While barrèd clouds bloom the soft-dying day,
And touch the stubble plains with rosy hue;
Then in a wailful choir the small gnats mourn
Among the river shallows, borne aloft
Or sinking as the light wind lives or dies;
30 And full-grown lambs loud bleat from hilly bourn;
Hedge crickets sing; and now with treble soft
The red-breast whistles from a garden croft;
And gathering swallows twitter in the skies.

ODE TO FANNY°

1

Physician Nature! let my spirit blood!
O ease my heart of verse and let me rest;
Throw me upon thy tripod, till the flood
Of stifling numbers ebbs from my full breast.
5 A theme! a theme! great Nature! give a theme;
Let me begin my dream.
I come—I see thee, as thou standest there,
Beckon me out into the wintry air.

2

Ah! dearest love, sweet home of all my fears,
10 And hopes, and joys, and panting miseries—
Tonight, if I may guess, thy beauty wears
A smile of such delight,
As brilliant and as bright,
As when with ravished, aching, vassal eyes,
15 Lost in soft amaze,
I gaze, I gaze!

3

Who now, with greedy looks, eats up my feast?

0 **Fanny** Fanny Brawne, to whom Keats was engaged during the last months of his life.

ODE TO FANNY

What stare outfaces now my silver moon!
Ah! Keep that hand unravished at the least;
    Let, let, the amorous burn—
    But, prithee, do not turn
The current of your heart from me so soon.
    O! save, in charity,
    The quickest pulse for me.

4

Save it for me, sweet love! though music breathe
   Voluptuous visions into the warm air;
Though swimming through the dance's dangerous wreath;
    Be like an April day,
    Smiling and cold and gay,
A temperate lily, temperate as fair;
    Then, heaven! there will be
    A warmer June for me.

5

Why, this—you'll say, my Fanny! is not true:
   Put your soft hand upon your snowy side,
Where the heart beats: confess—'tis nothing new—
    Must not a woman be
    A feather on the sea,
Swayed to and fro by every wind and tide?
    Of as uncertain speed
    As blow-ball from the mead?

6

I know it—and to know it is despair
   To one who loves you as I love, sweet Fanny!
Whose heart goes fluttering for you everywhere,
    Nor, when away you roam,
    Dare keep its wretched home,
Love, love alone, has pains severe and many:
    Then, loveliest! keep me free
    From torturing jealousy.

SONNETS

The Day Is Gone

The day is gone, and all its sweets are gone!
   Sweet voice, sweet lips, soft hand, and softer breast,
Warm breath, light whisper, tender semi-tone,
   Bright eyes, accomplished shape, and lang'rous waist!
5 Faded the flower and all its budded charms,
   Faded the sight of beauty from my eyes,
Faded the shape of beauty from my arms,
   Faded the voice, warmth, whiteness, paradise—
Vanished unseasonably at shut of eve,
10   When the dusk holiday—or holinight
Of fragrant-curtained love begins to weave
   The woof of darkness thick, for hid delight;
But, as I've read love's missal through today,
He'll let me sleep, seeing I fast and pray.

To Fanny°

I cry your mercy—pity—love!—aye, love!
   Merciful love that tantalizes not,
One-thoughted, never-wandering, guileless love,
   Unmasked, and being seen—without a blot!
5 O! let me have thee whole—all—all—be mine!
   That shape, that fairness, that sweet minor zest
Of love, your kiss—those hands, those eyes divine,

---

0 **Fanny** Both this sonnet and the following one were addressed to Fanny Brawne. "To Fanny" was written in October–November, 1819

BRIGHT STAR

That warm, white, lucent, million-pleasured breast—
Yourself—your soul—in pity give me all,
    Without no atom's atom or I die,
Or living on perhaps, your wretched thrall,
    Forget, in the mist of idle misery,
Life's purposes—the palate of my mind
Losing its gust, and my ambition blind!

Bright Star°

Bright star! would I were steadfast as thou art—
    Not in lone splendor hung aloft the night
And watching, with eternal lids apart,
    Like nature's patient, sleepless eremite,
The moving waters at their priest-like task
    Of pure ablution round earth's human shores,
Or gazing on the new soft fallen mask
    Of snow upon the mountains and the moors—
No—yet still steadfast, still unchangeable,
    Pillowed upon my fair love's ripening breast,
To feel forever its soft fall and swell,
    Awake forever in a sweet unrest,
Still, still to hear her tender-taken breath,
And so live ever—or else swoon to death.

° **Bright Star** frequently referred to as Keats's last sonnet. Since the discovery of an earlier version, the date is being questioned and no decisive argument has yet been made to settle the question. Suggested dates range from as early as February, 1819, till October, 1819. This later version was copied by Keats on a blank page of Shakespeare's poems when he was on his way to Italy on September 28, 1820.

TO ——°

What can I do to drive away
Remembrance from my eyes? for they have seen,
Aye, an hour ago, my brilliant queen!
Touch has a memory. O say, love, say,
What can I do to kill it and be free
In my old liberty?
When every fair one that I saw was fair,
Enough to catch me in but half a snare,
Not keep me there:
When, howe'er poor or particolored things,
My muse had wings,
And ever ready was to take her course
Whither I bent her force,
Unintellectual, yet divine to me;—
Divine, I say!—What seabird o'er the sea
Is a philosopher the while he goes
Winging along where the great water throes?

   How shall I do
   To get anew
Those molted feathers, and so mount once more
   Above, above
   The reach of fluttering Love,
And make him cower lowly while I soar?
Shall I gulp wine? No, that is vulgarism,
   A heresy and schism,
    Foisted into the canon law of love;—
No—wine is only sweet to happy men;
   More dismal cares
   Seize on me unawares—
Where shall I learn to get my peace again?
To banish thoughts of that most hateful land,

° To —— addressed to Fanny Brawne, October, 1819.

Dungeoner of my friends, that wicked strand
Where they were wrecked and live a wreckèd life;
That monstrous region, whose dull rivers pour,
Ever from their sordid urns unto the shore, 35
Unowned of any weedy-hairèd gods;
Whose winds, all zephyrless, hold scourging rods,
Iced in the great lakes, to afflict mankind;
Whose rank-grown forests, frosted, black, and blind,
Would fright a Dryad; whose harsh herbaged meads 40
Make lean and lank the starved ox while he feeds;
There bad flowers have no scent, birds no sweet song,
And great unerring nature once seems wrong.

O, for some sunny spell
To dissipate the shadows of this hell! 45
Say they are gone—with the new dawning light
Steps forth my lady bright!
O, let me once more rest
My soul upon that dazzling breast!
Let once again these aching arms be placed, 50
The tender gaolers of thy waist!
And let me feel that warm breath here and there
To spread a rapture in my very hair—
O, the sweetness of the pain!
Give me those lips again! 55
Enough! Enough! it is enough for me
To dream of thee!

THIS LIVING HAND°

This living hand,° now warm and capable
Of earnest grasping, would, if it were cold
And in the icy silence of the tomb,

---

0 **This Living Hand** The lines are written in a blank space on the page that goes on to Stanza 51 of the satirical poem *The Cap and Bells*.

So haunt thy days and chill thy dreaming nights
That thou wouldst wish thine own heart dry of blood
So in my veins red life might stream again,
And thou be conscience-calmed—see here it is—
I hold it towards you.

IV. Selected Letters

To Benjamin Bailey   22 November 1817

My dear Bailey:
... What occasions the greater part of the World's Quarrels? simply this, two Minds meet and do not understand each other time enough to prevent any shock or surprise at the conduct of either party—As soon as I had known Haydon three days I had got enough of his character not to have been surprised at such a Letter as he has hurt you with. Nor when I knew it was it a principle with me to drop his acquaintance although with you it would have been an imperious feeling. I wish you knew all that I think about Genius and the Heart—and yet I think you are thoroughly acquainted with my innermost breast in that respect or you could not have known me even thus long and still hold me worthy to be your dear friend. In passing however I must say of one thing that has pressed upon me lately and increased my Humility and capability of submission and that is this truth—Men of Genius are great as certain ethereal Chemicals operating on the Mass of neutral intellect—but they have not any individuality, any determined Character. I would call the top and head of those who have a proper self Men of Power—

But I am running my head into a Subject which I am certain I could not do justice to under five years study and 3 vols octavo—and moreover long to be talking about the Imagination—so my dear Bailey do not think of this unpleasant affair if possible—do not—I defy any harm to come of it—I defy—I'll shall write to Crips this Week and request him to tell me all his goings on from time to time by Letter wherever I may be—it will all go on well—so don't because you have suddenly discovered a Coldness in Haydon suffer yourself to be teased. Do not my dear fellow. O I wish I was as certain of the end of all your troubles as that of your momentary start about the authenticity of the Imagination. I am certain of nothing but of the holiness of the Heart's affections and the truth of Imagination—What the imagination seizes as Beauty must be truth—whether it existed before or not—for I have the same Idea of all our Passions as of Love they are all in their sublime, creative of essential Beauty—In a Word, you may know my favorite Speculation by my first Book and the little song I sent in my last—which is a representation from the fancy of the probable mode of operating in these Matters—The Imagination may be compared to Adam's dream—he awoke and found it truth. I am the more zealous in this affair, because I have never yet been able to perceive how anything can be known for truth by consequitive reasoning—and yet it must be—Can it be that even the greatest Philosopher ever when arrived at his goal without putting aside numerous objections—However it may be, O for a Life of Sensations rather than of Thoughts! It is "a Vision in the form of Youth," a Shadow of reality to come—and this consideration has further convinced me for it has come as auxiliary to another favorite Speculation of mine, that we shall enjoy ourselves here after by having what we called happiness on Earth repeated in a finer tone and so repeated—And yet such a fate can only befall those who delight in sensation rather than hunger as you do after Truth—Adam's dream will do here and seems to be a conviction that Imagination and its empyreal reflection is the same as human Life and its spiritual repetition. But as I was saying—the simple imaginative Mind may have its rewards in the repetition of its own silent Working coming continually on the spirit with a fine suddenness—to compare great things with small—have you never by being surprised with an old Melody—in a delicious place—by a delicious voice, felt over again your very speculations and surmises at the time it first operated on your soul—do you not remember forming to youself the singer's face more beautiful that it was possible and yet with the elevation of the Moment you did not think so—even then you were mounted on the Wings of Imagination so high —that the Prototype must be here after—that delicious face you will see—What a time! I am continually running away from the subject—sure this cannot be exactly the case with a complex Mind—one that is imaginative and at the same time careful of its fruits—who would exist partly on sensation partly on thought—to whom it is necessary that years should bring the philosophic Mind —such an one I consider your's and therefore it is necessary to your eternal Happiness that you not only drink this old Wine of Heaven which I shall call the redigestion of our most ethereal Musings on Earth; but also increase in knowledge and know all things. I am glad to hear you are in a fair Way for Easter—you will soon get through your unpleasant reading and then!—but the world is full of troubles and I have not much reason to think myself pestered with many—I think Jane or Marianne has a better opinion of me than I deserve—for really and truly I do not think my Brothers illness connected with mine— you know more of the real Cause than they do—nor have I any chance of being racked as you have been—you perhaps at one time thought there was such a thing as Worldly Happiness to be arrived at, at certain periods of time marked out—you have of necessity from your disposition been thus led away—I scarcely remember counting upon any Happiness—I look not for it if it be not in the present hour—nothing startles me beyond the Moment. The setting sun will always set me to rights—or if a Sparrow come before my Window I take part in its existence and pick about the Gravel. The first thing that strikes me on hearing a Misfortune having befallen another is this. "Well it cannot be helped—he will have the pleasure of trying the resources of his spirit, and I beg now my dear Bailey that hereafter should you observe anything cold in me not to but it to the account of heartlessness but abstraction—for I assure you I sometimes feel not the influence of a Passion or Affection during a whole week—and so long this sometimes continues I begin to suspect myself and the genuineness of my feelings at other times—thinking them a few barren Tragedy-tears—My Brother Tom is much improved—he is going to Devonshire—whither I shall follow him—at present I am just arrived at Dorking to change the Scene—change the Air and give me a spur to wind up my Poem, of which there are wanting 500 Lines. . . .

> Your affectionate friend
> John Keats—

To George and Tom Keats 21, 27 (?) December 1817

> Hampstead Sunday
> 22 December 1818

My dear Brothers
. . . I have had two very pleasant evenings with Dilke yesterday & today; & am at this moment just come from him & feel in the humor to go on with this, began in the morning, & from which he came to fetch me. I spent Friday evening with Wells & went the next morning to see *Death on the Pale Horse*. It is a wonderful picture, when West's age is considered; But there is nothing to be intense upon; no women one feels mad to kiss; no face swelling into reality. The excellence of every Art is its intensity, capable of making all disagreeables evaporate, from their being in close relationship with Beauty & Truth —Examine King Lear & you will find this exemplified throughout; but in this picture we have unpleasantness without any momentous depth of speculation excited, in which to bury its repulsiveness—The picture is larger than Christ rejected—I dined with Haydon the Sunday after you left, & had a very pleasant day, I dined too (for I have been out too much lately) with Horace Smith & met his two Brothers with Hill & Kingston & one Du Bois, they

only served to convince me, how superior humor is to wit in respect to enjoyment—These men say things which make one start, without making one feel, they are all alike; their manners are alike; they all know fashionables; they have a mannerism in their very eating & drinking, in their mere handling a Decanter—They talked of Kean & his low company—Would I were with that company instead of yours said I to myself! I know such like acquaintance will never do for me & yet I am going to Reynolds, on Wednesday—Brown & Dilke walked with me & back from the Christmas pantomime. I had not a dispute but a disquisition with Dilke, on various subjects; several things dovetailed in my mind, & at once it struck me, what quality went to form a Man of Achievement especially in Literature & which Shakespeare possessed so enormously—I mean *Negative Capability,* that is when man is capable of being in uncertainties, Mysteries, doubts, without any irritable reaching after fact & reason—Coleridge, for instance, would let go by a fine isolated verisimilitude caught from the Penetralium of mystery, from being incapable of remaining content with half knowledge. This pursued through Volumes would perhaps take us no further than this, that with a great poet the sense of Beauty overcomes every other consideration, or rather obliterates all consideration.

Shelley's poem is out & there are words about its being objected too, as much as Queen Mab was. Poor Shelley I think he has his Quota of good qualities, in sooth la!! Write soon to your most sincere friend & affectionate Brother

(Signed) John

To J. H. Reynolds 19 February 1818

My dear Reynolds,

I have an idea that a Man might pass a very pleasant life in this manner—let him on any certain day read a certain Page of full Poesy or distilled Prose and let him wander with it, and muse upon it, and reflect from it, and bring home to it, and prophesy upon it, and dream upon it—until it becomes stale—but when will it do so? Never —When Man has arrived at a certain ripeness in intellect any one grand and spiritual passage serves him as a starting post towards all "the two-and-thirty Pallaces" How happy is such a "voyage of conception," what delicious diligent Indolence! A doze upon a Sofa does not hinder it, and a nap upon Clover engenders ethereal finger-pointings—the prattle of a child gives it wings, and the converse of middle age a strength to beat them—a strain of music conducts to "an odd angle of the Isle" and when the leaves whisper it puts a "girdle round the earth." Nor will this sparing touch of noble Books be any irreverence to their Writers—for perhaps the honors paid by Man to Man are trifles in comparison to the Benefit done by great Works to the "Spirit and pulse of good" by their mere passive existence. Memory should not be called knowledge—Many have original Minds who do not think it— they are led away by Custom—Now it appears to me that almost any Man may like the Spider spin from his own inwards his own airy Citadel—the points of leaves and twigs on which the Spider begins her work are few and she fills the Air with a beautiful circuiting: man should be content with as few points to tip with the fine Web of his Soul and weave a tapestry empyrean—full of Symbols for his spiritual eye, of softness for his spiritual touch, of space for his wandering of distinctness for his Luxury— But the Minds of Mortals are so different and bent on such diverse Journeys that it may at first appear impossible for any common taste and fellowship to exist between two or three under these suppositions—It is, however, quite the contrary—Minds would leave each other in contrary directions, traverse each other in Numberless points, and all last greet each other at the Journey's end—A old Man and a child would talk together and the old Man be led on his Path, and the child left thinking— Man should not dispute or assert but whisper results to his neighbor, and thus by every germ of Spirit sucking the

Sap from mold ethereal every human might become great, and Humanity instead of being a wide heath of Furze and Briers with here and there a remote Oak or Pine, would become a grand democracy of Forest Trees. It has been an old Comparison for our urging on—the Beehive—however it seems to me that we should rather be the flower than the Bee—for it is a false notion that more is gained by receiving than giving—no, the receiver and the giver are equal in their benefits—The flower I doubt not receives a fair guerdon from the Bee—its leaves blush deeper in the next spring—and who shall say between Man and Woman which is the most delighted? Now it is more noble to sit like Jove than to fly like Mercury—let us not therefore go hurrying about and collecting honey-bee like, buzzing here and there impatiently from a knowledge of what is to be arrived at: but let us open our leaves like a flower and be passive and receptive—budding patiently under the eye of Apollo and taking hints from every noble insect that favors us with a visit—sap will be given us for Meat and dew for drink—I was led into these thoughts, my dear Reynolds, by the beauty of the morning operating on a sense of Idleness—I have not read any Books—the Morning said I was right—I had no Idea but of the Morning and the Thrush said I was right —seeming to say—

"O thou whose face hath felt the winter's wind; . . ."

Now I am sensible all this is a mere sophistication, however it may neighbor to any truths, to excuse my own indolence—so I will not deceive myself that Man should be equal with Jove—but think himself very well off as a sort of scullion-Mercury or even a humble Bee—It is not matter whether I am right or wrong either one way or another, if there is sufficient to lift a little time from your Shoulders.

Your affectionate friend
John Keats—

To J. H. Reynolds 3 May 1818

Teignmouth May 3ᵈ

My dear Reynolds.

What I complain of is that I have been in so an uneasy a state of Mind as not to be fit to write to an invalid. I cannot write to any length under a disguised feeling. I should have loaded you with an addition of gloom, which I am sure you do not want. I am now, thank God, in a humor to give you a good groat's worth—for Tom, after a Night without a Wink of sleep, and overburdened with fever, has got up after a refreshing day sleep and is better than he has been for a long time; and you I trust have been again round the Common without any effect but refreshment . . . Were I to study physic or rather Medicine again,—I feel it would not make the least difference in my Poetry; when the Mind is in its infancy a Bias is in reality a Bias, but when we have acquired more strength, a Bias becomes no Bias. Every department of knowledge we see excellent and calculated towards a great whole. I am so convinced of this, that I am glad at not having given away my medical Books, which I shall again look over to keep alive the little I know thitherwards; and moreover intend through you and Rice to become a sort of Pip-civilian. An extensive knowledge is needful to thinking people—it takes away the heat and fever; and helps, by widening speculation, to ease the Burden of the Mystery: a thing I begin to understand a little, and which weighed upon you in the most gloomy and true sentence in your Letter. The difference of high Sensations with and without knowledge appears to me this—in the latter case we are falling continually ten thousand fathoms deep and being blown up again without wings and with all the horror of a bare-shouldered Creature—in the former case, our shoulders are fledged, and we go through the same air and space without fear. This is running one's rigs on the score of abstracted benefit—when we come to human Life and the affections it is impossible how a parallel of breast and head can be drawn—(you will forgive me for thus privately treading out my depth and take it for treading as schoolboys tread the waters)—it is impossible to know how far knowledge will console us for the death of a friend and the ill "that flesh is heir too"—With respect to the affections and Poetry you must know by a sympathy my thoughts that way; and I dare say these few lines will be but a ratification: I wrote them on May-day —and intend to finish the ode all in good time.—

Mother of Hermes! and still youthful Maia! . . .

You may be anxious to know for fact to what sentence in your Letter I allude. You say "I fear there is little chance of anything else in this life." You seem by that to have been going through with a more painful and acute zest the same labyrinth that I have—I have come to the same conclusion thus far. My Branchings out therefrom have been numerous: one of them is the consideration of Wordsworth's genius and as a help, in the manner of gold being the meridian Line of worldly wealth—how he differs from Milton.—And here I have nothing but surmises, from an uncertainty whether Milton's apparently less anxiety for Humanity proceeds from his seeing further or no than Wordsworth: And whether Wordsworth has in truth epic passions, and martyrs himself to the human heart, the main region of his song—In regard to his genius alone—we find what he says true as far as we have experienced and we can judge no further but by larger experience—for axioms in philosophy are not axioms until they are proved upon our pulses: We read fine—— things but never feel them to thee full until we have gone the same steps as the Author.—I know this is not plain; you will know exactly my meaning when I say, that now I shall relish Hamlet more than I ever have done—Or, better—You are sensible no man can set down Venery as a bestial or joyless thing until he is sick of it and therefore all philosophizing on it would be mere wording. Until we are sick, we understand not;—in fine, as Byron says, "Knowledge is Sorrow"; and I go on to say that "Sorrow is Wisdom"—and further for aught we can know for certainty! "Wisdom is folly."—So you see how I have run away from Wordsworth, and Milton; and shall still run away from what was in my head, to observe, that some kind of letters are good squares others handsome ovals, and others some orbicular, others spheroid—and why should there not be another species with two rough edges like a rat-trap? I hope you will find all my long letters of that species, and all will be well; for by merely touching the spring delicately and ethereally, the rough-edged will fly immediately into a proper compactness, and thus you may make a good wholesome loaf, with your own leaven in it, of my fragments—If you cannot find this said rat-trap sufficiently tractable—alas for me, it being an impossibility in grain for my ink to stain otherwise: If I scribble long letters I must play my vagaries. I must be too heavy, or too light, for whole pages—I must be quaint and free of Tropes and figures—I must play my draughts as I please, and for my advantage and your erudition, crown a white with a black, or a black with a white, and move into black or white, far and near as I please—I must go from Hazlitt to Patmore, and make Wordsworth and Coleman play at leap-frog—or keep one of them down a whole half holiday at fly the garter—"From Gray to Gay, from Little to Shakespeare"—Also as a long cause requires two or more sittings of the Court, so a long letter will require two or more sittings of the Breech wherefore I shall resume after dinner.—

Have you not seen a Gull, an orc, a sea Mew, or anything to bring this Line to a proper length, and also fill up this clear part; that like the Gull I may *dip*—I hope, not out of sight—and also, like a Gull, I hope to be lucky in a good-sized fish—This crossing a letter is not without its association—for checker work leads us naturally to a Milkmaid, a Milkmaid to Hogarth, Hogarth to Shakespeare, Shakespeare to Hazlitt—Hazlitt to Shakespeare and thus by merely pulling an apron string we set a pretty peal of Chimes at work—Let them chime on while, with your patience—I will return to Wordsworth—whether or no he has an extended vision or a circumscribed grandeur—whether he is an eagle in his nest, or on the wing—And to be more explicit and to show you how tall I stand by the giant, I will put down a simile of human life as far as I now perceive it; that is, to the point to which I say we both have arrived at—Well—I compare human life to a large Mansion of Many Apartments, two of which I can only describe, the doors of the rest being as yet shut upon me—The first we step into we call the infant or thoughtless Chamber, in which we remain as long as we do not think—We remain there a long while, and notwithstanding the doors of the second Chamber remain wide open, showing a bright appearance, we care not to hasten to it; but are at length imperceptibly impelled by the awakening of the thinking principle—within us—we no sooner get into the second Chamber, which I shall call the Chamber of Maiden-Thought, than we become intoxicated with the light and the atmosphere, we see nothing but pleasant wonders, and think of delaying there forever in delight: However among the effects this breathing is father of is that tremendous one of sharpening one's vision into the heart and nature of Man—of convincing ones nerves that the World is full of Misery and Heartbreak, Pain, Sickness and oppression—whereby This Chamber of Maiden Thought becomes gradually darkened and at the same time on all sides of it many doors are set open—but all dark—all leading to dark passages—We see not the balance of good and evil. We are in a Mist—*We* are now in that state—We feel the "burden of the Mystery." To this point was Wordsworth come, as far as I can conceive when he wrote "Tintern Abbey" and it seems to me that his Genius is explorative of those dark Passages. Now if we live, and go on thinking, we too shall explore them. He is a Genius and superior to us, in so far as he can, more than we, make discoveries, and shed a light in them—Here I must think Wordsworth is deeper than Milton—though I think it has depended more upon the general and gregarious advance of intellect than individual greatness of Mind—From the Paradise Lost and the other Works of Milton, I hope it is not too presuming, even between ourselves to say, his Philosophy, human and divine, may be tolerably understood by one not much advanced in years. In his time Englishmen were just emancipated from a great superstition—and Men had got hold of certain points and resting places in reasoning which were too newly born to be doubted, and too much opposed by the Mass of Europe not to be thought ethereal and authentically divine—who could gainsay his ideas on virtue, vice, and Chastity in Comus, just at the time of the dismissal of cod-pieces and a hundred other disgraces? who would not rest satisfied with his hintings at good and evil in the Paradise Lost, when just free from the inquisition and burrning in Smithfield? The Reformation produced such immediate and great benefits, that Protestantism was considered under the immediate eye of heaven, and its own remaining Dogmas and superstitions, then, as it were, regenerated, constituted those resting places and seeming sure points of Reasoning—from that I have mentioned, Milton, whatever he may have thought in the sequel, appears to have been content with these by his writings—He did not think into the human heart, as Wordsworth has done—Yet Milton as a philosopher, had sure as great powers as Wordsworth—What is then to be inferred? O many things—It proves there is really a grand march of intellect—It proves that a mighty providence subdues the mightiest Minds to the service of the time being, whether it be in human Knowledge or Religion—I have often pitied a Tutor who has to hear "Nom: Musa"—so often dinned into his ears—I hope you may not have the same pain in this scribbling—I may have read these things before, but I never had even a thus dim perception of them; and moreover I like to say my lesson to one who will endure my tediousness for my own sake—After all there is certainly something real in the World—Moore's present to Hazlitt is real—I like that Moore, and am glad that I saw him at the Theatre just before I left Town. Tom has spit a leetle blood this afternoon, and that is rather a damper—but I know—the truth is there is something real in the World Your third Chamber of Life shall be a lucky and a gentle one—stored with the wine of love—and the

Bread of Friendship—When you see George if he should
not have received a letter from me tell him he will find
one at home most likely—tell Bailey I hope soon to see
him—Remember me to all The leaves have been out here,
for many a day—I have written to George for the first
stanzas of my Isabel—I shall have them soon and will
copy the whole out for you.

Your affectionate friend
John Keats.

To Richard Woodhouse 27 October 1818

My dear Woodhouse,
 Your Letter gave me a great satisfaction; more on ac-
count of its friendliness, than any relish of that matter in
it which is accounted so acceptable in the "genus irrita-
bile" The best answer I can give you is in a clerk-like
manner to make some observations on two principal
points, which seem to point like indices into the midst
of the whole pro and con, about genius, and views and
achievements and ambition and cœtera. 1st As to the
poetical Character itself, (I mean that sort of which, if I
am anything, I am a Member; that sort distinguished
from the Wordsworthian or egotistical sublime; which is
a thing per se and stands alone) it is not itself—it has no
self—it is everything and nothing—It has no character—
it enjoys light and shade; it lives in gusto, be it foul or
fair, high or low, rich or poor, mean or elevated—It has
as much delight in conceiving an Iago as an Imogen. What
shocks the virtuous philosopher, delights the chameleon
Poet. It does no harm from its relish of the dark side of
things any more than from its taste for the bright one;
because they both end in speculation. A Poet is the most
unpoetical of any thing in existence; because he has no
Identity—he is continually in for—and filling some other
Body—The Sun, the Moon, the Sea and Men and Women
who are creatures of impulse are poetical and have about

them an unchangeable attribute—the poet has none; no identity—he is certainly the most unpoetical of all God's Creatures. If then he has no self, and if I am a Poet, where is the Wonder that I should say I would write no more? Might I not at that very instant have been cogitating on the Characters of Saturn and Ops? It is a wretched thing to confess; but is a very fact that not one word I ever utter can be taken for granted as an opinion growing out of my identical nature—how can it, when I have no nature? When I am in a room with People if I ever am free from speculating on creations of my own brain, then not myself goes home to myself: but the identity of everyone in the room begins to to press upon me that, I am in a very little time annihilated—not only among Men; it would be the same in a Nursery of children: I know not whether I make myself wholly understood: I hope enough so to let you see that no dependence is to be placed on what I said that day.

In the second place I will speak of my views, and of the life I purpose to myself—I am ambitious of doing the world some good: if I should be spared that may be the work of maturer years—in the interval I will assay to reach to as high a summit in Poetry as the nerve bestowed upon me will suffer. The faint conceptions I have of Poems to come brings the blood frequently into my forehead—All I hope is that I may not lose all interest in human affairs—that the solitary indifference I feel for applause even from the finest Spirits will not blunt any acuteness of vision I may have. I do not think it will—I feel assured I should write from the mere yearning and fondness I have for the Beautiful even if my night's labors should be burned every morning and no eye ever shine upon them. But even now I am perhaps not speaking from myself; but from some character in whose soul I now live. I am sure however that this next sentence is from myself. I feel your anxiety, good opinion and friendliness in the highest degree, and am

Your's most sincerely
John Keats

To the George Keatses 19 March 1819

Friday 19th Yesterday I got a black eye—the first time I took a Cricket bat—Brown who is always one's friend in a disaster applied a leech to the eyelid, and there is no inflammation this morning though the ball hit me directly on the sight—'twas a white ball—I am glad it was not a clout—This is the second black eye I have had since leaving school—during all my school days I never had one at all—we must eat a peck before we die—This morning I am in a sort of temper indolent and supremely careless: I long after a stanza or two of Thompson's Castle of Indolence—My passions are all asleep from my having slumbered till nearly eleven and weakened the animal fiber all over me to a delightful sensation about three degrees on this side of faintness—if I had teeth of pearl and the breath of lilies I should call it languor—but as I am I must call it Laziness—In this state of effeminacy the fibers of the brain are relaxed in common with the rest of the body, and to such a happy degree that pleasure has no show of enticement and pain no unbearable frown. Neither Poetry, nor Ambition, nor Love have any alertness of countenance as they pass by me: they seem rather like three figures on a Greek vase—a Man and two women—whom no one but myself could distinguish in their disguisement. This is the only happiness; and is a rare instance of advantage in the body overpowering the Mind. I have this moment received a note from Haslam in which he expects the death of his Father who has been for some time in a state of insensibility—his mother bears up he says very well—I shall go to town tomorrow to see him. This is the world—thus we cannot expect to give way many hours to pleasure—Circumstances are like Clouds continually gathering and bursting—While we are laughing the seed of some trouble is put into he the wide arable land of events—while we are laughing it sprouts it grows and suddenly bears a poison fruit which we must pluck—Even so we have leisure to reason on the misfortunes of our friends; our own touch us too nearly for words. Very few men have ever arrived at a complete disinterestedness of Mind: very few have been influenced by a pure desire of the benefit of others—in the greater part of the Benefactors of & to Humanity some meretricious motive has sullied their greatness—some melodramatic scenery has fascinated them—From the manner in which I feel Haslam's misfortune I perceive how far I am from any humble standard of disinterestedness—Yet this feeling ought to be carried to its highest pitch, as there is no fear of its ever injuring society—which it would do I fear pushed to an extremity—For in wild nature the Hawk would loose his Breakfast of Robins and the Robin his of Worms The Lion must starve as well as the swallow—The greater part of Men make their way with the same instinctiveness, the same unwandering eye from their purposes, the same animal eagerness as the Hawk—The Hawk wants a Mate, so does the Man—look at them both they set about it and procure one in the same manner—They want both a nest and they both set about one in the same manner—they get their food in the same manner—The noble animal Man for his amusement smokes his pipe—the Hawk balances about the Clouds—that is the only difference of their leisures. This it is that makes the Amusement of Life—to a speculative Mind. I go among the Fields and catch a glimpse of a stoat or a fieldmouse peeping out of the withered grass—the creature hath a purpose and its eyes are bright with it—I go amongst the buildings of a city and I see a Man hurrying along—to what? The Creature has a purpose and his eyes are bright with it. But then as Wordsworth says, "we have all one human heart"—there is an electric fire in human nature tending to purify—so that among these human creatures there is continually some birth of new heroism—The pity is that we must wonder at it: as we should at finding a pearl in rubbish—I have no doubt that thousands of people never heard of have had hearts completely disinterested: I can remember but two—Socrates and Jesus—their Histories evince it—What I heard a little time ago, Taylor observe with respect to Socrates, may be said of Jesus—That he was so great as man that though he transmitted no writing of his own to posterity, we have his Mind and his sayings and his greatness handed to us by others. It is to be lamented that the history of the latter was written and revised by Men interested in the pious frauds of Religion. Yet through all this I see his splendor. Even here though I myself am pursuing the same instinctive course as the veriest human animal you can think of —I am however young writing at random—straining at particles of light in the midst of a great darkness—without knowing the bearing of any one assertion of any one opinion. Yet may I not in this be free from sin? May there not be superior beings amused with any graceful, though instinctive attitude my mind may fall into, as I am entertained with the alertness of a Stoat or the anxiety of a Deer? Though a quarrel in the streets is a thing to be hated, the energies displayed in it are fine; the commonest Man shows a grace in his quarrel—By a superior being our reasonings may take the same tone—though erroneous they may be fine—This is the very thing in which consists poetry; and if so it is not so fine a thing as philosophy— For the same reason that an eagle is not so fine a thing as a truth—Give me this credit—Do you not think I strive—to know myself? Give me this credit—and you will not think that on my own account I repeat Milton's lines

"How charming is divine Philosophy
Not harsh and crabbed as dull fools suppose
But musical as is Apollo's lute"—

No—no, for myself—feeling grateful as I do to have got into a state of mind to relish them properly—Nothing ever becomes real till it is experienced—Even a Proverb is no proverb to you till your Life has illustrated it—I am ever afraid that your anxiety for me will lead you to fear for the violence of my temperament continually smothered down: for that reason I did not intend to have sent you the following sonnet—but look over the two last pages and ask yourselves whether I have not that in me which will well bear the buffets of the world. It will be the best comment on my sonnet; it will show you that it was written with no Agony but that of ignorance; with no thirst of anything but knowledge when pushed to the point though the first steps to it were through my human passions—they went away, and I wrote with my Mind—and perhaps I must confess a little bit of my heart—

Why did I laugh tonight? No voice will tell . . .

I have been reading lately two very different books Robertson's America and Voltaire's Siecle De Louis XIV. It is like walking arm and arm between Pizarro and the great-little Monarch. In How lamentable a case do we see the great body of the people in both instances: in the first, where Men might seem to inherit quiet of Mind from unsophisticated senses; from uncontamination of civilization; and especially from their being as it were estranged from the mutual helps of Society and its mutual injuries—and thereby more immediately under the Protection of Providence—even there they had mortal pains to bear as bad; or even worse than Bailiffs, Debts and Poverties of civilized Life—The whole appears to resolve into this—that Man is originally "a poor forked creature" subject to the same mischances as the beasts of the forest, destined to hardships and disquietude of some kind or other. If he improves by degrees his bodily accommodations and comforts—at each stage, at each accent there are waiting for him a fresh set of annoyances—he is mortal and there is still a heaven with its Stars above his head. The most interesting question that can come before us is, How far by the persevering endeavors of a seldom appearing Socrates Mankind may be made happy—I can imagine such happiness carried to an extreme—but what must it end in?—Death—and who could in such a case bear with death—the whole troubles of life which are now frittered away in a series of years, would then be accumulated for the last days of a being who instead of hailing its approach, would leave this world as Eve left Paradise—

But in truth I do not at all believe in this sort of perfectibility—the nature of the world will not admit of it—the inhabitants of the world will correspond to itself—Let the fish philosophize the ice away from the Rivers in winter time and they shall be at continual play in the tepid delight of summer. Look at the Poles and at the sands of Africa, Whirlpools and volcanoes—Let men exterminate them and I will say that they may arrive at earthly Happiness—The point at which Man may arrive is as far as the parallel state in inanimate nature and no further—For instance, suppose a rose to have sensation, it blooms on a beautiful morning it enjoys itself—but there comes a cold wind, a hot sun—it cannot escape it, it cannot destroy its annoyances—they are as native to the world as itself: no more can man be happy in spite, the worldly elements will prey upon his nature—The common cognomen of this world among the misguided and superstitious is "a vale of tears" from which we are to be redeemed by a certain arbitrary interposition of God and taken to Heaven—What a little circumscribed straightened notion! Call the world if you Please "The vale of Soul-making." Then you will find out the use of the world (I am speaking now in the highest terms for human nature, admitting it to be immortal, which I will here take for granted for the purpose of showing a thought which has struck me concerning it) I say *"Soul-making"* Soul as distinguished from an Intelligence—There may be intelligences or sparks of the divinity in millions—but they are not Souls the till they acquire identities, till each one is personally itself. Intelligences are atoms of perception—they know and they see and they are pure, in short they are God— how then are Souls to be made? How then are these sparks which are God to have identity given them—so as ever to possess a bliss peculiar to each one's individual existence? How, but by the medium of a world like this? This point I sincerely wish to consider because I think it a grander system of salvation than the Christian religion— or rather it is a system of Spirit-creation—This is effected by three grand materials acting the one upon the other for a series of years—These three Materials are the *Intelli-*

gence—the *human heart* (as distinguished from intelligence or Mind) and the *World* or *Elemental space* suited for the proper action of *Mind and Heart* on each other for the purpose of forming the *Soul* or *Intelligence destined to possess the sense of Identity.* I can scarcely express what I but dimly perceive—and yet I think I perceive it—that you may judge the more clearly I will put it in the most homely form possible—I will call the *world* a School instituted for the purpose of teaching little children to read—I will call the *human heart* the *horn Book* used in that School—and I will call the *Child able to read, the Soul* made from that *school* and its *hornbook.* Do you not see how necessary a World of Pains and troubles is to school an Intelligence and make it a soul? A Place where the heart must feel and suffer in a thousand diverse ways! Not merely is the Heart a Hornbook, It is the Mind's Bible, it is the Mind's experience, it is the teat from which the Mind or intelligence sucks its identity— As various as the Lives of Men are—so various become their souls, and thus does God make individual beings, Souls, Identical Souls of the sparks of his own essence— This appears to me a faint sketch of a system of Salvation which does not affront our reason and humanity—I am convinced that many difficulties which Christians labor under would vanish before it—There is one which even now Strikes me—the Salvation of Children—In them the Spark or intelligence returns to God without any identity —it having had no time to learn of, and be altered by, the heart—or seat of the human Passions—It is pretty generally suspected that the Christian scheme has been copied from the ancient Persian and Greek Philosophers. Why may they not have made this simple thing even more simple for common apprehension by introducing Mediators and Personages in the same manner as in the heathen mythology abstractions are personified—Seriously I think it probable that this System of Soul-making—may have been the Parent of all the more palpable and personal Schemes of Redemption, among the Zoroastrians the Christians and the Hindoos. For as one part of the human species must have their carved Jupiter; so another part must have the palpable and named Mediatior and savior, their Christ their Oromanes and their Vishnu— If what I have said should not be plain enough, as I fear it may not be, I will but you in the place where I began in this series of thoughts—I mean, I began by seeing how man was formed by circumstances—and what are circumstances but touchstones of his heart? and what are touchstones but provings of his heart? and what are provings of his heart but fortifiers or alterers of his nature? and what is his altered nature but his Soul?—and what was his Soul before it came into the world and had these provings and alterations and perfectionings?—An intelligence without Identity—and how is this Identity to be made? Through the medium of the Heart? And how is the heart to become this Medium but in a world of Circumstances?—There now I think what with Poetry and Theology you may thank your Stars that my pen is not very long-winded—Yesterday I received two Letters from your Mother and Henry which I shall send by young Birkbeck with this . . .

To Fanny Brawne February (?) 1820

My dear Fanny,

Do not let your mother suppose that you hurt me by writing at night. For some reason or other your last night's note was not so treasurable as former ones. I would fain that you call me *Love* still. To see you happy and in high spirits is a great consolation to me—still let me believe that you are not half so happy as my restoration would make you. I am nervous, I own, and may think myself worse than I really am; if so you must indulge me, and pamper with that sort of tenderness you have manifested towards me in different Letters. My sweet creature when I look back upon the pains and torments I have suffered for you from the day I left you to go to the Isle of Wight; the ecstasies in which I have passed some days and the miseries in their turn, I wonder the more at the Beauty which has kept up the spell so fervently. When I send this round I shall be in the front parlor watching to see you show yourself for a minute in the garden. How illness stands as a barrier betwixt me and you! Even if I was well——I must make myself as good a Philosopher as possible. Now I have had opportunities of passing nights anxious and awake I have found other thoughts intrude upon me. "If I should die," said I to myself, "I have left no immortal work behind me—nothing to make my friends proud of my memory—but I have loved the principle of beauty in all things, and if I had had time I would have made myself remembered." Thoughts like these came very feebly whilst I was in health and every pulse beat for you—now you divide with this (may *I* say it?) "last infirmity of noble minds" all my reflection.

God bless you, Love.
J. Keats.

To Fanny Brawne August (?) 1820

> I do not write this till the last, that no eye may catch it.

My dearest Girl,

I wish you could invent some means to make me at all happy without you. Every hour I am more and more concentrated in you; everything else tastes like chaff in my Mouth. I feel it almost impossible to go to Italy—the fact is I cannot leave you, and shall never taste one minute's content until it pleases chance to let me live with you for good. But I will not go on at this rate. A person in health as you are can have no conception of the horrors that nerves and a temper like mine go through. What Island do your friends propose retiring to? I should be happy to go with you there alone, but in company I should object to it; the backbitings and jealousies of new colonists who

TO FANNY BRAWNE

have nothing else to amuse themselves is unbearable. Mr. Dilke came to see me yesterday, and gave me a very great deal more pain than pleasure. I shall never be able any more to endure to society of any of those who used to meet at Elm Cottage and Wentworth Place. The last two years taste like brass upon my Palate. If I cannot live with you I will live alone. I do not think my health will improve much while I am separated from you. For all this I am averse to seeing you—I cannot bear flashes of light and return into my glooms again. I am not so unhappy now as I should be if I had seen you yesterday. To be happy with you seems such an impossibility! it requires a luckier Star than mine! it will never be. I enclose a passage from one of your Letters which I want you to alter a little—I want (if you will have it so) the matter expressed less coldly to me. If my health would bear it, I could write a Poem which I have in my head, which would be a consolation for people in such a situation as mine. I would show some one in Love as I am, with a person living in such Liberty as you do. Shakespeare always sums up matters in the most sovereign manner. Hamlet's heart was full of such Misery as mine is when he said to Ophelia, "Go to a Nunnery, go, go!" Indeed I should like to give up the matter at once—I should like to die. I am sickened at the brute world which you are smiling with. I hate men and women more. I see nothing but thorns for the future—wherever I may be next winter in Italy or nowhere Brown will be living near you with his indecencies—I see no prospect of any rest. Suppose me in Rome—well, I should there see you as in a magic glass going to and from town at all hours,—I wish you could infuse a little confidence in human nature into my heart. I cannot muster any—the world is too brutal for me—I am glad there is such a thing as the grave—I am sure I shall never have any rest till I get there. At any rate I will indulge myself by never seeing any more Dilke or Brown or any of their Friends. I wish I was either in your arms full of faith or that a thunder bolt would strike me.

God bless you—J. K—

To Percy Bysshe Shelley 16 August 1820
Hampstead August 16th

My dear Shelley,

I am very much gratified that you, in a foreign country, and with a mind almost over occupied, should write to me in the strain of the Letter beside me. If I do not take advantage of your invitation it will be prevented by a circumstance I have very much at heart to prophesy— There is no doubt that an English winter would put an end to me, and do so in a lingering hateful manner, therefore I must either voyage or journey to Italy as a soldier marches up to a battery. My nerves at present are the worst part of me, yet they feel soothed when I think that come what extreme may, I shall not be destined to remain in one spot long enough to take a hatred of any four particular bedposts. I am glad you take any pleasure in my poor Poem;—which I would willingly take the trouble to unwrite, if possible, did I care so much as I have done about Reputation. I received a copy of the Cenci, as from yourself from Hunt. There is only one part of it I am judge of; the Poetry, and dramatic effect, which by many spirits now a days is considered the mammon. A modern work it is said must have a purpose, which may be the God—*an artist* must serve Mammon—he must have "self-concentration," selfishness perhaps. You I am sure will forgive me for sincerely remarking that you might curb your magnanimity and be more of an artist, and "load every rift" of your subject with ore. The thought of such discipline must fall like cold chains upon you, who perhaps never sat with your wings furled for six Months together. And is not this extraordinary talk for the writer of Endymion? whose mind was like a pack of scattered cards—I am picked up and sorted to a pip. My Imagination is a Monastry and I am its Monk—you must explain my metaphysics to yourself. I am in expectation of Prometheus every day. Could I have my own wish for its interest effected you would have it still in manuscript—

or be but now putting an end to the second act. I remember you advising me not to publish my first-blights, on Hampstead heath—I am returning advice upon your hands. Most of the Poems in the volume I send you have been written above two years, and would never have been published but from a hope of gain; so you see I am inclined enough to take your advice now. I must express once more my deep sense of your kindness, adding my sincere thanks and respects for Mrs. Shelley. In the hope of soon seeing you I remain

most sincerely yours
John Keats—

To Charles Brown 30 September 1820

Saturday Septr 28
Maria Crowther
off Yarmouth isle
of Wight—

My dear Brown,

The time has not yet come for a pleasant Letter from me. I have delayed writing to you from time to time because I felt how impossible it was to enliven you with one heartening hope of my recovery; this morning in bed the matter struck me in a different manner; I thought I would write "while I was in some liking" or I might become too ill to write at all and then if the desire to have written should become strong it would be a great affliction to me. I have many more Letters to write and I bless my stars that I have begun, for time seems to press,—this may be my best opportunity. We are in a calm and I am easy enough this morning. If my spirits seem too low you may in some degree impute it to our having been at sea a fortnight without making any way. I was very disappointed at not meeting you at bedhampton, and am very provoked at the thought of you being at Chichester today. I should have delighted in setting off for London for the sensation merely—for what should I do there? I could not leave my lungs or stomach or other worse things behind me. I wish to write on subjects that will not agitate me much—there is one I must mention and have done with it. Even if my body would recover of itself, this would prevent it—The very thing which I want to live most for will be a great occasion of my death. I cannot help it. Who can help it? Were I in health it would make me ill, and how can I bear it in my state? I daresay you will be able to guess on what subject I am harping—you know what was my greatest pain during the first part of my illness at your house. I wish for death every day and night to deliver me from these pains, and then I wish death away, for death would destroy even those pains which are better than nothing. Land and Sea, weakness and decline are great separaters, but death is the great divorcer forever. When the pang of this thought has passed through my mind, I may say the bitterness of death is passed. I often wish for you that you might flatter me with the best. I think without my mentioning it for my sake you would be a friend to Miss Brawne when I am dead. You think she has many faults—but, for my sake, think she has not one— —if there is anything you can do for her by word or deed, I know you will do it. I am in a state at present in which woman merely as woman can have not more power over me than stocks and stones, and yet the difference of my sensations with respect to Miss Brawne and my Sister is amazing. The one seems to absorb the other to a degree incredible, I seldom think of my Brother and Sister in America. The thought of leaving Miss Brawne is beyond everything horrible—the sense of darkness coming over me—I eternally see her figure eternally vanishing. Some of the phrases she was in the habit of using during my last nursing at Wentworth Place ring in my ears—Is there another Life? Shall I awake and find all this a dream? There must be, we cannot be created for this sort of suffering. The receiving of this letter is to be one of yours—I will say nothing about our friendship or rather yours to me more than that as you deserve to escape you will never be so unhappy as I am. I should think of

—you in my last moments. I shall endeavor to write to Miss Brawne if possible today. A sudden stop to my life in the middle of one of these Letters would be no bad thing for it keeps one in a sort of fever awhile. Though fatigued with a Letter longer than any I have written for a long while, it would be better to go on forever than awake to a sense of contrary winds. We expect to put into Portland roads tonight. The Captn the Crew and the Passengers are all ill-tempered and weary. I shall write to Dilke. I feel as if I was closing my last letter to you —My dear Brown

Your affectionate friend
John Keats

To Charles Brown 30 November 1820

Rome. 30 November 1820.
My dear Brown,
'Tis the most difficult thing in the world to me to write a letter. My stomach continues so bad, that I feel it worse on opening any book—yet I am much better than I was in Quarantine. Then I am afraid to encounter the proing and conning of anything interesting to me in England. I have an habitual feeling of my real life having past, and that I am leading a posthumous existence. God knows how it would have been—but it appears to me—however, I will not speak of that subject. I must have been at Bedhampton nearly at the time you were writing to me from Chichester—how unfortunate—and to pass on the river too! There was my star predominant! I cannot answer anything in your letter, which followed me from Naples to Rome, because I am afraid to look it over again. I am so weak (in mind) that I cannot bear the sight of any hand writing of a friend I love so much as I do you. Yet I ride the little horse—and, at my worst, even in quarantine, summoned up more puns, in a sort of desperation, in one week than in any year of my life. There is one

thought enough to kill me—I have been well, healthy, alert &c, walking with her—and now—the knowledge of contrast, feeling for light and shade, all that information (primitive sense) necessary for a poem are great enemies to the recovery of the stomach. There, you rogue, I put you to the torture,—but you must bring your philosophy to bear—as I do mine, really—or how should I be able to live? Dr. Clarke is very attentive to me; he says, there is very little the matter with my lungs, but my stomach, he says, is very bad. I am well disappointed in hearing good news from George—for it runs in my head we shall all die young. I have not written to Reynolds yet, which he must think very neglectful; being anxious to send him a good account of my health, I have delayed it from week to week. If I recover, I will do all in my power to correct the mistakes made during sickness; and if I should not, all my faults will be forgiven. . . . Severn is very well, though he leads so dull a life with me. Remember me to all friends, and tell Haslam I should not have left London without taking leave of him, but from being so low in body and mind. Write to George as soon as you receive this, and tell him how I am, as far as you can guess;—and also a note to my sister—who walks about my imagination like a ghost—she is so like Tom. I can scarcely bid you good-bye even in a letter. I always made an awkward bow.

God bless you!
John Keats